AN ARM AND FOUR LEGS

Stan Hey has written two crime novels and two books about sport – *A Golden Sky: The Liverpool Dream Team* and *Gary Lineker's Golden Boots*. He was born in Liverpool and was educated there and at St. Catherine's College, Cambridge. He now lives in Wiltshire, so he can be close to Wincanton and Cheltenham racecourses. He is married with two sons, who are already beginning to take an interest in the nags.

An Arm and Four Legs

a journey into racehorse ownership

STAN HEY

YELLOW JERSEY PRESS
LONDON

Revised and updated edition
published by Yellow Jersey Press 2000

2 4 6 8 10 9 7 5 3 1

First published in Great Britain in 1998 by
Yellow Jersey Press
Random House, 20 Vauxhall Bridge Road,
London SW1V 2SA

Random House Australia (Pty) Limited
20 Alfred Street, Milsons Point, Sydney,
New South Wales 2061, Australia

Random House New Zealand Limited
18 Poland Road, Glenfield,
Auckland 10, New Zealand

Random House (Pty) Limited
Endulini, 5A Jubilee Road, Parktown 2193, South Africa

The Random House Group Limited Reg. No. 954009

www.randomhouse.co.uk

A CIP catalogue record for this book
is available from the British Library

ISBN 0 224 06102 X

Papers used by Random House are natural,
recyclable products made from wood grown in sustainable forests.
The manufacturing processes conform to the environmental
regulations of the country of origin.

Typeset by SX Composing DTP, Rayleigh, Essex
Printed and bound in Great Britain by
Bookmarque Ltd, Croydon, Surrey

For my Dad and my Uncle Dick
for letting me in on the secret

Contents

Acknowledgements

This book would not have been possible without the co-operation and support given to me by Cliff and Janet Underwood, who were prepared to let me write about what turned into three difficult seasons for them as the breeders, owners and creators behind the Tally Ho Partnership. I offer them my profound thanks in the hope that the years we endured together were untypical of racehorse-owning partnerships and that a change of luck with the latest horse, Crowning Glory, will arrive next season. The other members of the partnership also deserve thanks for tolerating my presence among them, and for their various contributions to the manuscript.

I am equally grateful to my trainer Nigel Smith, his assistant and partner Liz Grainger, and to the jockeys mark Sharratt, David Creech, Brendan Powell and Ross Studholme for all their co-operation and their helpful input. It is a difficult enough task training or riding novice racehorses without having to cope with a novice owner as well. That they all did so with unfailing humour and civility is a great credit to the racing game. I owe much to various racing-made friends for their help, advice, anecdotes, companionship and hospitality on the journey. Andrew and Catherine Nickolds, Sean and Ceci Magee, Robert Cooper, Simon Kelner, Jon and Margaret Holmes, Chris Burt, Rev. David Seymour, Richard Edmondson, Sue Montgomery, Hugh McIlvanney, Brendan Hopkins, Peter Corrigan and Chris Coley all helped keep my spirits up when they might have failed. My former colleague Dudley Doust graciously gave me permission to quote from his excellent book on Peter Scudamore, and Liz Harrington of Conkwell Grange Stud kindly gave up time to brief me on the wonderful world of racehorse breeding. I'd also like to raise a glass to my long-suffering co-owner Steve Ludlam, but then we are not short of raised glasses every time we meet.

I would like to express my gratitude to my editor Rachel Cugnoni for her consistent support for the project despite the many frustrations which horse-owning seems to offer. Writing about nothing happening must have seemed a deadly prospect to an anxious editor. And I owe a debt of thanks to my agent Cat Ledger for getting me 'the ride' in the first place and for cracking the whip whenever I looked like pulling up. My wife Wendy and sons, Charlie and Jack, showed great tolerance for my expensive habit and frequent absences from home, and I hope they will not be too alarmed at what might have looked like my squandering what passes for the family wealth. It's an investment, honest.

Finally, I have to mention the real heroes and heroines of this book, who won't be able to read this expression of thanks and would prefer a packet of Polo mints in any case. Di's Last, Rowley John, Nova Scotia, Crowning Glory and Deadly Doris did all the real work and this is their story.

Stan Hey, Wiltshire, March 2000

Introduction

'Only 10 per cent of the horses in training ever get to win a race.' This remark may be in quotes but I can't ascribe it to any particular person. In fact I must have heard it from at least half-a-dozen different people when they were told that I'd bought my way into shares of horses for the 1997–8 National Hunt season. Whether this is folk wisdom or a matter of fact, I've no idea, but it has the feel of authenticity about it. And as I don't propose to go back through several seasons' statistics for analysis, I have to accept that this percentage must be about right. So why go into ownership knowing that the odds of seeing your horse win are so stacked against you?

Well, I'd say that in the first instance such negative omens are a challenge in much the same way as we defy the impossible odds of winning the lottery by buying a £1 ticket. By the time a more substantial sum of money is invested for a piece of horse you have to believe that your choice will be in the exceptional 10 per cent of horses that do win races and prize money for their owners. After all, there can't be too many people around who intentionally buy bad horses knowing that they can't win a race – if this is tax deductible I haven't heard about it from my accountant – so it follows that all owners undertake an initial act of wilful self-delusion when they cough up. This period of blind innocence may not last very long – their horse's first race usually – but it is the collective emotional point at which we all start.

When I had my first payment cheque for horses printed out last October, the girls in my local Stroud & Swindon Building Society made it plain that they thought I was mad, and I instantly felt hurt. Didn't they know that this was a sound investment? Didn't they realise that the two horses I was buying shares in were certain future winners? Did they appreciate that I would soon be glimpsed on the television leading one, or even both of them, into the winners' enclosure at one of the big jumping courses, Ascot perhaps, or Newbury or even Cheltenham?

I had spent my own money – not a huge amount, but a fair chunk in relation to my normal out-goings – and so it seemed to me to be only fair that I should be rewarded for my daring. For now I was taking control over events previously beyond my span as a small-time punter. My luck would change because I was an owner now, not just the poor sod who'd started his London life 24 years ago in a betting shop on Camden High Street doing a 10p each-way Yankee, trying to win the deficit between my £10.50 a week rent, and my £9.50 a week wages for writing the headlines on LBC's Saturday afternoon sports programme.

My route from there to here is not of much interest to this particular book, nor indeed any other come to that, except for the fact that trying to win money from backing horses has been a constant occurrence in my life, whether working successfully or otherwise. For me to end up having a ¼th share in two horses and, later, a quarter share in one may not seem much of an achievement, but in my private hinterland this was conquering Everest.

From the tone of this opening, you should have guessed by now that what was actually happening to me was something the psychotherapists might call 'the transfer of failure'. From being a 'mug punter', I was set to become a 'mug owner'. 'Mug' status involves the mute acceptance that if you are given a two-horse race to bet on, you will always back the loser; that if you take your umbrella out with you, a fine day will ensue; that if you don't, it will piss down. I knew deep in my internal organs that I was not about to become a successful owner, because my luck with racing has never gone that way. This didn't stop me drifting off into fantasies about winning, in much the same vein as imagining the prettiest woman in a restaurant making her way over to my table. It happens, but to other people.

Fortunately, what I think I discovered over the season with regard to racehorse ownership was that it is one of the few areas of life that does accept the co-existence of both 'herbivores' and 'carnivores' on the same terrain. Elsewhere in life, they seem pretty much segregated – the meat-eaters get to be big in business, the law, politics, the media and sport, while the grazers are cordoned off into the caring professions, the arts, teaching or the public services. The divide is there in racing too, but not to the exclusion of the 'herbivores'. There are those who regard horse ownership as a serious business investment, on which an annual profit must be made, and there are those who will be obliged to write off their money and explain it away in terms of 'having fun'. Both species are probably kidding themselves to some degree, but failure hurts the carnivores more, especially on those rare occasions when the herbivores win.

Coincidentally the very nature of racehorse ownership became the subject of a huge debate during the 1997–8 season, thanks to Sheikh Mohammed of Dubai, the world's richest racehorse owner, and a speech written by him and read out by one of his team, Michael Osborne, at the Gimcrack Dinner in York on 9 December. In the text, the Sheikh threatened a withdrawal of his racing and breeding interests from England if the level of prize-money for owners was not drastically improved.

'My hope,' the Sheikh declared, 'is that after we have emptied our pockets, we are at least allowed to keep the lining. At present the process of owing horses at any level is like driving on a flat tyre. All we seek is the luxury of a slow puncture.'

Sheikh Mohammed may have been talking essentially about Flat racing, where his fortune is invested – although he did have a Champion Hurdle win at Cheltenham in 1990 with Kribensis. But his argument inevitably spilled over into Jump racing, because it has less financial support due to the 60–40 per cent split in favour of the Flat in the annual distribution of money raised by the betting levy.

Not surprisingly two of the most successful owners of high-quality chasers, Paul Barber (See More Business) and Andrew Cohen (Suny Bay), joined in the debate. Barber took the 'it's all about having fun' line (he is a millionaire dairy farmer), while Cohen thought 'it has to be run as a business' (he is a millionaire executive in his own household goods company). Further ammunition was provided when the *Racing Post* published tables which showed the percentage return to owners in prize-money of their costs and investments in horses throughout the racing countries of the world.

South Korea finished top, ahead of the likes of Morocco, Turkey, Hong Kong, Qatar, Greece, Algeria and Chile. Britain was down in 36th place for the last audited year – 1995–6 – showing that owners could expect to get back an average of only 24 per cent of their costs. Or, to put it painfully, for every hundred pounds a British owner spent on his horse, he would 'lose' seventy-six of them. Of course, this was only an average figure, masking the truth that a small minority made profits, while the vast majority don't recover any costs at all.

The debate rumbled through the usually insular and introverted world of British racing like an Alabama twister, claiming the position of Lord 'Twelve Jobs' Wakeham, the incumbent Chairman of the British Horseracing Board, as his many other endeavours and his half-hearted response to a new 'business plan' for racing were deemed to be inappropriate responses to the perceived crisis.

All of which seemed to offer an extremely ironic

background to my minor involvement in ownership, as I trundled around such courses as Warwick, Towcester and Hereford in search of the seemingly impossible double of both 'fun' and 'prize-money', during which time I gradually began to realise what is the owner's true role in racing. What follows here is an account of my quest, partly in the form of a diary – from notes made at the time – and partly as an explanatory background to the various routes to becoming an owner, together with details of what it actually cost, and also what it felt like as I tried to make the transition from 'herbivore' to 'carnivore'. With regard to my inconsequential conclusions about British racing, I'll save them until last, always assuming, dear reader, that you stay the trip.

Why Horses?

If you are looking for some fun, with investment potential, there are probably a hundred more likely ideas before you'd get round to buying a racehorse. You could buy a boat or a canal-cruiser instead; you could shop around Bordeaux buying up top-quality clarets before they mature; you might prefer to take out a time-share in Tenerife; you could get yourself a classic sports car and do it up in the garage at weekends. Pleasure and investment are inherent to all these activities. There is a rational connection between the two elements, because the one doesn't consume the other. These are not wasteful ideas. The boat will always have a resale value; you can enjoy your wine at some stage in the future, gloating about what great value it will seem to be by then; you can always sell-on a time-share home, or let it at high rates to people you don't like; and the car will probably more than repay what you have spent on it when it is taken to one of those Chelsea auctions full of Jeremy Clarkson wannabes. But a National Hunt racehorse – *'what is this your business?'*, as my Jewish accountant asked me.

Even if you lay aside considerations about the likelihood of prize-money, and the costs of keeping a horse in training, there are other factors to consider. Most, if not all, male jump horses are geldings, that is, they have had their 'wedding tackle' surgically removed by vets in order that they should not be distracted by self-protective instincts when approaching a fence or hurdle. So even if they are successful they have no add-on value as future stallions at stud.

If your horse is a mare it may have some breeding potential, depending on the usefulness of the family it comes from and its own achievements on the racecourse. For instance, if her dad was the equivalent of 'Stan Ogden', who used to be the fat, chip-butty-munching window-cleaner in *Coronation Street* – and the form books and bloodstock annuals cover equine families more rigorously than the Social Services do humans – it will still count against her, no matter what she wins. Whereas there will always be a market for a filly from 'a good family', even if she does little more on the track than polish her fingernails. Racing pedigrees go back a long way.

Then there's the question of injury, a not uncommon experience when several tons of highly muscled horse-flesh are competing against each other, at speed, over birch fences, timber-framed hurdles, ditches and water-jumps, all on turf with the consistency of treacle sponge at one extreme, or the durability of an airport runway at the other. Once a horse is laid-up, its earnings potential is non-existent. Famous, successful jump horses can earn thousands after they retire by opening betting shops – a photo-appearance rather than the actual scissoring of the ribbon itself – or by more bizarre forms of marketing. I have a lawyer friend, one of whose earliest jobs it was to ascertain the precise percentage of the triple Grand National winner Red Rum's droppings that had to be included in a bag of manure before it could be sold as a 'genuine' souvenir to Japanese investors, or up-market compost to Cheshire gardeners. Obviously, it's not all *Murder One* in the legal profession.

But for horses which have yet to reach such a pinnacle as having their bodily waste revered, inaction brings their very existence into question. A lot of owners and trainers would rather have an injured horse put down than have it spending too much time in a stable recuperating. It is true, nevertheless, that several specialist equine insurance agencies – most notably Weatherby's, racing's civil service – will insure even National Hunt horses against injury or death. Naturally, the premiums are hefty due to the high risks involved, and also because the services of vets don't come cheap.

So let's just recap on these minor down-sides: your horse is unlikely to win a race, and even if it does, the prize-money will be on the low side; you will have all the horse's costs to bear, even when it's not running, and the insurance premiums and vets' bills simply push your out-goings into the realms of major expense. So, why horses?

Obviously I can only speak for myself, but I've got a pretty good idea that my path to ownership will also be the case for many others who have embarked on the great adventure. It began, as most sporting obsessions do, with a father's influence. Growing up in Liverpool in the 1950s and 60s, I was taken by my dad to all manner of sporting events from an early age. Quite apart from the inevitable devotion to football in general and to the Mighty Reds in particular, I was also offered chances to develop an affection for speedway at the now defunct Stanley Stadium in the Old Swan district; for rugby league with Liverpool City at the now defunct Knotty Ash Ground; and for boxing at the now defunct Liverpool Stadium. Although they held my interest for a short while, in a way that any vivid sporting spectacle takes a grip on a child's imagination, it was football that stuck. But bubbling away underneath was a fascination with horse-racing and gambling, partly derived from the presence of the Grand National at Aintree – I had my first ever bet, a shilling each way, on Oxo, who won the 1959 race at 8–1 – partly due to my dad's furtive activities, which I now know to be related to off-course betting, which wasn't actually legalised until 1961.

Two particular incidents stand out in my memory. The first must have been around 1959/1960, and took place one evening when we drove down to a pub called the Bow and Arrow in the West Derby area. Leaving me in the family Ford Popular, my dad went into the pub carrying a small brown bag. As I remember it, a few more cars pulled up moments later, spewing out a handful of official-looking blokes in suits. As soon as they entered the pub it was, as they used to say in Liverpool, a case of 'all hands bale out', with men climbing out of windows and running out of fire exits in Keystone Kops fashion. My dad ran to the car and did what would now be called 'burning some rubber', in what was an obvious getaway. He never spoke about the incident to me, but as I grew older I guessed that the gentlemen who had turned up that night must have been Inland Revenue officials or Customs Officers, and that what he had in the bag was probably betting money, taken from colleagues at work and now to be handed over to a bookmaker, for whom he was a 'runner'.

The second occasion was similar but the location was different. It took place during an early 1960s holiday to the Isle of Man, in which part of the daily routine was for my dad and his brother-in-law, Dick, to sit in their deck chairs with copies of the *Daily Mirror* and *Daily Express*, both open at the racing pages. At about eleven o'clock they would drift into Douglas and return with betting slips tucked into the pockets of their short-sleeved shirts. I was dimly aware that though there was a casino in Douglas, other forms of gambling were banned, and there were certainly none of the new betting shops that were sprouting up on the mainland after the 1961 legalisation of off-course gambling.

As a curious – all right, nosy – ten-year-old, I asked if I could accompany them one day, and they led me off through the back-streets of Douglas, finally turning down a blind alley, where a line of male holidaymakers were queuing up outside the open toilet window of an ordinary detached house. Money went in through the window, and a pair of hands passed betting slips out. The heady odour of illegality hung over the whole business. But the sudden arrival of a uniformed Manx policeman created instant chaos, with the toilet window slamming shut and everybody running off down the alley. A mad scramble ensued in which my dad lifted me over a fence and I was obliged, along with the other twenty or so holidaymakers, to leg it through somebody's garden and back out on to another street. As far as I recall, nobody was nicked, but the man in the toilet must have had some explaining to do. By the time we got back to the beach, I had been given the advice that this incident shouldn't be discussed in front of the 'wives', meaning my mum and her sister Madge. The point to this was obvious – that my dad and Uncle Dick would be well in the dog-house if it emerged that they had exposed a ten-year-old boy to such wanton criminality. So it was never discussed again, except in the male circles which used to form in the back kitchen at family do's at my grandmother's house, where it was the source of much boozy laughter. Nevertheless it had felt like a minor rite of male passage, and I knew that I was on to something.

A few years later, my father *did* detail to me some of the goings-on in the English Electric factory where he worked. Because the staff were effectively contained on the site from 8 a.m. to 5 p.m. – there was no going out to lunch, they just ate in the works canteen – a huge amount of gambling on the afternoon's races was there to be tapped. Accordingly, an 'unofficial' betting shop was set up in the main toilets with an unofficial 'bookie' – acting for a licensed one – laying bets for his co-workers. Think of Sergeant Bilko and some of his activities in the motor-pool, and you have some idea of how it seemed to me. I concluded much later that my dad must have been involved in all this, not just on his previous 'form', but also because of what happened in the late 1960s. One of his best friends left the company and set himself up with two book-making shops – they still styled themselves as 'turf accountants' in those days – and on Saturdays or Bank Holidays my dad would work in the back office of one of the shops as a 'settler', the most important figure to a punter because he's the person who calculates the return on the winning betting slips.

As this strand in my dad's life was also mingled with regular family trips to race meetings – mostly to Haydock Park and Chester – I was probably destined to inherit what might be called the psychopathology of the racehorse punter, although the pursuit of A-levels and university degree, not to mention student poverty, helped me to sublimate this for several years. It wouldn't be true to say that my childhood was completely filled with observations of gambling, or indeed contact with horses. The only ones we saw around our estate belonged to Mr Sowerby's milk-float and to Ken Dodd's coal merchant father. The only time I rode was in a 'Donkey Derby' at Pontin's Holiday Camp in Blackpool in 1965, and I'm proud to say that I won. But a few years ago, I discovered a photograph of myself as a tot, with a white running rail in the background, and found my nan's hand-writing on the back: 'Stan, aged 18 months at Newton Abbot'. This would make it the summer of 1953, and immediately I experienced a Proustian rush about just how much horse-racing was knitted into our family life.

Quite apart from the Saturday afternoon betting, and the holiday skirmishes, I remembered odd trips to York and Redcar, en route to a caravan site in Scarborough, or Bangor on our way back from a cottage in North Wales. I remembered being at Chester, leaning on the rail of the last bend into the straight, as a swirl of horses blurred past, cheering a nag called Selvedge home at 7–1, and then getting eight pound notes stuffed into my pocket. Then there were the visits to Aintree, not for the Grand National itself, but for the walk around the course and its battered fences the day after the big race – 'Jumps Sunday' it was called. In the 1960s, the Grand National was still looked on as an event for the toffs rather than the locals, to the extent that myself and several school-mates would usually venture no further than Speke Airport or the Adelphi Hotel to watch the likes of TV quiz host Hughie Green, actor Gregory Peck, celebrity hair-dresser Pierre 'Teasy Weasy' Raymond and assorted landed gentry setting out for the course. Indeed so comprehensive was this sense of exclusion from Aintree that only professional duties, as Chief Sports Writer for the short-lived *Sunday Correspondent*, forced me to go there in 1990, and I still felt as though I would be chased off by some big Scouse copper. Not surprisingly, I managed to experience a bizarre misfortune.

Travelling up to Liverpool by train on the Friday, with my wife Wendy and our first son Charlie, I fell into conversation with a little, grey-haired American lady who seemed keen to find out what the big race was like. Assuming she was a tourist I must have chatted to her for the best part of an hour without discovering her true purpose. The next day, as Mr Frisk romped home in a record time at odds of 16–1, there was the little old lady, Mrs Lois Duffey, waiting to welcome her now famous winner into the unsaddling enclosure. If only she'd tipped me the wink . . .

By this time, though, my adult passion for horse-racing and betting had been genetically triggered, rather like a disease or baldness. Although I somehow managed to spend three years at Cambridge without ever going to Newmarket, once I'd opted for the scuffling life of a writer – there being no other career opportunities available – having a bet became a daily routine, while going racing became the main escape from the existential *ennui* of having to think, write or meet deadlines.

I was helped to a great degree in this by my writing partner, Andrew Nickolds, with whom I worked from the mid-1970s until the early 1990s. Many of our television scripts had a sporting theme – our first play in 1977, *The Back Page*, was later developed into a BBC series, *Hold the Back Page!*, both dramas involving sports writers, which we'd been in an alternative, *Time Out* way. When Andrew suddenly developed a taste for racing, as part of the pursuit of a girl whose passion it was, the routine in our Windmill Street office became something like this: arrive 10.15 a.m., drink coffee; read paper, especially the racing pages; put a few bets on; have lunch, at the Spaghetti

House if funds allowed; wander up to the bookie's on Charlotte Street to watch our horses run; collect winnings; buy a bottle to celebrate; do a bit of work; go to the pub.

Whenever we could, we'd write a horse-racing scene into a drama just so we could get to the track. The high-point was probably a 1987 BBC film entitled *Blat*, which involved Alfred Molina as a Georgian gangster, trying to clean up on the newly deregulated British stock-market. One night-shoot near Basingstoke allowed us a day out at Newbury, but we also managed to persuade the producer to film a whole sequence at Lingfield Park. Being on location at a racecourse for two days, with catering, came close to paradise.

Andrew's enthusiasm eventually persuaded him to take a small share in an eight-year-old novice hurdler called Clever Fox, trained by former top-class jockey Jeff King. In a microcosm of all owners' experiences, the horse kept getting injured in training and even when it did get to the track it performed so badly that it was denounced by the trainer in his inimitably unvarnished style: the horse had either 'run like a c**t', or even worse, 'run like a *complete* c**t'.

With marriage and mortgage denying me such pleasures, I had to wait until 1997 to make that giant step. I was entering middle age, I was settled, had two children, an intermittently successful career and a bit of spare cash. The mature action would have been to buy a Personal Equity Plan or a TESSA, or to put a few bob into one of those football unit trusts which Alan Hansen had been advertising. But I knew that my passion for horses now exceeded my love of football, and I'd never invested much more than a few hundred quid in my whole life. My economic philosophy was still aligned with one expressed by actor Sid James in an episode of *Hancock*: 'If you haven't got it, get it: if you've got it, spend it.' But most of all I knew that my years of watching racing had always been from the outside, as just another punter. So it was inevitable – I had to become an owner, I had to buy a horse.

'I Gotta Horse!'

It was mid-September by now, and though the Flat season runs on till early November, the long shadows and the chilly nights always tell your body that the serious business of National Hunt racing will soon be under way. Statistically speaking, the Jumps year ends on the last Saturday of May, and begins again on the following Monday. The introduction four years previously of summer meetings at specified courses – Worcester, Newton Abbot, Perth, Stratford and so on – has achieved its purpose in letting some of the smaller yards stay active and earn some money while all the media attention is focused on Epsom, Royal Ascot and Newmarket's July course. As a December-born baby I suppose that I was destined to favour autumn and winter, and my inclinations in racing always tended to favour jumping. But this became especially so when I moved to the country and came to appreciate the wild, windy days at my local track, Wincanton, with its easy-going atmosphere, its glowing good cheer in the bars, its warming fish soups and its chunky cheese and onion pasties.

Flat racing is fine, but as Woody Allen once said about life, 'it's all over too quickly', not just in terms of the races themselves, but also with the horses passing through. The best Flat horses are usually glimpsed as two-year-olds in the later part of the season. But with four of the five Classic races over by the first week in June, they can often be whisked away as mere three-year-olds to stud in Ireland, France or Japan before you've even managed to get your tongue around their Arabic names. Jump horses stick around longer, achieve more,

14

embed themselves in the affections of the public – think of Arkle, Red Rum, Desert Orchid and One Man – and they give great value to punters and owner alike. They are also, by and large, cheaper to buy than a decent Flat horse. There is another, more subtle division too, with the Flat dominated by a handful of very wealthy patrons such as the Maktoum family of Dubai, Robert Sangster, former bookmaker Michael Tabor, and many captains of industry. Jumps owners tend to come from 'old money' backgrounds, a large number being farmers or landowners. Having been brought up in a council house in Liverpool, I belong in neither camp, despite going to Cambridge and developing a career in the 'class-less' media.

But there are significant differences if you apply what might be called 'social coding' to the animals in the two branches of horse-racing. It is very nearly impossible for a cheaply bought or lowly bred horse to win the very top prizes on the Flat, such is the dominance of the top thoroughbred blood-lines. In contrast, many of the less exalted members of the jumping stock have managed to achieve great things – Norton's Coin won the 1990 Cheltenham Gold Cup at 100–1, and this year's Grand National winner Earth Summit was bought for around £6,000 and has won more than a quarter of a million. This equine egalitarianism appeals to me greatly, as does the notion that when you buy a Jumps horse your dreams of an historic win can be sustained for much longer than would ever be possible on the Flat. That's the theory at any rate.

So I had my rationale established and had a few bob to spend – I'd budgeted on around £2,000–£3,000 as the initial expense – but I really had no idea of how to go about the business of acquiring a horse, other than in the vaguest terms. I knew that you could go to one of the many horse sales which run throughout the year, but also that you needed to know what you were looking for. With my riding career having been confined to a Blackpool donkey I was in no position to be a judge of a horse's configuration. A former show-jumping champion, Barbara Green, had lived in the stable complex next to our house for a few years until her untimely death, and she had once passed on a few 'horse-whisperer'-style tips to me in one of our daily conversations. 'Always go for one with big ears,' Barbara had told me mystically. 'A good horse will always look you straight in the eye,' was another of her equine *aperçus*.

I didn't doubt her sincerity, or the wisdom of her words, but it didn't seem quite the done thing for me to waltz into a fast-moving sales-ring at Ascot or Doncaster and start eye-balling the beasts for a positive reaction. It is also the practice at sales – which are conducted in much the same manner as the auctions of antiques or household effects – for potential vendors to have a trainer accompany them so that the right decisions can be made and apt prices be achieved. The etiquette of a horse-sale is also somewhat arcane – you can't just turn up with a credit card or a cheque, because they prefer banker's drafts or cash, and the deals are still done in guineas. The prospect of me turning up at Ascot's September sales with three grand in cash – or 2,857 guineas – and asking for the horse with the biggest ears did not appeal as the best route to fulfilment. Even if it succeeded, there was the problem of how to get the horse home – a cheap-day return on Great Western Trains is less viable than having your own or your trainer's horse-box to hand. What finally decided me against the sales, however, was the blunt verdict delivered by a racing correspondent of my acquaintance, who described the lots on view at many sales as 'dog-meat on legs'.

Fortunately, on one of Channel 4 Racing's broadcasts extended time was given to an initiative by the British Horseracing Board to encourage more people to take up ownership and a snazzy information pack and an explanatory video were promised to those who rang their Portman Square headquarters. I had a vague nervousness about mentioning my name to them in a phone-call as I'd occasionally gone into print for the *Independent on Sunday* with a stroppy, leftish opinion piece banging on to the BHB about the need for racing to be more open and democratic. I therefore imagined that my mast-head photo from the paper, with the eyes gouged out, might be taped to the wall of the receptionist's office, and that I would get a sneering 'Oh, it's *you*, is it?' But I was plainly overestimating both my own importance and also the size of the *Independent on Sunday*'s readership, because when I did get round to phoning the BHB, they couldn't have been more helpful and accommodating.

Indeed the very next day, an envelope arrived, albeit devoid of snazzy information pack and video. Inside was a three-page letter, with highlighted paragraphs in bold print, a folded leaflet entitled 'The Thrill of Ownership', and a card bearing the legend 'Your Reservation'. Inside, my name had been printed on an invitation to a two-day seminar on ownership, costing £225 plus VAT, or £150 plus VAT if I replied before 30 January 1997 – this latter option seemed unlikely given that it was now 18 September 1997. Equally disconcerting was one of the bold paragraphs in the letter which 'warned' me (their word) that 'places at the seminars, which take place twice a year, are limited in number, so if you want to attend an early reply is advisable. The next takes place at Newmarket on 29 and 30 September 1997.' Ten days' time, hmm?

No doubt well-intentioned, the letter and the 'reservation' nevertheless had the same tone as is usually found in those *Reader's Digest* prize draw brochures which drop through the letter-box shortly after you've busted through your overdraft limit of Christmas. You know, the sort which reads: 'Yes, you Mr Hey! Have Won a Prize! Just Take Out a 1,000-Year Subscription!'

So I found the response a little off-putting, or 'in yer face' in the modern idiom. The other wrong note to be struck came with the photo on the leaflet. One of the key elements of the initial broadcast had been to point out that the ownership of racehorses had become much more widespread and much more accessible over recent years – so what does the photo show? Two twats in top-hats and tails celebrating a win at Royal Ascot.

Equally intimidating was a small information panel inside the leaflet showing the purchase prices of some successful Flat and Jumps horses, and their subsequent winnings. The cheapest example from the Flat was Key to My Heart, which had cost 5,000 guineas – as a yearling, that is – at Doncaster sales. Mister Bailey's, the 1994 2,000 Guineas winner, had cost 10,000 guineas – as a foal – at Tattersalls sales in Newmarket. I half expected to see the price of an equine foetus quoted.

When it came to the Jumps examples, the prices were a little more realistic, although the cheapest example was probably an uninspiring choice. Killeshin is a rugged old staying chaser who usually needs a minimum trip of six miles to win, which is unfortunate given that the longest Jumps race is about four-and-a-half miles. Killeshin is also trained by the deeply eccentric Wiltshire trainer John Manners, nickname 'Bad', and was bought at a 'Horses-in-Training' (i.e., discard) sale at Ascot for just 1,550 guineas. The images brought to mind by this involved used Ford Cortinas and Alexei Sayle singing 'Hullo, John, Gotta New Motor?'

There was no doubt that the seminar's actual programme was worthwhile – a visit to a top yard, watching morning gallops, a tour of the National Stud, and then dinner at the Jockey Club rooms. And the fee would be repaid to me by the marketing division of the BHB should I actually take up racehorse ownership within the following year. But the timing seemed so at odds with the racing calendar – why hold a Flat seminar at Newmarket at the end of the season?

Wouldn't spring be a better time, leaving the autumn seminar for those who are trying to get into National Hunt ownership? Was the date designed to steer people towards the yearling sales at Tattersalls? Given that I wasn't interested in acquiring a baby horse for racing in a year's time, I reluctantly passed on the 'Reservation', bold highlighting and all.

There seemed, too, an assumption within the BHB's leaflet that entry-level ownership consisted merely of ringing up a trainer or agent and then toddling off to the sales. This might have been the case if I'd had ten grand to spend, but I'd met only a handful of trainers, none of whom would remember me, and none of whom would *want* to remember me once I'd mentioned my paltry wedge. I thought about being introduced to a couple of likely candidates – Kim Bailey perhaps, or Jim Old – by friends who were more well-connected in racing, but it still came down to me not having a bottomless pot of money to dip into. The nightmare scenario was getting in too deep, bull-shitting myself into a corner and then finding that I was looking at the wrong end of three hundred quid a week in training fees and seven or eight grand in capital outlay. I'd have probably been defaulted within the first six months, and then been warned off by the Jockey Club for non-payment of fees. I could see it all happening, as I lay sweating 'in my box'.

When this first fever of fear had passed, I decided I had two realistic options. The first was to go for the ultimate satisfaction and 'breed-your-own', which would effectively mean as long a wait as my kids had from birth to primary school. Specialist National Hunt horses are given a longer time to develop than their counterparts on the Flat, for the obvious reason that the minimum trip for 'beginners' is the 1 mile 6 furlongs to 2 miles NH Flat race known as a 'bumper', while the maximum for a first-year hurdler could be a 3 mile 2 furlong race. Most National Hunt horses come 'on stream' as four-year-olds, even those who have been bought after racing as two- and three-year-olds on the Flat. Even then, many of them are still 'babies', tall and lengthy enough but about as wide as an Orkney Island telephone directory. So, tempting as it was, B-Y-O was out and much as my wife Wendy loves horses – the type that just eat grass in the field and fart – she couldn't be persuaded that we should build a 'granny annexe', and then stable and feed young 'Trigger' for four years before he could go out and earn a living. Breeding your own must be a fantastic thrill, but it involves either having your own farm, or boxes, or field, with access to a suitable brood-mare, and a clear idea of who might be a suitable 'dad' for your racing offspring.

Still, out of curiosity, I phoned a local stud, Conkwell Grange, which I knew had housed three or four National Hunt sires at one time, including Nicholas Bill, Lyphento, Sula Bula and Bonny Scot. I wanted to know just what was involved in the long process of 'designing' your own race-horse. Liz Harrington runs Conkwell Grange, where the emphasis now is on the breeding of horses for the increasingly popular Arab racing. The 300 acres of the stud, high above the Limpley Stoke valley near Bath, are therefore dotted with over fifty Arab mares and their foals, many of whom are owned by Sheikh Mohammed. Of her four National Hunt sires, only Bonny Scot remains, with Nicholas Bill having died last year, and the other two being leased out to other studs. But Liz knows the breeding business inside out and her small, spartan office in a quiet corner of the stable blocks is stacked with manuals and reference books. So what would be involved if I chose the breeding route?

'Well, in the first instance – a long wait,' she said with a firm smile. 'A mare's pregnancy lasts eleven months, and then assuming the foal is born sound, it wouldn't be "broken" until it was three years old. Then it would be turned away into a field again to think about what it had learnt. You'd probably ride it a little after that for experience and then put it away again for the winter. In the spring of its fourth year, if it was strong enough, you'd then send it to your chosen trainer for its racing education. So the process takes about five years, and you may not even see your horse on a racecourse even then. Some don't run till they're five or six, and there's always the possibility that the trainer will think it's no good.'

Judging by the adverts I had seen from time to time in the racing press, the actual fee for covering a mare was pitched at a reasonable level. 'The average National Hunt stud fee is about £800,' Liz told me, 'although some are as low as £300, or as high as £1,500. Once you found your mare – and you can either buy one or just do a "rent-a-body" job – you'd bring her to be covered by your chosen stallion somewhere between 15 February and mid-July. The breeding season is shorter for the Flat. Traditionally, a mare is scanned on 1 October, and if she's in foal, that's when you pay up. If she's not, there's no charge. Once the foal is born, it can stay with its mother until it's weaned, longer if the mare is yours. A typical charge for housing a mare in foal would be around £10 a day, and for just looking after the foal, £6 a day. Vets' fees would be fairly basic provided nothing went amiss, say £300 a year. The foal could stay at the stud, grow up there and be prepared for training. Most studs can do all that for you.'

Without being able to reach a precise total, I could already see from what Liz had told me that there wouldn't be much change out of £15,000–£20,000 from the moment of my foal's conception and seeing it jump off for its first race.

'It's definitely cheaper to go and buy something ready-made from one of the National Hunt sales, at Doncaster or somewhere like that, because most of the work has been done on a horse by then. But you can't always know exactly what you're buying, not even if you've got a trainer with you. If you breed your own horse and it becomes a winner, I can tell you it's among the most satisfying feelings in the world. We know the Cole family very well, and they bred and trained Dubacilla [2nd in the 1995 Cheltenham Gold Cup] themselves and had a fantastic time with her. It all depends on how much time you're prepared to wait, and how much you want to spend. As a former owner of National Hunt horses, I have to tell you that you just can't make it pay, whether you've bred the horse or just bought it. The prize-money's just too low. But that doesn't mean you can't have lots of fun. I mean people spend thousands of pounds playing golf and don't get anything back for it. If racing's your hobby, you have to be prepared to accept that's the way it's going to be.'

Much as I was tempted to become an equine 'dad', the time-scale of setting up a home-bred horse was just too long. I'm sure that it's the sort of thing you can do once you've got horses in training and have some money coming in, but for a complete novice owner it just didn't seem viable.

This seemed to leave me with only one option – to form or join a partnership and limit my commitment to a percentage share of a horse and, perhaps more importantly, a percentage share of the costs. I discounted the idea of rounding up four or five friends with cash to spare – anyone who's ever tried to organise a weekend cricket team will know the agony this type of task can generate – and began to look for a suitable deal with an existing partnership.

This has been one of the great growth areas in both codes of horse-racing over the past decade or so, as two recessions have humbled trainers into the acceptance of partnerships as a means of staying in business when the rich single owners pull out their money after a stock-market crash. An equivalent, and equally welcome phenomenon, was the change in attitude of London cab-drivers as they too pursued custom, becoming first polite and, later, willing to go south of the river.

Now cab-drivers, wheel-clamp teams, ex-footballers and even journalists are accepted as racehorse-owning partnerships when they would have been lucky to get on a course without being shot as trespassers in the pre-war years. This social progress has obviously been helped by a greater distribution of wealth among the middle classes and the increasing perception of racing as another part of the leisure industry, rather than the private pursuit of the upper classes which it had been for most of its existence. In 1987, Channel 4 Racing's presenter Brough Scott, who has been in the game for four decades as first an amateur jockey and then an outstanding journalist, asked owner and Jockey Club member Lord Cadogan about the social changes in racing and was told casually, 'I think things have moved a long way. I mean, my grandfather would never have talked to someone like you.'

Lord Cadogan's grandfather would probably have been rendered entirely speechless had he been able to envisage that one day the descendants of his grooms, housekeepers, coachmen and chimney-sweeps would be able to share in the experience of racehorse ownership, but thanks to partnerships, syndicates and racing clubs, they do. Roughly speaking, partnerships may involve up to twenty people having shares in a horse, syndicates can be larger, while a racing club can involve hundreds owning shares in more than a dozen horses. One of the most high-profile of these is the Elite Racing Club, which has horses of both codes, stabled all over the country. Their best horse so far was the speedy hurdler Mysilv who cost over £150,000 to purchase and very nearly won most of that outlay back before she suffered a fatal accident on the Lambourn gallops. The club offers all the usual activities associated with ownership – stable visits, watching gallops, a regular newsletter and a 'confidential hot-line' for the word of intended gambles on the club's horses. I considered an investment here but ruled it out for three reasons.

Firstly, the annual all-in cost of £169 is – how can I put this? – almost too cheap, and a consequence of this is that the club must need God knows how many members in order to sustain its finances. This means, inevitably, that many of the activities offered are on a rota basis, including the actual business of being in the paddock before racing, one of the first pleasures an owner seeks. If you see an Elite Racing horse coming back into the winner's enclosure – which many of them do – they are usually followed by a charabanc-sized group of members, who are presumably the lucky ones for that particular day. I wanted something on a smaller scale, something more personal, with the guarantee that whenever 'my' horse was running, I could get an owner's badge to see it in action. The other considerations that came into play were the club's inclination towards Flat horses, and the wide geographical spread of the stables involved. Call me a fussy demanding bastard, but for my few grand I wanted a Jumps horse that had a chance of winning and which I could get to see both at its yard and on the track.

This left me one last option. Throughout late September I'd been scanning the classified advertisements which appear every Saturday in the *Racing Post* offering everything from racing trips abroad to jobs as stable lads. But throughout the year there are also adverts for horses for sale or syndication. I noted down a fair number and began to build up the nerve to make a few phone-calls. Most of the adverts are deliberately couched in teasing terms, designed both to attract the potential buyer, and to protect the vendor from nosy enquiries from others in the same trade. Some are also left vague because they don't want to name an up-front price, preferring to see what a caller has to spend before mentioning money. It's a curious etiquette, and one with which I wasn't entirely at ease.

For one thing, I didn't want to ring up about, say, a four-year-old gelding by top stallion Strong Gale and find that I was into the realms of thirty grand or more, and then meekly with-draw. Nor did I want to phone a number and find that it was in North Yorkshire. I wanted to sound keen but not gullible, shrewd but not aloof, knowledgeable but not an insider.

The first advert to interest me was one concerning a horse called Chabrol which, the text boasted, was a Champion Hurdle contender and would be running soon at Chepstow in early October. The price per share was £3,000, near the top of my range, and the number of 'an ambitious trainer' was given for a contact. I dickered a bit, liking the horse's name a lot because it belonged to a French film director I greatly admired — pretentious, *moi*? — but a long search through the dialling codes revealed that the trainer's number was in Newmarket. I wasn't sure about the boastfulness of the ad's tone either, because racing and betting have always seemed to me to be about shouting the odds *after* you've won, rather than before — very English. I managed to find some background on the horse through various handbooks and form guides and though he was sired by the unlucky Derby loser El Gran Señor, the word 'unreliable' occurred enough times to put me off making the call.

As it turned out, Chabrol would have been an entirely creditable investment, in more ways than one. In the first instance, he won a couple of decent races in the 1997–8 season — a Grade 2 hurdle at Uttoxeter in the mud at 14–1, and a less exalted race over 2 miles 6 furlongs at Windsor — and did indeed end up at Cheltenham, albeit not in the Champion Hurdle, finishing down the field in the Gold Card Handicap Hurdle. Secondly, the Chabrol Partnership was set up by a bloke called Terry Connors, a film and television production executive who was a close friend of a mate of mine, Chris Burt, of whom more later. Terry actually phoned me at one point in the season on another matter, when I had to confess to him that I'd chickened out of the partnership. He took it with good grace. It was my loss after all. Terry is a veteran racehorse owner with a lot of stories to tell and a good sense of humour, and I'm sure I would have enjoyed his company through the season.

But a week or so later I finally saw the advert that seemed

to hit all the right buttons. It was Saturday 11 October, when all eyes were on the big Italy v. England World Cup qualifying game in Rome, and it read as follows: '1997–8 NH Season: 2 horses currently in training with champion trainer. Fixed costs, no extras, small group. ¼, ½ or full share.'

This seemed ideal in every way. Buying into two horses rather than one would double my potential pleasure; the champion trainer had to be Martin Pipe, whose Pond House Stable at Nicholashayne in Somerset would be only about an hour's drive from my home; a small group of partners eased my fears about the regular availability of owners' badges; and the fixed costs with flexible share levels suggested that the overall deal wouldn't offer any unpleasant surprises. My trawl through the dialling codes revealed a South Wales number, which I called. I left my name and address so that more details, not least the identity of the two horses, could be sent. Two days later a fat envelope arrived with all the information, and a helpful, friendly hand-written letter from the man who ran the partnership, Cliff Underwood.

They called themselves 'The Tally-Ho Partnership', nothing to do with fox-hunting, but simply the name of the farm near Haverfordwest where Cliff and his wife Janet live and breed their horses. The two that were racing that year were revealed as Di's Last, a slightly unfortunate name given the events of 31 August, and Rowley John. Di, the information leaflet informed me, was a seven-year-old daughter of Ra Nova out of a mare called Dial Direct. The dam had won in Ireland and had family connections with the famous L'Escargot, who won both the Cheltenham Gold Cup and the Grand National, not to mention other well-known chasers such as The Pilgarlic, What a Buck, Havago and Flitgrove. The sire, Ra Nova, was a very successful hurdler in the 1980s, winning the Timeform Hurdle at Chepstow in 1983, the Tote Gold Trophy Handicap Hurdle (still better known as 'The Schweppes'), the Gerry Feilden Hurdle at

Newbury in 1984 at 16–1, and the Welsh Champion Hurdle the same year. As an 'entire' (i.e., wedding tackle intact) horse, Ra Nova had later become a useful recruit to the breeding of National Hunt horses.

This looked like a pretty good background to me. To support the good impression given by her breeding, Di's Last had apparently performed quite well during her first two seasons of racing, finishing 2nd, 4th and 4th in three 'bumper' races in 1995–6, and then finishing 5th, 3rd and 4th in her three hurdle races of 1996–7, before a cut on one of her legs finished her season. Champion jockey Tony McCoy had ridden her in one of the races, so, as the newsletter stated, she was 'highly thought of' by the Pipe stable. A novice chasing career was now planned for this year, and an enclosed photograph showing Di clearing a hurdle, with her hooves tucked-in in exemplary fashion, seemed to suggest that she might be rather good at it. A video of her races was also available should I want to see it – which I did. This wasn't some amateur cam-corder effort but a copy of the official recording of the race made by the company which provides the pictures both for the on-course stewards and for the off-course punters in the betting shops. Many winning owners automatically get a copy of the race in which their horse has triumphed as a present from the racecourse in question, but owners whose horses finish placed have to order them.

In contrast to Di's video career, Rowley John was an unfilmed, unraced four-year-old gelding, by Rymer out of Arctic Gipsy. Rymer's most famous son is Dublin Flyer, Tim Forster's great chaser, who was retired at the end of the 1998 season after a glittering career. Rowley is not yet a Dublin Flyer, but at least his photograph bore out the description of him as a strapping chestnut with a white blaze. Posed in the manner of a classical Stubbs painting on a track at the edge of a field, Rowley looked a bit like an equine Vinnie Jones eye-balling an opponent who'd complained about a tackle. 'Want

27

some more then, son?' was the unwritten sub-title to the confident look I detected in him. His season would be centred around a few bumper races before starting his hurdling career. All in all, this seemed like a good pairing, a fairly experienced horse without too many miles on the clock and with the promise of some progress to come, and a completely unknown quantity that, as all owners say until they see otherwise, 'could be anything'.

The only question now was the cost. The partnership consisted of 14 shares with 2½ being retained by Cliff and Janet Underwood as the owners of the two horses. The cost of a full share, all-in, was £140 a month for the period from 1 August 1997 to 1 June 1998, although I would only be liable for eight months' worth of fees due to my late entry into the partnership. The £1,120 total would include all those extras that many trainers don't include in their basic monthly fee but which soon mount up – the use of gallops, farrier's charges, transport costs, jockeys' riding fees and race entry charges. The only additional costs I was told that might arise would be vets' fees if either of the horses was injured and needed treatment, though even here, if the horse was unable to race, it would be returned to Cliff and Janet's farm with no further costs to the partnership. Any prize-money would be distributed in accordance with the share-holding at the end of the season.

This seemed an incredibly reasonable deal, so when Cliff phoned me up to see what I'd thought of the partnership and the horses, I simply told him to count me in. I thought about putting the payments on a standing order, but this seemed a bit of a puny option. I also knew that my freelance life meant that I wouldn't necessarily have the money at a specific time every month, because I simply don't get paid like that. Far better, and far more 'courageous', I thought, to pay up now and write off the money. So, on Thursday 16 October 1997, I walked into my building society in Bradford-on-Avon and eventually persuaded one of the highly amused girls working there to make out a cheque to the Tally-Ho Partnership for £1,120. I then walked the twenty yards or so from the building society to the letter-box in The Shambles and promptly posted the cheque off to Cliff before I could change my mind and find something sensible to do with the money. I knew that I wasn't exactly an 'owner' as such, nor did I have my racing colours to order, and my name was not about to be splashed all over the *Racing Post*, but to all intents and purposes I had two racehorses I could call 'mine' at long last. I went into my local bar, the Dandy Lion, and bought a large Calvados to celebrate, and to toast the memory of my dad, who I knew would have understood. A small adventure had begun.

Waiting

For the first few days, I walked around with the photos of the two horses in my jacket pocket, rather like a new father of twins, eager to show them to any of the other Bradford-on-Avon writers, artists, musicians and layabouts who meet every morning in the Dandy Lion for a few cups of cappuccino and a chat. It has become the fashion with our group that anyone with something new to reveal immediately gets the piss taken out of them in a major way, so a lunatic who had just spent over a grand on two horses was going to get more than his fair share. And I did. But apart from the expense, the most obvious source of ammunition for my colleagues was the simple question of when were they going to run, to which I had no immediate answer.

Cliff had told me that both horses had gone into Martin Pipe's yard in the late summer after spending time at the farm, and that Di was likely to run earlier than Rowley by dint of her greater experience. In fact, both Cliff and Janet had been down to the yard on 10 October to watch Di working and had come away impressed, reporting her to be 'stronger than last year'. She had, according to the partnership's first news-letter of the season, cantered three times both up and down the all-weather gallop at Pipe's yard, wearing something that sounded like it belonged to an Anne Summers catalogue, a grackle nose-band, to stop her running too freely.

Rowley – yes, I'd started to call them by their first names already – meanwhile had had just the one canter and was said to be 'learning well', being 'very laid back in his approach'. However, his blood test – something all trainers do on their

30

horses – was slightly wrong, and he would now be having 'a few quiet days' until he was all right again. The implications seemed fairly obvious to me, that Di would be running in the next weeks, with Rowley making his debut a little later. It looked, to my novice eyes, as though we'd get a couple of runs into both of them before Christmas.

The sense of anticipation about Di's return had been heightened by the subsequent achievements of horses she had run against with credit. Aerion (trainer, Olive Sherwood), Galatasori Jane (Paul Nicholls), Edgemoor Prince (Philip Hobbs), Maid for Adventure (Henrietta Knight), Dolce Notte (Pipe) and Connaught Cracker (Hobbs) had all recorded wins which, in racing parlance, had 'boosted the form'. So the simple question was 'When will she run?'

As a new member of the partnership I was a bit shy of showing any signs of impatience, and in any case it was made plain that the partnership as a whole deferred to Martin Pipe's decision about such matters. He was the man closest to our horses on a daily basis and, quite apart from his actual achievements, Pipe had made his reputation as a trainer who had his horses totally fit first time out, cleverly placing them in races that he thought they had every chance of winning. So it really was just a question of waiting to hear the word from his Pond House yard. I daresay that every owner in the country goes through this experience, apart from those few who are in a position to out-rank their trainers in terms of know-how. 'The owners you don't get on with,' said the trainer Mick Ryan once, 'are the ones who pay you the money to do a job and then want to do it themselves.'

There was no chance of us pressing Martin Pipe into getting the horses to race when he didn't think they were ready. It would have been akin to the eager father of some twelve-year-old schoolboy ringing up Glenn Hoddle and insisting that his lad be put into the England team. Quite apart from the fact that Pipe had over 150 horses in his yard, all with owners asking the same questions, he was now emphatically a trainer with all the big prizes of the National Hunt season at his mercy. At the latest Cheltenham Festival back in March 1997, Pipe had saddled four winners, including Make a Stand's spectacular triumph in the Champion Hurdle, his second hurdling crown after Granville Again in 1993. He'd won the Grand National with Freddie Starr's Miinnehoma in 1994, and a fistful of the Welsh and Scottish equivalents with horses such as Bonanza Boy, Run For Free, Riverside Boy and Carvill's Hill. From being what might be called purely a 'volume trainer', Pipe had progressed into the most formidable force in National Hunt racing. Having 'my' horses with him, though, seemed to me from the outset to be a double-edged sword.

The undoubted benefit we would enjoy would be the sheer professionalism of the Pipe approach that, over the last twelve years, had changed for ever the life-style and working methods of the typical NH trainer. Before Pipe made an impact, most of the bigger yards simply wouldn't race a horse outside the traditional 'book-ends' of the National Hunt season. The Mackeson, now the Murphy's, Gold Cup Chase at Cheltenham in early November was the first day of term at far as they were concerned, while the Whitbread at Sandown the following April was emphatically time for *exeunt omnes*. One simply didn't race outside those dates because it was considered vulgar and competitive, and one's owners understood that because they had also been to Eton or Harrow and knew the rules.

Pipe's new training methods – involving a gradual aggregation of shorter, bursting runs rather than just a conventional gallop – and his almost promiscuous pursuit of winning any sort of race, did not endear him to Jump racing's self-regarding, family-connected oligarchy. There was no doubt too that both social snobbery and suspicion were aroused by the fact that his father is one of the biggest independent bookmakers in South-West England.

Indeed at one period, you couldn't go racing without hearing a rumour or a bit of hearsay about Martin Pipe's methods, all of which culminated in an infamous episode of *The Cook Report* in May 1991. As I recall, Roger Cook's programme was essentially concerned with the allegedly high ratio of Pipe-trained horses that did not come back into training during the seasons between 1987–91. The implication being that he trained them too hard. Pipe, who appeared in the programme itself to counter the allegation, denounced it as 'total rubbish'.

Around this time, I remember discussing Pipe at a party with a trainer of the 'old school' whose attitude was as follows: 'I don't think Pipe's bent or anything, it's just that he and his stable are so damned competitive. They want to win everything, and work towards that goal. I was at a horse-racing charity dinner recently, and each stable had taken a table-for-ten. There was a racing quiz-sheet on each table and you had to fill it in over the course of the evening, and the winners would get a case of champagne or something. Well, there we were, scratching our heads over the questions in between getting pissed, and I just happened to look across to the Pipe table where one of his team was crouched under the table with a mobile phone to his ear. He was ringing back to Pond House to get someone to look up some of the answers they couldn't get. They just won't let a prize go un-won!'

But as the Pond House winners began to flood in from the mid-1980s onwards, so too did the new owners, and all the best and most ambitious jockeys – Peter Scudamore, Richard Dunwoody, Adrian Maguire and, most recently, the record-breaking Tony McCoy rode for the stable. They all wanted to buy into the Pipe dream. In the book *221 – Peter Scudamore's Record Season*, written by an old colleague of mine from the *Sunday Correspondent*, Dudley Doust, Scudamore outlined what he saw as the three crucial ingredients in Pipe's success.

'What I think, frankly, about Martin Pipe,' Scudamore said in 1989, 'is that what he does is so simple that to do it correctly is difficult. To do something better than somebody else in this sport, I can tell you, takes a touch of genius. Secondly, he knows horses. He knows their capabilities, which some trainers don't. He knows how to place them. In other words, he knows a goose from a swan and he'll make sure he doesn't enter a goose in a swan race. What I mean is, he won't go to Ascot or Cheltenham and socialise. He'll only go there to win. Thirdly, there's the blood-testing. He tests his horses scrupulously for virus and, as he puts it, they've got to be "spot-on" or they don't run.'

In one of our telephone conversations Cliff told me how Martin had been virtually the only trainer he could find who was prepared to offer an 'all-in' price for our two horses, such was his accessibility to smaller owners. Cliff also said, succinctly, that 'if Martin can't get our two to win a race, then nobody can'.

My main reservation about Pipe was not to do with old runners – a successful bet on Miinnehoma at 16–1 for the 1994 Grand National had helped dispel these – but with a fear that because he had so many horses in his yard, many of them high-flyers, our modest pair might somehow slip off the agenda. I didn't say anything to Cliff because it was only a private instinct. Instead, I practised 'Zen and the Art of the Owner's Patience', quietly clocking the stable's unending output of winners, hoping that ours would be soon among them.

What helped me enormously at this time of *equus interruptus* was a chance happening. For a year or so, I'd been doing bits and pieces for the *Night & Day* supplement of the *Mail on Sunday* – standing in as television critic, a few sports-related features. The magazine editor at the time was Simon Kelner, who had been my sports editor when I was writing for the *Sunday Correspondent* and who shared my passion for racing.

Simon had come up with an idea for a pre-Christmas feature involving five different people being given £1,000 to invest for a month, to see how much they could each make. There was to be a poker player, a stock-market trader, an antiques dealer and so on. I was cast as the racehorse gambler and commissioned to try and make money by betting, and then write an article on my success or, more likely, my failure. A cheque from the *Mail on Sunday* for a grand duly arrived.

Although I am a regular gambler, my stakes are usually fairly small – a £20 win single, or £2 win Lucky 15 are my normal strength. By habit, I bet only when I go to a meeting or when I can see a race on the television. I've grown out of the bad old days of spending entire afternoons in betting shops, chasing losses until I was ankle-deep in crumpled-up slips. Seven years ago, I opened an account with Tote Credit, so the bulk of my betting now is carried out over the phone, with a fortnightly statement detailing my losses and, just occasionally, my gains.

My two biggest wins, by a long margin, came in 1989 and then again in 1993. Both came about through basic £1 win Lucky 15 bets, which involve four horses and a stake of £15. If all four horses win, your fifteen bets come up – four singles, six doubles, four trebles and one four-timer. I have never quite achieved this, but even getting three horses up out of four can be rewarding if the prices are good. The 1989 bet had three winners – Vicario di Bray (11–1), Cuddy Dale (8–1) and Memberson (15–2) – which produced £1,363.50 winnings in cash. Had Wide Boy, at 10–1, won at Kempton I'd have picked up over £20,000. Surrey Racing, where I placed the bet, would have been reduced to Rutland Racing . . .

The second big win came courtesy of a splendid late summer Saturday on the Flat at Newbury. The first leg of the bet, Billy Cruncheon, went down, but the next three all came in – Polish Laughter (4–1), Lindon Lime (25–1) and Castoret (10–1) – producing a return of £1,926.50. On at least ten other occasions I've also come close to getting the complete Lucky 15 up, none more so than the day when, having had the first three winners, the appropriately named Does It Matter fell at the last at Kempton Park when 30 lengths clear in a novice chase. All of which goes to show that I'm neither a clever gambler nor a complete dunce.

But what happened over the next four weeks became something I have never experienced in 35 years of betting. From the grand I was sent I made a profit of £727.40, with 13 winners from 35 bets, the profit being donated to charity, the grand being returned to Lord Rothermere. The principal contributor to this total was Suny Bay, who won me over £300 with his victories in the Edward Hanmer Memorial Chase at Haydock, and the Hennessy Gold Cup at Newbury. I didn't have any inside information – except for a coincidence tip from a Canadian friend which put me on to Breeders' Cup winner Chief Bearhart, which was trained by her friend Mark Frostad. But I became convinced that my new status as an 'owner', combined with the heavy responsibility of looking after Lord Rothermere's grand, and the obligation of going public on the outcome, had suddenly made me a more thoughtful bettor.

On Wednesday 12 November I was invited – at the last minute, so somebody more important must have cried off – to a box at Newbury hosted by the highly successful sports agent Jon Holmes. His clients include many of the top names, although most of them are now more active in broadcasting and newspaper work than in actual sport itself. The likes of Gary Lineker, Alan Hansen, John Barnes, David Gower and Will Carling are on his books, together with such racing personalities as Brough Scott, Clare Balding and that little Italian chappie called Frankie Dettori.

I'd first met Jon at the 1989 Ryder Cup at The Belfry, which I was covering for the *Sunday Correspondent*. Jon had been a fan of *The Manageress*, the series I'd written for

Channel 4, and wanted to meet up, so an introduction was made and we swapped a few drinks and stories. Our relationship developed into a firm friendship, and our families once shared a holiday together in Devon in 1991. I'd written quite a number of speeches for some of Jon's high-profile clients – for three England captains in fact, Lineker, Carling and Mike Atherton – and I'd also helped Jon and Gary develop a drama series for ITV. Our latest collaboration was a World Cup documentary for the BBC, presented by Gary, about the top scorers at each competition, the *Golden Boots*.

Not surprisingly, the guests in the box included some of Jon's broadcasting contacts – the then Head of BBC Sport, Brian Barwick (soon to defect to ITV), Gary Newbon of ITV, Niall Sloane, editor of *Match of the Day*, and Peter Fincham, executive producer of *They Think It's All Over*. I was a relative minnow among these 'honchos' but my status as owner at least won me a little serious respect, along with the inevitable burden of providing tips for the rest of the guests. The perception is that somehow an owner must be 'in the know', not just about his own horse but all horses. That first newsletter from Cliff had pointed out that 'our horses will be run on their merits', in other words, there would be no nonsense about 'hiding' form. I was also advised of the 'Pipeline' telephone number, on which Martin or Chester Barnes, his assistant, give their tips from the stable's runners, but presumably only *after* the relevant owners have had first word. That was about as close as I'd come so far to 'inside information', so finding winners for the box's guests was no easy task, even with the pitifully small number of runners on the Newbury card. I managed to tip, and back, Copper Boy in the Novice Chase, which brought me some credibility, and another small profit towards the *Night & Day* gambling competition.

During this month of mystical betting, I received the second 'Tally-Ho Partnership' newsletter from Cliff, dated 12

November, with more frustrating news. It read as follows:

Janet and I visited the yard on Friday 7 November to see the horses. Unfortunately they had literally swapped places since the last visit. Di's Last had a slight infection after working on the gallops about ten days ago, and had to go on a course of antibiotics for five days, which in the end meant ten days' box rest. We saw her, and Martin said that she had picked up and was much brighter in herself. He informed us that the vet would see her again on the 10th and that he would ring us, which he duly did. Di's blood test is fine and she has scoped clear and is now back in work. This has put her back a couple of weeks in preparation of course, but she was not far off peak, so hopefully it won't be for too long.

Rowley John's blood picture is fine and he is now in fast work. We watched him work on the gallops three times up, three down. He worked with no effort and looked really well. He worked with Cyborgo and Big Strand, and besides dwarfing them both, did not look out of place. Gerry Supple, his work rider, reports him a very cool customer, laid-back and doing everything asked of him so far.

A photo of Rowley working with his two exalted companions was enclosed – Cyborgo, a top-class staying hurdler, now embarking on a chasing career, and Big Strand, winner of the Coral Cup at that year's Cheltenham Festival. From what was written, it now seemed that Rowley was more likely to run before Di.

The Jumps season was well and truly under way now, whether you went by the old or new calendar, with Señor El Betrutti having won the Murphy's Gold Cup at Cheltenham – an encouraging victory for the three-horse yard of Susan Nock over the bigger stables – and the Hennessy looming. I was brought out of semi-retirement by the *Independent on Sunday* to cover the race, or, to be precise, to write a piece about the last working day of the BBC's iconic race-caller Sir Peter O'Sullevan. The great man's television commentary was broadcast over the racecourse tannoy as Suny Bay survived a nose-diving error at the fourth fence to go on to win with supreme ease, despite the burden of my – sorry, make that Lord Rothermere's – sixty quid.

It was a great scene in the winner's enclosure afterwards with all the jockeys coming out to present O'Sullevan with a magnum of champagne. His voice had played so much a part in my childhood that I was at one time convinced he must be a lodger. Now it was silenced and I reflected, a touch selfishly I admit, that the glorious possibility of Sir Peter calling home Di's Last or Rowley John no longer existed. That pleasure had gone to Andrew Cohen, the owner of Suny Bay, and I bet that in time the videotape of the race, with O'Sullevan's voice over it, will be as cherishable as the winner's trophy itself, perhaps even more so.

To provide a photo for the *Night & Day* feature, I'd also been to Ascot on 21 November and the only winner I'd backed was something called Ela Agapi Mou, Greek for 'I Love You', in the last race. This was a horse owned by script-writer Lynda La Plante, whom I'd interviewed a few weeks previously for another *N&D* feature. While I was pleased to win money on what had been purely a coincidence bet, the sight of somebody I knew in the winner's enclosure brought out one of the basic emotions of ownership, jealousy. When this was combined with the wistfulness of my day at the Hennessy, it created a tremendous sense of frustration at the non-appearance of the two horses I'd bought into. I began to feel that I was personally responsible for this failure, on the old pessimist's logic that 'everything I touch turns to shit'. It felt like I'd stopped backing losing horses, but had taken to buying them instead. The imminence of my 46th birthday on

8 December probably had something to do with it as well.

Indeed, one day after passing this minor landmark no less a personage than Sheikh Mohammed threw another spanner into my life with the bomb-shell speech that was delivered on his behalf at the Gimcrack Dinner at York. As I noted in the Introduction, it was a measured but deeply felt complaint about the levels of prize-money available in English racing, when set against the costs of ownership. Since his speech was made, the Sheikh has made several dramatic gestures, including the buying of the former French racecourse at Evry, with a view to turning it into a private training centre for many of his best two-year-old horses, run by one of his most favoured Newmarket handlers, David Loder.

In amongst all the racing industry reactions at the time – from the stony-faced bookmakers who the Sheikh had accused of milking racing's profits, to the querulous trainers worried about their future – was my own sharp realisation that if one of the richest men in the world couldn't make the game pay, what chance did I have? I worked out that if I was paying £140 per month as my ¹⁄₁₄th share of the costs of training Di and Rowley, then the total outlay for the ten-month season for the whole partnership was a whopping £19,600. Given that the average winning prize-money for a bog-standard National Hunt hurdles race is usually around the £1,500 mark, our two horses would have to win about twelve races between them just to break even. To add to this gloomy perspective was the simple fact that the NH season was very nearly half-way through. Depression descended upon me once again.

I was also beginning to become completely paranoid about the partnership being some kind of elaborate 'sting'. I'd asked for the video of Di's races early on, but it had never been sent, and the longer this went on so I began to believe that the horses didn't actually exist, or that they had died some months ago. And because there had been no chance to meet up with Cliff or the rest of the partners, I didn't really have a clue about the people to whom I'd handed over my £1,120. I kept reassuring myself that nobody pulling such a stroke would give out their home and business addresses, but then again I thought they might be a front. I wondered about going down to the Martin Pipe stable, but as visits had to be arranged through Cliff or Janet, I started to fantasise about how easy it would be just to stick any old horse on the gallops and I wouldn't have known otherwise. And then I realised what was going on – apart from a depression about the horses' apparent inactivity, my script-writer's brain was trying to construct a plot because that's how I see life.

Fortunately, Cliff phoned a few days later to say that Rowley was continuing his education by completing the essential task of learning to run round bends – something I'd always assumed horses did naturally – and that he was looking good, 'though still a bit green and big'. The stable reckoned he would be best on good-to-soft ground, and would probably go well on heavy. Martin was now said to be looking for a suitable bumper race in which to introduce Rowley to racing.

Meanwhile Di had passed her latest blood test with 100 per cent and 'seemed OK'. More enticingly, thanks to further wins by two horses that Di had raced against last season – Spring Gale and Galatasori Jane – one of the partners, who is a student of racing statistics, had worked out that her current handicap mark of 86 was effectively 24lb below what she should have. For those baffled by such technical references, let me attempt a clarification. All horses in training are allocated an 'official weight' or 'handicap mark' by the BHB's team of handicappers as a means of expressing how good they are. The very best horses are at the top of a theoretical handicap, while the worst are at the bottom. But if a horse shows improvement, he or she is moved up the handicap, or down if they under-perform. The official marks are based on actual performances, cross-referenced with other form. But as Di hadn't run for the best part of nine months her rating hadn't been changed, while those of horses she'd run well against had risen because of their improvement. I'm not sure even *I* understand it now . . .

The main point of this information, though, was that once Di was ready to run, she could be placed in a race surrounded by other horses on roughly the same mark, but only we would know that she would be well ahead of them! In short, we could fill our boots betting on her. Cliff told me that Martin was eyeing a maiden handicap hurdle in the first or second week of January. I just hoped that I could survive Christmas with enough money to have a decent bet.

Another call from Cliff on 16 December suggested that Rowley would almost certainly run at one of the Boxing Day meetings, possibly even Kempton Park. I began to cheer up a bit, and now comforting images of going to the races with a party of friends over the festive season started to fill my head in idle moments. Whether this is a trait peculiar to writers, who have to spend most of their working day stuck behind a desk, lost in their thoughts, I don't know. But somehow I feel that I need something to look forward to, in order to cope with the internal miseries and physical constraints of the creative process. I'm sure that assembly-line workers suffer worse mental tortures. I know that I did when I worked in a steamily oppressive tobacco warehouse in Liverpool docks for four months. But there are compensations in being able to interact socially within a factory, and in knowing that work can be left behind as soon as the big bell sounds. Writers work alone, and even when they stop, the black dog of anxiety falls into step behind them, often going on to roger their leg until well into the night.

Saturday 20 December 1997

Perversely, there is no better cure for the blues than a day out at the races. So having finished my pre-Christmas work (ho, ho!), I decided a trip to Ascot as just another punter would help keep things in perspective, not least by backing six straight losers as I usually do. I arranged to meet my friend Chris Burt, who also fancied the day for the slightly less deserving reason that he was going to Cuba for three weeks and needed a fix of harmless fun before really enjoying himself.

Chris is a long-standing film and television producer with a list of major credits to his name, most popularly *Inspector Morse*. I worked with him on a less successful drama series five years ago, but we got on very well – not a normal occurrence in the writer–producer relationship, I have to tell you. It certainly helped that we shared more than an interest in many of the same things: horse-racing, football, jazz and drink. On New Year's Day 1994, we had managed to shake off the self-inflicted hangovers we'd ended up with after a mutual friend's party in Southwell, and headed straight off to the Notting-hamshire town's all-weather track for an afternoon of quite appalling racing.

The good thing about Chris as a racing companion is that he quite enjoys being a hopeless punter, or can at least see the funny side of it. There are plenty of people with whom I've been racing who become quite murderously aggressive if they back a loser, or see their Placepot go down in the first race. Chris just roars with self-mocking laughter. He also likes what are known as the 'gaff' tracks for the same reasons that I do, because being perceived as lesser racecourses often encourages the people running them into greater efforts to please their public. There's a more relaxed atmosphere at the places we've been to together, such as Bath and Wincanton, than at some of the more prestigious tracks where you are forever being scrutinised by 'jobsworths' for the correctness of your badge or the presence of silk neck-ties.

Having said that, neither of us is particularly averse to smart days out at Newbury or Sandown, or especially York, to where I took Chris for his first time in August 1997 on Ebor Day. I'd booked us on to the Tote Credit train at £125 each, a price that may seem steep, but is in fact one of the bargains of the century. Consider what you get for your money: a day-return trip on a Pullman-style train (the ones with upholstered seats and table-lamps and fictional Belgian detectives); a champagne breakfast on the way up, with a *Racing Post* and the day's racecard to study; coach to the course and a member's badge; a suite to use as a base for the day; coach back to the station; and then a three-course dinner as the train trundles back through the warm summer evening to King's Cross. Our return trip also included an episode in which the four 'Manny Cripes'-style London cab-drivers installed at the table opposite us, embarked on a typical 'Enoch Powell was the best Prime Minister we never had' routine, only to be silenced by our withering looks. Convinced that our eye-balling had done the trick, we later left the carriage for a smoke in the next car, but I just had time before I left to overhear one of the cabbies say, 'Best be careful, I think those two are plain-clothes coppers.' Chris's early years of working on *The Sweeney* had obviously stood him in good stead.

Chris was bowled over by the whole experience, which also happens to include top-class racing and sightings of very beautiful Northern women in their designer gear. York's August meeting is Royal Ascot without the Windsors, a garden party stripped of all the suffocating stuffiness of the

English class system.

Going to Ascot for the Jumps, just before Christmas, is entirely different again, however. The toffs from the Flat have already legged it to Barbados for their winter holidays, so the course is handed over to the National Hunt enthusiasts, racing's foul-weather friends, for a few months. Ascot is owned by the Crown Estates, so the pace of change has always been in keeping with the monarch's view of society. Indeed Jump racing wasn't staged there until 1965, so it still feels a bit like they're letting the servants use the outdoor pool in winter.

As it happened, this particular Saturday wasn't too inclement and Chris and I headed straight for the Champagne and Seafood Bar, which overlooks the summer paddock. During Royal Ascot this bar is packed to the rafters, and has plastic tables and chairs on a terrace for the overspill. But now these were stacked away, and there was plenty of space for lunchers or drinkers. Among these was none other than 'my' trainer Martin Pipe, perched on a stool near the door, tucking into a plate of poached salmon. This seemed a rare moment of stillness in Pipe's life, because he's normally seen cycling around his yard, or buzzing around a racecourse with a quick, clockwork-mouse walk, or with a mobile phone glued to the side of his head.

So while I was at the bar buying our first bottle of champagne, I resolved to introduce myself to him as one of his owners and find out what was going on with the two horses. I was served pretty quickly, but by the time I turned round, Pipe had already wolfed down his lunch and moved off, and was now haring across the paddock towards the saddling boxes, having left but a few fragments of salmon on his plate. God knows what his digestion is like.

Chris was keen to know about my ownership experiences, having had shares in a couple of horses himself in the mid-1990s, one called Wizzy Lizzy with David Elsworth, the other called Father Dan with Gay Kellaway. Though work had always managed to prevent him getting to the track to see them, he had at least made some money back, not just in the odd places which the horses picked up, but most notably when Wizzy Lizzy won at Newton Abbot at 6–1 one Boxing Day. He was staying in Faringdon, on the fringes of the Lambourn valley, with friends and freely tipped the horse to anyone he met in the pub. The win made a big hole in the local bookie's Christmas, and the celebration party went on till the early hours in the pub. This is exactly the sort of stuff anyone buying a horse dreams about – not only being on the inside, but being *seen* to be on the inside.

I bemoaned the complete lack of action in the two-and-a-half months of my involvement with the partnership and we chatted, drank another bottle of champagne, and got through a few losers between us. My six selections went at follows: Ground Nut (fell), Polydamas (3rd), Go-Informal (4th), Callisoe Bay (fell), Lord Dorcet (2nd), and L'Opera (last). Cool Dawn won the feature race of the day, the Betterware Cup, which is sponsored by Andrew Cohen, owner of Hennessy Gold Cup hero, Suny Bay. If only we could have guessed that day that Cool Dawn would go on to win the 1998 Cheltenham Gold Cup in three months' time, Chris and I might have recouped some of our losses. But we didn't, so we didn't.

But during one of the breaks between races, I noticed Chris studying the 'Horses for Sale' adverts in the *Racing Post*, as though our conversation had triggered a memory or an instinct. Then he pointed to one ad near the bottom of the page. It read: 'Due to unfortunate circumstances, 2 shares have become available in small partnership who have 2 horses with champion trainer. No capital outlay, fixed costs.' Underneath was Janet Underwood's name and number. I tried to guess what the unfortunate circumstances might be, and assumed they involved somebody dropping out of the partnership rather than anything more serious. But it seemed like another cloud on an already dark horizon. Had I not already gone through my conspiracy-theory phase, this might have triggered it.

While I brooded, the soon-to-be-divorced Chris was writing his phone number on a losing Tote ticket, with a view to passing it over to two attractive women in the bar. Chris may be in his mid-50s, but he's a teenager at heart. We wished each other all the best over a last brandy, and shook hands. He was off to Cuba, I was heading for Reading station.

I'd only been home about ten minutes when the phone rang. It was Chris. 'I'm in,' he said, and I wondered why he was telling me he'd got home in one piece. 'I'm in the partnership,' he clarified, 'I phoned Janet Underwood and I've bought myself a share.'

'You mad bastard!' I said with a laugh.

Tuesday 23 December 1997

Racing has now closed down until Boxing Day, so, as the sad punter arriving at Kempton Park once said, 'I hope I break even today, because I need the money.' But the money is needed elsewhere at this time of year, and anyway about the only thing you can bet on is whether or not it will snow on Christmas Day. Nevertheless the *Racing Post* publishes today, with form guides for the big race, the King George VI Chase at Kempton Park. In order to fill the space it has also printed one of its regular features, 'Trainer File', and the subject of today's profile is Martin Pipe.

The format is a simple one: a boxed CV of the trainer's most exalted winners, and a list of his total wins for the past five seasons, which reveals the numerical dominance Pipe has asserted over the racing world. His totals have been as follows: 194, 126, 137, 176 and 212. So far in this 1997–8 season he has already trained 120 winners from 339 attempts, a strike rate of 35 per cent. He has also achieved the fastest 100 winners ever, while preferred jockey Tony McCoy has racked up the fastest 150 victories ever recorded by a NH jockey. Not surprisingly, Pipe heads the Trainers' Championship, determined by prize-money won, having amassed £578,148 for his owners. None of this has come my way, of course.

The feature also includes short 'pen-pictures' of some of the horses to follow from the Pipe yard, listing 64 names in alphabetical order. Di's Last doesn't appear in the 'D's, and Rowley John certainly isn't among the 'R's. I suppose this is to be expected because they haven't run yet, but it reaffirms some of my initial instincts that our horses would be better placed in a smaller yard. Against that, Di's form might not have been so good without Pipe's expertise.

But then it's sobering to read that even some of Pipe's best horses have their set-backs and problems. Make a Stand, the reigning champion hurdler, has been ruled out for the entire season with 'heat in a leg', and one of his other Cheltenham winners, Big Strand, hasn't been out yet due to 'niggling problems'.

The one amusing thing about the 'pen-pictures' of the horses is that they are plainly taken down verbatim and therefore replicate Pipe's lopsided-mouth vocal style, which is virtually the same as comedian Paul Whitehouse's 'Ron Manager' character in *The Fast Show*: 'I really like this horse. He's had his problems on the way, but is a lovely sort.' And that's a cheery thought for Christmas, isn't it? Christmas. Nice word, isn't it? You know, snow, berries, chestnuts roasting on an open fire. Christmas. Isn't it?

Saturday 27 December 1997

See More Business was an emphatic winner of the King George yesterday, with my fancy Suny Bay tiring a furlong out to finish fifth. But then, as the Mafia dons say, 'He owes me nothing.' But the big news for today is that Cliff phoned to say that Rowley is entered in a bumper race at Warwick next Wednesday, New Year's Eve. Before I could get too excited, Cliff added that this was subject to a satisfactory blood test at the Pond House laboratory, and also to the minor complication that 44 other horses have been entered for the same race. This will almost certainly mean that a ballot will have to take place in order to reduce the field to its maximum for safety purposes – the idea of 45 burly novice National Hunt horses charging around any course outside of the Crimea is too awful to contemplate.

Both today and the next few days are spent in a frenzy of preparation for something that may not actually happen. As one of my Christmas presents Wendy had bought me a bizarre little book entitled *The Aerofilms Guide to Race Courses*, the unique selling point of which is that is has photographs of all British courses taken from an aeroplane. At first I thought that my wife might have overestimated my intentions regarding travel to the tracks when the horses were running, thinking perhaps that I'd be flying in Martin Pipe's helicopter. The book therefore looked destined to gather dust on the shelf, but once I began to flick through it, two hours passed as I assessed every detail of Warwick racecourse, which was one I'd never been to before. Such was the grip of Rowley's debut on my imagination. Then came the study of my railway timetables, to see if I could get there in good time for the first race, and back home in time to cook a New Year's dinner. By Monday I'd worked out my route – Bradford to Bath, across to Reading, up to Leamington Spa, and then one stop along to Warwick itself. Sweet as a bun, provided he gets a run.

Tuesday 30 December 1997

This is probably the saddest thing I've ever done since I studied aerial views of racecourses, but this morning finds me watching Ceefax waiting for tomorrow's declarations to come up, to see if Rowley's got into the race. They usually appear at about 10.45 a.m., but there's a delay for some reason. Eventually Warwick's pages come on, and because bumper races are traditionally the last on the card – the hurdles have to be cleared from the course – the wait for the pages to scroll over becomes excruciating. But then there he is – Rowley John, number 12 in the 3.30 race, to be ridden by Chris Maude. The betting forecast has him down as an 11–2 chance. A few minutes later Cliff phones and he says, almost breathlessly, 'We go!' When we've both calmed down, he tells me that Rowley blood-tested 100 per cent fine. The same will not be true of this owner if he wins tomorrow.

Wednesday 31 December 1997

I am up well before seven o'clock and through the bathroom window can just about see a few shafts of dawn above the Wiltshire downs to the east. The late weather forecast on BBC 2 predicted a sunny last day of the year, and by the time I've shaved, sorted out the right clothes to wear – shirt and tie for smartness, baggy brown cords for country-cred – it's becoming a glorious morning. I tune in to Radio 5, where a friend of mind, Robert Cooper, sometimes does the horse-racing bulletins at five minutes to the hour. But today it's the BBC Radio racing correspondent Cornelius Lysaght – apparently known as 'Ghastly', an anagram of his surname. Almost unbelievably, his tip for the day is in the 3.30 at Warwick – and it's not Rowley John, but Jenny Pitman's runner Ardfinnan. We'll make the cheeky bastard eat his words.

Because I'm new to the partnership, Cliff has arranged that I should get one of the free owners' badges which the course will make available. The growth of large partnerships has obviously put a strain on some elements of racecourse hospitality, but the Racehorse Owners' Association has been able to negotiate various levels for owners' badges, and also a reduced-entry scheme where the maximum for that course is exceeded. I still don't know how many partners there are in Tally-Ho, because although there are 14 shares, some have been sold in fractions. And during a period of public holiday we could have upwards of twenty people turning up at Warwick today. Rather like a blind date, Cliff and I have exchanged physical descriptions and clothing details so that

53

we can recognise each other in the Owners' and Trainers' Bar at the course.

I told him I looked a bit like David Ginola . . . (To: the legal representatives of D. Ginola, Esq.: An apology). No, my actual summary was 'six foot tall, glasses, big nose, brown hair greying rapidly at the edges, brown winter coat'. Cliff's description was 'leather cap, glasses, beard and Barbour, with Janet and two teenage children in tow'.

I made sure that I had my notes on this description, and also on the location of the bar, as part of a ritual check-list before departure. My wife says this side of me is all anal, but I just think it's good organisation. So I made sure that I had with me the following items: £120 in cash; Tote Credit Club card; two pens, the second one as cover for the first; a small notebook for when my race-trained eyes spot future winners; my mobile phone, so that I will be able to ring friends up 'live' from the winner's enclosure; my binoculars (minus their missing case and strap). I decided to leave the hip-flask at home today because I didn't want to create the wrong (i.e., right) impression with my new colleagues that I like a drink or two when I go racing, but I *did* take the cigar case, because there's no knowing whether you can get Havanas at Warwick, and I'd hate to have to celebrate our win with a bleeding Castella.

At 8 o'clock, I get down to the newsagents in Bradford where I have the *Racing Post* on daily order, but Clive, the man who runs it, has shut up shop while he takes his other copy of the *Post* up to Janet at Backhouse the bookie's. Bradford is like this – when I write about the town I always hear the Beatles song 'Penny Lane' playing in my head, because of the picture it paints of a small community. Almost everybody here is on first-name terms with each other, without necessarily knowing second names. This marks a sensible compromise between recognising who someone is, without having to find out what they do or where they come from. If this makes the town sound like Trumpton, tough on you, because I happen to like it that way. Anyway, I haven't got time to wait for Clive to come back, so I sprint – well jog, actually – round to the station. I'll pick up a paper in Bath.

The second snag of the day now becomes apparent. The 8.10 a.m. train coming up from Portsmouth is fifteen minutes late, which means I'll miss my 8.27 a.m. connection at Bath. There's nothing for it but to take a taxi from Ashley Cabs office, outside the station, over to Chippenham where I can get on the same train. I make it on time, but I'm already £17.00 down on the day.

Changing at Reading, I can't find either a *Sporting Life* or a *Racing Post* at the big newsagents on the main concourse. (The subsequent fate of both newspapers in 1998 – the *Post* sold to the Mirror Group by Sheikh Mohammed for £1, and the *Life* closed down – was probably not unconnected with this sort of piss-poor distribution.) But at least the much-derided Virgin Cross Country train is on time, both leaving Reading and arriving at Leamington Spa. Here there's a quick change to a train which arcs round the south Midlands to Stratford. The first stop is Warwick and thankfully there's a cab waiting and ready to go to the course – somebody up there likes me after all, because just over three hours after leaving home, I'm safely at the racecourse.

The aerial view of the Warwick train from my new book doesn't do it justice, for, as the taxi journey revealed, the course is right next to the pretty Georgian town centre, which must make it a terrific place for an overnight stay, either before or after racing. Even though there's a good hour to the first race at 12.30, a big crowd is already filing in. A touch too self-consciously I go into the racecourse office and ask for my owner's badge. Still trained to expect the gloved hand of authority on my shoulder, there are a few sweaty moments while the steward checks a computer print-out, but then he sees my name and a badge is handed over with great politeness.

'You can collect your complimentary racecard at the weighing-room, Mr Hey,' the steward says, and I automatically look round to see if there's another, more exalted Mr Hey behind me. But, no, it's me and I'm in, and through to the stands which spread along the town-side of the course in a pleasing higgledy-piggledy fashion. I finally acquire a *Racing Post* and turn to the card for the seventh race, the 3.30, to see what the comments are for Rowley John.

The Spotlight section describes him as 'Out of a poor hurdler; stable to be feared', while in the Verdict panel it says that 'a number of powerful stables have runners here and Prancing Blade, Rowley John, Winter Gale, Stefphonic and Wilmott's Fancy are all interesting newcomers, but it will take a useful performance to beat ARDFINNAN (nap) if he comes on from his promising Towcester debut.' The betting forecast is 11–2 for Rowley, but nobody in the list of National Newspaper Tipsters tips him. Oh, well.

As I move off to find the Owners' Bar, I bump straight into Robert Cooper who's presenting for the Racing Channel. Robert is one of the nicest men I've met and it's always a pleasure to chat to him, not just because he's a gent, but also because he gets the odd decent tip in the line of duty. He's had a good word for Robin Dickin's Macy in the 2.30, but seems more impressed by my new status of 'owner'. I can't offer any sort of inside information, but he does seriously ask me if I'll come and be interviewed for the Racing Channel if Rowley wins. I point out to him that I will almost certainly be too pissed by then, but Robert kindly takes this as a joke, before going off in search of his favourite lunchtime fancy at Warwick, mushy peas.

I walk the line of stands, which culminates in a splendid Victorian number which looks more like a cricket pavilion than a racecourse grandstand. Inside there's a lovely, red-walled bar that is already humming with seasonal cheer. But I'm an owner now, so I'm determined to enjoy the privileges that my new status accords me – if only I can find the bloody Owners' Bar. Dodging the lines of coal braziers that are taking the chill off this bright winter's day, I eventually have to admit my 'nouveau' status and ask someone where it is. I'm directed to a more modern annexe set back from the main enclosure. I make my way across, ensuring that my badge is clearly visible, and go into the bar, trying to look as though I've always belonged there.

The bar is already quite full, with a majority of the people present being prosperous men in their mid-50s, accompanied by younger women with leopard-skin accessories. I buy a small bottle of red wine and a turkey sandwich from the bar, and begin to scan the room discreetly for Cliff with his beard and glasses. Nobody quite fits that description, so I settle down to study the form, not that I'm all that interested in any horse other than Rowley. This shows itself in my betting, which is distracted and half-hearted to say the least. Koathary disappoints me in the first, and in the second I have £20 on a horse I picked up from a tipping line 'by mistake' the previous night on the Teletext pages of Channel 4. The mistake I made was seeing the advert announcing 'a serious horse is about to be unleashed at Warwick tomorrow', and then thinking it might be Rowley. But when I phoned, it wasn't him but a novice chaser called Sierra Bay. When he is unleashed, however, Sierra Bay continually jumps to his right, not a good thing to do on a left-handed track. Into the back straights he jumps so far to the right that he runs out through the wings of a fence and is pulled up. In the next, Carlito Brigante is nowhere. I'm £40 down already.

In between these races I keep popping back to the Owners' Bar, trying to spot Cliff. And as I embark on my second small bottle of red, I realise I'm probably standing next to him – the leather cap, the Barbour bearing a Pembrokeshire Fox

Hounds badge, the glasses, the beard.

'Hello, Cliff?'

'Stan.'

We shake hands and a smile of instant fraternity passes between us. From the phone calls and correspondence, I know that Cliff leads a slightly bizarre working life. He's the senior instruments engineer for an oil technology company based in Great Yarmouth, but lives on the opposite side of Britain near Haverfordwest. Obviously, he doesn't commute, but does ten-day working spells alternated with four or five days off. Since much of his work involves travel to the Persian Gulf or the Caribbean, going racing has become a vital part of his leisure, especially as Janet runs the small breeding operation at their farm. I'm introduced to a few other members of the partnership, including Darren who's driven all the way down from Wakefield. Darren is our stats-man, and has taken objection to the description of Rowley's mum as a 'poor novice hurdler'. 'She were placed in quite a few races,' he tells me. But the other names don't really register as yet. A couple of burly Welsh chaps in their late 40s are part of the group but they're soon off in search of a pint of the local bitter, which is presumably deemed too vulgar for the Owners' Bar.

Although Rowley has arrived at the course, Martin isn't coming – he has three runners down at Fontwell today, but isn't going there either. I can see the headline in the racing press – 'Pipe Takes Day Off Shock'. I discover that the bar has an internal staircase leading up to the owners' and trainers' viewing area in the stand, and from there I watch Nickle Joe lose me another ten quid in the fourth race. I find myself standing among the likes of top trainers Charlie Brooks and Nicky Henderson, not to mention England full-back Stuart 'Psycho' Pearce. To my surprise, nobody challenges my right to be there. In the fifth race, I forget to back Robert Cooper's tip, Macy, which promptly wins at 9–1. In the next I back

Brooks's Mr Moonlight, but it falls when well-placed in the back straight, and I watch the trainer's face contort with disappointment.

While I'm in the owners' area I overhear the kind of story I always imagined was bandied around such an incestuous enclosure. It goes back a few years, but concerns a small stable whose horse had unexpectedly beaten a well-backed horse from one of the top yards, and ridden by a leading jockey. About five days after the race, the leading jockey rings up the small trainer and asks if he can have the ride the next time the horse is out, because he was so impressed. The small trainer is suitably flattered and books the top jockey. When it comes to the horse's next race, the leading jockey promptly defies the small trainer's instructions and rides the horse vigorously to the front. Then he pulls it back, and then rides it to the front again, repeating the process a few more times to give the poor horse a tortuous and exhausting ride. When it arrives back in the unsaddling enclosure after being well beaten, the horse is close to being a nervous wreck. The top jockey then tosses the reins back at the small trainer and says firmly, 'You cost us a lot of money last time, don't do it again,' before walking back to the weighing-room. If I ever get round to writing my Dick Francis-style thriller, I'll have to include this, whether it's true or not.

But now it's time for the seventh race, or to give it its full title, the Christmas Standard Open National Hunt Flat Race (Class H), over two miles. I get a touch of the Sheikh Mohammeds when I see that the prize-money for the winner is a meagre £787, with the second horse getting £256 and the third £128. This latter sum would barely cover the cost of racing, once the entry fee, the travel costs and the jockey's riding fee had been deducted. So we're racing for the honour, not the money, for sure. I make a quick trip to the betting ring, where Rowley is chalked up on most bookmakers' boards at 8–1, having opened at 7–1. The show on the Tote is nearer 11–1, so I take that as a cue to put my first ever bet on one of my own horses – £20 to win, no messing around with each way.

I scoot back to rejoin the other Tally-Ho Partnership members, and there are over a dozen of us as we now watch Rowley being led from the saddling box and into the parade ring. We follow behind him, entering the holy-of-holies. Chester Barnes, the former champion table-tennis player who is now Pipe's trusted assistant, waddles into the ring in his trademark padded coat and tweed cap. His walk is almost a replica of his boss's, though he's much shorter in height. I've observed Chester on television and around the racecourses, and he's always struck me as a cheerful, Jack-the-lad type, although a recent heart operation is said to have mellowed him considerably.

Chester dutifully does the round of handshakes, cracking a quip, although we are all too nervous to take it in. Chester says he's been on the phone to Martin and the riding instructions for the jockey Chris Maude are to 'send him on quickly, get him into the race and see what happens'. But Chester adds his own warning that this will be very much 'a learning experience for the horse'. My £20 seems doomed already.

Rowley himself looks very relaxed. He's a tall horse with a white blaze on his face, and one white sock front and rear. He looks a bit on the narrow side to me, and has plainly got some growing to do. Maude arrives to be teased by Barnes about not having the sun as an excuse this time round – his mount Luv-U-Frank blundered and unseated him in the previous race, when Maude claimed to have been blinded in the back straight by the sinking winter sun. Then the bell sounds for the jockeys to mount, and Rowley makes his way out on to the course, lobbing easily down to the start. He looks a nice mover. I think about having another 'score' on him but decide against it.

I make my way up to the back of the Owners' Stand, where there's a television set to assist the watching of the race. About a third of the crowd has already drifted away by now, the usual procedure before a bumper race, leaving the spectacle to the die-hards, the drunks and the dedicated connections of the horses who are competing. I get my binoculars fixed on the Tally-Ho colours – light blue body, black cross-belts, sleeves and star on cap – and wait for the off with my heart beating fast. I've been nervous before races in the past, but only because of the sense of occasion that something like the Gold Cup or the Grand National can generate, or when I've had some money rolling up on a horse. But I've never felt quite like this before. It's almost personal, as if one of my children was about to do a party piece in the school's Christmas show.

And then they're off! Within a few seconds, it becomes apparent that far from jumping Rowley off quickly, Chris Maude is having a tough job getting him to run at all. And when the horse does move, he's rolling his head around like Stevie Wonder in concert. Two furlongs up the home straight and Maude is scrubbing Rowley along, trying not to let the field get away from him. As he reaches the turn out of the straight, Rowley at last seems to be responding, going up the inside rail, but he's already in last place, about ten lengths off the nearest horse.

About the only unhelpful feature of the Warwick course is the large mound that obscures the punters' view of the horses as they move across the shorter part of the course and into the straight on the far side. Indeed the whole field disappears for around half a minute. When they all reappear, Rowley is not with them, only emerging about twenty seconds later, as though he has been through some sort of equine Bermuda Triangle. He is now roughly a furlong down on the rest of the horses as they continue their way down the far side. Maude keeps him going but only at the sort of pace usually associated with a fully laden hearse.

As the field strings out into the soft ground, Rowley actually passes one of the other horses which is downing tools, and eventually lobs his way round to finish, albeit several counties behind the rest. I've no idea what won the race, because my binoculars were trained in the opposite direction at the time. As the watchers in the Owners' Stand disperse, I catch sight of Cliff on the staircase and he sees me shrugging. He draws his right index finger across his throat to sum up the race.

As we gather round Rowley in the unsaddling area, there are no end of desperately glum faces, no more so than Janet Underwood who helped in Rowley's difficult birth. Maude tries to stay upbeat as most jockeys are trained to do. 'He's still a baby,' the jockey says. 'He didn't like the ground, and needs it better. Probably needs further. He'll make a great 'chaser, though. Cheers.'

Even as a novice owner I recognise these terms as the necessary platitudes given to those connected with a hopeless horse as some measure of comfort. Yet this is a runner from the champion trainer's stable, so there must be more to it than just sheer inexperience. Good money has been paid over to the Pipe yard for nearly five months of training, and nothing has been said to indicate that Rowley was not up to the task. Of course, I don't say anything about what I'm thinking. I just watch my shoes sink into the mud for a short while. Cliff tries to form a plan of action. He says he'll call Martin tomorrow to see if the horse wasn't right, find out what the plan is, see if better ground might do the trick.

Meanwhile a tall, thirty-something bloke in a tweed jacket and cap wanders over to the group. He's wearing a National Trainers' Federation badge, but I've no idea who he is.

'I'm sorry to say this,' he offers in what sounds like a Brummie accent, 'but that must be one of the weakest horses I've ever seen on a racecourse.' He is pointing with a little biro in his left hand at Rowley, as the horse is washed down after his 'efforts'.

'He shouldn't have been put in a race yet, he's not strong enough, he's a baby. Put him away in a field or go point-to-pointing with him, and he might make a nice horse in about two years' time. You should save your money and go and buy something else, because you're cheating yourselves by having him put on a racecourse. He's not ready.'

Janet's face is close to crumpling at this dramatic intervention, and part of me – the old Scouse part I suppose – wants to tell this bloke to bugger off and mind his own business. Through whispered conversation, I manage to glean that this is Nigel Smith, the trainer of one of the other horses that the Underwoods have bred, and which they have leased out to another owner. It also emerges that Nigel is not being wise after the event, having already had a word with Cliff and Janet about Rowley's apparent lack of physique. So I mistook his blunt speaking. He was, in his way, trying to be helpful and constructive. Better to be realistic than stuck in fantasy land.

The various partners disperse to their cars, while I walk along the empty stands feeling confused and almost humiliated by the experience. My best friends will probably tell you that I'm not essentially a competitive person – a definitive herbivore – but that I get along by doing my best, and that failures and disappointments can wound me deeply. But I also recover quickly, having come to regard most experiences as essential compost for nurturing what passes as my sense of humour.

So as I make my way out of the course, I manage to buy myself a large 'Romeo y Julieta' Churchill cigar from a kiosk – so they do have Havanas at Warwick – and I take comfort in this and the wonderful art deco panelling of Leamington Spa's station buffet, a real train-spotter's delight. The taxi-driver from Warwick had taken one look at me and said: 'You must have had a few winners today, mate!'

I didn't challenge his assumption and gave him a large tip for a New Year's Eve drink when he was off duty. It was the end of a tired old year. But my Virgin train was on time again, and as it pulled out of the station I could see that there was a beautiful indigo sky over Leamington Spa, with Venus studded in it like a diamond. So things, as the anthem of 1997 promised, could only get better.

Expenses: Taxi to Chippenham, £17; train fare, £85; taxi to Warwick racecourse, £5; drinks and turkey sandwiches, £12; losing bets, £90; cigar, £14; taxi to Leamington Spa, £5; coffee and jam doughnut at Leamington Spa station buffet, £1.50. Total: £229.50.

Thursday 1 January 1998

Always a fairly bleak day, despite the racing from Cheltenham on Channel 4. The results section in the *Racing Post* tells me that Rowley finished 20th out of the 21 runners: 'behind, ridden 10 furlongs out, soon tailed off' is the summary of the race reader, and the betting digest shows that he opened at 6–1, but drifted out to 10–1, so there was certainly no stable confidence behind him, or tips on its 'Pipeline' telephone tipping service. It is small consolation that the heavily tipped Ardfinnan was beaten into second place by Wilmott's Fancy, losing several largish bets – indeed a total of £3,500 in recorded bets went astray, so there were some people who had a worse day than us at least.

There is no phone call from Cliff, but I'm sure that he and Janet are still licking their wounds. It must be a terrible disappointment to a horse's breeders after four years of feeding and attention to see that their charge is either not ready yet, or even worse, not up to it. I feel particularly sorry for Janet, who I gather had gone through hell bringing Rowley through the trauma of his birth. Rowley's mum, Arctic Gipsy, fell over after foaling and broke her pelvis, and had to be put down. After contacting the National Foaling Bank a foster mare was brought in, together with her dead foal. In order to get the mare to accept Rowley, the dead foal was skinned and its coat was placed over the infant Rowley. The mare was allowed to sniff the skin in order to convince her that Rowley was her original baby, and soon she began to feed him as normal.

I don't know if horse psychology in any way mirrors its

human equivalent, but something as traumatic as this birth for a human would probably have had them in therapy for several years. Who knows what Rowley remembers? But I certainly feel more sympathetically disposed to him today than I did at 3.40 p.m. yesterday. I suppose the decision on his future will have to be made by Martin, as only he knows what the horse was really showing on the gallops. Cliff was adamant yesterday about Rowley's bumper career being over, so the only question now is whether he's up to hurdling after reacting so badly to the hurly-burly which always plays a part in National Hunt flat races. My own instinct, for what it's worth, is in line with Nigel Smith's assessment that Rowley should be allowed some more time to grow physically and mature mentally.

Meanwhile the. Pipe Machine seemed to stutter yesterday despite a horse called Unsinkable Boxer winning at Fontwell. His other two runners there, Damier Blanc and Robert's Toy, were both beaten. And today at Cheltenham, his Vent D'Août was turned over at odds of 4–7, and Joliver was beaten at Exeter at 8–11. In addition, his Rainbow Star was beaten seven lengths into second, with another Pipe horse, Kasterlee, only 4th in the same race. D'Naan was well beaten in the last, with Kiniohio tailed off. Over at Leicester, Jazz Track was ten lengths second, but Brighstone won, albeit in a selling hurdle. This is not normal form for the Pipe stable, so maybe there's a virus or something in the yard? This is almost certainly clutching at straws time, but maybe Rowley was sickening for something too? He may yet have a chance of a reprieve.

Tuesday 6 January 1998

Cliff phones in the morning and I can tell immediately from his tone that it is bad news. And it is. After a conversation with Martin, Cliff has agreed to have Rowley John released from the yard and sent back to the Underwoods' farm so that he can have more time to grow. They are thinking in terms of giving him two years off rather than one, such is the disparity between Rowley's impressive height and his less than robust physique. Rowley has now been 'let down' – that is, disengaged from training and all attendant routines – prior to being shipped back to the farm and turned out into one of the fields so that he can eat, grow and forget about his adolescent inadequacy on the racecourse. This seems eminently fair given the presence in our language of the phrase 'flogging a dead horse'.

But there is also bad news about Di's Last too. She has apparently been suffering from a lung problem, which has resulted in some bleeding, one of the major danger signals that all is not well with a horse. Martin has suggested that she be retired with immediate effect and that she should be able to take up a career as a useful brood-mare at Underwoods' farm. Cliff professes some shock at this news. While Rowley's withdrawal from racing was hardly a surprise, Di's sudden illness and vulnerability is. Since she had an infection in October there had been little or no word from the stable that something was amiss. Indeed she had been cleared by Martin's vet to resume training. Cliff and Janet have agreed to take Di back, but want to submit her for a 'second opinion' to the Department of Veterinary Science at Bristol University, which houses a special equine unit.

While I'm disappointed at the outcome, I can't claim to have come into ownership blind to the injuries and illnesses that afflict equine athletes, so I give Cliff a sympathetic response rather than a surly one. It's the least that he and Janet deserve. Moreover, Cliff has already worked out a Plan B – part of which is to repay me some of my original investment. But the main constituent is for the partnership to take a 'half-share' in Nova Scotia, the horse that the Underwoods had leased out to an owner, Derek Newberry, in Nigel Smith's yard. Nova Scotia is, Cliff tells me, a seven-year-old mare, who is a half-sister to both Di's Last and Rowley John, having had the same dad as Di, Ra Nova, and the same mum as Rowley, Arctic Gipsy. This may seem a bit incestuous, and also a poor omen given the 'family's' recent results, but she has yet to race, and therefore has to be given the benefit of the doubt. Besides, Cliff has behaved very honourably over this matter. I know it's my first experience of a racing partnership, but I would imagine that a few of them, given the same circumstances, might be economical with the truth and try to hang on to the partners' money for as long as possible. But here I am with a rebate and a new horse, so despite the sad incidents with Di and Rowley, I can't allow myself to be too disappointed or to feel morally compromised. There are probably many owners who, faced with two semi-redundant racehorses, would simply ring up the knacker. But Cliff and Janet love their horses, whatever their frailties may be.

Thursday 8 January 1998

A letter from Cliff arrives, enclosing a cheque from the Tally-Ho Partnership account for £400, having worked out what had been used up so far from my original £1,120, and what would be required for the remainder of Nova Scotia's season. The letter reads as follows:

Dear Stan,

Thank you very much for your support and kind words. It has been a rather frustrating time. If only horses were humans they could tell us what was going on. Let's hope we have some fun with Nova Scotia whatever she does. As soon as we know what Bristol say about Di, we will inform everybody. And Rowley will return in two seasons' time, a stronger horse and a three-mile chaser. (Dreams are a good thing.) It was nice meeting you at last. I have written to Chris Burt explaining the situation. Let's hope he still decides to join anyway. I will ring as soon as I have news.

Cliff

I wondered how I was going to break the news to Chris when he got back from Cuba. I obviously felt responsible for him being involved, and for him to have joined the partnership only to 'lose' both horses so quickly would be an embarrassment for me, and a severe disappointment to him, even allowing for his sense of humour.

Meanwhile, I took the cheque back to the Stroud & Swindon Building Society in Bradford-on-Avon and banked it, pretending to the sceptical girls there that this was only the first of my many winnings from my horses. OK, it was a white lie, but only a small one.

Tuesday 13 January 1998

Another communication arrives. This time it's the official Tally-Ho Partnership newsletter, with more details of the Di and Rowley situation. Both horses are now back at the farm. According to Cliff, Rowley has 'run up very light, so we will pamper him a bit until he can get on to the spring grass. Janet rode him yesterday and he will be hacked out so that it is not a sudden change from full training to nothing. Di has a lot more condition than Rowley and looks well in herself. She enjoyed a good roll and took off round the field in her first time out in many months. We have the vet's report and it seems they have basically not been able to get her blood right since the viral infection she had. We will talk to Bristol University and our own vet and see if we have a post-viral/stress/permanent problem. I will let everyone know as soon as we hear.'

With regard to our new horse, the news was that Cliff had 'talked to Nigel Smith on 12 January about Ruby (pet name for Nova Scotia), and she is fine and he has pencilled in Sedgefield on 28 January or Doncaster on 30th. Nigel has apparently decided against a "bumper" race as two miles would be too short for her, so why waste a run? She jumps really well and so will go straight to hurdling. The Sedgefield race is a mares-only event, over 2 miles 6 furlongs.'

Attached to the newsletter was a copy of a letter sent from Martin Pipe to Cliff regarding Di and Rowley. It read:

Dear Cliff and Janet,

Di's Last has been a really genuine mare, having raced

six times for us, being placed 2nd and 3rd, and 4th on three occasions, and only once finishing out of the frame. This season, however, the Ra Nova mare just couldn't seem to stand up to her racing. Her lungs seemed to give us plenty to worry about. She is a very consistent mare and to be fair to her I think she deserves to fulfil her potential as a brood-mare. Rowley John, a 16 hh [hands high] son of Rymer, is a big, strong four-year-old who we gave a run at Warwick on 31 December 1997 for experience. Chris Maude said that he was very backward and immature, and still needed plenty of time to strengthen up. He should grow into a nice horse. We wish you all the best with them both in the future.

Yours sincerely,

Martin

And that was it – just a matter-of-fact 'good-bye, folks, thanks a lot'. To me, Pipe's letter left several questions begging. Such as when was Di's condition diagnosed? And why did it take a race to reveal that Rowley wasn't up to scratch – surely this should have been evident in his training? Of course, it wasn't my business to ring up Martin Pipe and pose these questions, because I wasn't technically an owner. But fortunately Cliff was also sufficiently unhappy to take matters further and an exchange of phone-calls and letters with Martin began, designed to get to the bottom of what had gone wrong with the two horses.

All owners have dust-ups with their trainers at some stage in their relationship, even the most successful ones. Sheikh Mohammed had one of the most dominant periods of his ownership while his best horses were with Henry Cecil, but that all counted for nothing when he apparently decided that he was 'no longer being listened to enough'. In the National Hunt game, owners regularly move their string of horses from one stable to another, as a response to poor results or an unsatisfactory relationship with the trainer. It's part of the fabric of racing, and essentially involves a battle of wills between the owner, who, because he's paid out money, sees his concerns as paramount, and the trainer, who sees himself as the professional, the person who really knows about horses and racing, and doesn't like owners giving their opinions or, even worse, telling him what to do or when to race. Usually, the trainer wins any such battle because he has more direct control over the day-to-day condition of the horses, but if the owner gets the hump in a big way he has the ultimate sanction available to him, to go elsewhere.

With the partnership's two 'crocked' horses already back home, Cliff was obviously denied this course of action. But because he and Janet know horses inside out, having bred and reared them, they were at least in a stronger position to pursue their case than somebody like me, who wouldn't know a fetlock from a kick in the arse. A few days after the newsletter, I received a follow-up phone-call from Cliff, who reported that Rowley had been assessed by their vet as a 'mentally and physically worn-out horse'. The assumption was that the training regime at Pond House might just have been too tough for him to cope with. Cliff was also waiting for the report from Pipe's vet on Di, so that it could be sent to Bristol. Despite Martin's suggestion that she should be retired, Cliff retained a hope that Di might yet be able to race again, pending veterinary advice.

Meanwhile, the Sedgefield race for Nova Scotia had been ruled out as being 'a bit far' for her first time out, so a two-mile intermediate bumper race at Towcester on 5 February was being looked at as a more likely alternative.

Saturday 17 January 1998

Simon Kelner, the editor of the *Night & Day* supplement of the *Mail on Sunday*, has wangled a box at Ascot for today, and I've been invited along with several other friends and contributors. I've also been in touch with Chris Burt about the news while he's been away in Cuba, and he's going as well, so we've made a loose arrangement to meet up. Chris has decided to stay in the Tally-Ho Partnership, despite the less than auspicious omens. The main race of the day is the Victor Chandler Chase over two miles, which often turns out to be a good rehearsal for the Queen Mother Champion Chase at the Cheltenham Festival.

A 'brunch' is served in the box from about midday onwards and apart from Simon and myself, the other guests include Peter Corrigan of the *Independent on Sunday*, Simon's brother Martin who broadcasts on Radio 2 and writes for the *Guardian* on TV sport, and two rock music writers, Robert Sandall and Adrian Deevoy. In normal circumstances, the burden of tipping the winners for the day might have fallen on me – though Peter Corrigan is no slouch at backing horses – but fortunately Simon has asked Mike Dillon of Ladbrokes to drop by and 'mark our card'. Mike is officially Ladbrokes' Public Relations man but he's also one of the shrewdest judges of horses in the game, and has very good connections with many of the big stables, particularly Aidan O'Brien's in Ireland. It's worth noting that Mike is well-liked throughout the industry, a rare feat for a bookmaker. Some informed people wish that Dillon could be deployed at the highest levels of organisation and planning of the racing industry, but

I fear he cherishes his current job too much. Mike gives us his reading of the form and then leaves us to make of it what we will.

But while I'm browsing through the card, I notice that my 'new trainer', Nigel Smith, has a runner in the fourth race, Tarakhel. Despite having won a 1 mile 6 furlongs maiden race on the flat for John Oxx in Ireland as a three-year-old, this form was misleading since there was only one other horse in the race. Tarakhel's two subsequent hurdle races were unimpressive. He also hasn't run for 458 days, so he is well down in the betting today. Indeed, looking at Nigel's form in the 'Today's Trainers' section of the *Racing Post*, I see that the stable is without a winner from 24 runs over the jumps. This doesn't look too promising, and is a complete contrast to the Pipe operation, which has racked up 128 winners before today's racing.

Perhaps distracted by this, and the recent bad news, I bet like a dog and fail to find any of the winners as Ever Blessed, Oban, Or Royal, Simon's Castle, Wayward King and Riparius all go AWOL. Meanwhile Tarakhel finishes tailed off in tenth place. The small consolation is that Mike Dillon's tips prove equally duff, so I feel I'm in good company. I also fail to meet up with Chris Burt, dodging around various bars to try and catch up with him, but he's like the Scarlet Pimpernel today. Naturally, I suspect it's a case of *cherchez la femme*, but when I speak to Chris later in the evening he claims to have spent the afternoon with a male friend from Brazil. By the time our party adjourns to the bar next to Ascot station, I have a tenner left in my pocket, but just manage to buy a round of beers before trudging through the darkness and the drizzle to catch my train back to the West Country.

You can fall out of love with racing on days such as this, when your years of accumulated judgement of horses seem to have been rendered useless. I can remember leaving Wincanton a few years back with so little money that I had to fake a donation into one of the charity collectors' buckets at the gate by hiding the copper coinage in a clenched fist before dropping it in. Today probably feels even worse, given my eunuch status as a hopeless owner as well. But then I always tell myself that this sort of stuff is character-forming and that the good days will soon follow the bad. This almost turns out to be true, as the following week I'm asked by *Night & Day* to try and get an interview with Sheikh Mohammed in Dubai. I write a letter to him via the Embassy of the United Arab Emirates, citing my status as a poverty-stricken owner as an attempted badge of brotherhood, and I dream of a few days in the sunshine of the Gulf.

Monday 19 January 1998

Nigel Smith has two runners at Fontwell Park today, Lady Pendragon in the first and Fortytwo Dee in the second. The former finishes tailed off at 66–1, but in the Houghton Novices' Chase, Fortytwo Dee manages to stay on to finish a remote second to Kilmington at odds of 25–1, netting £1,190 for the horse's owners. As you might guess by the name, there is more to this than meets the eye. The mare's sire was a horse called Amazing Bust, so Fortytwo Dee is the sort of witty name that will keep Channel 4's Derek Thompson in smirking puns for a few seasons. She also happens to be owned by the Swindon-based bra-making company, Triumph International. Suddenly, thoughts of sharing a hospitality box with Melinda Messenger begin to take shape.

Sunday 25 January 1998

I land my first successful bet in ages by backing the Denver Broncos at 4–1 against the red-hot Super-Bowl favourites, the Green Bay Packers. The Broncos win by 31–24, giving me a £120 profit. But there's a swift downer the next day as one of Sheikh Mohammed's English-based employees writes to tell me that His Highness has nothing more to add to the words of his Gimcrack speech. The letter signs off with the thinly disguised sardonic put-down, 'good luck with your horses!' I am tempted to write back with a reciprocal message, but think better of it.

Wednesday 28 January 1998

The horse manure really hits the fan today as the *Racing Post* leads with the dramatic news that three National Hunt jockeys, Leighton Aspell, Dean Gallagher and the high-profile Jamie Osborne, have been arrested in connection with an investigation into race-fixing. There is a popular perception that horse-racing is a bent sport, as opposed to those paragons of virtue boxing, cycling, swimming and athletics. The fact that big-money betting is such an integral part of the game leads to this belief, with the assumption that anyone desperate enough to risk several thousand pounds on a horse is capable of making sure that his wager will be a winning one. Yet the vast majority of punters, myself included, actually enjoy the element of uncertainty that a bet involves and the occasional thrill of getting it right either through good judgement or even good luck. But around the margins of the sport – the small races, the gaff tracks – there are a soulless few who want to know the result of a race before it happens, and it's here that these parasites operate.

Racing's image probably isn't helped by the fact that three former jump jockeys, Dick Francis, John Francome and Richard Pitman, make some of their living by writing fictional tales of racing skulduggery. Because of their status, it probably appears that these stories must have more than a grain of truth in them. I have no specialist knowledge in such matters but can recall a few dodgy incidents that have taken place over the years. The running of a 'ringer' (a horse with a false identity and better form than the one it is pretending to be), a jockey accepting 'presents' for inside information, and the outright doping of a horse are the three principal offences in racing.

Nevertheless, this case looks like a serious one because Scotland Yard's Organised Crime Group is involved, and the Jockey Club is moving to suspend the three jockeys while charges are considered. The two doping incidents relate to the running of a Josh Gifford-trained horse, Lively Knight, who was beaten when an odds-on chance at Plumpton with Leighton Aspell on board, and Avanti Express, ridden by Osborne when beaten at Exeter. Both horses tested positive for the tranquillising drug ACP. The police are also said to be looking at other races. Given the recent row about prize-money, this is the last thing racing needed, particularly the National Hunt division. I can already hear the comments of my doubting friends, 'Is that why your horses aren't winning, because they were doped?'

Saturday 31 January 1998

Although I gave up regular sports-writing for the *Independent on Sunday* last summer – partly due to fatigue, partly due to my psychopathic reactions to late-running trains – I am occasionally hauled out to write what they term a 'colour' piece or 'sidebar', which goes alongside the main correspondent's report if the event warrants such attention. Doing Sir Peter O'Sullevan's last commentary at Newbury was one such occasion, and now today's racing at Cheltenham has taken on a new dimension, given the arrests. It is, in any case, a decent meeting in its own right, with lots of form pointers for the Festival itself. But today I'm here to do a 'vox pop', a tour of the punters and bookies to see if their confidence in racing has been dented.

I collect my 'complimentary' badge at the main entrance and make my way across to the press room at the foot of the main stand. Here, I am met by a not untypical response from the man on the door, who will only allow 'metal badge' holders into the room. The 'metal' press badges are issued sparingly to the full-time racing correspondents of the national and regional papers and are jealously guarded because of the access they give to every course and its unsaddling enclosure. Inevitably, some abuse of the system has taken place over the years with people who are not racing journalists 'borrowing' them from the sports desk so that they can have a free day out. So a more rigorous policing has come in. This doesn't help me today, because unless I get into the press room I have no base from which to write, nor access to Sue Montgomery the 'Sindy's' racing correspondent, in order to ensure that we are not covering the same territory.

So while the man on the door is within his rights, I have to point out to him the fallacy of the Cheltenham authority issuing me with a badge but him denying me the facilities to use it. I do this in a calm and reasonable manner because these are specialist 'jobsworths' whose first reaction to bad temper is to dig in their heels even further. They are impervious to rage and questions about their parentage, which is the usual currency of exchange, so being reasonable actually disconcerts them. After a few minutes of gentle pleading he allows me in, on the basis that the press room isn't very busy today anyway, a fact he must have known in the first place, but which his training told him to ignore in favour of obstructionism.

Once inside, I can see that there is indeed a fairly desultory turn-out, which makes me want to go back and confront him, but that would only risk my little victory. I meet up with Sue and deliberately don't mention my troubles because she has been known to 'sort out' a few doormen in her own inimitable fashion many times. Having clarified our respective missions, I drift off to the paddock to listen to views and collect some 'colour'.

I spend a few moments in the winner's enclosure imagining what it would be like to lead Nova Scotia in one day. I have stood here before, when Norton's Coin shocked everybody, including his trainer Sirrell Griffiths, by winning the 1990 Gold Cup at odds of 100–1, and I managed to get myself on to the front of the Tote's Christmas card, my head appearing above the crowd, just to the left of the Queen Mother and Lord Wyatt of Weeford, the then Chairman of the Tote.

But today the privilege of being first into the winner's enclosure belongs to the eight-year-old gelding Gutteridge, and his party of owners from BCD Steels, a Midlands-based company. They seem a jovial group, much the same as the Tally-Ho Partnership, even though the prize money is only £2,811, which seems a paltry sum for a Cheltenham race.

After the presentations, they are invited to a room for a champagne by Cheltenham's managing director, the suave Edward Gillespie. I manage a quick word with one of the party, who declares that despite its troubles 'racing is still a great afternoon out'.

I begin to do my rounds of the bookies, exchanging a word with an old acquaintance, Mark Sturman, who trades in the betting ring under the unglamorous name of Fred Binns. He reports that 'business is quiet but holding up', but he still sports a winter tan like most of the denizens of the ring. Mark shrugs off the notion that the public's confidence will take a knock. 'People will still want a bet, won't they? It's part of our lives, isn't it?'

Well, it isn't for me today, as I've always found that working and punting just don't go together. Having a bet without thinking about it is just throwing money away, as I know to my cost. So I content myself with watching the big race of the day, the Pillar Property Chase over 3 miles 1 furlong, which Paul Nicholls's See More Business wins impressively, to put himself in pole position for the Gold Cup in March. I've already booked my three-day badge in the somewhat naïve belief that I can get away from work and the phone for the duration of the entire meeting. Being here today has certainly sharpened my appetite for it. Now all we need is a decent run from Nova Scotia to lift the spirits.

Wednesday 4 February 1998

Nova Scotia has been declared for the bumper on Towcester's card tomorrow, but a few meetings have been lost to the frost this week, and fingers are being crossed that the milder weather which is forecast will wing its way in. By coincidence, Nigel Smith appears in today's *Racing Post*, pictured alongside his stable 'star' Fortytwo Dee who is running today at Leicester. Apparently the horse is known as 'Booby' in the yard, and races wherever Triumph International is holding one of its parties for business clients. All the usual puns are wheeled out involving 'knockers' and 'big cups'. The stable's form remains resolutely flat-chested, however, without a winner now in 28 outings so far this season.

Meanwhile racing continues to plummet into the mire. There have been more arrests in the race-fixing enquiry, bringing the total to six. However, due to pressure from various lobbies, the Jockey Club is about to lift the suspensions it imposed on jockeys Osborne, Aspell and Gallagher, and indeed Leighton Aspell is down to ride at Towcester tomorrow, which should ensure a big press turn-out. The other unwelcome development is the opening of a High Court libel case brought by trainer Lynda Ramsden and champion Flat jockey Keiren Fallon against the *Sporting Life*, because of comments made about the running of Top Cees in a handicap at Newmarket and subsequently when winning the Chester Cup. Unlike Fortytwo Dee's moment of fame, this story will run and run. I've just seen on Ceefax that the Leicester meeting this afternoon is off because of the frost.

Taking a chance on the weather, I arrange to stay at Chris

Burt's house in Chiswick to catch up on news of his Cuba trip. Although he's definitely in the partnership now, he has to attend a script meeting tomorrow on a film he's producing for ITV and can't get away. On a whim, we go off to the Barbican to see jazz saxophonist David Sanborn playing with the Danish Radio Jazz Orchestra in a tribute to the work of composer and arranger Gil Evans. Despite looking like a collection of Jan Molbys in suits, the Danes swing and Sanborn blazes away on the alto. Chris has his eyes on Maria Schneider, the conductor and arranger for the evening, but I don't think they have 'stage-door Johnnies' at the Barbican, so we go up to Islington to have dinner at Lola's afterwards.

While he was away in Cuba, I got Chris an application form for the Tote Credit Club, which he's now joined. I get a free umbrella from them as a reward for this 'introduction' – yes, folks, racing is that exciting. The music and the dinner at least create a mutual sense of optimism and I promise to give Chris a ring when I get back from the meeting.

Back at his house, Chris gives me a fistful of cigars brought back from Cuba, so at least I won't have to hunt round Towcester to sate my depraved taste for tobacco.

Thursday 5 February 1998

Up very early to hear confirmation that Towcester has passed a 7.30 a.m. inspection. So the travel plan I had mapped out last night is immediately put into action – across London to Euston station for a train up to Milton Keynes, from where a taxi ride to the course should be available. Cliff phoned yesterday to say that I would have to have a 'half-price' owner's badge rather than a free one due to a high turn-out of partnership members, and to arrange a rendezvous at one of Towcester's bars. It is another course to which I've never been, so if nothing else, becoming an owner has widened my geographical horizons.

This time I manage to get a *Racing Post* from the news-agents on the Euston complex, although it doesn't say much about Nova Scotia, other than her background: 'fourth foal of a staying novice hurdler/chaser'. She isn't even mentioned in the betting forecast, being somewhere in the '33–1 bar' category.

The next fast train up to Milton Keynes is heading for Manchester so I look conspicuously *louche* in the first-class carriages, carrying binoculars and racing paper, while all round me there are executives studying flow charts or making calls on their mobile phones. I have to admit that this is the part of the ritual of going racing which I enjoy greatly. The blatant exhibitionism of somebody taking a day off is a small revenge on all those 'suits' who either turned me down for jobs, or who consistently rubbished my life-style when I was the epitome of the struggling writer in the mid-1970s. No doubt people will think this an extreme pettiness, but having been regarded with a mixture of condescension and amusement by 'achieving' friends for so long, I now get an extreme pleasure out of these mid-week indulgences. So going to the races is not only an act of freedom in its own right but also a statement about my facility to do something when I want to, rather than when employers permit. I don't go as far as ringing these 'friends' up from the course, because that *would* be petty, but if Nova Scotia wins today, I may break that particular protocol and give them a drunken earful down the Nokia.

At least Virgin Trains are maintaining their 100 per cent record for me, leaving and arriving on time, but I'm not sure about the individual *cafetières* of coffee which are brought to your table, prior to a bill for a couple of quid. At least the train's conductor belongs in the real world. Seeing my *Racing Post* he offers me a tip for Wild Rita in the third race.

From Milton Keynes station, I take a taxi up to Towcester racecourse, which is about eight miles away on the old A5 road. As we leave behind the bizarre constructs of Milton Keynes, the sweeping fields of Northamptonshire fill the horizon. It's a bright, mild day with a hint of spring in the air, and as we approach the course, there is already a line of cars filing through a stone archway that is probably a relic from a country estate. Unfortunately, what appeared to be a large bouncy castle on the horizon is in fact a new pavilion and stand, with gaudy turrets and a mustard-coloured wash on its walls. The older stands and the course itself are a delight. The finishing straight is a stiff uphill climb while the back straight is a steep descent. But there's a great view across the course, and to the picturesque town beyond.

I make my way round to the racecourse office, and collect my owner's badge for a £6 charge. Once inside, there's a small whitewashed hut which houses one of Barry Cope's seafood operations, and as there's still an hour to the first race, I park myself in there for a fish pie and white wine lunch. Reading the racecard notes I see that they think Nova Scotia is 'making a belated racecourse debut here today and is sure to benefit for the run', which when decoded means they don't think she has much chance.

Through the window, I catch sight of Cliff arriving. He has driven across from Great Yarmouth, while Janet and the children are coming from Haverfordwest. I give Cliff a shout, and he points to a bar on the ground floor of the 'bouncy castle' where he has arranged to rendezvous with Janet. 'That's our base for today,' he says before moving off.

After my lunch, I do a circuit of the stands and find quite a few familiar journalistic faces outside the weighing-room. They include Robert Cooper of the Racing Channel and the wonderfully droll Richard Edmondson of the *Independent*. They are here, as anticipated, because Leighton Aspell is riding again after his suspension was lifted. A gaggle of photographers adds to the scrum, which goes to show how big a story this is becoming. Richard tugs his forelock mockingly when he hears that I'm here to see 'my horse' run, and I tell him I expect to find a few paragraphs in tomorrow's paper if she wins.

Leaving the press to their long wait, I make my way across to the bar and meet up with Cliff and Janet. I recognise some of the other faces from the afternoon at Warwick, and am now able to put a few names to them. Jill Heslop is a Nottingham-based partner in a racing events company called Bowood Leisure and, apart from coming to see Nova Scotia run, she is making contact with the Towcester officials with regard to packages in the future. And Darren Roberts has travelled down from Wakefield again, armed with his usual informative statistics. This time he has worked out that from Di's six races no fewer than 44 winners have emerged, which is a frustrating reminder of how much potential was lost when she was forced into retirement.

Cliff reports the horse to be well in herself, although he's having difficulty finding out exactly what happened to her. It seems that Martin Pipe's vet has yet to release his full file on

Di, despite several calls from the Underwoods' own vet, so a definitive diagnosis cannot yet be made. Cliff also reports a telephone conversation with Martin in which the trainer apparently 'got quite shirty' over Cliff's continued enquiries into what happened to Di. I get the impression that Cliff isn't going to let this go away as easily as Martin might wish.

After drinks and chat are exchanged, we all go our separate ways to get some bets on. Given my recent form I restrict myself to a £3 Lucky 15 on Tote Credit, and a £20 win bet with Bryan West on Wild Rita. I give the first race, a twenty-one-runner selling handicap hurdle, a very wide berth, as it is the sort of race that ought to be sub-titled Bookmakers' Holiday Fund. In the second, I'm on General Pongo who battles up the hill well but can't get closer than second to the winner, Sail By the Stars. Wild Rita can only finish a remote eighth in the second race, so I make a vow never to take tips off train conductors ever again. This now joins my collected lessons on life, such as 'if you find yourself drinking with a man called Spike it's time to go home'.

In the fourth race, however, I actually have a winner. Ramallah, trained by Henrietta Knight, is a son of Ra Nova, the sire of Nova Scotia and Di's Last. The race is a 2 mile 6 furlong Novice Chase, and Ramallah jumps well and stays on strongly to win by eight lengths at odds of 5–1. I am greatly cheered up by this, not only because of the winning bet, but also because of the 'family connection' and the good omens it offers for Nova Scotia later in the afternoon. The final leg of my Lucky 15, Sylvan Sabre, finishes tailed off, so I'm down over £50 on bets so far, and we still haven't got to Nova Scotia's race. This is one of the hazards of having your horses run in bumpers, which are tagged on to the end of meetings. You have a whole afternoon of drinking and betting to get through before you can concentrate on your own horse, so that by the time it comes around you're either broke or pissed, or possibly both in my case. When the outsider of four wins the penultimate race and my bet finishes last, I'm down to emergency rations again.

The partnership gathers as Nova Scotia is saddled up, with Cliff buzzing around taking photographs. She got her name from the 'Nova' part of her sire's name, and the 'Arctic' bit of her dam's – Nigel having come up with the idea of linking her name to a cold place, hence Nova Scotia. Derek Newberry, the original owner who has now sold back a half-share to the partnership, only arrives about half-an-hour before the race, having got lost on his way through Buckingham. I give him my spare racecard as a souvenir and wish him good luck.

Then with the gloom gathering, we file into the parade ring to meet up with trainer Nigel Smith and jockey Mark Sharratt. Nigel reports that Nova Scotia has been schooling well over hurdles and has such a light action that she hardly leaves a print in the ground when she's landed. 'She's a sweet horse with a nice nature, and is a good mover,' he says encouragingly but then adds more darkly, 'but today is very much make or break time, see if she's got a future in racing.'

Such a warning seems a touch out of place at this early stage, but Nigel's rationale is that seven-year-old horses have to make a pretty immediate impact in order to suggest that they have a racing career. Most of the horses in today's eighteen-runner field are five or six years old, and a few of them have already raced. Nova Scotia has had to wait until she was fully grown before racing, so this is a catching-up exercise as well as a test of Nova Scotia's potential. She looks to me to be a little on the small side, but there are three or four horses going around the parade ring that are even smaller.

'Look at that one over there,' Nigel says, pointing. 'My Little Pony, that is.'

Mark Sharratt arrives from the weighing-room in dark blue colours with yellow stars. He taps his helmet to say hello. A smiling, open-faced chap, Mark is both Nigel's work-rider and stable jockey. I had checked in a recent Timeform book on his record and he hasn't got a great number of winners to his name – just four in the past five seasons. But there are an awful lot of unsung jockeys like this who ride the lesser horses around the lesser tracks at just £85 per ride. Nigel's instructions are fairly straightforward, to try and keep her handy and see how she stays on. The two-mile race is expected to be a bit on the short side for her, and there are genuinely no expectations of a win, just a promising run and a safe return will do. And even though the race is only offering £999 to the winner, there are at least half-a-dozen horses from the top stables competing – Russell Road from David Nicholson's yard; Brush Off (Henrietta Knight); Gullible Guy trained by the rising star of National Hunt, Venetia Williams; Quick Succession for Nick Gaselee; and Rockcliffe Gossip from the in-form Nigel Twiston-Davies stable. It just goes to show how little chance the small owners and trainers have of picking up winnings when even the scraps are fought over by the big boys and girls of the Jumps world. At least there isn't a Martin Pipe horse in the race.

The bell sounds for the jockeys to mount, and soon the horses file out of the parade ring against a sky becoming inkier by the minute. I find a place between the stands that has a good view over the course, and is within squinting distance of a television screen above one of the Tote windows. Nigel Smith stands next to me.

'Nervous?' I ask lamely.

'A bit,' he confesses with a smile. 'We very nearly weren't allowed to race because the Clerk spotted some equine vaccination infringement on her passport. Cost me a hundred-and-fifteen-fucking-quid in fines! So even if she wins I'll be down on the day.'

And then they're off. Starting down at the bottom of the hill on the finishing straight, the pack of horses comes out of the gathering mist towards us. I can make out Nova Scotia's blue and yellow sleeves on the outside of the leading pack, and as they come up the hill past us, she's going quite well in about sixth or seventh place of the eighteen runners. They turn out of the straight and head towards Towcester, the sounds of their hooves fading away. It's a mute spectacle now, just a blur of coloured specks set against a winter sky. As they pound down the hill on the far side, I can see through my binoculars that she's beginning to lose touch. The pace is quickening against her. The field comes around the lowest part of the course and begins the climb up the hill towards the winning post.

I've moved out to the rail by now, standing alone, and I don't even turn as the leading pack of horses thunder past in a cacophony of jockeys' shouts and whip-cracks. Instead I watch Nova Scotia stay on bravely up the hill, passing a couple of tiring horses on the way. Mark rides her right to the line and she finishes in what I reckon is thirteenth or fourteenth place. I've no idea what the winner is, and I don't care. Our little horse has run pretty well and shown plenty of guts to keep going, and she plainly stays. So although my superstitious £5 each way on the Tote is a loser, I feel like a winner none the less.

The group of partners streams towards the unsaddling area at the rear of the weighing-room, and Nova Scotia arrives back, breathing quite heavily, to a little round of self-conscious applause. The assistant trainer, Liz Grainger, takes the reins and Mark jumps off, still panting himself with the effort of driving Nova up the hill. His helmet has several clumps of mud and turf on it, and his face is splattered with muddy streaks, but he seems cheerful.

'We have got a future!' Nigel announces buoyantly as he arrives to pat the horse. 'Looks like you've eaten half of Towcester on the way round, mate,' he says to Mark as he picks the earth off his jockey's helmet, the manner being distinctly Blackadder to Baldrick.

'She's run pretty well for me,' Mark reports. 'She got a little outpaced when they quickened on the far side, and she also hit a patch of false ground round the bottom bend. She was always pulling out to the left a bit as well, and losing ground, so she'll definitely be better going round left-handed tracks. Apart from that, fine. Very promising.'

We say our thanks to Mark as he walks off to the weighing-room with his saddle. Liz now collects a bucket of water and begins to wash the sweat from Nova Scotia, who's gradually getting her breath back. We wait for Nigel's post-race speech.

'Well, I was chuffed with that,' he says. 'Given that we know she needs a lot further, that was a bloody good run first time out. She knows how to race and she stays. She'll do for me, all right.'

All around us, the beaten connections are getting the same sort of encouraging words, but I think that Nigel is probably being genuine in what he says. His bluff manner doesn't really allow for bullshit, I would guess, and if Nova Scotia had run badly and finished tailed off or pulled up, I think he would have told us straight to forget it. Being a relatively unsuccessful trainer probably doesn't allow much room for transparent hype.

We all give Nova Scotia a pat on the neck or stroke her ears, and then she's led off towards the horse-box. Nigel says he'll look out for a more suitable race, over a longer distance, in the next few weeks, and then jogs off to catch up Liz and the horse. We say our farewells to each other and this time there's some optimism in the air, not the sour depression of anti-climax as at Warwick.

I light myself a celebratory cigar and head off up towards the arch where I hope my taxi-driver from Milton Keynes will be waiting for me. The course is emptying rapidly. The press has long gone, having got themselves a story of sorts – Leighton Aspell wouldn't talk to them but then went and broke his collar-bone when his only ride, New Rising, fell in the third race, a novice hurdler. So tomorrow's racing pages will be about the 'up' of his return from suspension and the 'down' of the injury which will now keep him out for several weeks. It is, as people keep telling me, a cruel game.

Out on the road outside the course, there's a nose-to-tail line of cars heading south, their tail-lights flashing on and off as they brake. There's no sign of my taxi, so I begin to contemplate how long it might take to walk into Towcester. Two other blokes, well-dressed and well-spoken, join me at the road-side.

'Are you waiting for a taxi?' one of them asks me.

'Well, I've got one booked but it's beginning to look like he's forgotten. Where are you heading?'

'Our hotel in Stony Stratford.'

Hotel? I think to myself. The flash bastards. That's the way to come racing.

'Well, I'm going to Milton Keynes station, if that's any use?'

'That would be great if you don't mind dropping us off. Cheers.'

And then the inevitable question.

'You had a good day?' the other one asks me.

'Not bad. One winner . . .' (I pause for effect) 'and my horse didn't do too badly in the last either.'

'Ours won at Kelso,' they say together, topping me in an instant.

At this moment, the taxi appears, just about completing a U-turn and parking on the grass verge. I wave my two 'companions' forward and we all get in, and I ask the driver to make the short detour to Stony Stratford. As we move off, I try as casually as I can to tease out who this pair might be and, more importantly, who their horse is, and why they're at Towcester if it was running at Kelso.

From a fragmented conversation they appear to be connected to, or members of, a partnership called, wouldn't you know it, 'The County Set', and the horse in question is called Deep Water, in training with Micky Hammond up at

Middleham in Yorkshire.

'Got it for twenty grand out of Paul Cole's yard, but we had two grand on it first time out and it won at 7–2, so we're on our way to making the money back. I think one of our chaps was having a big bet on it again this afternoon. Beat Mary Reveley's horse easily. Probably aim him at the Triumph Hurdle at Cheltenham now.'

I realise that I am, so to speak, in deepish water, trying to trade ownership stories with these two. But I manage to bluff my way through a few minutes' worth of tales of misfortune about Di's Last and Rowley John, and hint at Nova Scotia's promise, before we reach their hotel, a smart-looking place in the pretty main street. They offer me some money towards the fare, but I wave them away, citing the fraternity of ownership. But then when I get to Milton Keynes and pay off the taxi, I find that I've exactly £2.14 left in my pocket. So my return journey has to become a coffee-free zone.

By the time I get back, Chris Burt has already been on the phone trying to find out what happened. He has obviously checked Ceefax and found no trace of Nova Scotia in the results. So I phone him and give him a full run-down of the day's events, with the encouraging news that another run is on the cards very soon. Because he's in the middle of shooting his film at the moment, he could only get there if it was a Saturday, so I promise to lobby for a weekend run. If, by chance, it were to be on television it would be even better.

Expenses: Train fares, Bradford–Bath–Milton Keynes, £101.10; taxies to and from Towcester racecourse, £35; reduced-price admission to course, £6; additional racecard, £1; fish pie and white wine at Barry Cope's Seafood Bar, £9.70; drinks, £15; losing bets (including Placepot), £72; *cafetière* of coffee on Virgin Trains, £2. Total: £241.80.

Friday 6 February 1998

The optimism generated by yesterday's run has survived the night, but is somewhat punctured by the race report in the back of the *Racing Post*. This puts Nova Scotia in fifteenth place out of eighteen and the comments are equally depressing: 'always behind, tailed off from halfway'. But for the fact that I've witnessed race readers at work, and know that they meticulously study the video before writing their reports, I would have called this a gross distortion of the truth. I'm so annoyed and irritated that I actually add up the distances recorded between each horse in order to see how far Nova Scotia finished behind the winner, Russell Road. It totals just over 59 lengths. Trying to be rational about this, however, the helter-skelter pace of a two-mile bumper race is a totally different kettle of fish to the one Nova Scotia will experience when she takes on hurdles over two-and-a-half miles. I realise there is some degree of wishful thinking at work here, but barring an outright win, what else have owners got to keep them going.

On checking Deep Water's win at Kelso, I find that he won by 14 lengths at odds of 4–5, with somebody winning £12,000 by putting £15,000 on him, and I just hope it wasn't on behalf of my taxi companions. Leaving envy aside, this was obviously a seriously good prospect, and I make a note to start backing him once the Triumph Hurdle ante-post odds are published. But the main questions now are when will Nova Scotia run again, and where?

Thursday 12 February 1998

Things have become a bit tangled as far as Nova's entries are concerned. Cliff phoned to say that Nigel had found two possible races for her, both on Saturday 21st, one at Windsor, one at Chepstow. The fact that it's a Saturday is great news for Chris, who can finally see a run for his money, and when I phone him he's really excited at the prospect. He'd prefer Windsor for the sake of convenience, but if it's to be Chepstow, he'll come and stay at ours and we can go over to Wales together. No sooner had I put the phone down, than Cliff phoned again. A change of plan – Nigel thought the horse was ready to race earlier, having shown no signs of trouble after her exertions, and he's put her into a two-and-a-half-mile hurdle at Hereford next Monday. I explain to Cliff what I've just arranged and he points out, quite fairly, that he and his family would have loved it to be a Saturday at Chepstow for *their* convenience.

But the guiding principle of the partnership is that the trainer has the decisive say where the horse runs, irrespective of what suits any members. So Hereford it is. I phone Chris back immediately with the news, and he's pretty pissed off about it all, but there's nothing I can do. I tell him a few rude jokes I've heard and he cheers up.

I feel a bit agitated by this messing around. The principle of the trainer deciding is all very well, but if the bra company can dictate where Fortytwo Dee runs, I think we should direct Nigel a bit more towards particular meetings. The partners are spread all over the country – Yorkshire, Nottingham, Birmingham, Runcorn, Essex, South Wales,

Chris in London, me in Wiltshire – so it should be possible to nominate a meeting that's best for a certain number of partners each time. (In the event, Chris Burt went to Windsor on the 21st anyway and met up with his old friend Terry Connors, owner of Chabrol, who went and won at 8–1, so all was well for him in the end.) In the meantime it's out with the old aerial view book again, to see what Hereford looks like.

But today I'm off to my local track, Wincanton, for a stress-free day's racing. Since Wendy needs the car, I'm going by train and meeting up with a writer friend John Fletcher at Bruton station. John comes racing with me two or three times a year, and actually enjoys it once he's there, despite having a much larger reservoir of 'writer's guilt' than I do. He drives a thirty-year-old Rover 110 so when we trundle into the Wincanton car-park, we probably look like a pair of old country poofs.

It is a quite bizarre day in any case, since the temperature must be in the high fifties and there's a clear blue sky. I'm actually wearing an open-necked shirt and a sports jacket, so I have to keep pinching myself that it is mid-February. We make a bee-line for the seafood bar – in fact one end of a long wooden pavilion – where delightful old ladies serve Mediterranean fish soup, smoked salmon sandwiches and so on. John and I have co-written two radio plays together, and we've known each other and our respective families for over eight years now. So we're relaxed in each other's company, and even when John starts to talk about work, as he always does, I can joke him out of it. The only downside is that John expects me to bring my superior knowledge of racing to bear on his choice of horses and I invariably give him a bum steer.

It's a thinnish card today, however, despite the decent prize-money available in the two feature races. There's a £9,466 purse for the Première 'National Hunt' Auction Novices' Hurdle that attracts only seven runners, while the

Wessex Chase (£5,402 to the winner) has only five runners. Examples such as these are always used against the Jumps game when owners start whinging about prize-money, and it's difficult to come up with a convincing response. Despite the paucity of runners, John and I can't manage a winner between us, but the day is enlivened by a chance meeting with sports-writer and author Laura Thompson and trainer Charlie Brooks, who are working on a book together. The four of us have afternoon tea, indulging in a bit of metro-politan gossip and writers' bitching. Charlie has already embarked on a journalistic career with the London *Evening Standard*, and wants to know how he should react to sub-editors' comments. I tell him to just ignore them, and to moan loudly if they interfere with his copy. He's the name after all. I tell him about my frustrating time with ownership and he sympathises. His best horse, Suny Bay, has picked up a muscle injury and with less than a month till the Gold Cup at Cheltenham, he's worried about getting him fully fit in time. The burden of both the owner's and the public's expectation seems to be bearing down on him.

Monday 16 February 1998

It's half-term so my first job before I slip away to the races at Hereford is to explain to my sons Charlie and Jack that I'm 'working' today, not just avoiding taking them to the pictures. Fortunately they took so well to horse-racing when I took them both to Bath a few summers ago that they seem to understand the importance of 'daddy's horse' running and why I have to be there. It doesn't lessen my guilt, but it will make it easier when I get back with exciting tales of how Nova Scotia romped home.

This isn't the view in the *Racing Post* when I open it up on the train across to Newport. Their brutal preview is that she was 'tailed off in a Towcester bumper 11 days ago'. But at least she's mentioned in the betting forecast, albeit at 25–1. I'll have some of that when I get to the course. The first race is at 2.00 p.m., a sure sign that the days are becoming longer now, after the 12.15 starts of midwinter. The train up from Newport rattles through some glorious countryside, but it's a journey fraught with memories of the Saturday last August when I went to cover Hereford United against Welling Town in the Vauxhall Conference for the *Independent on Sunday*. I suffered a Kafkaesque experience at the hands of Railtrack staff on Newport station. With my train from Bradford running five minutes late, I naïvely thought they might hold the connecting service up to Hereford. But no – the four-minute gap between trains was deemed to be 'not an official connection' so they sent the Hereford train off on time, leaving me stranded for another hour, during which time I tried to debate with them the merits of serving the travelling public. I eventually arrived at the Edgar Street ground ten minutes after kick-off, and wouldn't you just know that Welling had scored in the opening minutes. I managed to cobble together what had happened from press-box colleagues, but missing the start hurt my professional pride. The perverse delay and the searing heat combined to make me a near-murderous individual for the rest of the day, and it was as a result of this that I packed in Saturday match reporting. Buying into horses was probably, in part, another act of escape from the stress.

Today the connection at Newport and the Hereford train are both spot-on, so I return to the town as a relaxed individual, not Freddie Kruger. The taxi out to the course never seems to leave the town behind, however. Far from being a country track, Hereford is hemmed in on two sides by industrial warehouses and DIY superstores. This deflationary impression is made worse by having to queue up outside what looks like a garden shed in order to collect my owner's badge. It takes fifteen minutes for the line of owners to pass through, one of the reasons being an iron turnstile inside the shed. The other is a girl at the counter who can't, or won't, find the right names on the list of owners, and is more concerned about whether I have a 'swipe' card than letting me through in time for the race. Short of making us walk through a sheep-dip, the welcome couldn't have been less effusive.

The racecard, which I have to pay for because I haven't got the 'swipe card', is another bummer. With the same typescript and cheap paper consistency as the take-away menu of a Chinese restaurant, this is a real rip-off at £1, by about 99p. It doesn't help my mood that the entire front page of the card is given over to listing the double-barrelled names, army ranks and honours of the Stewards. Much of the space inside is given over to warnings of drinking outside, using a mobile phone or exercising dogs. I half-expect to see a notice stating that the working class will be shot if they are found enjoying themselves too much. Overall, it makes the colourful, well-laid-out, helpful racecards at Warwick and Tow-cester look like the Caxton Bible by comparison.

I wouldn't mind if this was a picturesque course, but it looks like Wormwood Scrubs with a few stands stuck on to it. If the BHB eventually decides to cut costs by reducing the number of British racecourses, Hereford will get my vote as being first for the chop. My irritation increases even more on arriving in the Owners' and Trainers' Bar. I can forgive the fact that it's a glorified Portakabin that looks more like a dentist's waiting-room than a bar, but today on every plastic chair they've placed a leaflet and a car sticker advertising the 'Countryside March' that's coming up soon. The leaflet is full of the usual guff about the 'dangers to our way of life', when all they are really concerned with is the proposed Bill to ban fox-hunting.

One of the few teeth-grinders about Jump racing is this wanton assumption that anyone who attends is automatically a supporter of field sports. As it happens, I don't care about them one way or the other, but I object to being lobbied with leaflets and hectored by tannoy announcements on a day out. There also seems to be an unchallenged belief that racing is an entirely rural sport, rather than something dependent on the money of urban betting-shop punters and sharp-suited bookmakers. The old argument about the link between hunting and the Jumps is just that, an old argument. Do they really think that a multi-billion-pound betting industry, not to mention a huge horse-training infrastructure, would collapse if fox-hunting was banned? Happily I was gratified to see throughout the ensuing afternoon the large number of leaflets and stickers which had been dumped into the waste-bins by like-minded punters.

When I've cooled down, I manage to find some of the partnership members gathered in the main restaurant and bar, with Darren once again having made the journey down from Wakefield. Three of the Welsh boys are there as well, already filling in their Placepot tickets. Cliff and Janet arrive shortly afterwards and we swap stories and dreams for half-an-hour or so. I hear an outrageous tale from one of the members I've not met before. He was once involved in a Flat syndicate up North, which owned a fairly hopeless sprinter. When they met up with the horse's trainer, they wondered if the drop back to 5 furlongs from 6 would help today and he said 'no', advising them to keep their betting money in their pockets. The race comes round, and to general surprise the sprinter whizzes in at 25–1. While the victory is welcome, the sight of the trainer collecting a wad of cash in winnings from a bookie is not. The partnership broke up in revolt that very afternoon.

Such an occurrence seems unlikely this afternoon, not least because Nigel is not too bullish about Nova Scotia's prospects. This is probably to do with the race – snappily titled the Hoechst Roussel Panacur European Breeders Fund Mares' 'National Hunt' Novices Hurdle (Qualifier) (Class E) – has attracted a couple of runners from the powerful yards of Paul 'See More Business' Nicholls and Nigel Twiston-Davies. The latter's horse, Madam Muck, has close form with Mary Reveley's Marello, which is entered in the Champion Hurdle. In short, she totally outclasses the rest of the field and looks to be the deadest of dead certs. So we can forget the £2,752 first prize, and look at the £772 for second place, or the £376 for third instead. Even Darren the stats man can't come up with a convincing argument for Madam Muck not winning.

I drift away to the Tote Credit office and construct a desultory £2 win Lucky 15 for four of the races – Catempo, Dr Rocket, King of the Blues and Supermick. With four of the races classed 'F', two as 'E' and one as 'H' – the further down the alphabet the worse the standard of horses – this is clearly a low-rent card, staged with the bookmakers' profits in mind. It should carry a punters' wealth warning. A few drinks in the Butlin's-style bar help ease some of the depression, but my bet soon brings it back. Catempo finishes down the field in the first race, as the 33–1 chance, Funny Genie, wins. I do a £10 single in the next on Nigel Twiston-Davies's Snowshill Shaker but that pulls up after ploughing through a fence like a drunk driver. And then it's us.

Being in the 3.00 p.m. race at least means we can get the agony over relatively early. We make our way into the parade ring where Nigel is shuttling between our group and the owners of his other runner in the same race, Lady Pendragon. Mark Sharratt arrives with his usual cheery face and guesses that this 2 mile 3 furlong trip will suit Nova Scotia much better. 'What's the plan?' Mark asks Nigel in his best Baldrick fashion. Nigel tells him to get her out early, stay handy and see how she jumps. 'Make her stay on at the end,' Nigel adds optimistically. The ground is officially 'good', which may not suit her as well as good-to-soft. As for the lurching to the left, well, Hereford is another right-handed course like Towcester but much flatter, and Nova has been fitted with a special bit on her bridle. So the theory is that the turns won't affect her too much. Mark gets a leg-up on to the horse and we wish him good luck.

I make my way down to a Tote window and look at the odds on the win-pool for Number 6, as Nova Scotia is numbered. She is currently trading at odds of 82.1–1, so I lump my £5 each way on and the odds remain the same. I rejoin the others on the lower steps of the main stand, and we watch Nova Scotia (or 'Ruby' as she is known) canter down to the start on the far side. The fourteen runners circle around and then line up, going off at the first time of asking. Nova is quite handy as they move down the far straight. She is jumping quite fluently, although Madam Muck, as expected, is taken to the front early in a bid to make her obvious class tell. As they swing round and into the short straight in front of the stands, Nova is still in the leading pack and hurdling well. They are close enough for the spectators to hear a loud 'thwacking' noise as a few of the horses hit the hurdles, dislodging some of the wooden struts. It must hurt them in the same way as barking your shins on a coffee table.

As they turn away from us Madam Muck steps up the pace, and the field begins to string out. Nova hangs on until the far turn, but then begins to lose contact as a group of four horses make their way ahead of the rest. She is starting to jump more deliberately now, but stays on gamely none the less. Madam Muck surges clear in the straight to win by a comfortable nine lengths, with Lady Pendragon a distant but gallant fifth. Nova meanwhile has jumped to her left at the third last and Mark appears to be trying to pull her up, but she jumps the next flight before slowing down to a trot. She is among the five horses who don't finish.

It is a pretty subdued group as Nova returns to the unsaddling enclosure. Mark dismounts. 'They went too fast for her, it was lickety-lip' (I think he means 'lickety-split'), 'but she jumped well for the first circuit,' he says breathlessly. Then he adds ominously, 'I think she rapped her knee on the third last. I was trying to pull her up, but she still went on to jump the second last. She's game all right.'

Mark drifts away as Nigel begins to run his hands down her near foreleg. 'Might be a bit of swelling there in the morning, I think,' Nigel says. Then Nova is led away and Nigel shrugs and says, 'We'll have to try three miles now. She just needs a trip. Anything less they're just going to out-run her.'

We adjourn to the bar, where Nigel buys a round of drinks. He seems quiet compared to his normal cheer-leading manner. Whether it's the injury or just the size of the task in turning Nova Scotia into a contender, I can't tell. He's annoyed that he couldn't get Lady Pendragon into the card's 'Claiming Hurdle' later, as he fancied her chances in that. The banality of the next race is on us almost too soon, and I have to switch my head back to my useless bet. Dr Rocket finishes second, as does King of the Blues in the next. It's one of those days. I phone Chris Burt on my 'banned' mobile phone and tell him he hasn't missed much. But then he quite enjoys miserable days at the races, and this is certainly one of them.

By the time Supermick comes home fourth in the last race, I'm jumping into a taxi to beat the expected traffic jam. Cliff has said he'll phone with news of 'Ruby's' leg. There are no plans until that has been assessed. My misery is pretty much completed by the taxi-driver who, on learning that I live in Wiltshire, immediately launches into a speech about how 'there's got to be something in those crop circles, you know'. I briefly wonder if they still have the death penalty in Hereford.

On the train home my thoughts become even darker. Given that racehorse ownership is supposed to be about fun or money, I feel I'm not getting much of either. I think, meanly, that all the partners in Tally-Ho are really doing is underwriting Cliff and Janet's dreams of breeding a good racehorse which, since the retirement of Di's Last, have come to nothing. I begin to believe that, in Scouse parlance, I have been sold a pup. No run from Di, a farcical debut for Rowley John, and now two pretty mediocre races from Nova Scotia – all this doesn't add up to much. Maybe I should have invested more money in a more credible horse. The ghost of Chabrol, the horse I rejected, begins to haunt me.

And then I snap out of it. Cliff and Janet are transparently good and fair people, and the other members of the partnership are enjoyable companions in their different ways. Nigel seems like a good bloke, and whatever his success rate is or isn't, he has the great redeeming feature of a sense of humour. I'm quite lucky really. I'm out of the house, away from the pressure of work, going racing, having a few drinks and cigars. Life should always be like this.

Expenses: Train fare, £20.60; coffee at Bristol Temple Meads station, £1.30; taxi to Hereford racecourse, £5; reduced-price owner's badge, £6.50; racecard, £1; drinks and sandwiches, £12.50; losing bets, £50; taxi to station, £5. Total: £101.90.

Thursday 19 February 1998

Cliff phones. Nova Scotia has a knee injury, but they don't know the full extent of it yet. Nigel's vet has examined her and is coming back to the yard tomorrow with a mobile X-ray machine when all will be revealed. Meanwhile, there's further news of Di, who has been examined by the vets at Bristol University. They have found no signs of a post-viral illness but there is some minor problem with her lungs. There's a chance that antibiotics could help this and that she may yet race again. We live in hope.

Sunday 22 February 1998

Cliff phones again. The diagnosis on Nova Scotia is not good. She has broken a bone in her knee and is unlikely to race again this season, if at all. She has been strapped up and will come back to the farm in about six weeks, provided no further complications set in. There is no question of putting her down, though, as she can be used to breed from, and can still enjoy a useful and happy life in the fields of Tally-Ho farm. But as far as the partnership is concerned, 'it's over for the season'. Cliff offers to work out a further refund on my original investment, but there are vets' bills to come on 'Ruby', so I tell him not to bother. I can't quite use the phrase 'a good run for my money', but then it wasn't much money in the first place.

A partnership newsletter arrives a few days later. It reads as follows:

> Although I have now managed to talk to everybody, I thought I would put pen to paper for an update. The bone that Ruby (Nova Scotia) shattered means that her athletic career is over for good. What remains to be seen is how much movement she retains in the leg. We understand from the vet (Paula Williams) that it is a common injury in NH racing and ends the careers of a lot of horses.
>
> Nigel reports that Ruby is a model patient. Her painkillers have been reduced by ¾ and she is eating up and not distressed at all. We estimate six weeks at Nigel's yard, then hopefully she can travel home. She then faces another two months' box rest after that, when we hope she will be

well enough to go out into a small paddock. Janet and I are presently discussing whether she can be served this year – we will let everyone know if she gets in foal. We both thank you all for your kind words and support at the end of what has been a dreadful season, and we are encouraged that almost everyone wants to carry on again next season.

Irrespective of the final decision on Di's Last – (we had a reply finally from Martin's vet which consisted of a single paragraph and NO clinical notes. Also Martin has got involved ringing up Janet and our vet, and we are still talking to the Royal College of Veterinary Surgeons, but with Martin blocking things we wonder if we will ever learn the truth!) – all being well, the Rakaposhi King filly (four years old, stable name 'Kelly') will be ready for August. We have yet to name her and we thought it would be nice if the partners had a go – the breeding is Rakaposhi King–Miss Lizzie (Push On). So please let us have your suggestions. We'll sort out a prize for the name that is selected and is available at Weatherby's.

As everyone is hopefully aware by now, because of what happened to Di and Rowley we cannot advocate going back to Martin Pipe next season. The consensus of opinion is to stick with Nigel Smith who at least ensures that we have some fun and feel part of the racing game. But please tell us if you have any other ideas. Once Ruby has returned home, the costs to the partnership will cease. But thanks again for the vote of confidence. Other matters: Ginger Maid is due to foal on 31 March. Fassbinder is due on 1 June. Rowley John has filled out and is taking much more interest in everything now, but will not be brought back into serious work for at least another eighteen months. Di's Last seems physically fine but is very insecure now and subject to panic attacks. Time will tell. Kelly had a good winter, and has been broken and ridden with no stress or problems. She will come in around June for her preparations. Sid (that's new to most of you, but some of you saw him as a foal) is out of the same dam as Kelly, by Still Time Left, a Teenoso stallion. He is only two years old but is already looking like another Rowley John, but a bit finer. He has long-term prospects, and he is BIG! Everybody is welcome to visit to see the horses. There is nothing like seeing them at first hand.

Best wishes,
Cliff and Janet

Fall-Out

From the tone of the above letter, and several conversations I'd had with Cliff, either at the track or over the phone, it seems plain that both he and Janet were somewhat unhappy with the way they had been treated by Martin Pipe. Since I never met him, or went to the stables, I can't comment personally. But what follows is an account, based on a long conversation I had with Cliff, about what he and Janet experienced as the owners of Di's Last and Rowley John. Given the sudden 'retirements' of both horses, I feel that it is appropriate to present this, not just because you have been reading about them, but also because it shows some of the less publicised difficulties owners have with their horses and trainers. The words are Cliff's, verbatim.

Towards the end of October, Di's Last had a slight infection and missed some work. Janet and I went down to see her later, when she was back in training and everything seemed OK. About two weeks later, Martin Pipe rang Janet at home. He said that Di had exercised that morning, but when they went to check on her in her box later, the staff found that she had collapsed and was in respiratory distress. The stable's resident vet was called over and he gave her some medical treatment, and within an hour she was back on her feet. She had a high temperature. Martin said that they had thought at one point that they were going to lose her.

Janet drove down to the yard the next day, phoning ahead twenty minutes before she arrived, and went to see the horse. She was up, eating, seemed happy and was in no obvious distress. Janet was gob-smacked. Martin's vet called it a 'miraculous recovery'. She asked the vet what it might have been, and what the blood tests showed. Martin turned up and Janet asked him if something had gone wrong, like a rug being left off. 'We don't make mistakes at Pond House,' Martin said to her sharply. The vet's view was that it may have been viral pneumonia. Neither of them said that Di would never race again.

On 10 December Di's blood tested clear, and she was allowed to go back into training. There were no apparent problems, it had just been a set-back. We saw Di do road-work and Rowley do fast work on the all-weather gallops, and there were no problems. Later in the week, we met David Pipe (Martin's son) at Chepstow and he told us he had 'watched Di work on the gallops that morning and she was fine'. Then, just before Christmas, we were told that they couldn't get her blood right and that Di was showing signs of distress after galloping. She was just not taking her heavy work. At this point, Martin recommended she be retired to become a brood-mare.

Naturally, Janet wanted to talk to Martin's vet on site, but he wouldn't let us talk to him. He wouldn't even give us his name or his phone number. He wasn't very forthcoming. The vet who had treated Di had left by this time. So Martin's opinion was put to us as a *fait accompli*.

We wanted to get Di to Bristol University once we'd brought her home. Our vet checked her, and her blood was fine. He asked Martin's vet *five* times for the horse's clinical notes and report but got nowhere. He then mentioned that he might have to take up the matter with the Royal College, and soon after we finally got a letter of one paragraph saying that the horse had not been his patient but believed that she had had viral pneumonia.

Di by now was showing us problems. She'd always had

a wonderful temperament, but since she'd come back to us, she would just stand by the gate in her field and not move for hours or mix with the other horses. She was having panic attacks. And it took her months to go out with the other horses. So we just don't know what happened to her. We *do* know that Martin had put her in an isolation box that was in the shed where he kept his helicopter, and kept her there even when she was cleared to return to work.

When we had her examined at Bristol University, her blood was fine and they could find no post-viral symptoms. They said that she was producing some mucus after exercise, and had what they term 'small airway disease'. Apart from that she was fine. They thought that within the limits of her lung capacity, and with a regime of antibiotics and fresh air, she could go back into training. But we decided we did not want to take the risk.

My personal view is that, as this was her third season at the stable, and she had shown reasonable toughness, Martin pushed her too far in training and went over her limit. In that situation, something breaks down. When we saw her once on the gallops she was sweating up, something she hadn't done before. I think Martin tried too much with her, too early, and stressed her too much, and that that came out as a respiratory condition. He always wants his horses super-fit, and while some horses like Pridwell can take the regime, others can't. And once that happens he doesn't want to know. After being with him for three seasons, he dismissed us with a wave of his hand. And though I've called him, he won't be questioned, he's just pulled the shutters down on us.

With regard to Rowley John, we knew that he was inexperienced when we sent him to Martin. Rymer's offspring generally don't mature until they're six or seven years old. All we asked Martin to do was to find him a few quiet bumper races in his first year. He had the horse for four months, and we got no negative feedback from the stable. But when I saw Rowley at Warwick, I was shocked. He was a donkey. He'd always been laid-back but not that laid-back. I think that the horse was literally mentally and physically exhausted. If Rowley hadn't stood up to his training, why couldn't Martin have let us know that, rather than let us go through that farce at Warwick? Yet within ten minutes of that race finishing, he was on the phone to Chester Barnes telling him to tell me that Rowley was backward, he was weak and he needed a lot more time and should go home immediately.

We must have had ten or eleven races with Martin over the three years, and in that period he came to watch our horses race just three times. He should support his owners by being there. But I think that the real trouble is that he's only interested in success, and if your horse is not successful, he's just not interested.

At Last – Di's Last: the Video

Several months after joining the partnership, Cliff finally managed to get Race-Tech to produce another video compilation of Di's races and forwarded one to me. It seems that the original tape was sent out to somebody and not returned. Originally meant as both a factual record of her progress and a sales pitch for prospective shareholders, the video assumed the nature of a touching epitaph for a career that was now over. As I sat and watched it, I began to realise why Cliff and Janet held Di in such affection, and why they should go to so much trouble and expense to find out what had happened to her, to get her the best treatment, and to assist her recovery so that she could enjoy a new life.

Di's first appearance was at Ludlow on 4 December 1995 in a bumper race. Ridden by David Bridgewater, then Pipe's stable jockey, she shows lots of early pace and is able to hold her position in about fifth throughout most of the race. With some of the horses behind her beginning to come off the bridle, Bridgewater kicks Di on into the straight and she takes a lead of about five lengths on her rivals. She looks a certain winner, but then over the last 50 yards a horse called Come on Penny finds an extra gear and goes past Di with about 20 yards to go to the line. It's a fantastic first run, and anyone who was there must have been thrilled with her performance.

The next two races are also bumpers, the first at Wincanton on 21 March 1996. Here Di jumps off straight into the lead in typical Pipe-horse fashion. She leads all the way, at a good pace until, at about 2 furlongs out, Aerion cruises past her and goes on to win easily. Two other horses, Wentworth and

Warner For Players, relegate her to fourth place. The next bumper is at Hereford on 4 May 1996. Again she leads all the way, still on the bridle, only to be overtaken in the last furlong by the strong-finishing Cool Virtue and Wynyard Lady.

Di's first hurdle race is at Warwick on 16 December 1996, with promising young Irish jockey Richard Hughes in the saddle. He jumps her off into the lead from the start and at one stage in the back straight is more than ten lengths up on the field. This is typical Pipe style, in which he tries to use his horse's superior fitness to burn off the opposition. Unfortunately, Di doesn't quite last the trip, weakening in the straight to be passed by Konvekta King, Joy For Life, Maylin Magic and Priory Gale. Fifth will be her lowest finish of all her races.

In the next hurdle Di found herself up against two very strong horses in Maid For Adventure and Galatasori Jane. This time she was ridden with more restraint, tucked in the field in about fifth place. She jumps very fluently and with three flights left cruises up to take the lead. But a jumping error at this hurdle slows her down, though I doubt that she could have held off Maid For Adventure anyway. Galatasori Jane, who just pipped Di for second place, is now famous in racing circles for winning no fewer than eight times in the 1997–8 National Hunt season.

In what was to be her last ever race, at Taunton on 16 January 1997, Di was again tried with waiting tactics, presumably in a bid to preserve her stamina. She is always well-placed throughout the race and is moving into third place when she makes a slight mistake at a hurdle. Nevertheless she stays on gamely to finish fourth behind the winner Spring Gale, Edgemoor Prince and Weather Wise.

I suppose if I was to be emotionally detached, I would say from the video evidence that it looks as though she lacked a bit of pace at the end of a race. But that doesn't do justice to those horses that finished in front of her, nor indeed to the many who finished behind her. The steadier tempo of a steeplechase would almost certainly have suited her better. But now we will never know. At least Di finished the game in one piece, despite her illness, which is more than can be said for many horses. What surprises me is how possessive I feel about a horse I've only previously seen in a photograph. And far from being a depressing experience, watching Di in action reminds me why I wanted to get involved in ownership in the first place – yes, for a bit of fun, and perhaps some money, but above all for a bit of genuine sport.

I began to get the blues now about the 'ownership' season being over. But like the junkie who has stashed away a last fragment of gear in a secret place for emergency use, I knew in the furtive recesses of my mind that there had been an advert in the *Racing Post* last Saturday that had read: '4 YEAR OLD FILLY to run in bumpers. Must be seen. Serious contender. £5,000 for a quarter share. Contact Trainer N.A. Smith, Worcestershire.'

I agonised for what seemed like days but was in fact only hours. I just about had the money for this scale of investment, and I'd developed a logic, admittedly dangerous, that a bit more expense on horses might bring me more reward rather than less. This isn't the same as thinking that the more money you bet on a horse, the more likely it is to win. No, it was more like the difference between a cheap pair of shoes and an expensive one. You hope that by buying the expensive pair they will last longer, that you will get better value for money than if you bought two or three cheap pairs in the same period. The only trouble being that horses are not shoes.

The fact that I knew and liked Nigel also helped make me interested. Even over this relatively short period of ownership I'd realised that having some kind of rapport with your trainer, even if it was only at the superficial level of a few jokes, could make a difference to the whole experience. I also knew that this was an approach I could make without too much evasiveness. If I liked the horse and its prospects, fine, I was prepared to spend the money. If I didn't, I felt that it was unlikely that I'd end up being condemned as a 'time-waster' by Nigel. With an effective 'value' of twenty grand on this unknown horse I was entitled to a good look before committing myself. So, the conversation went something like this.

'Hello, Nigel?'

'Yeah?'

'It's Stan Hey. The Scouser with the big nose from the Tally-Ho mob.'

'Hello, mate! What can I do for you?'

'About this horse of yours in the *Racing Post*?'

Back in the Saddle

Because Nigel could at least place my face, there was less need for the usual defensive protocol that these 'horses for sale' advertisers use as the first line of defence against nosy-parkers and time-wasters. So he could tell me that the filly was unraced, and had been sired by a Flat horse called Ron's Victory, out of a mare by the name of Camp Chair. The mare had had five foals, three of which had won races, so this daughter technically had what they term 'a winning background'. Nigel had originally intended to race her on the Flat – he holds full training licences for both codes – but the horse had startled him by growing so big. So he'd decided to let her develop physically and then introduce her gradually to a career in bumper races and then over hurdles. She had already been doing light training work and was in good shape, so much so that when she had been taken for a racecourse gallop at Towcester she had seen off her more experienced galloping companion. Nigel was convinced that 'she' – no name, not even the stable one was mentioned – had a very bright future. There were four shares available, of which Nigel was going to retain one, and he'd already received a preliminary enquiry from a businessman in Derby.

'Come on up and have a look if you want,' Nigel said cheerfully, 'no obligation.'

Like hell, I thought to myself, knowing that, barring the horse having one eye and only three legs, I was bound to get out my cheque book.

'What about tomorrow?' I asked, probably giving the game away in an instant.

'Fine. The yard's in Upton Snodsbury, on the Stratford road out of Worcester. There's a pub on the main road called the Coventry Arms. Meet me in there about 10.30 and we'll get the horse out for some exercise. See you.'

I put the phone down, giddy with excitement, yet stomach-rumblingly anxious about making a bad decision. My normal approach to major purchases is an instinctive, no-messing-around, 'I'll have that, thanks'. This is partly due to an abiding hatred of shopping – when I was a kid I used to collapse on the floor in most of Liverpool's department stores and then wail my lungs out. The other factor was the brief residency of any substantial sums of money in my accounts.

When I was working with Andrew Nickolds in a house in Cambridge for a fortnight in 1980 – the third series of *Agony* it must have been – I got a cheque for just over £5,000 on the second Monday morning of our stay. That same evening we went for a walk on the way to the pub and there in this car showroom was a silver-coloured, 1972 Porsche 911S, for £4,750. I went back the next day in my jeans and T-shirt, and managed to blag a test drive out of the salesman. As I took the car out on the Newmarket Road, I found myself not only grinning at the driving experience, but also at the knowledge that I could actually afford this. When we got back to the showroom, in one piece, I took out my cheque book and asked for a discount for an outright purchase. By the end of the week the AA had done a report to say that it was a serviceable car, and on the Saturday I drove it back to London, with Andrew holding on to every handle he could find in sheer terror. Despite being an old, flash car, it lasted a good twelve years for me, before the onset of family responsibility forced me to sell it in favour of a sensible Renault Espace.

So, if I see something I want that I can also afford, I just buy it there and then. I can't bring myself to shop around, I hate going home to make my mind up, and even on cars and houses, I'm happy to trust my own instincts and let the experts have their say later. That doesn't mean to say that I'm a complete impulse buyer. Within a few minutes of putting down the phone on Nigel, I'd managed to find an entry for Ron's Victory in a 1991 Timeform annual. They described him as 'quite attractive colt; high class performer at 3 years'. His best effort had come when winning the Group 3 Krug Diadem Stakes at Ascot in 1990 by 10 lengths. It also referred to an even better run in a race at Longchamp in which he had finished a close third. In twelve races, he'd won three times, come second four times, and third once, never finishing lower than sixth.

This was all very impressive and I spoke to an old friend, Sean Magee, the well-established racing author, to see if he remembered anything about Ron's Victory. It turned out that Sean did indeed remember 'Ron', not least because he'd backed him when he won the Diadem. 'A very good horse,' was Sean's verdict, but he was less sure about the potential of Ron's offspring in National Hunt. 'As far as I know he only ran over 5–7 furlongs, which wouldn't make him a big influence for stamina. Who was the mare?'

I had found nothing on Camp Chair in my admittedly limited selection of racing reference books and Sean had never heard of her. This didn't necessarily mean bad news, because many brood-mares never actually raced, but they are still regarded as OK because of their blood-lines (decent mum and dad, solid grandparents and so on).

So on Friday 27 February 1998 I set off in the car from Bradford after dropping the boys off at school. 'What are you doing today, dad?' 'Buying a racehorse, what else would I be doing?' With a reasonable run up to the M4 and then through to the M5, I thought I'd be able to do the trip in about an hour and a quarter. Well, twenty minutes of this was spent stuck on the A46 north of Bath where they have a new by-pass that speeds you through to an absolute bastard of a bottleneck. As I sat there, with the everyday traffic of ordinary life at a standstill around me, I began to think this was a message – 'turn again' or 'go home'. I became convinced that Nigel would think I wasn't coming and that I'd be put down as a 'time-waster'. Then the traffic finally started moving.

Once I'd got on to the M4, it was a relatively straight-forward trip up on to the M5 even at a steady gallop. My days of driving the Porsche are a distant memory now so I get a nosebleed if I go into the outside lane. By 10.30 a.m. I was turning off at Junction 7 and heading out on the A422 towards Stratford-on-Avon. About seven miles on, the sign for Upton Snodsbury appeared – no twinning, as yet, with Upper Harlem – and the Coventry Arms was practically the first building on the left. A handsome-looking pub with cream-painted walls and blue trimming, it had a large car-park and children's play area, and I instantly had images of the family coming up to see the horse on a Sunday morning.

The pub didn't look open but Nigel was sitting at the bar with a mug of coffee in his hand, as though he owned the place. The beamed interior of the pub and the cosy furnishings suggested that this was more than just your average local boozer. A quick introduction to the resident chef confirmed as much. Nigel then showed me some of his racing memorabilia that line the walls of one of the bars. They are mostly pictures of the stable's main Flat horse, Petraco, who had the distinction to win the first-ever race under floodlights at Wolverhampton's all-weather track. The star item is probably the photo of Nigel with Petraco and jockey Frankie Dettori after winning a sprint at Warwick.

Nigel then led me out to my car for the short trip to the stables. Off a country track, they are tucked away between open countryside one side, where Nigel's gallops run up a ridge, and a jumble of farm buildings. Two sides of the yard are made up of charming, red-brick boxes, the third is a tall hedge and the fourth a large agricultural shed that has been partitioned into several boxes. I parked by the hedge and as I got out two horses were being saddled up, with Liz Grainger, Nigel's partner and assistant trainer, on one, and stable jockey Mark Sharratt on the other.

The other inmates of the yard included Tarakhel, Silent Action, Lady Pendragon and the injured Nova Scotia. I went across to see the poor little horse, with her damaged leg totally bandaged. I could have sworn she gave me a dirty look, as if to say, 'Look what you and your racing mates did to me, you bastard,' but in fact she seemed quite cheerful when I stroked her face and chatted to her.

A few years back, I spent four months of a fairly nasty winter feeding our late neighbour's two horses, morning and night, trudging up a steep field with a bale of hay on my back, before breaking the ice on their water trough. During this time, I fondly imagined that I'd developed a 'relationship' with the horses, talking to them, getting to know where they liked their feeding buckets and so on. In the early spring, when some other people came to take over their care, the horses displayed not one flicker of regret or disturbance at my departure from their daily routine. It was at this point that I realised that all they saw when I was approaching was food, and not the human being carrying it.

So even though I was on the threshold of a deeper commitment to ownership, I remained fairly sceptical about there being a genuine relationship between man and beast, other than the merely functional. My feeding of the two horses in my care had been reciprocated by Nova Scotia's brief racing services to the partnership. And though I was sorry she'd been injured, and happy that she could still lead another life, I didn't feel anything approaching guilt. As a punter of long standing I'd grown used to developing attachments to certain horses that had won for me, such as Mtoto, at 16–1 at Sandown one night before he became famous, and Wayward Lad, three times the winner of the King George Chase. I'd also regretted when any of them had been killed in action, but never to the extent of wanting to stop racing. That might seem like a heartless, almost colonial attitude, but I took the view that racehorses actually enjoyed their sport, and contributed to the general happiness of the nation.

But then Nigel pointed to the horse that Liz was now coaxing gently out of the yard – a tall, handsome, well-muscled bay filly with lovely big ears and two white diamond-shaped blazes on her face. This was Dee-Dee, as they called her, the horse for sale. And I was smitten in an instant. As she walked away down the track with her galloping companion, Nigel filled me in on the bizarre circumstances by which they had both come into the yard.

'It was just over three years ago. Gerald Spencer, a horse transporter, was in the yard and he told me he'd seen two smashing-looking yearlings in a field in mid-Wales, looking a bit sorry for themselves. He gave me directions and Liz and I drove over there one freezing cold day. We had a look at them and they were slipping and sliding around on the frozen turf. But they were both obviously thoroughbreds, with good conformations, and Liz wanted us to take them home. So we went in to see the chap who'd got them, and I made him an offer. He'd bought them at a sale in Ireland but hadn't worked out what he was going to do with them. I checked their breeding. Dee-Dee was by Ron's Victory, and the other filly by Roi Danzig. Taking them on was an act of faith really.'

Nigel and Liz duly acquired the two fillies and nurtured them for a year. At two, they were both 'broken' and then galloped on the all-weather at Wolverhampton. 'They both needed more time, so we let them feed and grow for another year with a view to racing them on the Flat as three-year-olds,' Nigel explained.

By that time, Dee-Dee – so called because of the 'double-diamonds' on her face – had become so big that it was decided to save her for jumping. Liz now explained the basics of the training that Dee-Dee underwent.

'We put them both into serious training over the winter of their third and fourth years, which really involves giving the horses discipline, and harnessing their will to run. Vitamins and diet are a big part of the equation too. Gradually you build up their muscles and stamina through exercise, and make sure that you know when to give them some time off. A horse can't grow and race at the same time.'

Nigel took up the last leg of the story. 'We then gave Dee-Dee a racecourse gallop at Towcester alongside a more experienced horse, Silent Action (known as "Dozy" in the yard), which we'd bought in Ireland for one of our owners. In that gallop Dee-Dee just took Silent Action to the cleaners, and Mark jumped off her with an amazed look on his face. We knew then that we'd got a good horse.'

We went back to my car and drove out across the Stratford road, deeper into the countryside, with Bredon Hill now looming in the distance. Dee-Dee and her companion – later to be named Bosom Pal when the Triumph bra company bought her as a companion for Fortytwo Dee – were heading for one of the huge open fields owned by Nigel's farming father, where a pair of home-made starting stalls stood in one corner, alongside the foundations for Nigel's planned equine swimming pool. As the cold February wind sliced in off the hill, Dee-Dee and Bosom Pal cantered around the field a couple of times, moving easily and, in Dee-Dee's case, with a bouncy eagerness, occasionally bucking with excess energy. After the two circuits they pulled up, with Dee-Dee hardly drawing breath. She plainly wanted to go round again. 'She's got a real engine,' Nigel said with passion.

While the horses walked back to the yard, Nigel filled me in on the plans for Dee-Dee – firstly to get the partnership up and running, and then to find her a couple of bumper races for experience in April or May, before the 'official' end of the 1997–8 season. We drove back to the yard, and while Liz and

Mark unsaddled the horses, I went into Nigel's office that adjoins the red-brick boxes. The low, beamed room was filled with clutter – an old desk and filing cabinet, a big but battered television and a long sofa. All around the walls were his racing mementoes. These consisted mostly of photos of Nigel riding as an amateur jockey, and others of horses, such as Master Nova and Holt Place, that had won for him during his ten years as a trainer. Nigel was initially a permit-holder (a trainer with a small yard of only two or three horses), and then acquired a full licence for first the Jumps, and later the Flat.

As a farmer's son, riding had been a natural pastime for Nigel, first at pony club and then hunting. He then rode several times as an amateur jockey over the jumps, winning a hunter chase at Cheltenham, though not at the Festival.

'I remember going out to walk the course in the morning, and there was a ground staff guy by one of the fences. "This is the one where they all fall off and break their collar-bones," he told me. So when I came to that fence in the race I was bricking myself, so I just closed my eyes and then opened them after I'd cleared it.'

More inclined to training than farming, Nigel began with £400 in his pocket at the Doncaster sales and, after buying a horse, applied for a permit. He was turned down the first time, probably for being a 'bit flippant' in his interview before the licensing committee of the Jockey Club.

'It's a bloody terrifying experience. They were all sat at one end of this huge table while I stood at the other. Only the secretary called me "Mr Smith", to the rest I was just "Smith". The second time I applied, in March 1987, I behaved myself and got my permit. My first winner as a permit-holder was a horse called Au Revoir Joan, which the owner had named after the wife he was divorcing. Then a couple of years later I got my full licence and had my first winner as a registered trainer in November 1989. Through my friendship with another trainer I got to know Mick

O'Toole from Ireland, who's one of their best handlers and a great character. I was having a drink with him one night while he was over here, and telling him what a struggle it was. About two days later these horse-boxes pulled up outside my stable with six of Mick's untried horses inside. He wanted me to have a go at assessing them, at the same time as giving me a chance to prove myself and expand my yard. It was a lovely gesture.'

In 1993, Nigel took on a Flat licence, and Petraco became his first success. With just nine horses in his yard now, Nigel exists mainly on selling shares in horses he's acquired, and on the training fees from his owners. The infrequent earnings from a 10 per cent share of win and place prize-money would appear to be fairly negligible. In the past five seasons he's had just two winners over the sticks, but there are plenty of other trainers for whom this would represent giddy success. He remains undaunted and ambitious and, with Liz's intelligent support, manages to enjoy things on the way. 'I love training,' Nigel insists, 'but it's bloody hard making ends meet.'

So there I was in his office making my mind up about whether this was a sound investment or not. Well, the investment didn't come into it really. Once the capital sum of buying a quarter-share had been paid, the main burden would be my portion of the monthly fees for Dee-Dee's training and feed, which would work out at around £120–£150. I liked Nigel, and I liked the horse. It was no contest. I opened my cheque book and made out a deposit for £2,500 as the first payment for a share of Dee-Dee. Nigel wrote me a receipt and we shook hands. 'We'll have some fun with this horse, I promise,' he said.

Nigel then announced that as I was the first one in the new partnership, I could choose the racing colours. He showed me those of his existing owners, dangling on wire coat-hangers in an old wardrobe on the top of which was a budgie in a cage.

'The only tips are to choose something that'll be visible on a filthy winter's day at Hereford, and don't pick green because that's regarded as bad luck.'

He gave me a four-sided form from his filing cabinet. On it were the basic designs and colours for owners' silks. There are different combinations for the jockey's cap, and even more design combinations and patterns for the body and the sleeves of the silks. The colours are relatively limited in number. Once I'd decided, Nigel would send the form on to Weatherby's and, assuming the chosen design and colours weren't identical to anybody else's or didn't infringe any dress code, they would then be officially registered and he'd have the colours made up at the Roy Mangan Saddlery Foundation in Stow-on-the-Wold.

I went back out into the yard to take another look at Dee-Dee in her box, where Liz was grooming her after the canter. Seeing the horse close-up, it was noticeable how alert she was, how she watched me carefully and how she pricked her ears as we talked. And then in an absolutely heart-melting moment, Dee-Dee lifted her off foreleg in a begging gesture.

'She wants a Polo mint,' Liz said. 'This is her party-piece. Any time she wants something, she gives you a nudge and then lifts her leg.'

I didn't have any on me, unfortunately, but Liz had a supply in her jacket pocket, and as she reached for some, Dee-Dee instantly spotted their location and nuzzled in to try and get at the packet. This was one clever horse. I gave her a stroke on the face and patted her neck. She gave no sign of recognition that I was now her one-quarter owner, but hey, it was only a first date.

We adjourned to the Coventry Arms for a drink to celebrate the new partnership, with Liz joining us after finishing the grooming. The subject of a name was broached and I said I didn't have any ideas yet. But Nigel and Liz had already developed a notion from Dee-Dee's stable name, taking the alliterative initials and making a name from these. What they'd come up with was 'Deadly Doris'. I like to think that my smile didn't freeze on my face when I heard this. All through my punting career there had been a received wisdom that horses with daft names didn't win races. It didn't always apply of course, with animals such as Hellcatmudwrestler, Muff Driver and Mary Hinge proving the purists wrong. Why, even Flakey Dove was a bit on the weird side, and she'd won a Champion Hurdle. I could tell that Liz and Nigel had settled on Deadly Doris as a name, so I resisted the temptation to protest and nodded mutely.

'Thanks for supporting the yard and taking Dee-Dee on,' Liz said sweetly as I left for my car. I joked about the real challenge being them taking me on as an owner. On the way back down the M5, I kept repeating Deadly Doris to myself, and creating imaginary racecourse commentaries. 'And it's Deadly Doris clear at the last now, storming up the hill, she's spread-eagled this field, no mistake. Deadly Doris is the winner!'

By the time I'd got home the image of this bright-eyed, good-looking horse and her slightly silly name had begun to gel. There was no doubt that she was a character, and that something puckish would suit her. When I picked up Charlie and Jack from school, I told them that I'd gone ahead and bought a quarter-share in a horse called Deadly Doris. They both loved it, probably because it sounded like a cyber-heroine in the Lara Croft mode. But as I told them I realised that the name was now tripping off my tongue as though it had always been right.

Doing the Business

Over the next few weeks, in the run-up to Cheltenham, I busied myself – in between work – with some of the minor bureaucracies of being a quarter-shareholder in a racehorse. The first priority was to decide on our racing colours. Nigel had phoned soon after my visit to confirm that Steve Ludlam was going to buy one of the other quarter-shares, which left the final one up for grabs. There was a possibility that Nigel's father would take that, but I was asked by Nigel to 'keep an ear open' for any friends or contacts who might like to buy in. Nigel was fairly determined that he wanted the partnership to remain small because he found dealing with a dozen or more owners milling around a parade ring a bit of a strain at times, not knowing names, or whether anybody might be offended by his fairly repetitive swearing. So we had three, possibly four male partners with a female horse. It was the equivalent of a social dilemma in the agony columns of the *Tatler* – 'Dear Abby, one is choosing one's colours for one's horse, do the same rules apply as for humans, viz: blue for boys, pink for girls?'

While I was wrestling with the actual colours, the design was much easier to decide upon. Though you could have all sorts of chevrons on the body and sleeves, or quartered colours, or hoops or even large circles, I knew I wanted something on the plain side, not too busy, rather than have the jockey turning out in something resembling a modern rugby league shirt. I almost favoured a single colour for the body, but because this is deemed to be the classic style in National Hunt racing, most of the colours have long been claimed by various Lords, Ladies, Viscounts and Earls.

I thought the next best thing would be to have the body colours split into two vertical halves, with contrasting sleeves and a classic quartered cap, all of this with just two colours. I began to think seriously about pink because of Doris's sex, and then the solution, so to speak, came out of the blue. The colours of my college at Cambridge were maroon and pink! I'd worn the maroon shirt when I played football for the First XI, and still had a 'Catz' cricket sweater with a maroon and pink vee. They went together well, it seemed, and the idea of using these colours for a horse struck me as a vaguely amusing, even subversive gesture. I thought about writing in to the 'News of Old Members' section of the college's annual magazine. This is usually filled with notes about knighthoods and other 'Buck House gongs', as one Fellow referred to them during my time there. As one of the college's under-achievers, I would enjoy seeing my entry in this year's edition: 'Hey, S.B. (1971), writes to say that he has still not found a proper job, but has recently bought a racehorse called Deadly Doris, who runs in the college colours.'

Somewhat pathetically, I now sketched in the colours on the chosen design, using my children's coloured pencils. I thought the finished result looked quite classy, even if it erred towards the territory occupied by Harry Enfield's camp jockey character. So I filled in the form and sent it back to Nigel, leaving him the option of saying no, but didn't receive any immediate reaction from him, which I took as a sign of approval. I also sent off another cheque for £2,500 to complete the purchase of the quarter-share.

Later that week Nigel phoned to say that the colours had been sent off to Weatherby's for a 'search' and then registration once they had been cleared. At my prompting, he announced that the fees for Deadly Doris's training would commence from 1 April, with no slight being intended by the starting date. I didn't ask what the fees would be, there didn't seem any point now that I was in the partnership. It was rather like the old story of the man looking at Rolls-Royces who asked what the price of one particular model was, his social blunder being that if he could afford to buy, he didn't need to ask. Deadly Doris was by no means a Roller, but she might yet turn into one. This thought touched on the subject of insurance. I'd mentioned this to Nigel at the pub when we'd met, and he was of the view that we should go through Weatherby's for a policy on Doris, the going rate being something between 5 and 10 per cent of the horse's estimated value. I guessed that this would be included in my first bill at the end of April.

So I had completed all the preliminaries of ownership – paid for my share, selected the colours, accepted a name for the horse. All I could do now was wait for her to race. I knew that I would have to be patient on this. Nigel had stressed how much he thought of Doris – 'the best horse in the yard by far' – and also that he wouldn't 'rush her unnecessarily'. The bureaucratic details would probably take another month to complete in any case. In the meantime, the Cheltenham Festival was looming large on my horizon, and that would certainly occupy my mind. Not least in the small matter of investing a few bob on Deep Water for the Triumph Hurdle. I shopped around for ante-post prices, and put £20 on with Tote Credit at 25–1, and then had another £10 each way at 33–1 with Janet at my local branch of H. Backhouse in Bradford-on-Avon. If Deep Water won, I'd be £912.50 better off, and that would certainly help pay a few bills for Doris. My pulse began to quicken. The National Hunt season was heading towards it climax with the Cheltenham and Aintree meetings, and I felt more involved than ever before, because this time round I was an owner.

Monday 9 March 1998

The perfect appetiser for Cheltenham arrived with a commission from *Night & Day* to write a 'Personal Space' feature on trainer Charlie Brooks. I accepted it straight away, of course, despite the initial requirement to be in Lambourn, the centre of National Hunt training, at 7.30 a.m. This was later amended to a more civilised 9.30 a.m., after Brooks had dealt with his 'second lot' of horses. Brooks had nominated his training gallops as his 'personal space', so it was a chance to penetrate one of the most exclusive inner sanctums of National Hunt racing, since the trainer had the use of private gallops bought for him by his main owner and patron, Andrew Cohen. Cohen had bought Uplands House, Charlie's yard, in the mid-1990s as the recession took its toll on racing, with owners cutting back on their commitments as a first reaction to the latest financial crisis. There was a time when large wars and Wall Street crashes wouldn't have made the slightest impact on British racing, so deeply entrenched and secure were the aristocracy in the sport's finances. But things were different now.

I drove across to Lambourn with a painter friend from Bradford, Tim Williams, who had once been a 'dray-man' for Usher's brewery, and who therefore knew every back lane and every pub in Wiltshire and Berkshire. It was a fairly grey morning, and still chilly. By the time we arrived in Lambourn village itself, lines of horses were already on the streets, on their way back to their stables after training. I dropped Tim off so that he could have a browse around old haunts and make a few sketches if the mood took him.

I headed out of the village towards Upper Lambourn, looking for Uplands Lane on my right. As I paused at the turning, a silver Mercedes saloon flashed past and turned in, heading up the lane. One of Brooks's rich owners, I presumed, and I followed behind in the humble Espace. The Merc parked in the yard itself and I pulled alongside. Out of the car stepped the photographer, Paul Massey, together with his assistant and the picture editor of *Night & Day*, Tim Leith. I asked Tim if the writer was going to get the same rate as the photographer, because I'd always fancied a Merc myself one day.

We found Charlie Brooks, who was very accommodating despite the imminence of Cheltenham, and we drove the short distance up to his gallops. Here, on the very roof of Lambourn, were magnificent views out across 'The Valley of the Horse' as it styles itself. The facilities were fantastic, the sort of set-up Nigel and many other trainers would envy: a circular, railed, all-weather warm-up/cool-down ring, and then, sloping away down into a valley, a six-furlong wood-chip gallop, along which several of his horses were already working, racing up from the bottom of the valley in pairs. While Paul the photographer scouted locations with his assistant, I watched the horses alongside Charlie and asked him how Suny Bay, his main entry for the Cheltenham Gold Cup, was coming along after his muscle injury.

'He's still short of peak fitness, by about two weeks I'd say,' Brooks confided with some pessimism. 'I wish I had a bit more time to work on him, but that's the nature of racing. You're always chasing targets that you may not be able to reach. Andrew wants to run him whatever, though I'd be tempted to let him miss the Gold Cup and go straight to the Grand National for another crack.'

Suny Bay, who had become my second favourite racehorse after Deadly Doris by virtue of his big wins at Haydock Park in October and Newbury in November, had finished runner-up to Lord Gyllene in the 1997 Grand National. Lord Gyllene had been injured in training and was out for the year. So even though Suny Bay was lumbered with top weight, he looked to have a good chance of taking the Aintree showpiece. But the feature I was to write was timed to come out on the very next Sunday, four days before the Cheltenham Gold Cup, so I was a bit alarmed at the possibility that Brooks might yet pull him from the race. He said a gallop on Friday would probably make up his mind, but by then *Night & Day* would be at the printers. So I would have to 'hedge' in my copy about Suny Bay making it to Cheltenham, otherwise the feature would look a little stupid.

Paul took a few preliminary photos of Charlie watching his horses in the warm-up ring, but the sky was still so grey that the sweeping backdrop of the valley was almost impossible to pick up. I took Charlie back down to the yard while Paul waited for a break in the cloud, and sat down in his small but pleasantly furnished office for our chat. Like Nigel's, it was lined with racing memorabilia, albeit more substantial given the quality of horses that Brooks trained. Brooks had also been a very successful amateur jockey before becoming assistant at Uplands to the great Fred Winter, the legendary jump jockey and trainer, who had won all the major prizes in both of his careers.

Winter had ridden two Gold Cup winners, Saffron Tartan in 1961 and Mandarin in 1962; two Champion Hurdle winners, Fare Time in 1959 and Eborneezer in 1961; and won two Grand Nationals, on Sundew in 1957 and Kilmore in 1962. As a trainer he won the National with Jay Trump in 1965 and Anglo in 1966; the Gold Cup with Midnight Court in 1978; and three Champion Hurdles with Bula in 1971 and 1972, and Lanzarote in 1974. He was also credited with Celtic Shot's 1988 Champion Hurdle win, despite the fact that Charlie Brooks had prepared the horses after the domestic fall which had effectively ended Winter's training career.

Despite following in Winter's giant footsteps, Brooks had acquitted himself honourably since taking over the famous Uplands yard, and had laid to rest the cliché of the dim, snotty Old Etonian trainer by being a bright, accessible Old Etonian trainer. The main text of our interview was obviously unique to Brooks, but I think that there were elements of it that apply to most trainers in relation to what happens on their gallops. This is what he said:

This is my real 'office' up here. It's where I do my job, and I'm lucky in that a lot of the other Lambourn trainers have to use communal gallops. This is very much my own space. I do what I want and I can make the rules. It's the most beautiful place on a fine winter's morning because the sun hits the gallops as it rises. Even on a cold morning, it's amazing how the sun can warm you, and it's just a wonderful view. The most unsatisfactory part of being a trainer is the amount of time one spends on the phone. But up on the gallops I can get peace and quiet and focus on the horses. Up here is where I start to put it all together, where the possibilities start to unfold. Here is where the real decisions are made. The real joy of training horses is seeing a good young one suddenly come together. Suny Bay couldn't really have been expected to make a significant improvement after finishing second in last year's Grand National, but his work here one morning told me he'd made a massive leap forward. This is where the dreams begin.

After the interview I wished Charlie good luck with Suny Bay, and left him to the attentions of Paul the photographer. I collected Tim Williams from the centre of Lambourn just as the rain began to fall. But by waiting another hour or so for the weather to clear, Paul was able to get an absolutely fantastic photo of Charlie with Suny Bay, with the valley dropping away behind them. When I got home I typed up my copy and faxed it through to the *Night & Day* office, and the feature duly appeared on Sunday 15 March. By then Suny Bay had passed his 'fitness test' on the Friday morning and was announced as a 'probable runner' for the Gold Cup on Thursday 19th. Unfortunately, on checking through my Ceefax five-day declaration pages I couldn't find any trace of Deep Water in the entries for the Triumph Hurdle. My two ante-post bets were sunk, and so even before the Cheltenham Festival had begun I was already forty quid down.

Friday 13 March 1998

My first opportunity to test out Deadly Doris's collateral form arrives with Silent Action declared for the bumper race on Market Rasen's card today. Silent Action was the horse that Doris saw off in no uncertain terms during their racehorse gallop at Towcester. So a good run by this horse this afternoon will give me a rough guide as to Doris's potential, always allowing for the fact that she was a complete baby at the time of the work, and also for the fact that it was a gallop, not a race. Silent Action's Irish form involves two races. In the first, a bumper race over two miles at Punchestown on 18 February 1996, he finished a length second to a horse called Glebe Lad in a field of seven runners. In his second race, another bumper, this time at Leopardstown, he finished fifth out of ten, beaten by about twelve lengths by a horse called Graduated. Since I can't track down the form of the horses that beat him I don't know how good these performances were, but they at least seemed promising in absolute terms. But his debut in an English bumper was less auspicious, albeit after a break of nearly eighteen months. He finished twelfth out of a field of fourteen runners and the race report describes him as 'prominent, led 7f out, quickened 4f out, headed and weakened 3f out, beaten 26 lengths'.

Today's race is over 'just' 1 mile 5½ furlongs, which is well short of the normal bumper race. But it will still be interesting, not to mention nerve-racking to watch. I go down to the Backhouse betting shop in Bradford-on-Avon and stick a fiver on him to win, just in case. To the ordinary punters in the shop this is just a 'nothing race' at the fag end of the day, and Janet the bookie gives me one of her 'are you mad?' looks as I place my bet. The race starts and I watch the SIS coverage, eyes glued to Silent Action's red and black colours. He is quite prominent for roughly a mile or so, but then gets hampered badly on the turn into the home straight, and drops back. But as the winner, Belisario, speeds home, it looks to me as though Silent Action stays on again and has come home fast in about sixth or seventh place in the sixteen-runner field.

But in the race report in the *Racing Post* the following morning, he is placed ninth and their view is that he was 'held up and behind, headway on outside 5f out, never near leaders', which goes to show how one-eyed you can be when one of 'yours' is racing. It's not too bad a run though, and leaves me with enough optimism to look forward to Doris's debut, whenever that may be.

Festival Time

For those who have never been to a Cheltenham Festival, it will require considerable detail to convey even a small slice of what it is like. In the first instance, the fact that every other festival at Cheltenham has to insert a prefix with a more precise definition – as in 'literary' or 'jazz' – gives some indication of racing's predominant claim on the title. It's true that the three days are now often classified as the National Hunt Festival, presumably for marketing purposes or perhaps because some whizz-kid found that the letters NH are together in the word Cheltenham. But for most Jump racing fans, it's either simply 'Cheltenham' or 'the Festival'. To us, it's the equivalent of the FA Cup Final, the Last Night of the Proms, Glastonbury, the Second Test at Lords, a feeding frenzy on the Stock Exchange or Glyndebourne – sometimes all of these rolled into one.

The basic structure of the three days of racing is built on three championship races, one on each day. On the first day, Tuesday, it's the Champion Hurdle, run over two miles and half a furlong, with horses from four years old upwards competing for a first prize of over £100,000. On the Wednesday, the feature race is the Queen Mother Champion Chase over two miles, the minimum trip for a steeplechase. Because of this there is as much emphasis on speed as on jumping, and the race is often the most exciting spectacle of the Festival, with horses taking fences at speeds close to 35 m.p.h. On the Thursday, the centre-piece and the climax of the meeting is the Gold Cup, a 3 mile 2 furlong Chase for those horses with stamina as well as class in their genes, with a winner's prize of £148,962 at stake this year.

Around these three highlights are races for all other types of National Hunt horse, both British and Irish – the promising youngsters of both hurdling and chasing, the old lags, the handicap trundlers, the hunter chasers, the dour stayers and even the bumper horses with no experience of jumping just yet. All this takes place in the most spectacular setting, with a line of craggy Cotswold hills framing the far side of the course, and a half-mile wall of grandstands and hospitality boxes overlooking the finishing straight. If you add into this mix a daily crowd of 50,000 people from all walks of British and Irish society, on-course betting that easily exceeds a million pounds a day, and a variety of bars pumping out champagne and Guinness like there's no tomorrow, then you might have a clearer idea of what you've been missing.

While it's true that Cheltenham doesn't have the fashion parade or society ball element that Royal Ascot generates, or the stylish high-summer glamour of Glorious Goodwood and the Ebor meeting at York, the Festival manages to be either as smart or as informal as you wish to make it. The two basic survival rules are to work out how much money you want to take with you, and then double it, and to make sure that you wear comfortable but durable shoes. For a lot of people it's the equivalent of an annual holiday, with a four-night stay away from home in a hotel that would have been booked almost a year in advance. The alternatives are to stay with friends in the area, or to travel up on one of the special trains from Paddington station that can provide you with a champagne breakfast on the way up and a three-course dinner on the way back.

For me, it's about an hour and a half on the train via Bristol. I would never think of driving there, partly because of my alcohol intake, partly because it can take two or three hours to get on to or off the course if your timing is wrong. This time round I'd accepted an invitation to stay with Sean Magee and his wife Ceci who live in west Oxfordshire. Apart from the attraction of their excellent hospitality, Sean also knows the back routes and can usually manage the door-to-course journey in about 45 minutes. I'd also arranged to meet Simon Kelner and a group of his journalist colleagues from *Night & Day* in the Arkle Bar at the foot of the main grandstand on the first day. To complete my social calendar, Nigel Smith had phoned to say that he was running Fortytwo Dee in Wednesday's National Hunt Steeple Chase, and had suggested we might meet up for a drink.

I'd 'tooled up' for the Festival with a dozen prime Havanas from Tranter's cigar shop in Bath and also with Timeform's Cheltenham 'Black Book', a comprehensive form guide to all the runners at the meeting. I'd also worked all weekend on the *Golden Boots* scripts to make sure that I wasn't called away to a meeting, or that the black dog of guilt would not make an unwelcome appearance.

So, armed with a wallet stocked with £200 in readies from the Stroud & Swindon Building Society, I set off for Cheltenham on Tuesday 17 March with a rare lightness of step. By 11.30 a.m. I was in the Arkle Bar waiting for Simon and friends, but the first person I bumped into was the vicar of one of Bradford's churches, David Seymour. Unlike his Irish counterparts, David doesn't wear his dog-collar to the meeting, nor does he drink or bet. He's there just to watch the races, and is a fair expert on form and history. We spent a cheerful half-hour chatting about the prospects for the day, before he went off to catch up with his group of race-goers from Bradford. I scoured the bar again for Kelner and Co., but there was still no sign. I'd heard that they were planning to stop off at Raymond Blanc's Manoir aux Quat' Saisons for breakfast, so a delay seemed inevitable.

On my next pass through the bar, I met Hugh McIlvanney, Britain's greatest ever sports-writer. Although I am no more than a mere tick on the great elephant's arse of sports journalism, Hugh always seems pleased to see me. This may not be unconnected to the fact that he also has a taste for Havanas and knows that I am a reliable source. He too is waiting for a rendezvous with Kelner, and suggests an adjournment to the small outdoor champagne bar around the corner while we both wait. I get the first bottle and we light up our first smokes of the day – Romeo y Julieta Exhibitions – and fall into chat about the horses we might back.

Hugh is currently working on an authorised biography of Manchester United manager Alex Ferguson, who has recently become a racehorse owner himself. Alex, though, had immaculate connections, being guided in his search for horses by both Mike Dillon and Aidan O'Brien. I tell Hugh about my venture into ownership and he responds by suggesting I may be in need of protective custody. But the mention of Ireland's wonder-boy trainer Aidan O'Brien brings out good inside information from Hugh that Istabraq is a certainty for that afternoon's Champion Hurdle. Those who have doubted the horse's ability to quicken suddenly over this minimum trip of two miles are apparently in for a rude surprise because O'Brien has spent the season working on this particular aspect of the horse's preparation. It hasn't been on display in his races so far this season, although he is unbeaten, but will be revealed to devastating effect today. Hugh is sitting pretty, having backed Istabraq at odds of 14–1 last autumn. The horse is currently hovering around the 2–1 mark, even before the Irish punters on the course get stuck into backing him. After more amiable chat and a further bottle of champagne, we discover that it is now approaching 1.30 p.m., just half-an-hour away from the first race, so we make our way back into the Arkle and immediately find Simon and colleagues surrounding a heavily laden table.

Far from having a luxurious morning, Simon and his party have been the victims of two set-backs. Firstly, the people at the Manoir had no record of their breakfast booking and turned them away. Secondly, a side-window of their chauffeur-driven car has been shot out by a disaffected youth with an air-rifle on the approaches to the course. It makes my ham and mustard sandwich on the train seem like the height of pleasure. The immediate business of the first race is discussed and because it is often won by an Irish horse, we scan the likely candidates. Opinion suggests that His Song is their best, although I mulishly ignore this advice in favour of Native Estates. We are both wrong, as the classy French Ballerina, another Irish horse, storms home to get St Patrick's Day off to a flying start. Not for me, of course, as the first of six £20 win bets goes down.

In the second I back Wade Road, but he weakens quickly and Martin Pipe's Champlève gets home by a short head from the Irish runner, Hill Society. I should have had more faith in my former trainer. But now it's Champion Hurdle time. Simon is also holding a 14–1 voucher from last autumn on Istabraq. I'm tempted to join in, albeit at the much shorter odds which now prevail, but like many punters there is a stubborn streak once I've missed the boat. So I opt for Shadow Leader. We all go out on to the lawn to watch the race, which turns into a masterful display by Istabraq, quickening clear three flights out to win by at least a dozen lengths. Hughie was spot-on, and I should have followed his advice. The mood of the group is ecstatic, apart from myself because Shadow Leader has taken a horrible tumble at the last flight when beaten, and now the green screens, the harbingers of a humane killing, are all around him.

Sickened by the death of such a good horse, I find a quiet place for a few moments to pay my respects. This probably sounds corny, but most race-goers are genuinely grieved by the deaths of horses on the track. The moral ambivalence it brings to our sport is not easily dismissed, and I'm all the more aware now that I'm an owner of what a price we expect from horses in pursuit of our entertainment. The defensive rationales are that the horses are not deliberately hurt as part of the game – unlike the competitors in boxing or other martial arts – and also that the victims have enjoyed a caring and pampered existence in preparation for their exertions. The ratio of deaths due to racing accidents is also relatively low, at around 1 per cent of the horses-in-training population. These considerations are no comfort to the connections of the unfortunate few who are killed, though, and I dread the thought of anything happening to Doris.

Suddenly sobered, I return to the Arkle Bar and meekly join the celebrations being orchestrated by Simon and Hugh who have each copped for a few thousand quid on their Istabraq bets. The rest of the afternoon passes in an oblivion of drink, more cigars and a full set of losing bets which leaves me well down on the day. By the time I meet up with Sean, I am probably not the sort of person he wants to invite into his house, but the invitation still stands.

As the car clears the hills above Cheltenham, most of the afternoon's tumult has subsided and the crushing humiliation of backing six losers has become the source of amusement and self-mockery rather than recrimination. Martin Pipe has also had another win, Unsinkable Boxer in the last race, so I'm mercilessly teased along the lines of a rat who has deserted a ship that wasn't sinking at all.

The evening passes pleasantly, with a few drinks in the local pub and then Robert Cooper joining us for dinner. None of us appears to have had a winner, and watching the re-run of the races late on Channel 4 therefore becomes an act of pure masochism. Sean and I talk about the business of ownership, including some of his own experiences with Clever Fox. He recalls that when it finished placed in a terrible race at Worcester, the jockey Steve Smith Eccles jumped off it and predicted that it would now win 'five or six novice chases on the trot'. The horse had other ideas, however, getting itself injured on a regular basis in training and ultimately being retired to the hunting fields. We joke, blackly, that maybe it should be the jockeys who get shot.

During the night, I wake with a throbbing hangover, which is instantly made worse as I attempt to go for a pee and plant my head into a low beam. Company apart, it has not been a great first day at the Festival. But a bright, sunny morning and a couple of sachets of 'Resolve' bring new optimism. I phone home to speak to the boys, always aware that I might seem to them a disloyal and wasteful father. But they seem happy to buy the line that this is 'daddy's holiday', perhaps because they expect me to return with presents at the end of it. There are two messages on my mobile phone. One is from Nigel suggesting we meet at the Dawn Run statue by the parade ring at 1 p.m., and the other from the production office of the *Golden Boots* programme requesting my urgent presence at a meeting tomorrow, Gold Cup day. Damn, damn, damn!

Today is the day that Ceci prepares one of her brilliant picnics for a pre-race lunch in the car-park. Robert Cooper takes me in his car, while Sean and Ceci and a barrister friend travel in the other. Robert, who is probably among the most self-effacing of men, has nevertheless found some celebrity with his appearances on the Racing Channel, and this certainly comes in handy when negotiating a passage into one of the prime car-parks. The jobsworth who spotted me lifting a rope to gain access would probably have had me before the Stewards' public execution committee but for Robert's 'famous' face and placatory demeanour. It's now become a really warm day and the picnics abound in the car-park, just another way to enjoy yourself at Cheltenham. Nearby, a Range Rover pulls up with what looks like a classic collection of tweed-suited English landowners and their 'gals'. But far from being braying, 'county' stereotypes, our barrister companion identifies them as belonging to one of the leading law firms in Dublin and goes over to say a professional 'hello'.

He returns a few minutes later with a 'nailed-on' Irish tip for this afternoon – not Florida Pearl, but Impulsive Dream in the Coral Cup.

Armed with this information, I make my way off to the Dawn Run statue to meet Nigel. Unfortunately there are about a hundred other people using the same spot as a rendezvous, and either I miss him, or he misses me. After half-an-hour, I give up and get my bets on, this time on Tote Credit, as my cash mountain has now become a molehill after just one day.

After the first two races, Tote Credit has become Tote Debit in my case, as Borazon finishes tailed off, and Klairon Davis has no answer to One Man's brilliant display of jumping and speed in the Queen Mother Champion Chase. The grey horse has had his detractors, myself among them, for his failures to stay in certain key races, but today, over a drastically shorter trip, his instinctively thrilling pace is too much for a high-class field. But now I'm £40 down already, to add to first-day losses.

Now it's time for Impulsive Dream to get me out of trouble, and as he turns into the straight he hits the front and looks all over the winner. Until, that is, Top Cees, the horse at the centre of the Ramsden–*Sporting Life* libel trial, rockets up the hill for a win that's greeted with a smattering of surly booing from the crowds on the lawn. Dazed and depressed by my continuing gullibility to other people's tips, I wander over to the pre-parade ring and wait for Nigel to appear with Fortytwo Dee. When he does, I realise why I may have missed him at the statue – he is wearing a smart blue suit, not his usual tweed jacket and flat cap. He is also accompanied by several people from the Triumph International Bra Company, so I decide that it would be impolite of me to gatecrash. Next year, it will be Deadly Doris circling the ring before one of the novice hurdle races. Dream on.

I watch Fortytwo Dee run well enough before she runs out

of steam and fades down the field. Ironically, my prevailing form is almost identical. I'm winner-less, very nearly pot-less, tired and hot. After just one-and-a-half days I've pulled up. So either I need to go into more serious training, or I have to accept that I don't get the trip these days. With a journey to London looming tomorrow, I quit the field and head for the taxi rank, £240 down on all my bets.

During my meeting the following day, I manage to persuade the producers to switch the television on for the races, but my luck is no better. Darapour is well beaten, Splendid Thyne is a close second at 10–1, and my sentimental bet on Suny Bay proves that Charlie Brooks was right to worry about the horse not being quite ready for Cheltenham. He finishes fifth behind shock winner Cool Dawn, after the favourite See More Business has been carried out at a fence by the injured Cyborgo trying to pull up. Martin Pipe, Cyborgo's trainer, nevertheless picks up the last two races with Cyfor Malta and Blowing Wind, to collect four winners for the second successive Festival. Di's Last and Rowley John may be evidence that not everything he touches turns to gold, but it seems that he's not far short of that achievement. On checking Ceefax, I see that Edredon Bleu at 7–2 has become my only winner of the meeting – Mike Dillon, Victor Chandler, William Hill, Joe Coral, Tote Credit, your boys took one hell of a beating!

Winnings: £70. Losses: £300.

Waiting, Part Two

Nigel phoned on the Friday after Cheltenham to apologise for missing me at the Dawn Run statue. There was nothing complicated about the explanation, like too many other bodies being in the way, or the unfamiliarity of us both being in suits; it was simply that he was being entertained by Triumph International in a box that they had taken, and couldn't get away. When it comes to seeing their owners, trainers have to apply the concept of first among equals, giving priority to those with horses running on the day. I didn't have one running, Triumph did. And I suppose the box helped as well. Never mind, the news of Doris's progress in training is good, and she will be taken up to Wolverhampton for a racecourse gallop on the all-weather surface very soon. I still felt that it was too early for me to start asking specifically when she might race – I hadn't even paid a bill yet – so I contented myself with the image of her doing well.

I suppose having a horse in training is not that different to having children away at boarding school. Like an anxious parent, you will phone occasionally and be lied to, albeit creatively, by the house-master, about little Johnny's progress; you pay the odd visit to the school to reassure yourself that he's all right and that the fees are still worth paying; until one day when he sits an exam and fails, and then you wonder where all the money was being spent. That's when you begin looking around for another school – or perhaps even another child.

Then on 24 March, Silent Action could only finish in twelfth place out of fourteen runners on his hurdling debut at Chepstow, beaten 64 lengths at odds of 66–1. It appears that Doris may have been sitting next to the naughtiest boy in the class, and that her work was not all it was cracked up to be.

Six days later, Nigel wrote to me to give me an update on the Deadly Doris share issue. The fourth share was still available, and Nigel wanted to get this sold before registering the partnership with Weatherby's, because chopping and changing names involves building up administrative costs. He said that he would consider advertising again in the *Racing Post* but felt it might be better if we could complete the sale 'in house', as he termed it. So the question was whether I had anybody in mind who might be willing to come in for the share. Nigel also offered an open invitation to join him racing over the next week – he had horses running at Ascot, Taunton, Hereford and Fontwell Park in the coming weeks.

He concluded by writing: 'all is going well with the horse and I am aiming to run her towards the back end of April in a bumper, probably at Market Rasen over 1m 5f. However, she is coming to hand nicely and it may be sooner.'

I was still sufficiently naïve at this stage to get excited by this news, and out came the book containing the aerial photographs of British racecourses, and my British Rail map. Even though the intended race was at least three weeks away, I was already at the planning stage for the trip. Sad, isn't it? Anyway, Market Rasen looked jolly nice from the air, with a big wide, open course, framed by a pine forest, and a pair of small lakes or reservoirs inside the course itself. I could see that the journey would almost certainly need an overnight stay, either before or afterwards, since Market Rasen station is on a looping line from Newark or Lincoln. So then I started to 'recce' likely hotels or pubs in the *Good Food Guide*. So much nervous energy goes into being an owner, even before the horse runs.

But with the end of April as a target, I now set about trying to recruit friends as other potential owners in Doris. I'd mentioned to Nigel that two possible candidates had sprung to mind, Chris Burt and Simon Kelner. Given the choice, they would be among the first people I would go racing with, so it seemed only right that I should approach both of them simultaneously, having extracted from Nigel the concession that the remaining share could be split into two, at £2,500 each. So I wrote an identical letter to both, having mentioned the possibility to them in passing during phone-calls. I tried to pitch as neutrally as possible. Getting a friend into a partnership is one thing, but getting them in at considerable expense is another. I still felt guilty about my inadvertent recruitment of Chris into the Tally-Ho Partnership, from which he had got diddly-squat for his money. Anyway, the letter read as follows:

2 April 1998

Re: 'Deadly Doris'

Dear Chris/Simon,
Further details on the horse of which I am one-quarter owner. Nigel Smith, the trainer, has taken a quarter-share for himself, while a businessman from Derby has bought the third quarter – all at £5,000 each. This leaves one remaining to be sold, but Nigel is happy – at my suggestion – to consider offers for it in two one-eighth shares of £2,500 each – ideally, one for you, one for Simon Kelner/Chris Burt, who is also interested.
The horse in question is a four-year-old filly by Ron's Victory out of Camp Chair. The sire was a top-class 6f–7f sprinter, winning the Group 3 Diadem Stakes at Ascot in 1990 by 10 lengths. He also won Group races at Longchamp before being retired to stud in Newmarket as a 4 y.o. The dam I know nothing about so far, except that she was a specialist NH brood-mare, but the hope is that

the speed of the sire will have been passed down, to mingle with the stamina of the dam and produce something worth racing.

I've been up to see her at the stables and she's certainly a good size and a good mover – she's had one racecourse gallop so far, at Towcester over 1m 6f, where she comfortably out-paced Silent Action, who had been second in a bumper in Ireland. He has just finished 3rd, beaten just 2½ lengths in a hurdle race at Taunton. If Doris could do this to an experienced horse first go, the hope is that some success, and fun, is to be had with her, initially in a few bumper races this season and then over hurdles next.

Nigel isn't the world's most successful trainer, but he's a good lad and a trier, and a straight-talker. The stable is also right next to a pub, for social gatherings, overnight stays, work-watching etc. If you're interested at all, give him a ring at the stables – Court Farm, Upton Snodsbury, just outside Worcester – on 01905 381077, or on his mobile: 0589 808 202. Training fees are about £500 per month, which would work out at £100 a head if we achieve the five-person partnership. It's a small but friendly yard, which is only too happy to see its owners involved.

This isn't meant as a test of our friendship or anything, so if you don't fancy it I won't be offended. Call me if you need any further details.

All the best,

Stan

I didn't expect an immediate response from either Chris or Simon and I made a vow to myself that I wouldn't indulge in chase-up phone-calls. But, with my usual gift for bad timing, my letter went out just as two more bad occurrences cropped up in racing. In the first instance, the BBC's pro-gramme *Watchdog* did a special segment entirely about what bad value racehorse ownership was in Britain. The programme asserted that up to 25,000 people had shares in racehorses and quoted, in an ironic voice, from the very same BHB brochure that I'd received last autumn. The programme then featured the *Daily Mirror*'s former royal correspondent, the unctuous James Whittaker – an old mate of Anne Robinson's – about what he termed his 'five very expensive months of ownership' by the end of which he claimed to be 'about £8,000 out of pocket'.

Other moaning owners were then interviewed, one of whom complained about 'having no control over my horse's destiny', while Channel 4's John McCririck was wheeled on to say 'don't expect to make any money. If you put £3,000 into a syndicate or partnership, you're going to lose it all.' A BHB spokesman made a feeble attempt to 'accentuate the positive' but I'd guess that the overall impact of the programme would have been to put many prospective owners off the idea for life.

The second downer occurred on Friday 3 April, when the most popular and high-profile National Hunt horse in training, One Man, was killed in a terrible accident at Aintree. Running in the Mumm Melling Chase, just sixteen days after his triumph at Cheltenham, the beautiful grey seemed to dive into a fence on the far side and went crashing through it in a horribly graphic fall. Although the race continued, you could tell by the commentator Jim McGrath's downbeat voice that the worst had happened, and we were soon given the news that the horse had been put down after serious injury. My immediate reaction was to switch the television off. Although I'd never backed the horse, and had never quite fancied him that much, he was the undoubted figurehead for our sport as far as the wider public was concerned. To lose him in such desperate circumstances, a grey, rainy day and a sodden track, was a sickening blow. Apart from the cruel fact of the horse's own death, and the obvious grief for his owner John Hales and trainer Gordon Richards, the implications for Jump racing would be enormous, especially coming just a day before the Grand National itself, which has become a rallying point for those animal welfare activists who want to ban Jump racing.

Sure enough, One Man's demise became front-page news the next day, and cast a shadow over the National, and indeed all racing. The *Racing Post* had to carry a two-page obituary on the one day of the year when it can normally guarantee to achieve maximum sales. The fat pages of eager previews for the Grand National therefore sat queasily alongside this *memento mori*, as if those endless financial services adverts had finally been obliged to print in large type that 'investments can go down instead of up'. Anyone seriously considering going into racehorse ownership over these days would surely have paused for deep thought, not just at the implications of losing money, but also at the likelihood of losing their horse in a racing accident.

However, the people who make up the racing community are a resilient force, which allows for grievous moments and due sympathy before getting back to normality. They, and I suppose I could now say 'we', use a wonderful word in talking and writing about the ever-rolling racing calendar, and that word is 'renewal'. Its strategic deployment offers both a kind of certainty, and certainly a form of optimism, that however bad things get, racing will go on. I had achieved a 'renewal' of sorts on the Thursday, the first day of the Grand National meeting, when my old pal Deep Water turned out in the Glenlivet Novice Hurdle and I'd lumped £50 on him to try and recoup my losses on the ante-post bets for Cheltenham. Deep Water had duly delivered in emphatic style, cruising through the soft ground to beat the 3–1 favourite Rainbow Frontier, by eleven lengths at odds of 8–1. My £400 winnings more than made up for the disappointments I'd suffered at Cheltenham.

But now a more significant 'renewal' was at hand with the Grand National itself. With various pundits beating their breasts about the heavy going and the prospect of more equine fatalities, what was needed was a great race to restore not only the public's confidence in racing, but also racing's confidence in racing. And we got it. As the heavy ground took its toll, stringing out the field into a huge crocodile line of tired horses, Earth Summit and the top-weight Suny Bay battled alone up front for the last three furlongs of the four-and-a-half-mile race. But approaching the last Earth Summit, carrying 10 stone 5lb, finally exploited his huge weight advantage and eased clear of Suny Bay, carrying 12 stone. Both horses were heroes in their own right – the cheaply acquired Earth Summit had fulfilled the small owner's dream by taking the £212,569 prize, while Suny Bay had confirmed what a class horse he was. The race didn't entirely escape controversy, with three horses being killed in action – Griffin's Bar, Pashto and Do Rightly – re-opening the debate not just about the race's toughness, but also about the entry of vulnerable older horses in such a competitive event. Only six runners finished in the end, including John Manners's old rogue Killeshin, so maybe the BHB were right to include him in their promotional brochure on ownership after all. My apologies to all concerned.

I had tipped Earth Summit to quite a few people earlier in the week, but had stayed loyal to Suny Bay in the end, backing him each way, and also doing the dual forecast with Earth Summit, which netted me £250. I'd also been successful with bets on Bellator (9–4) in the first race and Jeffell (3–1) in the second, and so ended the three days of the meeting around £700 up. This was a stark improvement on a year earlier, when I'd been covering the race for the *Independent on Sunday* but was suddenly transformed from a sports journalist into a war correspondent as the IRA bomb warning forced the abandonment of the race. Filing instant copy on my mobile phone from outside the course in an increasingly chaotic environment had proved a huge strain, while later searching for somewhere for myself, Robert Cooper and Mr and Mrs Magee to stay also proved equally taxing. Finding a B&B on the Wirral with three spare rooms, as we did at about eight o'clock at night, was a pure stroke of luck compared to what many other race-goers had to go through that weekend. But racing is about nothing more than ups and downs, the only certainty being that if one happens, the other can't be far behind.

Within a few days of my 'lucky' 1998 Aintree, I received the following letter from Cliff Underwood with regard to the condition of Di's Last, and confirmation of the news that had seemed inevitable once she had been returned from the Martin Pipe stable:

Thank you all for your patience. We have had word from Bristol regarding Di's examination so I thought I would write, although I will also try to ring everybody. Basically, she has 'small airway disease' (mild COPD), as a result of what happened at Martin's last year. They found no post-viral indications so we can only assume she was stressed when not ready for it. This means that her lungs are not perfect, although she is fine in every other way. Bristol says that with careful monitoring, full-time antibiotics, a dust-free environment, preferably outside, and constant tracheal washes, she could go back into training. It would be difficult and has been done before, but there are no guarantees. The main thing we have to consider is if we try, and do not get it right, there is a possibility of her breaking down completely. We are not prepared to take that risk and as such, Di has been retired.

I know that you will understand that her well-being must come first. We will be taking Di to Shade Oak Stud in the next couple of weeks where she will go either to Bob's Return (1993 St Leger winner) or Alflora (triple

156

Group 2 winner). We will keep you informed of progress. One piece of good news is that we have solved Di's behavioural problems, and she is a lot happier, mixing with the other mares all the time now.

We had an update on Ruby (Nova Scotia) today, and although she is not yet recovered enough to come home she is now progressing well and we hope that she will be fit enough to travel in the first week of May. Ginger Maid is enormous, two weeks overdue now, but really well. Janet is on the night shift, waiting for the moment. Rowley John is out all the time unless the weather is bad and looks more like himself these days. 'Kelly' is being brought in regularly now and is getting a lot of attention to prepare her for work. The response on a name for her has been very slow, so come on all you racing buffs!

Cliff phoned shortly afterwards for a chat and offered me a further rebate on my partnership costs, now that all three of that season's horses were definitely out of training, but I declined, knowing that there must be stabling costs and vets' bills for the convalescence of Nova Scotia. Cliff had also heard from Nigel about me buying the share in Deadly Doris, so it hardly seemed appropriate to take money back from him when I'd already invested elsewhere. Cliff was intrigued by Doris's prospects, but I couldn't tell him any more because I didn't know anything other than that a race might be in the offing. I promised that I would call Cliff once I knew the date of the race, so that he could come along as a supporter, or at least watch Doris run on the telly in his local betting shop in Great Yarmouth. That was the least I could do in the circumstances, and though I'm sure every partnership is competitive in wanting its own horse to win before anybody else's, I knew that Cliff would be equally enthusiastic for 'mine' to have some success. His main worry was that now I'd gone 'big-time', certainly in terms of costs, I wouldn't be interested in coming back into the Tally-Ho Partnership for the next season with the as-yet-unnamed 'Kelly'. But I promised him that I would. And I meant it.

I had checked on my racing calendar that there was a Market Rasen meeting on Saturday 25 April, and guessed that this must have been the meeting that Nigel had in mind for Doris. I didn't want to pester the poor bugger any further, having already phoned him once to find that his yard was half under water after the spring floods which burst the banks of the Avon. So rather than spend my time fretting, I filled my time with work, and also managed a day out at Ascot on Wednesday 8 April, the penultimate fixture of the course's National Hunt season. (They also have a highly popular evening Jumps meeting towards the end of April, the first three races of which are televised on BBC 2, a rare outing for a sport other than snooker or skiing on the cultural channel.) But those who claim that nothing happens in the Jumps after Aintree should think again and make a date for this early April meeting, which features the Long Distance Hurdle, sponsored by Grosvenor Casinos this year, as its centre-piece.

A seven-race card included several horses that had either won or run well at Cheltenham, not to mention some of those who had run badly and that were here on what the trade terms 'a recovery mission', a euphemism for getting back money lost on bets at the Festival. I checked the racecard, as I now did with those in the *Racing Post* every day, in order to see if any offspring of Ron's Victory were running, so that I could get a clue about the merits of Doris's breeding. But there were none, and hadn't been any that I'd noticed so far. This could mean one of two things, either that 'Ron' hadn't been too prolific as a stud – they probably didn't have an equine Viagra in his day – or that his children weren't up to staying two miles in National Hunt racing, which was my one, deeply repressed, reservation about Doris.

So with no 'family' implications to be gleaned, I just had a quiet day losing money, as I returned to my usual form. Polydamas was second in the first race behind Better Offer, while Lightening Lad made a mistake and unseated his jockey at the fourth last fence. The big race, over three miles, went to Mary Reveley's impressive Marello, and not to my unimpressive selection Red Blazer. I gambled on a sudden return to form by the once useful but now ageing Dancing Paddy in the fourth, but I couldn't have been more wrong because he finished stone last. In the three-horse Kestrel Novices' Chase, the 12–1 outsider beat Wade Road, who therefore aborted both my, and his own, recovery mission after Cheltenham. Abit More Business – no doubt weighed down by my ten pounds – blundered his way out of the Merlin Novice Hunters' Chase, which was won by Joy For Life. This happened to be the only horse in the race running on behalf of a 'drag' hunt, in which the hounds chase a scented bag rather than a real fox, a victory that must have pissed off the serious, blood-lust hunt supporters no end. Then it was my turn to feel the same emotion, as Another Night could do no better than fifth place in the last race. I couldn't even win the raffle for the Racing Welfare Charities, for which I'd bought five tickets at a pound apiece.

The only redeeming feature of a rather ho-hum day came when I ran into a long-time racing friend who is a senior civil servant in the Foreign Office. He therefore cannot be identified as a fun-loving racing fan, just in case a member of New Labour's 'Pleasure Police' reads this bit of the book. Mr X, as I shall call him – is he really a man or am I just bluffing? – did not go to this year's Cheltenham Festival due to official duties, but gleefully recounted how he'd been able to pick up highlights of the races on satellite television in the Caribbean island of Dominica. In fact, whenever he goes around the world, Mr X usually visits a local racecourse if he possibly can, rather like those people who've been to every Football League ground in England, and to my certain knowledge can claim Barbados, Macau, Hong Kong and Italy among his 'scalps'. Maybe I shouldn't worry too much about my friend's identity, since the Foreign Secretary himself, Robin Cook, is an avid race-goer, and used to contribute a column on horse-racing to a Scottish paper until less weighty matters such as Iraq and Sierra Leone seized his attention.

As it transpired, I was on the verge of a small slice of foreign racing myself. Dispatched as a member of a team of writers sent to France by *Night & Day* to compile an assortment of features on their way of life – I got the tough assignment of reviewing restaurants – I was able to slip away on the Sunday afternoon to Longchamp. This fulfilled a long-standing desire to rub shoulders with the Parisian *turfistes* whom I'd always assumed, from coverage of the Arc, to be a collection of sophisticated Sacha Distel lookalikes, complete with their bleach-blonde girlfriends in Max Mara outfits.

What I in fact encountered was a rather desultory, down-beat experience, with a paltry, largely shell-suited crowd despite a fine spring afternoon and the presence of three Group races on the seven-race card. The Longchamp complex, with its huge stands and open terraces, is sophistication itself, but Sunday racing there would seem to make our much-maligned seventh-day efforts look positively Bacchanalian. It probably doesn't help Longchamp that roughly 75 per cent of Parisians bugger off to the country at the weekends, but critics of French racing here cite their tote monopoly as the real reason behind the desultory attendances. I can't really buy this, even on the evidence of one meeting, since the betting was brisk enough up in the Tribune restaurant where I eventually stationed myself.

It seemed to me like a failure of marketing the product more than anything else. The racecard, a double-sided printed sheet of thin paper, bearing just the bare details of jockeys, colours, horses' names, trainers, weights and form, made Hereford's puny effort look like the Magna Carta by comparison. But then there is barely any coverage of racing in France's main sports paper *L'Equipe*, while *Paris-Turf*, their specialist racing paper, isn't much better. And yet the fact that the French have a tote monopoly means that the prize-money for owners is impressive. The two Group 3 races on the card offered roughly £22,000 to the winner, while the Group 2 race gave up £42,500. Even the lowest purse offered £10,000 to the winning owners. No wonder Sheikh Mohammed is switching more of his horses to a country where the blood-sucking bookmakers *n'existent pas*.

My personal contribution to the funds of French racing that afternoon totalled 500 francs, just short of fifty quid, as my betting continued its patch of duff form. Worst of all was the 200 francs thrown away on Finally, a five-year-old son of Ron's Victory, who finished tenth in a field of ten in a 2,400-metre claiming race. Not only did Finally not stay the trip, it hardly broke into a run either. I can only hope that this particular member of the family is the one that became a tattooed layabout living in a trailer park on a diet of oven chips and deep-fried Mars bars.

When I got back from France, about a stone heavier, there was even worse news. A letter from Nigel was waiting on my desk congratulating me, ironically, on receiving my first invoice, but also revealing that Doris had 'bruised a muscle in her back during a gallop'. Though this was deemed to be 'a minor setback', she was 'confined to walking for a few days' and wasn't expected to see the track until mid-May at the earliest. Nevertheless my chosen colours had been accepted by Weatherby's and duly registered, and were now being made up. The bill for four weeks' training, stabling and feeding was £480, with a further £40 required for blacksmith's charges. My share was therefore £130. So I sent Nigel a cheque with news of Finally blotting the family escutcheon in France and resigned myself to another period of Waiting for Doris.

Pear-Shaped

That first invoice of Nigel's had some small print running across the bottom of the page that read 'every care taken but no responsibility accepted for accident or disease'. I presumed that this was a standard trainer's disclaimer, rather than Nigel's individual declaration of policy, but it brought home to me the precarious nature of a horse's fitness. All owners of horses probably accept that injuries can occur in racing, especially over the jumps, but the realisation that something relatively simple like pulling a muscle in training can put a horse out is harder to accept. We are constantly fed the line that 'horses are not machines', and indeed they are not, being more like finely honed ballerinas where every strenuous movement is a threat. Human athletes, from the Olympic sprinter to the urban jogger, may have the self-knowledge of their limits and when they are reaching them but a horse, being less self-aware, almost certainly has a smaller instinct for self-preservation. Even in my own limited sphere, I've seen horses in the fields that adjoin my house clatter into the post-and-rail fences, slip over on a patch of wet ground, bang their heads on a water trough or eat too much grass until they are so full of wind they can't move an inch.

Among the routine injuries all horses suffer, apart from the seemingly inevitable viruses, are sore shins from training or running on ground that's too firm, tendon strains, over-reaching, where one of the back legs hits a front leg causing a cut or bruise, or being 'cast in their box'. This latter experience is a common one and involves the horse lying down in the confines of its box in a fashion that makes it impossible to get up without human assistance. The result is usually a stiff muscle somewhere in its back or near the top of its legs. This is what owners are up against, even while the horse isn't actually racing.

I spoke to Nigel on the phone about Doris, and he seemed quite matter-of-fact about the muscle strain. 'Happens all the time, mate,' he told me, before reassuring me that she wouldn't be seriously affected. Even so, ten days of walking rather than working means that it takes a further twenty days to get back to the level of fitness enjoyed before the injury. Horses are like us in that they are not naturally fit, but have to work and train in order to achieve it.

During this set-back I began to become an owner by proxy, following Silent Action's races as though I was involved with that horse rather than Doris. Whatever he did on the track reflected on Doris's potential, for better or worse, and my interest in him became almost morbid. After his promising third at Taunton in April, he'd been well beaten into sixth on soft ground at Plumpton, in a Class E Novice Hurdle. Now, on Friday 15 May, he was at the other end of the country, in a Class D Hurdle at Aintree's evening meeting. I thought about asking my brother Keith, who still lives in Liverpool, to pop over and watch him, but thought that this was getting to be a bit absurd. Instead, I watched Ceefax's live betting shows and 'saw' him finish third, behind Wynyard Lady and Just Bayard. When I checked the result later in my *Racing Post* I found that he had finished third, beaten by about seven lengths, at 16–1. More encouragingly, he had 'kept on from two out' to achieve his place.

A fortnight later, Silent Action dropped down to a Class E hurdle again at Uttoxeter, still over two miles, though the papers reckoned he needed further. Nevertheless I had a tenner each way on him, and he stayed on again to finish third at odds of 20–1. So I got £50 back, my first winnings from my connection to the new stable. Who says ownership isn't profitable?

By coincidence, that night's episode of *Sergeant Bilko* – a formative influence on me since childhood – featured a story in which Bilko backs a useless horse at the track with a pot of the soldiers' money. But when one of the recruits, a farm boy from Kentucky, spots that the horse's form may be due to a leg problem, they buy the horse at a knock-down price, in the hope of making a killing once he's cured. They hide the horse on the army base, feeding it oats that Bilko wangles out of the supply depot by pretending they are for an experimental diet for his men. They exercise the horse at night around the base, with the horse wearing lights to enable it to see, but then when they get back to the track, find that it is useless anyway. I feel honoured to be in such exalted, albeit fictional, company.

However, my elation was ended quickly by another letter from Cliff Underwood. It read as follows:

I unfortunately have to start with bad news again. Ginger Maid lost her foal during birth. Basically, although we never put a maiden mare to a stallion that throws big stock, and did not do so this time, Ginger put a lot into the foal and also went three weeks overdue. This meant it was a monster of a foal – a black colt – and he unfortunately spent too long coming out and suffocated. Ginger herself is fine and has recovered well, more so than Janet who had spent three weeks hardly going to bed waiting for the foaling. Decisions had to be made fairly quickly, and so Ginger has gone to stud with Di's Last at Shade Oak. Di is being covered by Bob's Return, and Ginger will visit Rakaposhi King. There is some good news though. We brought Ruby (Nova Scotia) home from Nigel's and though she is still bandaged up, she is very well in herself. She has not lost a great deal of condition, is flexing the injured leg and is not on pain-killers. We expect another two months of box rest, followed by another X-ray, and then hopefully she can go out into a small paddock.

These bad tidings were added to a few days later when I phoned Nigel's yard, and spoke to Liz. It appears that Doris's muscle injury was slightly more serious than they thought. The vet had diagnosed a tear in the muscle tissue near the sacrum joint, the pelvis, and complete rest was needed to assist the recovery. So all bets, and all races, were off for the time being. The vet's fees (£23.50) were included in my new monthly bill, together with the charge for making up the silks (£89.45), the registration of the horse and partnership at Weatherby's (£221.79), the blacksmith's charges (£40), and Nigel's training fees (£480), totalling £854.74. My share was therefore £213.68, and a run seemed more remote than ever.

Meanwhile, I heard back from both Simon Kelner and Chris Burt that they would not be joining me in a share of Doris, which was disappointing, but probably best for my friendship with them, given the news about her. (Nigel had allocated the fourth share to his father to complete the partnership, but it remains 'on sale' if we come across a buyer.) Simon had just been head-hunted to become the new editor of the *Independent*, which I knew wouldn't leave him much room for the frivolous business of horse-racing. Worcester was also a bit far for stable visits from Canary Wharf. He didn't say so, but I also thought that it might not have been too seemly to have the editor of a national newspaper swanning around the gaff tracks while the affairs of state required much-needed critical comment. Chris's excuse was equally valid. He had emerged from his divorce settlement without the means to make such a hefty commitment to a horse. However, he said he would rejoin the Tally-Ho Partnership for the next season.

This prompted me, in a rare idle moment, to start thinking about a name for the new horse. The traditional approach is to derive something from the names of the sire and the dam, ideally witty or imaginative rather than something that sounds like the name-plate on a suburban bungalow. The ingredients were a filly by Rakaposhi King out of Miss Lizzie, and so a few possibilities suggested themselves. 'Posh Liz' was a basic attempt at the genre, but was plainly a bit on the dull side. From this I had a wild stab at calling the horse 'Elizabeth Hurley' – a posh Liz if ever there was one – the hidden agenda being for the actress to come and meet us and pour champagne over the horse's head to christen her, and then over mine to christen me. That didn't seem too promising either. And then I came up with a more abstract number, based on the royal connotations of 'king' and 'lizzie' – Crowning Glory. It seemed a little grand for an unknown quantity, whose future lay over hurdles at Ludlow, Hereford and Warwick, but when I sent the suggestions off to Cliff, he phoned back a few days later to say that Crowning Glory had hit the right note. He was going to clear it with Weatherby's, and then get her registered.

Shortly after this, the details for next year's partnership arrived from Cliff, via another newsletter. It read:

The time has come to look at the 1998–9 season, which we can only hope will be better than last season. One issue that is not in doubt is that we will have more fun with Nigel than with Martin. The update on the two mares is that they have both now been covered, Di by Bob's Return, Ginger by Rakaposhi King. We await the results of the scan to see if they are in foal. Ruby is well in herself and is still a model patient. She was redressed last week but our vet pointed out that we are still in a 50–50 situation with her, and it may never improve beyond that, with the long-term prognosis not good. Therefore we have one horse to go with for 98–99, the four-year-old filly (16 hands high), for which we have now reserved the name 'Crowning Glory'. We were quite surprised the name was available.

As you all know, we have had some problems in the past few seasons with people promising to join the partnership, but then not actually doing so, leaving the onus to fall on myself and Janet. We have a wonderful core of people now, and hope that we do not have to go outside the group this season. We are therefore looking at ten shares only, which should work far better than before. The agreement is the usual all-in cost. The season will start on 1 July, running for a period of ten months to 30 April 1999. 'Kelly' will actually start work on 8 June. In July, she will have all her vaccinations, worming, farrier-work, and also be ridden out by the leading novice point-to-point rider in Wales, Paul Sheldrake. On 1 August, earlier than we have ever tried before, 'Kelly' will go to Nigel Smith's yard. Part of the reason for this is to try and achieve some early runs, as we have always seemed to reach December in the past before getting a run. The cost in relation to ten shares is £80 per month per full share, £40 for a half-share and £20 for a quarter-share.

I didn't see that much harm in joining up again, nor a conflict of interest with both horses stabled at Nigel's. I got on well with Cliff at all levels, and was beginning to enjoy the social interaction between the partners when calamity had struck over January and February. So I confirmed my decision to rejoin with Cliff and decided that I would mark this step up into multiple ownership by joining the Racehorse Owners' Association, the official body representing 'our' interests on the British Horse-Racing Board. The act seemed propitious, in relation to the fact that Peter Savill, the President of the ROA, had just been appointed to the Chairmanship of the BHB, filling the vacancy left by Lord Wakeham's resignation. I have tried to cover some of the implications of this in the final chapter, but, in brief, it seemed to me that an Owners' Revolution had effectively taken place with Savill's appointment. They were seizing, if not the means of production, then certainly some of the machinery.

So I sent off my cheque for £50, not least as a gesture of support.

A week or so later, I received an envelope containing the glossy *Owner* magazine, some forms and leaflets, and a car-park pass with the ROA initials on it. The conditions of the pass seemed to make its use fairly limited, with most of the major meetings and racecourses excluded. No matter, since I rarely drive to the races. But the racecourse pass, giving an owner free access to a course when his horse was running, was also limited to those who had 100 per cent ownership of a horse, or shares that added up to that amount. So with 25 per cent of Deadly Doris, and 10 per cent of Crowning Glory, I wouldn't qualify. I would have to face the Hereford 'sheep-dip' all over again.

The official end of the 1997–8 National Hunt season was nearing by now, with the statistical data being compiled after the evening meeting at Market Rasen on Saturday 30 May. Within a few days the *Racing Post* published the full table of several hundred trainers, showing their winners and prize-money for the season. It confirmed that Nigel had had no winners from 40 runs during the season, with just £3,511 in prize-money for the half-a-dozen or so places his horses had earned, which seemed poor in every sense, but there were many more trainers below him in the table. At the top sat my former trainer, Martin Pipe, with 208 winners, and £1,505,520 in win and place prize-money. On Monday 1 June, the circus started all over again, with an evening meeting at Hereford, and everyone who had suffered a bad season – trainers, owners and jockeys – would probably feel a completely irrational surge of optimism at another beginning, another 'renewal'. Why, even Deadly Doris would be able to put her 0 per cent record behind her, no runs, no wins. But we'd soon change that, wouldn't we?

Flaming June

With the World Cup beginning in France on 10 June, I really didn't have that much time to notice that another month was slipping away without an appearance on the racecourse by madam Doris. Writing a three-times-a-week column on the televised football for the *Independent* and a fictional diary of a yuppie, football-loving *arriviste* couple for the *Independent on Sunday* meant watching nearly all the matches, and putting horse-racing on the back-burner. This was probably just as well in the financial sense because my selection in the Derby had been King of Kings, who finished last, while I was only able to find one winner at Royal Ascot. Even my football bets went astray, as Spain quickly, and Argentina later, both departed the tournament without a pay-out. I think that I noticed somewhere in all the football that Silent Action had another run – at Worcester? – this time over 2 miles 2 furlongs, but didn't do anything startling like winning. I saw that Nigel's Flat horse hero Petraco was placed a couple of times, but that was about as much as I could take in, as my eyeballs began to develop Adidas logos.

Eventually, on the morning before England's fateful clash with Argentina, I saw what they term 'a window' in my schedule and, having cleared it with Nigel, set off to Upton Snodsbury to have another look at Doris. I wanted to see how she was, if she still existed, and whether I'd just imagined writing out cheques to the value of £5,000. When I'd spoken to him, Nigel had told me she was now back in serious training, and was completely over her muscle problem, to the extent that she was due to work on trainer John Spearing's all-weather gallop at nearby Kinnersley later that very morning. We arranged to meet in the Coventry Arms at about ten-thirty.

When I arrived the horse-box was already loaded with Doris and her galloping companion Bosom Pal waiting to go, so I tucked in behind it as it travelled down through Pershore, over the M5 and then turned off on to a B-road for Kinnersley. Nigel has an open arrangement with Mr Spearing to make use of the all-weather gallop when conditions on his own natural run are too extreme. The torrents of rain in June had saturated most of the fields, and the main gallop up along the ridge around Nigel's stable, so giving Doris a blow was essential if her recovery was to be tested.

With Liz on Doris and Mark Sharratt on Bosom Pal, the two horses set off down the strip of woodchip carved into the turf and did two pieces of fairly vigorous work. John Spearing is best known as a sprint trainer, although, like Nigel, he operates in both codes of racing, and had already told Nigel that he liked the look of Doris when he'd first seen her. To me, not having seen her for nearly four months, she seemed an even bigger, stronger horse than I remembered.

'She ain't stopped growing yet,' Nigel said. 'She'd eat buckets of food if we let her.' As the two horses pulled up after their work, Liz reported that Doris was beginning 'to show tremendous aggression in her work, and even tried to take a bite at her galloping companion when they were alongside each other'. 'Deadly' may not have been a bad name for her after all. I could have sworn she gave me the eye, as if to say, 'Who's this bastard, and has he got any Polo mints?'

I'd forgotten to bring some, which probably didn't endear me to the horse, but by the time she was back in her box at the stable, having been washed down and groomed just a little, she permitted me to stroke her face and ears. But she's a watchful and alert animal, apparently aware of everything that's going on around her. There are other horses in Nigel's yard that will happily loll around, looking relaxed and dozy, but Doris doesn't seem to be one of them. She's on the case all the time, looking for what you might have for her, or weighing up the other horses in the boxes opposite her.

I had been on guard from day one of my ownership adventures for instances of the 'pathetic fallacy', John Ruskin's phrase for the attribution of human emotions to animals by humans. I knew that I was vulnerable to this because our house and its garden contain seven cats, a rabbit, four hens, a rooster, and three goldfish, as well as the neighbour's horses in the fields. Thanks to daily contact, I've established what I imagine to be a two-way dialogue with all bar the fish. This didn't happen with Rowley John or Nova Scotia, because I didn't see that much of them, and then only in their racing environment.

But there is a world of difference between that, and seeing a horse in its domestic setting, when it's no longer a racing component, but just another animal dependent on human kindness and attention for its comfort and well-being. The use of stable-names by staff for horses is not just because they are easier to say than their racing names, but also because a master and pet relationship develops despite the fact that they are all in it for business purposes. But I know already that extended exposure to Doris's charms will render me less liable to complain about her ability once it is established, and more vulnerable to distress if she gets hurt. A sensible balance will have to be struck, otherwise I could end up tucking her in at night and reading her stories.

After the horses were put away, Nigel and I adjourned to the pub for lunch and talked through a few possible plans for Doris and about the business of knowing when she's fit enough to race.

'It's just something you see,' Nigel says. 'I don't think you can measure it, although blood tests and such will help. You just have to go on how the horse looks and behaves. And that comes with experience. I've been going ten years now, but I'm still learning every day.'

Nigel seems much more relaxed now than when I first met him at Warwick six months ago. I assume that he's made an assessment of me that he can accept, or would that be a pathetic fallacy on his behalf? I suspect that as long as you don't cross Nigel, or try and tell him his business, he'll be fine with his owners, although a certain level of bluffing must have to take place. I've worked out that I'm going to try and be a relaxed owner rather than a worrier, because there doesn't seem much point in being any other way. I want Doris to succeed not primarily for me, but rather for her. I suppose that after the experiences with the other three horses over the past year, I'm just happy to work on the basis that it can't get any worse.

After lunch, I go back to see Doris again, and Liz gets her out of the box to walk around the yard a little. She immediately begins to pick at the longish grass in a small display, having spotted a snack opportunity. And then out of the blue, she does it again – she lifts her off-fore in a gesture of what? Happiness, desire, thanks, self-admiration, attention-seeking? I'll need to get to know her better, and the only way to achieve that is to see her racing. And soon. Nigel says as I leave for the car-park that it won't be long now, and I make a self-protecting guess at late September, early October.

'Bugger that,' he says. 'I'm talking about her running in less than three weeks!'

Wetter than July

Waiting for your horse to run over an undefined period of time is bad enough, but when that period becomes specific, the agony changes to a form of exquisite torture. Your sense of anticipation is heightened, but so too is the fear that something will happen to deny you the big day. Nigel's 'gift' of an approximate date had me scrabbling through my diary as soon as I got home, cross-referencing the commitments I had in July with that month's National Hunt fixtures on my desktop calendar. There were only thirteen, but two or three of these looked potentially inconvenient. Stratford on the Sunday of the World Cup Final, 12 July, would be a tough one because I would still be writing reviews of the tournament's television coverage up to and including that date. Market Rasen or Stratford on 25 July would clash with the big Flat race at Ascot, the King George VI and Queen Elizabeth Diamond Stakes, while Sedgefield on Tuesday 29, Newton Abbot on Wednesday 30, and Bangor-on-Dee on Thursday 31 July would compete directly with 'Glorious Goodwood'. Not that I would prefer to watch this than see Doris running – that would be no contest. I'd just like to be able to take it all in, ideally.

One other complication was that the boys would be breaking up on Wednesday 22 July, the day of a meeting at Nigel's nearest course, Worcester, so slipping away from the traditional end-of-term parental ceremonies in favour of the race wouldn't go down too well with 'the management'. The final snag was the almost certain onset of a load of journalism, because somewhere in the databases of two or three newspapers I am listed under the category of 'Holiday Replacement' for all those with staff jobs taking paid holidays in the Dordogne and Tuscany. Like an ice-cream salesman, albeit less well paid, I bank on my annual income being boosted during the summer season. I could say 'no' to this extra work, of course, but freelance anxiety is a condition for life, not just for the early years of the career.

The other major factor in my craven acceptance of any work offered at this time is the new self-assessment tax regime. This is specifically designed to nail casual labour such as myself to the floor using every available body part, culminating in the last day of July when cheques have to be sent to both the Inland Revenue and the VAT. This is the revenge of the bureaucrats over those who don't work in offices. They hate us for what they see as our freedom, we hate them for what we see as their sense of power.

So the first weeks of July found me writing an instant piece about the over-the-top reactions to David Beckham's sending-off against Argentina, a report on the semi-finals of the Boys and Girls Tennis Championship at Wimbledon, plus another half-a-dozen World Cup television reviews. I was also desperately trying to finish this book and then start the third of my highly unsuccessful series of crime novels. Racing couldn't get much of a look-in at all. Despite the work-load, however, I did manage to recover my losses on the World Cup by getting a £20 bet on France at 5–2 with Tote Credit just after it was announced on television that Ronaldo was only a substitute. Even while I was congratulating myself at getting in quick, the news came through that Ronaldo *would* be playing after all. Suddenly I didn't feel such a smart-arse, but then the French surprisingly delivered the goods. My losing bets – £20 on Argentina to win, £20 on Gabriel Batistuta to be Golden Boot, £10 on an Argentina–Spain Final – were wiped off, and after 33 days and 64 matches I'd broken even.

The Final meant that I'd come to the end of my stint of writing for the *Independent* and the *Independent on Sunday* and could therefore get back to worrying about when Doris would run. But then came yet another reminder of the costs of being a racehorse owner. A feature in the *Racing Post* on Thursday 16 July outlined how a Flat horse called Lady Rockstar, who had won eight races in succession in just 32 days, still hadn't delivered any profit to the five-man partnership which owns her. One of the partners, Phil Donnison – a tax adviser, no less – detailed how the owners' share of prize-money had come to £18,000 but that the costs exceeded this by £850, and that was after excluding the horse's purchase price of £15,000.

'Top owners moan about prize-money in the top races but they don't understand that it is the smaller owners who should be encouraged to enter the sport,' Donnison said in the report. 'I don't want anyone to get the impression that we are moaning. We are quite philosophical about the situation, but the prize-money at the lower end is crap. If you didn't love the game you wouldn't invest in a share you knew basically would go down in value.'

Fortunately the following day there were two optimistic signs on the unfolding road to ruin, the first being delivered by my former trainer Martin Pipe, the second by my current trainer, Nigel Smith. Pipe saddled a horse called Ron's Round to win a 1 mile 3 furlong handicap on the all-weather at Southwell. This half-brother to Doris won easily by eleven lengths. Apart from the simple fact of a 'family' win, the significant cheer for me was that a Ron's Victory horse could win over that distance, which offered some hope that Doris might have more of a chance of staying two miles than I had imagined.

Then, in the evening, Nigel managed to coax another win out of his ten-year-old sprinter Petraco at Salisbury at odds of 14–1 (23.1–1 on the Tote), thereby registering his first win of the Flat season. I hadn't backed the horse, but it was still a moment to celebrate in the context of a small stable battling to keep its head above water. I phoned Nigel the next morning to congratulate him, with only the vaguest of ulterior motives of getting some news on Doris. Nigel said he was just about to take Doris off for another gallop at Kinnersley and would give her a racecourse gallop within a week. 'She'll be racing in about three weeks,' he said, apparently unaware that it was now nearly three weeks since the last mention of 'a race in three weeks'. Perhaps this is the standard unit of procrastination for all trainers, given that it sounds better than saying 'a month' and puts less pressure on them than suggesting 'a fortnight' to their inquisitive owners. I didn't mind that much, partly because it took some of the immediate fretting away from me, and partly because it continued to suggest that Nigel was taking Doris's preparations very seriously. In any case, July's absolutely foul weather had reduced the prospects of finding a NH course with decent going, and even I didn't want Doris ploughing through unseasonal mud on her debut.

My new-found mellowness may have had something to do with having landed a few successful bets that week. Apart from backing the French football team, I'd won over £70 on Mawared and Brave Edge at Newbury's Sunday meeting on the same day. Later, on the same day that I'd talked to Nigel, I had two more decent winners in Grazia at Newbury and Princess Topaz at Newmarket. Winning bets certainly generate 'good karma', but I think that they also require a calm state of mind in order to be successful in the first place. Just occasionally, about two or three times a year, I manage to achieve this higher state of consciousness in which the racing form suddenly seems obvious, and the right stakes and structure for my bet can be glimpsed shimmering on the horizon before the usual storm clouds close in again.

The feel-good factor spilled over into the following week

too, first in the shape of another win for Ron's Round, this time at Wolverhampton over the lesser distance of 1 mile 1½ furlongs. It was reported afterwards that the horse would now be aimed at a hurdling career, raising the piquant possibility that Doris and her half-brother Ron could end up racing against each other some time. But the best news came in a phone-call from Cliff on the same day, in which he reported that both Di's Last and Ginger Maid had been successfully covered by their respective sires and were now back at the farm preparing for their long state of maternity. Even better was the latest veterinary opinion on Nova Scotia, which concluded that the horse now 'had a very good flexion' in the knee she'd injured at Hereford way back in February. The prognosis for her was much better, with a try at motherhood now a distinct possibility next spring. Given all the disappointments that the Tally-Ho Partnership had suffered during the season, the successful recovery of all three horses – and Rowley John was now 'right as rain', according to Cliff – was both a happy coda to the 1997–8 season, and a good omen for 1998–9. With Crowning Glory due to arrive at Nigel's yard on Sunday 2 August to prepare for her Tally-Ho campaign, it seemed that the tide had turned from ebb to flow for once. A sudden, albeit brief, improvement in the weather and a commission from the *Independent on Sunday* for me to write a 'sidebar' on the King George at Ascot completed a rare sequence of harmonious events in my racing curriculum. But I knew that this couldn't last, and it didn't.

Once I knew that I was covering the King George, I phoned Chris Burt because I know he always goes to it. This time round he was taking one of his new 'friends' – since his divorce Chris had decided to 'play the field' again – and we arranged to meet in the champagne and seafood bar for a drink before the first race. I arrived much earlier to make sure of getting my press badge for the day, and then bagged a space in the press room, which is housed under the main stand.

Lined with outsize wooden desks with large lids, the room has distinct echoes of Bob Cratchit about it. But then it was probably a kennel for the Royal corgis before it was handed over to the press. I'm rarely comfortable in racing press rooms because there is a hard-core clique of reporters who travel around together on a daily basis, and who therefore have little or no time to welcome newcomers. Most of them are desperately defending their own territory anyway. The fall of the *Sporting Life* dumped an awful lot of labour on to the market and now, after the years of plenty, there is genuine job insecurity in the world of racing journalism. So, basically, I'm happy to mind my own business, apart from having a chat with those few that I do know, such as Sue Montgomery, Richard Edmondson and Brough Scott.

After preparing my notes on the race, it seems that the likeliest story is a victory for one of the two three-year-old runners, Derby winner High-Rise, or Royal Ascot winner Royal Anthem. The older generation of horses – and this is the element that makes the King George such a compelling event – are represented by the likes of the 1997 St Leger winner Silver Patriarch, and the six-year-old Swain, who won the King George last year in desperate conditions. I remember this clearly because I backed him at 14–1 on the day.

Happy with my background notes, I wander off to the champagne bar to find Chris and 'friend'. This is the same bar that we met in just before last Christmas, but now the lawn in front of it is a mass of people sitting at tables under parasols, quaffing champagne and shovelling seafood into their mouths. Fair enough, it's the first warm sunny day of the month and there's a spirit of revelry in the air, but I know that many of these people are here just for that, and not for the racing itself. Some of them sit there all afternoon without even going to watch a race. I order a modest half-bottle of champagne on the basis that, if Chris doesn't turn up, I won't have to sit there like some sad lush and finish off a whole bottle on my own. But at that very moment Chris swans in, suntanned lady-friend behind. I upgrade the order to a full bottle, and because everybody is outside, we easily find a space and stools at a spot by one of the windows. It's not yet two o'clock, and the big race isn't until 3.50, so I can allow myself to relax a little. Normally I never drink when I'm writing a live report because I found that when I did I was (a) writing complete bollocks, and (b) thinking it to be quite good. There seems no harm, though, in sharing a bottle between three.

However, in a private moment when the lady has gone off to powder her nose, Chris announces a complication. Another of his current girlfriends telephoned him that morning to tell him she was also going to Ascot and would meet him in the bar. Since neither girlfriend knows about the other, Chris now wants me to hang around with him in order to give the impression of an innocent grouping. I tell him that I can manage up to about 3.15, but then after that I really will have to get busy and find some colour and detail for my piece, rather than ad-lib my way through the Feydeau farce he has constructed for himself.

I now break my rules by going off to have a bet on a working day. Bloated with champagne-fuelled arrogance, I find myself casually writing out four selections for a £5 win Lucky 15, making a total of £75. At this moment, the calm, responsible core of my being can step outside its earthly body and watch this cigar-chomping, boozy alternative persona filling out his Tote Credit form with an air of complete arrogance. But then my fall was imminent. My four selections would all prove to be duff, which meant that lost bets and the cost of the champagne would exceed my writing fee for the afternoon.

What is worse, I am now obliged to shuffle between the pre-parade ring, where the eight runners for the big race are being walked prior to saddling, and the champagne bar where Chris will be, prior to being gelded. But each time I go, he's not there. I guess that he might have done a runner, or perhaps even have planted the two women in separate bars. But now race-time approached and I had to get back up to the press box, otherwise the paper will have a 700-word hole in the sports pages.

The race turns out to be an absolute cracker. Swain's stable, Sheikh Mohammed's Godolphin operation, provides a pace-maker, Happy Valentine, to bring Swain's proven stamina into play against the fast-finishers in the race like High-Rise and Silver Patriarch. The plan works perfectly, with a scorching pace being set to the straight, whereupon Swain's multi-geared but powerful acceleration takes him away from his two main challengers, High-Rise and Royal Anthem, to win the race for the second year in succession.

The famous successes of five- and six-year-olds like Swain, Pilsudski and Singspiel prove that horses can indeed reach their peak just when you're starting to dismiss them as being past it. Meanwhile, the winning owner copped for £279,720, taking Godolphin's earnings for the season to £1,750,271. If this represents, as the Sheikh said in his Gimcrack speech, 'the luxury of a slow puncture', I wouldn't mind being the bloke doing his tyre repairs.

After the race, Ascot now lays on a formal press conference instead of leaving it to the usual scrum in the winner's enclosure. But this takes place in a tiny, grotto-like space next to the weighing-room, as if they had only planned it for use by jockey-sized journos. Frankie Dettori, the winning rider, hardly looks as though he has broken sweat and gives his usual bubbling performance. National Hunt could do with a personality jockey such as Frankie to promote the sport, but perhaps the inherent danger of the Jumps inhibits too much exhibitionism for fear of bringing on disaster.

This brings me to Chris Burt's adventures on the day. When I finally catch up with him after I've filed my copy, he reports that Ascot's summery champagne bar was transformed into the frozen tundra when his two friends eventually met and realised what was going on. Now he's looking for a scapegoat – me. But there isn't a jury in the land who will find any other verdict than that Mr Burt was the author of his own misfortune.

My betting form over the following week of 'Glorious Goodwood' carried on where it had left off at Ascot, going from bad to abysmal. By Sunday 2 August I had almost convinced myself that I would never back a winner again, so in an instinctive act of defiant madness I found myself phoning through to Tote Credit a £2 each way Jackpot for that afternoon's meeting at Chester. What happened then is one of those tales that punters carry around with them for years as something akin to a battle wound, a source of pain and pride. The meeting wasn't televised but while I was working I kept one eye on the results coming up on Ceefax, and then started to pay more attention as I got the first three winners – Nasheed, Likely Story and Hyde Park – together with the second in the third race, Bollin Frank. So my Jackpot (picking the winners of all six races) was still going, as was the each-way element, the Placepot, of which I had two lines running on. When my choice in the fourth race, Mawared, also won I stopped work and started to pace my office anxiously. I was two-thirds of the way towards a potentially big pay-out – the Jackpot pool for the day had started at £67,656 and was certain to have grown as more punters waded in with their bets.

The clock ticked slowly towards the off-time of the 4.30 race in which I had two selections running for me, Highborn and Philistar. I watched the live betting show on Ceefax and then the 'off' sign started to flash. I tried to visualise the race around the tight turns of the Chester track with both my horses flying off the final bend and up the short straight to the finishing post. And then the result flashed up – neither Highborn nor Philistar were in the first three. I lingered for a while, hoping for a stewards' enquiry, but nothing was called. Both my Jackpot and my Placepot had gone down. All punters will know what happened next – one of my choices in the last race won. So I had five winners and six placed horses but nothing to show for my £64 stake. The odds for the winning horses, though immaterial, ran as follows: 1–2, 5–1, 7–2, 7–4, 11–2. If I'd had, say, just a £2 accumulator bet on these five horses it would have paid out £1,447.87. The next day, I checked the dividends for both Jackpot and Placepot. The Jackpot paid £21,421.10 to a £1 unit, while the Placepot paid £1,834. Given that my two selections for the fateful fifth race had been at decent odds, if either had won I'd have probably been looking at a total pay-out in the region of £50,000. But they didn't.

Normally I don't confide such near misses to my wife Wendy, because it only fuels her belief that I am a born loser when it comes to gambling. In many ways this is true, because despite the odd big win now and then, I've never made an absolute killing on either horses or pools, just enough to keep me coming back for another try. I've only once had three numbers up on the lottery, and I can only recall one instance when I won something in a raffle. It was at my junior school's Christmas Fair and I won a tennis racket – just the job for December.

In the early days of our relationship I tried to overcome Wendy's resistance to my betting by celebrating any wins with the purchase of 'white goods' for the kitchen – microwave oven, fridge, blender and so on – and then sticking labels on them bearing the names of the successful horses. Indeed the likes of Green Dollar, Mtoto, Twin Oaks and Father Time were at one time responsible for most of the stuff in our small Chiswick flat. I expected a volley this time around, but she was surprisingly supportive, perhaps because I didn't get round to mentioning that I'd actually lost sixty-four quid. I suppose the healthy aspect of my betting is that

I neither let it get out of control, nor become too depressed when I'm on a losing streak. It has, in any case, certainly gone down in volume since I became an owner, partly on the grounds of expense, but mainly because the horses take up most of the mental exertions that would otherwise go into betting.

To emphasise this fact, any lingering depression I had over my long losing streak disappeared in an instant on Wednesday 5 August, when Nigel phoned unexpectedly to report that he had finally found a suitable race for Doris and had entered her for it. It was to be a 2-mile bumper on Wednesday 26 August, and he was looking to book a conditional jockey (i.e., an apprentice with a weight allowance) to take some of the load off her back. He added that Doris had 'been working lovely'. I put down the phone in a daze. Three weeks, then.

Doris's Debut

In contrast to the previous spell of waiting for Doris to run, this one rocketed by. The factual certainty of a selected race no doubt helped. So much of the currency of both horse-racing and ownership is mere possibility that it was quite exhilarating to begin trading in the almost definite. I knew that Doris could do all sorts of things to herself to prevent her running, and that the lousy summer weather might also lend a hand. But she had suddenly made that transition from being just an untried horse in training to one that now existed in the official bureaucracy of the sport as a competitor. Her name was being processed through the information systems at Weatherby's, and soon she would appear in the list of entries in the trade paper the *Racing Post*, like the news of a ship being launched in *Lloyds List*. I was also able to sense that Nigel was neither bluffing nor stalling this time round because he had sounded as excited as I was over the phone. Suddenly he was talking as a part owner of Doris, not just as her trainer.

I immediately cross-hatched 26 August in my diary with a blue felt-tip pen, an early-warning system I deploy to write off a whole day as my own territory. Only five days of the year so far had received such treatment – the three days of the Cheltenham Festival, Wendy's fiftieth birthday in June, and the imminent day-trip to the Ebor at York with Chris Burt. Doris's debut now joined them. My 'holiday replace-ment' work was still flowing in, together with a new com-mission for the script of the official film of the 1998 World Cup. So I had to make sure that I protected that Wednesday from outside demands with the same combination of zeal and low cunning that I'd used for the other special days. I'd already lost one day of Cheltenham to work and couldn't face a repeat now. Being freelance means that you're regarded as part of the service industry, on a par with a pizza delivery or emergency plumbers. Television producers and the section editors of newspapers expect you to be available at a moment's notice and, while I'm normally pretty obliging, there was no way I could miss Doris stepping out for the first time. I have a fairly standard repertoire of excuses – a dental appointment, doing something special with my children, sudden illness, fictional train strikes – but I knew that I would even resort to the Doomsday scenario of a 'family funeral', if necessary, in order to get me to Worcester racecourse.

Without recourse to such measures, I managed to negotiate the two other days of racing that I had planned, at Bath on Tuesday 11 August, and at York eight days later. Both outings were with Chris Burt, who had finished all his work on the latest *Inspector Morse* and was keen to 'play'. Bath was just fine – a sunny day and five winners between us. I'd also got a hot tip for a horse at another meeting from a member of the Tally-Ho Partnership that landed quite a gamble for him, over £20,000, and a more modest £100 for Chris and myself. So we were both buoyed up for York. Like last year, it was another enjoyable trip on the Tote Credit train, with a champagne breakfast on the way up and a three-course dinner on the way back. Chris met up with a formidable bunch of racing ladies of his acquaintance and they made the day go with a swing, even if our bets didn't. The other memorable moment of the day was seeing the drinks we'd ordered for our dinner on the train stretched out in a line across the table. At the time of filling out the list in the morning it had looked to me like a suicide note, but somehow we got through them without any illness or disrepute.

But now Saturday 22 August was approaching, the day

when the 'five-day entries' for Worcester's card would be printed in the *Racing Post*. I was down at my newsagent's first thing and there was Deadly Doris along with fifteen other entries for the 5 p.m. race, the Wichenford Intermediate National Hunt Flat Race (Class H). A jockey's name, D. Creech, was alongside Doris's, which was as sure a sign as anything that she was going to run. Seven of the entries had previous experience, and there were horses from two of the most powerful stables in Jump racing, those of David Nicholson and Nigel Twiston-Davies, so it would obviously not be easy. On Monday afternoon Nigel phoned to say that Doris would definitely race barring a dodgy result on the blood test which he had sent off to the vet's that morning. It was time to get out my book of aerial photographs again and check the train times.

The major feature about the Worcester course in the photograph was the River Severn running right along its eastern edge. Nigel had told me to meet him at the Owners' and Trainers' Bar, which he'd described as 'being built on stilts to stop the annual floods washing it away'. Now I could see what he'd meant. It sounded like a scene from *Titanic*, and I imagined that it would certainly be awash with drink if Doris won. Nigel wouldn't be at the course until about three o'clock, having driven Doris the short distance from Upton Snodsbury in the stable's horse-box. So I could create a fairly relaxed train schedule, especially as the rest of the card didn't look up to much. And just for a change, I certainly didn't want to end up broke and pissed by the time Doris ran at the end of the meeting.

By Tuesday evening I'd bought a few Havanas in Bath and worked out my route and my timings – 11.32 a.m. from Bradford to Bristol Temple Meads; 12.10 from Bristol to Cheltenham Spa, arriving at 12.54; then the 13.13 from Cheltenham to Worcester, arriving at 13.40. I checked the declarations on Ceefax and Doris was still in, though the field had now been reduced to thirteen runners. She wasn't mentioned in the betting, being somewhere in the '12–1 bar' category after five shorter-priced horses. The twice-raced Meldrum Park was predicted as the 9–4 favourite. Other runners included such names as Springfield Scally, Captain Biggles, Steady Eddy and Country Buzzard, which seemed to make Deadly Doris sound quite classy by comparison. I went to bed relaxed but woke up in a sweat of anxiety on Wednesday morning at 4 a.m. and started to visualise the race that was now only thirteen hours away. Would Doris be a complete embarrassment? Would our racing colours look naff? Would she run off and jump in the river?

I managed to get back to sleep again, but took ages to get myself organised. There had been two technological upheavals recently which would affect today. In the first instance, I'd bought a new pair of lightweight binoculars at York to replace my old ones that had neither strap nor case. Secondly, after my trip to the stable in June, when I'd taken photographs of Doris, I'd discovered that there was (a) no film in the camera despite what Wendy had said, and (b) that the camera was broken anyway. So now my morning round in Bradford-on-Avon included buying one of those idiot-proof instant cameras, as well as teasing some dosh out of the cashpoint and getting my *Racing Post*. I managed to raise about £120 by shuttling between Bradford's two cashpoints and using a combination of three cards. Despite all the work I'd done over the summer, I was pretty strapped because it takes an average of two to three months for freelancers to get paid by papers and production companies, who know that they can treat us with contempt and get away with it because we need the work. This is why what we desire most is some 'fuck you' money. I'm not there yet, probably never will be, but maybe Doris can help raise it.

My last call was to Clive the newsagent's. This would be a moment to savour – my horse, colours and name in the *Racing*

Post. 'Top of the world, mate . . .' But then my heart sank as I saw Clive's hand-written cardboard sign on the door: 'Back in 5 minutes'. As I've pointed out to him on several occasions, this isn't very helpful, because you don't know whether you are in the first of the five minutes or the last. Clive's absences are often more like ten or fifteen minutes anyway. I browsed through some of the other papers in the rack while I waited. As far as I could see, nobody was tipping Doris. After ten minutes I gave up and walked to the station.

More frustration. When you ask for a day-return to Worcester and the bloke behind the glass asks: 'Which way were you planning to go, sir?' you know that there is something wrong. The use of the word 'planning' is the clue. It is almost sarcastic, the underlying notion being that nobody 'plans' rail journeys these days, they just try to get to their destinations as best they can. The two sources of trouble were signal works outside Chippenham – not my problem today – and the delay these had caused to the train that was supposed to be forming the 11.32 a.m. to Bristol.

'I think your train will be cancelled, sir.'

'It's still showing on the screen behind you.'

'The information on that is sometimes well behind.'

'What am I supposed to do then? I have a connection at Bristol at 12.10.'

'You'll not get that . . .'

'Yes, I know . . .'

'You could take the 11.48 train across to Newport . . .'

'I'm going to Worcester, not Newport.'

'But you can change at Newport for Worcester.'

'At what time would I get there, please?'

He goes off to check on his computer and a minute later comes back to tell me that with luck I might be able to get to Worcester for about 3 p.m. This is OK, but Newport station and I have a bad history. I get my ticket and cross the footbridge. It's 11.35 a.m. now, and it looks as though the man in the glass booth is right. My train has been cancelled. Then he appears on the opposite platform.

'Your train's running after all,' he says with a high note of surprise in his voice. 'Six minutes late.'

This leaves me with about four minutes to spare at Bristol to make the connection. Scary, but I've had worse. I make it to Bristol on time, and manage to get a *Racing Post* before boarding the Virgin Cross Country train for Cheltenham. On page 29 Deadly Doris is listed, along with my name and one of the other quarter shareholders, Steve Ludlam. A little graphic shows our colours. In the Spotlight section below, it says this about Doris: 'By a smart sprinter out of Ela-Mana-Mou mare so measure of speed in pedigree; others preferred on paper.' Doris is priced at 16–1 in their betting forecast. But the revelation that Doris's maternal grand-dad was Ela-Mana-Mou should make a few form historians sit up a bit. It certainly had that effect on me, because he was one of the best horses of 1979 and 80. He won the King George VI and Queen Elizabeth Diamond Stakes, the Eclipse Stakes and finished third in the Prix de L'Arc de Triomphe. I know NH purists are not supposed to like Flat-bred horses coming into the game, but with this kind of pedigree Doris should in theory be a decent asset to the Jumps, given the speed of her dad and the stamina of her grand-dad. The paper's 'Verdict', however, doesn't mention Doris, preferring the chances of Karenas Lass, Steady Eddy and favourite Meldrum Park, whom they say 'sets a fair standard for the others to aspire to'.

Almost as an afterthought I check the prize-money that we're competing for this afternoon: £1,203 to the winner, £333 for the second, and a stupendous £159 for the third. After the trainer's 10 per cent share, the jockey's riding fee (now up to £87.35) and the £15 fee for entering the race there wouldn't be a lot left to get excited about. Let alone be classified as 'fuck you' money.

A D.J.-style voice announces the train's details as it pulls away – 'sit back, relax and enjoy Virgin Cross Country' – but the soothing doesn't extend to running a full buffet. There's just a trolley at the front of the train serving sandwiches but no hot drinks. When I ask for wine I get the 'I'll have to check' response that belongs in a collapsing economy some-where in the Balkans. Ten minutes later we grind to a halt and the D.J. masquerading as a train conductor falls strangely silent.

Someone should have a go at rewriting the Edward Thomas poem 'Adlestrop' to take account of the modern age of railways, for now we have 'drawn up unwontedly' and there is an awful silence broken only by creaking and the cries of babies in other carriages. Across the way, I can see a punter and his wife beginning to twitch. I can afford to stay cool in view of our late race, but the delay is irritating anyway. By the time we move off, we're running twenty minutes late, so if they let us get ahead of the Worcester train we should still be all right. But they don't. They let that into Cheltenham first and then send it on its way. On the platform the punter starts to go ballistic as the implications of the delay sink in – he'll be lucky to get there for the third race now. He screams at a 'blazer' and then stomps for a taxi shouting, 'How far's Worcester?'

I recognise the familiar signs of 'rail rage', which I used to suffer from on my match-reporting Saturdays. But now I'm calmer. I'll just go across the road here, buy a lottery ticket for tonight and when I win, I'll make Richard Branson an offer he can't refuse to sod off out of railways. That's why they call it Virgin, because you really know when you've been f . . . Stop. That's enough. I construct a lottery sequence out of today's date, 26 and 8, Doris's racecard number, 10, and the time of race, 5. I add the month of my birth, 12, and then my age, 46. It feels like a winner to me.

The next Worcester train arrives on time, albeit caked in grime, and once I'm out of the station I take a taxi to the course. Nigel had warned me of traffic problems because of market day and Worcester's byzantine one-way system. But now that the races have started there's a clear run through. The course is only just off the city centre, looking like a stretch of public park that has been converted for racing. The Owners' and Trainers' entrance is just a small wooden hut with an open flap. I explain who I am and my badge is handed over without question, though there are apparently no racecards left.

'Try the weighing-room, sir,' the lady suggests politely.

The third race is just finishing as I walk the line of stands, and there seems to be a decent crowd, certainly more than the racecourse expected in terms of racecards. At the hut of one vendor – possibly a relative of Clive the newsagent – a hand-written cardboard sign hangs, saying 'Race Cards Sold Out' with an irritated exclamation mark at the end to suggest that he's fed up with the people asking. I buy a Timeform card instead. Walking past the front of the main stand, I then come to a line of Tote booths and the unmistakable owners' and trainers' bar on its brick stilts. Of wooden construction, it looks as though it might actually float away if the Severn did rise quickly. Beyond this is the weighing-room, built in the style of an Edwardian cricket pavilion. The parade ring and unsaddling enclosure are just opposite, squeezed on to a narrow strip of land between the course and the river.

I wander into the weighing-room hall and spot a woman of a certain age smiling at me. Like a Moscow hotel concierge of the Soviet era, she knows instantly what I'm after, but I will obviously have to play the game to get my racecard. Anger would be a no-no, as would pomposity, so I return her smile and try to look sad. I explain that my horse is making its debut today and that I really wanted a souvenir of this great occasion, so would it be possible? Without a word, she slides a card out from under her large handbag and slips it to me.

Next I visit the bar, but there is no sign of Nigel. Since I haven't met or spoken to my co-owner Steve Ludlam yet, it's really just a case of standing still and watching the crowd. For the first time ever, I am not the least bit interested in any race but Doris's. I don't even have a bet, such is the gravitational pull of my own horse being here. Eventually, I spot Nigel weaving his way through the crowds, in his usual attire of tweed jacket and flat cap. We stand on the steps of the weighing-room looking out for Steve, and Nigel tells me that he'd had the results of Doris's blood test back, and though they were not quite right, they were by no means bad enough to stop her running. He thinks she may be about to go down with a cold or virus, or has perhaps just come out of one.

'There's a lot of green snot around the yard,' he tells me graphically. 'Otherwise she seems fine. I'm really looking forward to it.'

We are about to adjourn for a drink when Nigel spots Steve and introduces us – two apparently sensible, married men, randomly brought together by a horse advert. Steve is a fair bit younger than me, I reckon, and he has close-cropped hair and a fashionable goatee beard. He works in Derby as a manager for one of the major construction companies, and although he's always liked racing, his experience of it and of ownership is, by his own admission, quite limited. So while we have a drink Nigel gives him a crash course on the etiquette and routines of race-going. By the time this is over, it's close to 4.15. Doris will be in the pre-parade ring by now, being walked around by assistant trainer Liz.

Nigel leads us down to the ring at the far end of the course's enclosures and Steve reacts as he sees Doris for the first time since he bought his share in early March.

'Bloody hell, she's filled out a bit, hasn't she?'

Indeed Doris has, and even though my last stable visit was only at the end of June, she appears to me to have become more muscular since then. She's also walking round calmly and with an easy grace, head up, alert, no slouching, but no fretting either. Only when the horses in the 4.30 race thunder past just fifty yards away does she become agitated, as do many of her companions. The horses' natural herd instinct is compelling them to try and join in the race. Fortunately Doris doesn't break free, but when she gets into one of the saddling boxes she seems genuinely spooked. Training is just nursery school compared to the Bash Street Comprehensive experience of actually going racing.

Liz is beginning to struggle with Doris, so Nigel takes over, letting Liz put the saddle on. Nigel's a strong lad, but he needs all his strength to keep a firm hold on Doris as she acts up.

'She's being a bit of a cow, which is only natural,' he pants to Steve and I as we watch. 'But if I let her get away with it today, she'll always be like this.'

In one of the saddling boxes further up another novice horse is agitated to the extent of rearing up and banging her head on the roof of the box. But by the time they are saddled and parading again they have all calmed down and Doris is placid again. Nigel leads Steve and I into the parade ring proper. A lot of the crowd is already on its way home, with the grey, chilly afternoon an additional incentive to quit well before our little novice bumper race.

Doris begins to parade now and looks really good. She is certainly bigger than some of the geldings in the ring, most of whom are older than her. 'Thing is,' Nigel says to Steve, 'she ain't finished growing yet. Can you imagine what she's going to be like at six?'

Our jockey for the day, David Creech, comes across to us as he and his fellow riders spill out of the weighing-room. I shake hands with him in what still may be regarded as a breach of Dickensian protocol – maybe I should have offered him one of my boots to shine. David is only a youngster, learning the trade with, as far as I can gather, just one win to his credit so far. As he becomes more experienced and wins more races the weight allowance he gets will be reduced from 7lb, to 5lb, to 3lb and then after a certain number of winners or years of experience, he'll become a full professional. He looks pretty good in the colours, although it's stark staring obvious that they are brand new, and stand out a bit like a waxed Barbour at a point-to-point.

Nigel briefs David quickly, but simply. 'Don't go too fast too early. Get her settled. Get her round this big bend at this end of the straight, and see how she's going. Hold her up round the bottom bend, then see what she's got left in the finishing straight. But for Christ's sake don't panic if they go off fast.'

David nods and smiles and eyes up the horse, which he's only ridden once in a training gallop. 'She's a good-looking horse, isn't she?' he says, and we all nod.

The bell sounds and Nigel gives David a leg-up onto Doris. Liz leads the horse and jockey towards the exit onto the course, and Nigel, Steve and I watch as Doris sets off up the track with the others. By now, my armpits are like shower-heads at full blast. Conversely, my mouth is so dry that I haven't even been tempted to stick a cigar into it. I can feel my pulse beating too. Steve drifts away to the betting ring, although he can't be sure of anything because there is so little form to go on. I watch Doris gallop back down the course towards the start. She seems to be moving easily.

'Ground's no problem for her,' Nigel says expertly, dousing one fear that the good-to-firm going might be against such a young horse. As the horses disappear down to the start Liz sighs in relief and lights up a much-needed cigarette. The back of her shirt is soaked with sweat, partly with the effort of getting Doris saddled, partly from sheer nerves. Liz is sentimentally attached to Doris, as I'm sure Nigel is too, but she's not afraid to show it. It's three-and-a-half years since they effectively rescued the one-year-old Doris from a freezing Welsh field. Now all the care and attention they've given her is about to be put to the test.

I join a line at one of the Tote windows. I'd almost forgot to have a bet on Doris, such was the tension of the last hour. I can see on the screen that Number 10 is trading at just over 20–1, which seems a decent each-way price. But now the idiot in front of me is trying to get a bet on Number 6, which is a non-runner. While he tries to pick another, I nudge past him and get £20 each way on Doris. I find Nigel and go to the foot of the stands to watch.

'This bend up here's a real swine to get round because it's so tight,' Nigel tells me. 'I've ridden here and it throws horses right off balance.'

Over the tannoy, the announcer calls 'starter's orders' and then a very quick 'they're off'. I get my new binoculars out and train them down the straight. The colours stand out well, with the pink arm towards us on this side. Doris is about fourth or fifth and the pace is respectable. As they pass us Nigel says simply, 'That's all right.' Indeed, Doris seems to be moving well, not pulling or shaking her head around. The twelve runners disappear around the bend which is masked by catering wagons and coaches. Emerging on the far straight, Doris is still only two lengths off the leading horse and is still moving well. Nigel and I move off quickly to a Tote screen to watch the action on the far side in close-up. As they come down the straight towards the camera it becomes clear that a group of five horses are leaving the others behind. Doris is still among the leading group. These five begin to take the bottom bend. Two of the horses are already off the bridle. Doris still looks comfortable.

'He's just having to niggle her a little there,' Nigel observes, with both our faces glued to the screen. As the pack moves around the sweeping bend, Doris cruises up into a distinct second place. And then, just before the bend becomes the finishing straight, Doris eases past the horse on her inside and GOES INTO THE FUCKING LEAD!

Nigel grabs my arms, lets rip a volley of expletives and drags me back off towards the rail. We scamper over the tarmac concourse like schoolboys escaping through the yard. As we strain to see I can hear the tannoy saying, 'It's still Deadly Doris leading . . .', and I briefly remember my own imaginary commentaries just after I'd bought her.

But now Doris, who has been racing alone for about two furlongs, looks to be tightening up. There's less than a furlong-and-a-half to go. One horse drives past her, Steady Eddy, I think, then another . . . but she stays on alongside another two . . . and as they hit the finishing line, I can't tell from my angle whether she's finished third, fourth or fifth. It's certainly no worse than fifth because the next horse after her is a good twenty lengths back.

I pat Nigel on the back, but all he can say is 'fucking hell', repeatedly, but not in the disappointed tone of defeat. This is one of exhilaration. 'I thought she was a good horse but, Christ, that's some run . . .'

I'm equally dazed, with the overwhelming emotions being pride and excitement. The tannoy says the judge has called for a photo for third place, it's that close. But it's between Just Jenny and Solway Rose. Steady Eddy won, with Springfield Scally second. Meldrum Park, the hot favourite, must have been behind Doris, along with six other horses.

Nigel and I go out onto the track to greet horse and jockey as they come back. There won't be a place in the winner's enclosure this time round, so it's a walk back down the course to the unsaddling area. Liz is a bag of nerves. She tells me she got through two cigarettes during the race. David Creech jumps off Doris and we congratulate him on a sympathetic and dutiful ride.

'She's some horse, I tell you. Great engine. She was just cruising past them. When I got into the straight I really couldn't hear anything behind me. That's when she swerved a bit, ran a little green. But she was staying on well into the last two before they got to her. And then she stayed on again, even though she was tired.'

David gives the horse a pat, and tells Nigel that he wouldn't mind riding her again if Nigel wants some weight taking off. We lead Doris down the course. She's breathing quite heavily and lathered in sweat. But she's not distressed or anxious. Steve catches up with us.

'I thought she were going to bloody win. She was 12–1 in the betting. My stomach turned over.'

'Mine too,' I say.

We hear the result of the photo – Just Jenny is third by a short head. Doris is half a length back in fifth. We were that close to a massive £159 in prize-money. Nigel begins to wash Doris down, giving his analysis of the race as he does so.

'That was some race for a first time, I tell you. She's the best I've had since Holt Place' (a 50–1 winner for Nigel at Cheltenham in the early 1990s). 'And we know her blood wasn't quite right. She's got a good cruising speed. She acts on this ground. We've just got to see how she comes on for the experience. David may have gone a little too early on her, but she was moving so well that I don't think he had much choice. But I'm telling you, for a first run by a young, inexperienced horse, that was smashing. I'm well chuffed.'

The course is emptying now, and the adrenaline surge is ebbing from my body at the same rate. The race seems a blur of fragments, slurred sound-bites and tunnel vision. Nigel tosses a rug over Doris and Liz begins to lead her across the course to the horse-box.

'Right. Drink,' Nigel says to Steve and I.

But first we drop into the weighing-room, and go through to the jockeys' quarters. The long, wood-floored room looks like a Victorian work-house, with chapel-style clothes pegs and three huge wooden benches down the centre of the room for saddles and tack. We watch a re-run of the race on the racecourse video. It still looks as though Doris might win. But you can see her visibly tiring inside the two-furlong pole. Even so, the other four horses all have to be strongly ridden to get past her. We drift out onto the near-deserted course and manage to get three bottles of Beck's off a mobile bar before it closes. Steve is well pleased. 'Couldn't have asked for more,' he says in deep, Northern tones. But Nigel is already plotting.

'Right, we give her a little rest now. Let the experience sink in. Make sure she's all right. And then I'll start looking for another race. Maybe a 1 mile 6 furlong bumper, or a "mares only" race. But she's beaten some horses with racing experience here today. And she can only get better, I promise you.'

We say our goodbyes, and Steve goes off to drive Nigel back to the horse-box in the far corner of the course. I walk across and then into the town. My brain is still in a sort of hyperventilation mode, with images of the race strobing across it. I've only been to Worcester once before, but now I'm more or less walking through it blindly, looking for signs to the station. But the walk is doing me good, draining the tension out of me. Even when I have a Kafkaesque experience at Worcester's Foregate Street station, I'm almost narcotically passive about it. The screen says there's a train going to Worcester's other station, Shrub Hill, that will get me there in time to catch my train to Cheltenham. But the man in the station office says there's no such train. I walk across to the timetable and point to the train in question.

'Those timetables aren't relevant at the moment – you should look at the temporary ones around the corner.'

The old 'me' might have performed a Terminator act now, punching my fist through his glass screen and then dragging him out by the throat before ramming his head into the non-relevant timetable, while asking in my best Schwarzenegger why there was 'nussink to inform ze publik of ziss'. But I'm mysteriously calm and serene. I just walk away. Check the street map and do the fifteen-minute walk across to Shrub Hill. While I'm walking, the greyness finally clears and the sun comes out. I feel deliriously happy that Doris has done so well, and will do so again if she stays healthy. After nearly a year of ownership, I can see that it isn't quite so polarised an experience as I'd imagined up to now. It's not money owners are after, but that would be nice. It's not even fun we're after, but that's easier to achieve. I think that all we want from our horses is what Doris delivered today – a run for our money.

I reach Shrub Hill station in good time. The evening sun has really set Worcester's red-brick core alight now. It's a glorious sight. And yet I must be the only man in town looking forward to the winter . . . and, no, my lottery ticket didn't win.

Expenses: Train fare, £15.50; instant camera, £5.99; wine and sandwich on train, £5.30; lottery ticket, £1; taxi to course, £5; drinks, £6.50; Timeform card, £5.50; bet on Deadly Doris, £40; taxi from Bath to home, £13. Total: £97.79.

Tail Piece

Of all the years to venture into racehorse ownership, I doubt if I could have picked one more troublesome. If I list some of the negative events, 'bulleted' in true Public Relations style, you will see what a huge background of turmoil there was going on behind my small experiences. Try to imagine the openings 'bongs' of *News at Ten* as you read.

• Sheikh Mohammed, the biggest owner in the world, threatens to pull out of British racing if owners' prize-money is not improved in the near future.

• The Chairman of the BHB, Lord Wakeham, resigns after failing to back the Industry Committee's new Business Plan for Racing.

• Three Jump jockeys, Jamie Osborne, Dean Gallagher and Leighton Aspell, are arrested by Scotland Yard's Serious Crime Squad during an investigation into race-fixing. Aspell is subsequently dropped from the enquiry.

• National Hunt's most famous horse of the past few years, One Man, is killed in a chase at Aintree. Three other horses die in the Grand National.

• The *Sporting Life*, racing's oldest newspaper, closes after the Mirror Group acquire the *Racing Post* from Sheikh Mohammed for just £1.

• Two courses, Windsor and Lingfield Park, announce that they are to drop National Hunt racing from the fixtures.

• The Countryside Alliance is discredited after it is revealed that it has been sending the names and addresses of its supporters to the Conservative Party.

• Labour Chancellor Gordon Brown suggests that the privatisation of the government-owned Tote might be a possibility in the near future.

With headlines like these, it is obvious that 1997–8 has been a difficult, turbulent year for racing in general, and the National Hunt in particular. While it is true that an air of crisis can be generated over most British sports on issues such as funding, corruption and injuries, racing is perhaps the most vulnerable of all because its image is already fairly suspect and its finances fragile. The combination of a high-profile debate about owners' prize-money, the death in action of the sport's most popular horse, the possible scandal of race-fixing by a highly organised criminal gang, and the dismissal in some quarters of a vital business plan as 'a wish list', represented four serious blows to the sport's self-esteem. If ownership is perceived as a poor investment, races as either horse-killers or potentially 'bent', and the financial organisation as unrealistic, why should people pay out good money to be involved with the sport? How long before owners come to recognise that what they are pursuing is nothing more than 'fool's gold'?

At various times during my multiple ownership, I asked myself some of these questions, usually at low moments, of which there were quite a few. As I have written earlier, at the heart of the debate is the issue of whether owning a racehorse is for fun or for money. Ideally it should be both and certainly winning a race would in itself be fun enough. But none of the horses I invested in returned any money to me, either in prizes or in winning bets, despite the promising run by Doris at Worcester. I therefore found myself constantly rationalising what I was actually in it for, and whether or not the small pleasures were enough compensation for the larger miseries. On the day, Doris's fifth place was a genuine thrill but, for the rest of the season, becoming an owner brought me a new perspective on the game, and it was not, for the most part, a particularly flattering one.

Certainly that February Monday at Hereford, when Nova Scotia was injured to the extent of ending her career, will stay with me for a long time, as my bleakest thoughts proved almost insurmountable. As an owner I was treated with no great courtesy by the racecourse's organisation, and was subjected to unwelcome propaganda. The horses running that day were generally of the most mediocre quality, and would hardly have qualified for the term 'sportsman' had they been human. One hundred and three of them were competing for total win and place prize-money of £22,400 on the day, yet only 23 of them could win anything. So no fewer than 80 horses, including our own, left the course with nothing to show for the expense of travel, entry fees and staff labour, not to mention their owners' time and money.

In addition, as it were, to the sums not adding up, that day at Hereford was the first time I'd glimpsed the relationship between racing and the bookmakers stripped to its bare essentials. Three of the races were won by favourites, but four weren't. Can you imagine how much money the bookmakers up and down the country in thousands of big and small betting shops took on the Hereford card? A hell of a lot more than £22,400, I bet. The 103 horses were running for the bookies' profits, a load of third-rate nags with little or no future, cynically enticed out onto an ugly little racecourse for scraps of prize-money just to keep the mug punters in the shops handing over their money. That's what it seemed like to me, a huge capitalistic edifice manipulating events from a distance and just counting the money rolling in. That was the sole justification for the day. No wonder the bookmakers continue to moan about Sunday racing, which has proved a great hit with new and family race-goers who tend to bet very little. It's the bookies' worst nightmare to have half-empty shops, with their normal punters detained at home by leisure or family duties, while on-course the betting turnover is negligible. As top Flat trainer John Gosden once said, 'All the big bookmakers are interested in is servicing an endless fruit machine of mug punters in betting shops.'

But we also have to consider the complicity of racehorse owners in this great scam. We take our low-rent horses to these downbeat tracks, dreaming gormlessly that fun can be had out of competing for £164 in third-place prize-money, never questioning our place in the scheme of things, never seeing how our innocence is being abused. We content ourselves with a few drinks, the abysmal catering, the poor viewing facilities and the minimal hospitality from the racecourse. We then kid ourselves that we are having a good time, despite the fact that we're the ones actually under-writing the whole show, by paying for our horses to be trained and entered in these two-bit races. And it happens every day of the racing year.

If you follow this bleak line of thought, you might also ask yourself why the bookmakers make substantial profits from racing but have to be dragged to the table every year to make a contribution to the Betting Levy, which is one of the sport's chief sources of finance. One of the reasons for this chicken and rooster situation is that when off-course betting was legalised in 1961, the Conservative government rejected a state-run Tote monopoly and instead allowed the book-makers to set up their chains of betting shops. Vast fortunes have since gone to the bookmakers rather than into racing itself, and the contrast with French and Australian racing, where a Tote monopoly exists off-course, and our own game is stark. In both countries, prize-money is substantially higher than in Britain, with a much better return to owners to set against their expenses.

How the Tote deal was rejected is still shrouded in mystery, but there are plenty of stories of how an Establishment stitch-up and behind-the-scenes lobbying helped the bookmakers win the vote. It is well known, for example, that the Eton and Cambridge-educated bookmaker Archie Scott was Chairman of the National Bookmakers' and Associated Bodies' Joint Protection Association from 1957 to 1964, and acted for them in the complex negotiations for the Betting and Gaming Act which legalised off-course bookmaking in 1961. Scott also acted as an adviser to Home Secretary 'Rab' Butler on the establishment of betting shops after the Act was passed. Scott is generally credited with uniting the book-making industry to fight against the prospect of a Tote off-course monopoly, which had seemed almost certain to be enacted when legalisation was first mooted. What actually happened to deny this possibility would make a wonderful drama, if the documents relating to it, Cabinet papers and so on, could be comprehensively scrutinised, and the various eye-witness testimonies assembled. Even so, I suspect that the influential moments in the decision-making probably happened off-stage, either in the smoking rooms of the Gentlemen's Clubs, or at country-house weekends.

But that's all getting on for forty years ago now, and it seems a distant part of our social history. Had the administrators known how racing and gambling were to become boom activities from the 1970s onwards, they might have thought twice before handing over such a money-making concession to the bookies, thereby denying the sport, and government, considerable revenue. In his controversial Gimcrack speech, Sheikh Mohammed said at one point, 'I know that there will never be a Tote monopoly in this country – the stable door that allowed that horse to bolt was irresponsibly left open many years ago.'

The irony now is that we are getting closer than ever to a bookmaking monopoly. What was once the 'Big Four' of firms – Mecca, William Hill, Ladbrokes and Coral – is virtu-ally the big two, Ladbrokes and Hill's, always assuming that Ladbrokes' current take-over bid for Coral's is approved by the Monopoly and Mergers Commission and the Department of Trade. William Hill took over Mecca several years ago, but is now owned by a Japanese securities company, and with many of the smaller bookmakers either selling up or closing down, we are faced with the genuine prospect of a private monopoly. The old argument that the market would serve the punters' interests best would therefore be completely invalid. If we are heading towards what will be close to a monopoly for off-course betting, how much better that it should be the Tote, whose profits would be ploughed back into racing, rather than a private bookmaking giant whose profits wouldn't.

The on-course bookies would still have their business and bring the colour and variety to racecourses, qualities that are alleged to be so deeply cherished by punters. A state-owned Tote monopoly off-course would simply offer an alternative form of betting that helps the industry rather than bleeds it of funds. If some betting-shop punters found this system restrictive, they might even be encouraged to go to the racecourses and bet, which would help both attendance and turnover. In any case, my experience suggests that most punters are happy enough just to get a winner, without worrying about whether they'd have got better odds with 'Honest Ernie' or on the Tote.

Where racing will get its money from in the future lies at the heart of the 'Business Plan' which the BHB has now endorsed under its new Chairman, Peter Savill. As a successful owner – Celtic Swing has probably been his best horse so far – and a very rich and shrewd businessman, Savill seems ideally placed to take racing's case into battle with both government and bookmakers. When the Plan was first unveiled last January, on the historic day after Lord Wakeham actually left the job, it was widely welcomed as an intelligent document with a good chance of success. Since those heady few hours, however, there have been dissenting voices, among which some might have been expected to be supporters. Junior

Labour Ministers, with a genuine interest in racing, expressed disappointment with the document, although there must be a suspicion that they were moving early to dispel any notion that this government could ever be helpful to racing. New Labour wouldn't be seen dead in betting shops, while Old Labour grew up in them.

Later the main proposals of the plan were conveniently rubbished by accountants Coopers & Lybrand in a study commissioned by BOLA, the betting shop bookmakers' 'umbrella' organisation. This reaction was hardly surprising, given that two of the key elements in the plan involve getting the bookmakers to pay up more money, and widening the opportunities for betting beyond the bookies' shops and into pubs and clubs. However, the long-desired and, to my mind, utterly logical aim of the BHB to take over the Tote appears to have been put on a back-burner, while the initial campaign to get a better deal with the bookmakers is waged.

Let me just outline the main points of the plan, to confirm the seriousness of the crisis in which racing finds itself.

- Racing needs an extra annual investment of £105 million to ensure a sound financial basis.
- Racing can generate £25 million of that figure itself, but the outstanding £80 million must come via an increased return from horse-race betting turnover, which requires government intervention.
- If this were to happen, the following benefits would accrue:
  - A doubling of prize-money, thus enabling owners to recoup up to 50 per cent of keep and training costs.
  - The creation of 9,000 jobs in the racing industry, and the recruitment of 2,400 new owners and 3,400 new horses.
  - An increase of £450 million in betting turnover through bigger fields, better marketing and limited

expansion of the fixture list, which would also bring £50 million more profit to the bookmakers. The government would benefit from the generation of £100 million in new direct taxation.

You would not need to be a racing fan, nor indeed a rocket scientist, to see that these aims are expansionist in nature, rather than reductive. The plan's essence is that growth is necessary for survival, not pruning. This is a bold view, not only because it seems to go against the prevailing trend of decline, but also because it is predicated on the existence of a greater appetite for horse-racing among the public than already exists. But the most audacious stroke is the notion that government would be prepared to forgo £80 million in revenue by adjusting the level of their take from betting duty. Given that a good deal of the planning for this document took place in the mid-1990s, it may well be that there was an assumption that the Conservatives might still be in office, an administration which had already made a VAT concession to owners and breeders. But to think that 'Iron Chancellor' Gordon Brown might buy the notion of giving money to racing now in the expectation of getting more back later seems optimistic in the extreme. Indeed, that £25 million to be raised by racing itself, and the £80 million from government, looks more like the two fishes and five loaves of an earlier miracle.

If I were to be asked for my opinion, which I'm sure I wouldn't be, I would insist that the increased promotion of racing is a necessary first step. This would not only test the market's appetite for more racing, but also automatically deliver a natural, organic growth, rather than the hormone-injected expansion from a sudden injection of cash. At the moment I get the impression that the BHB actually spends very little on advertising and promoting racing, although it should be encouraged by what it has achieved with the increased attendance for Sunday meetings. The more people are introduced to our sport, the higher the percentage of future punters and owners. Racing has to be sold as a great day out for men, women and children and families, as better value for money than a Premiership football game and as a more thrilling spectacle than motor-racing or tennis. All of which I believe to be the case, and I speak as a fairly well-travelled sports-writer and as a parent of two young boys. Last year it cost me £54 just for the tickets to take them to Anfield to watch Liverpool play. In contrast, their admission to a racecourse would be free.

With regard to the expansion of the number of horses in training, I can only judge from my largely downbeat year as an owner, that there are actually too many horses, of mediocre quality, chasing too little prize-money already to make expansion feasible or desirable. Racing has its own in-built economy, but it isn't divorced from that of the country, so any imminent recession would have a destructive effect on a manufactured boom. If expansion is going to happen it will be because racing attracts more people to the racecourses, and encourages them to make the step into affordable ownership, with the prospect of a decent return for their money.

On a more basic level, it seems obvious that the financial burden of supporting racing in inequitable, given that it is estimated that owners contribute the majority sum of £156 million per annum (52 per cent). Meanwhile the racecourses chip in £88 million (29 per cent) and the punters, via the levy, currently give £56 million (19 per cent). I have a couple of small but I hope practical suggestions to improve this imbalance. Rather than battle the bookmakers for increased fractions of the levy, the BHB could try to get them to underwrite directly certain race-going costs that bear down on owners, punters and racecourses. In the first instance, the on-course bookmakers should be made to pay for the cost of printing the racecards, so that they could be distributed free of charge to punters as they arrive. Secondly, the off-course bookmaking companies should be required to make a contribution towards either the entry fees of owners or the riding fees of jockeys. After all, the more horses that run, the greater the chance of the bookmakers making a profit. Both of these elements are quantifiable and both are burdens on the people who support racing with their money. Extracting a measure of direct subsidy from those making a profit out of the punters' betting money and the owners' financial commitment should be a guiding principle behind all that racing does to improve its finances.

I should say that this book wasn't originally intended to stray into these areas. But the larger events in the background of my year made some comment inevitable. I have a cartoon by Ray Lowry on my toilet wall, and it shows the New York police trying to deal with a King Kong figure menacing the skyline. One of the policemen is shouting from a roof, 'This is worse than we thought, the ape is only a giant furry glove-puppet.' I am constantly identifying with this policeman.

But what I didn't want to do was to give the impression that I have come to dislike racing because of being an owner. On the contrary, that has mostly enhanced my pleasure of going racing in so many ways. Of all my excursions over the year, either connected with my horses or not, I only had one really bad experience, and that was at Hereford the day that Nova Scotia was injured. Even Rowley John's poor run at Warwick was preceded by a wonderful winter's day out that couldn't have been bettered as a refreshing change from my normal dull routine. And as for Doris, I'm still tingling with the excitement.

Indeed, days at the races have been among the most memorable of my life so far. In December 1991, I celebrated my fortieth birthday by hiring a box at Cheltenham and inviting a dozen close friends to enjoy steak and kidney pie, red wine, a clear blue sky, and some fairly decent races, and it was probably the best birthday party I've ever had. In 1987, Andrew Nickolds and I, in the days when we were successful writers, hired a chalet at Lingfield for the last Saturday's racing before Christmas and invited a bunch of actors we'd worked with to join us. The bookies looked on in terror as such formidable faces as Warren Clarke and Peter Vaughan moved among them. In November 1989, I covered the Melbourne Cup in Australia, an event that would probably do for my dying day, such is its celebration of earthly pleasures. I was in the seething throngs at Leopardstown when Carvill's Hill won a chase, and the Irish race fans believed for a short while that they had a second Arkle. And in August 1990, I was at York to cover the Nunthorpe sprint in which Dayjur blistered along the sun-baked track as if he was one of those machines in the Arizona desert out to break the land-speed record.

But there are countless other minor days, at the likes of Wincanton, Fontwell and Windsor, which have also registered their mark on me. In moments of depression, or when the winter seems endless, these days can keep you alive with their equine spectacle, with their boozy comradeship and their bucolic beauty − Hereford excepted. Above all, these days are one of the few escape routes left open to us as our leisure becomes ever more pre-packaged and homogenised by way of multiplex cinemas, fast-food restaurants, satellite television, shopping malls and computer-game technology.

Going racing, especially as an owner, puts you back in touch with two key relationships in our collective folk memory − that between man and horse, and between man and countryside. It isn't so long ago since we became a largely urban species. My paternal grandfather, born in the last century, worked on farms in Yorkshire until he was forced to seek manual work in industrial Liverpool after an agricultural recession. I'm not a believer in reincarnation or anything like that, but I do think we hear distant echoes in our lives of those of our forebears, not just in our behavioural patterns but also in our reactions to things we have not previously experienced in our own lifetime.

When I took my two sons, Charlie and Jack, racing for the first time, I could see on their faces the same expressions of intrigue and amusement as I'd felt myself four decades ago. They were fascinated by the horses' movements, and in stitches when one of them unleashed a pile of droppings in the parade ring. One runner with a visor was immediately christened 'Bat-Horse'. When they picked out a few vivid names that appealed to them from the racecard, I faked putting money on for them, and of course three of their selections won, leaving me to hand over their winnings from my own pocket. On the drive home, I could tell that they were enchanted with the experience of their afternoon's racing, and so I already knew, when I asked them both what they'd made of it all, that I'd get a positive response.

'It was great, because the horses really run fast,' Charlie said.

'And they look really cool,' Jack offered as his opinion.

And then, out of the blue, Charlie asked, 'Could we get a horse one day, Dad?'

And now I have.

What Happened Next . . .

Anybody who has been within smelling distance of owning a horse will know only too well what usually happens after a promising first run. It involves a fruit that is not round and which is used by Cockneys to describe stairs. In the case of Doris everything went pear-shaped twice. In the first instance, it soon became obvious that running her on the good-to-firm ground at Worcester had not been to her liking, and that her legs were a bit jarred up, requiring a period of rest in her box. This didn't quite square with what Nigel and I had seen in the race, in which she appeared to be travelling smoothly before running out of steam two furlongs out. But, as Nigel pointed out, a horse will have a go on any surface on its initial run because it doesn't know how to do otherwise. I was reminded here of an old Liverpool joke about two blokes who'd started an argument in a pub and had gone outside to settle it with their fists in the car-park. One of the men is much stronger than the other and gives him a right battering. With his opponent on the deck, the winner stands over him and asks if he has had enough yet. Whereupon the loser replies, 'I don't know yet, it's my first fight.' Doris had lost her first fight with honour, but both she, and we, her human guardians, now knew that the next time she wouldn't run on a surface as hard as a pub car-park.

A week or so later, I ordered a video of the Worcester race from Race-Tech, a facility available to every owner at a discounted charge of around £20. Having received the video and watched it three of four times, two things became apparent. On the serious side, it was possible to see Doris weaving about on her run up the straight, a sure sign of 'greenness', and also lifting her head in the final stages of the race. This was an equally clear indication that she was tiring and that the turf had too much of a sting in it for her to run flat out. On the plus side, I could see that as the video built into a collection of her races – and her wins – I could bore my friends and neighbours more successfully than with any compilation of slides of holidays. Not that there'd been any since the boys were born. Both they and Wendy get car-sick just going to Tesco's so an overseas trip had always seemed way beyond the power of *Kwells*.

However, as September ebbed away, it seemed that serious tranquillisers might be required, not just in my capacity as a part-owner of Doris, but also as a renewed member of the Tally-Ho Partnership. Crowning Glory, the partnership's sole horse for the 1998–9 season, had been safely delivered to Nigel's yard in August and had been put through her initial acclimatisation to serious training. But then out of the blue, in a phone-call to me about Doris's progress, Nigel suddenly announced that he was thinking about handing in his licence because he could no longer make training pay. Though it had been stark staring obvious that Nigel hadn't picked up much in the way of prize-money over the past few seasons, it was still a shock to hear him stricken by doubt all of a sudden. A couple of horses, including the infamously-named Forty-Two Dee and her companion Bosom Pal, had been removed from the yard by their bra company owners, which only left perhaps eight or nine horses. Nigel's fees err on the reasonable side compared to most stables – a basic £120 per week for Doris – so though a total weekly income for the stable of close to a grand might seem manageable, it's not that much for him and Liz to live on.

I offered Nigel my sympathy and support and told him about the time in the early 1980s when my five-year television writing career had appeared to grind to a complete halt after the collapse of several projects. I'd been so strapped one week that I'd tried to flog a couple of old suits to a second-hand shop in Edgware Road. Unfortunately the two cool black guys running the operation had rejected my threads, probably on the grounds that wide lapels and bell-bottoms weren't ready for a comeback just yet. Apart from family bereavements and broken relationships, that particular day remains in my mind as probably the most miserable in my life, trudging back through the February slush with my unwanted suits over my shoulder. Yet, as I told Nigel, about ten days later I got a call from a producer inviting me to join the writing team on a fairly unlikely project about Geordie builders going out to Germany to find work. So I urged Nigel not to say '*Auf Wiedersehen, Pet*' just yet. He thought it might make his life simpler if he became what is termed a 'permit holder', officially a trainer who works only with horses owned by himself or his immediate family. This would plainly lead to complications about the ownership of Doris – would Steve Ludlam and I have to sell out our shares? Would Nigel have to adopt me as a long-lost son who was four years older than himself?

The complications became worse when Cliff Underwood, the organiser of the Tally-Ho Partnership, went to visit the yard and Nigel told him about his troubles. With the stable's future looking uncertain Cliff and Janet decided that it would be unfair on Crowning Glory to be prepared for action in one yard when it seemed she would abruptly have to be found another. So they withdrew the horse from Nigel and sent her down to Jim Neville just outside Newport. It was a purely pragmatic decision, and Nigel took it with good grace, but together with Doris's lay-off, this development effectively closed off the chance of an imminent run from either horse.

Within a month, Nigel had reversed his decision and vowed to train on. He combined this with a prospective move from his currently rented stables to a small, home-built yard in one corner of his dad's land. Despite his lack of major successes Nigel is a born competitor, though fortunately not one of those types that has to blinker themselves from reality in order to achieve that state of mind. I didn't enquire too much about his change of heart, being simply grateful for myself and happy for both him and Liz that the show was back on the road. However he did let slip that he'd managed to sell a set of racing colours at Sotheby's for a few grand. These auctions take place a couple of times a year with high prices being achieved for the classier, predominantly one-colour silks. Maybe I should have taken my old suits down to a Bond Street auction house instead. 'Lot 37. One brown, John Travolta in *Saturday Night Fever* number, what am I bid?'

The renewed surge of optimism couldn't help the stable steer clear of a virus, however, and by mid-November the Green Snot was all over the yard again, with Doris sidelined for a further period. Inevitably, this began to raise questions within the Hey household about what I was doing with my money. As a painter and illustrator who has often lived in Bohemian style, my wife Wendy isn't by nature a 'nagger' but she has occasional moments when she has to cross-examine me about what she sees as my cavalier attitude to money. I would guess that a lot of racehorse owners undergo this process from family or friends because the expense is hard to justify in the face of world poverty, let alone domestic bills. My case for the defence, available free of charge to anybody who needs it, is this.

1. Life is short and mostly miserable so anything that cheers us up is worth a try.
2. Two of the things I don't try are drugs or golf, so I am neither adding to the problems caused by crime, or encouraging the continued despoliation of the planet with another bleeding golf course.
3. My happiness is not only good for my health, it stops me being a miserable bastard around the house and

bringing everybody else down with me. *Ergo*, things that make me happy – like Liverpool tonking Everton or Manchester United, or me owning a racehorse – create a ripple effect of happiness that then touches my friends and family, people I buy drinks for, the people at Tote Credit who accept my hopeless bets and so on.

4. I am not religious, but if I were, I think I might lean towards Buddhism in which the notion of reincarnation seems a bit more cheerful than eternal darkness or damnation. It follows then that we should be kind to animals, which I am, because we might end up as one in a future life. Who knows whom Doris might have been, Joan of Arc, Marilyn Monroe?

5. You never know, the horse might win some big money one day.

If these arguments fail to convince your inquisitor, there's always the trip to the stable to fall back on, an event that can work magic on even the hardest of hearts. With this notion in mind, I decided that it was time for the family to meet Nigel, Liz and Doris, so I booked us all in for a Saturday night in the Coventry Arms next to the yard. By combining this with a visit to Stratford-upon-Avon, so that the boys could see the Royal Shakespeare Company's new production of *The Lion, the Witch and the Wardrobe*, I was hoping for above-average brownie points and a long-term acceptance that my involvement with Doris was fine by the family. The trip worked a treat.

After lunch at the pub, we spent a couple of hours at the stable, with Wendy feeding Doris Polo mints and stroking her ears in the same smitten trance that I had initially experienced. While Charlie and Jack also liked Doris, they were more taken with Nigel's Jack Russell terrier who gladly performed his array of tricks for them. The one they particularly loved involved the dog retrieving a stone from a large plastic bucket full of freezing water by diving in head-first after balancing on all four paws on the rim of the bucket. Who needs a PlayStation? Unfortunately, trampling around the yard on a winter's afternoon left shoes and trouser bottoms caked in mud and horse-shit, so we were not the most fragrant of theatre-goers later that evening as the family completed this multi-cultural double. The following morning dawned with a blanket of white frost stretched out over the fields and a vast pink sky on every horizon. Though we live in the country, this felt even more like it, with the combination of cosy pub, racing stable and agricultural land striking an almost Edwardian note of bucolic bliss. After breakfast we went round to the stable to watch and help with the morning feed and then left Liz and Nigel to what was left of their Sunday. By the time we got back to Bradford, it was clear that Doris had been assimilated into our family life along with the rest of the pets. Within days the boys were asking me what I was always asking Nigel – 'When is she going to run?'

Christmas and New Year passed without substantial wins on any of my seasonal bets – the biggest, on See More Business, got stuck in the mud with the horse at Kempton in the King George as Teeton Mill followed up his Hennessy win with ease. However, news soon came through of Doris's improved health and decent work and, a race at Southwell – on the turf – was pencilled for mid-January. In fact Doris was actually declared for this bumper and appeared in the list of runners when the last-minute result of a blood-test forced her out. The blood wasn't completely wrong, just wrong enough to add to the disadvantage of not having had a run for 146 days. There were only eight runners for the race and Doris was listed as fourth favourite in the betting at 5–1 earning two 'ticks' out of three for 'ability' in the *Racing Post*'s data file on the race. The *Guardian* had even gone as far as tipping her to win.

Nigel already had another imminent race in mind at

Huntingdon on Thursday 28 January and the extra week allowed Doris's blood to come right at last. The snag was that having been booked to face just seven opponents at Southwell, Doris was now up against twenty at the Cambridgeshire track. Nobody was tipping her this time as I prowled through the *Racing Post* on the train heading for London, and she was listed at 25–1 in the betting forecast. I'd never been to Huntingdon before, although I'd once worked on a traffic census outside the town in one of my many impecunious years after university. This involved sitting in a tin Nissen hut for a ten-hour stretch counting vehicle totals for each of the hours. My particular stretch was on a bleak by-pass with nothing but a hurricane lamp and a flask of coffee for company. Unfortunately, as darkness fell, I made a mess of lighting the lamp and managed to set fire to the hut. I retreated to a distant pub and made up the numbers for the last few hours based on an average of the previous totals. Although this seemed to pass the council's scrutiny at the time, I became guiltily convinced in later life that my faked numbers were somehow responsible for the M11's bizarre curve at the end of its trajectory north from Cambridge.

Fortunately nobody in authority was waiting for me at the racecourse, and I quickly met up with Nigel and my co-owner Steve Ludlam. I liked Huntingdon instantly, its array of low-level buildings and stands giving it a true country feel, despite the looming presence of a flyover on the A14, filled by the constant passage of container lorries from Felixstowe. The usual problem with having a horse in a bumper soon surfaced – it's the last race so there's even more time to fret, lose money and get drunk. I managed to avoid the latter, but was sufficiently emboldened to go round sticking several £10 each-way bets on Doris as soon as the market opened. She was 33–1 in the betting ring, even more on the Tote, and then her price drifted out to 50-1, so I was treble-handed by the time she set off down the course.

Nigel had booked Ross Studholme for the ride, a conditional jockey whom he and Liz had met when they'd taken Petraco to race in Jersey. Ross was with Graham McCourt's stable at Wantage, and seemed a bright, attentive lad. His five-pounds allowance took Doris's weight down to 10 stone 4lbs, a big help in what were clearly very soft conditions. Having established that the horse didn't like firm going, we were now about to find out if she could act on the opposite extreme. Nigel was reasonably confident that she would, the main doubt being how much the soft ground would sap her slightly dubious stamina. He'd therefore asked Ross to try and hold her up in midfield for as long as possible and this he duly did as they went out into the back straight. Doris seemed to be travelling perfectly on the ground, although nowhere near as easily as the hot favourite, Mark Pitman's Devil's Advocate who was powering through the mud at what looked no more than an exercise canter. As the field began to string out on the long turn for home, Doris suddenly found a great position on the inside and began to scoot through to be in the first five or six. For a few brief seconds she looked as though she could get closer but her run began to stall about a furlong out, though she stayed on really well to take fourth place behind the winning favourite, Henrietta Knight's Roman Lord in second and Paul Webber's Dromdoran in third.

This was a much better ran than expected for a 50–1 chance and I became convinced that I would get a pay-out for fourth place. But because the race was not a handicap there was prize- and place-money only for the first three home. My bets were done for, but this was the next best thing to a win. Liz defiantly led Doris into the fourth-place berth in the winner's enclosure and we all gathered round to give our horse our congratulations on her valiant effort. As darkness fell, Nigel joined Steve and I in one of the rapidly emptying bars and reported himself to be 'chuffed' with the horse's effort. I went back to the racecourse stables with Nigel to see Doris, now washed down and rugged up, and fed her a few Polo mints. All races tell you something about your horse, and Doris had added to our knowledge by showing that she could act on very soft ground and still get the two-mile trip. With slightly better ground, she'd be in contention for a win. 'One more bumper, and then we're going hurdling,' Nigel announced.

I left Liz and Nigel to load up the horse-box – his other runner Miss Nova had also run in the race, but a slipped saddle had put paid to her chances – and found myself wandering the road alone in the dark. I saw a taxi light in the near distance and approached. The driver had been booked but had been waiting more than ten minutes beyond the pick-up time so agreed to take me back to the station. I can honestly say that I have never left a racecourse happier than I did on that day.

Within a week, Nigel had plotted Doris's next outing – Cheltenham. Before I could get too excited about Doris running at the Festival, he added 'in April'. She had apparently qualified to run in a major, end of season 'Mares Only' bumper race that boasted a £14,000 winner's prize. The race distance was 2 miles 1 furlong, but Nigel thought that Doris stood a chance of getting the trip. I was not so lucky when it came to the Cheltenham Festival itself in March. Unseasonally warm weather lured several associates and myself to overdo the champagne on the first two days, as we managed to bag a place on the small outdoor terrace of the Arkle Ear. This unheralded double of being able to drink and watch the racing at the crowded Festival is usually only achieved by those in the private boxes, or those who get to the bars at 10.31 a.m., one minute after the gates have opened.

Sun and alcohol are potent destabilisers at any time, but in the context of a serious betting arena they can discombobulate even the strongest of wills. Mine isn't that strong, so I ended up not only fairly drunk but also arrogantly confident about my betting strategy, doing £5 win Lucky 15s and £10 dual forecasts as well as single bets. I lost heavily on the first day, even though I fluked the Fulke – the Fulke Walwyn & Kim Muir Cup for Amateur Riders – by finding 20–1 winner Celtic Giant.

On the Wednesday, I managed to ignore a strong tip for Barton (won at 2–1), and then tipped Khayrawani to everybody I knew but somehow failed to back it myself, watching with a mixture of pain and pride (99 per cent of the former) when it came in at 16–1. When the Festival 'banker', Major Dundee, fell and injured himself in Sun Alliance Chase, I lost heart for the rest of the day and my stamina gave out. Watching the final day at home, I began suddenly to bet with clarity, picking both See More Business in the Gold Cup (16–1) and Sir Talbot (10–1) in the County Hurdle. I suppose the lesson to be learned from this is that if I want to make money on the Festival I should stay at home and stay sober. On the other hand, just being at Cheltenham, in fine weather, with good friends around you is enough of a pleasure without backing winners. . . . Nah, that's sentimental tosh. You still need the winners.

A month later I was back at Cheltenham, with Wendy, but without 48,000 of the people who had been there on my last day in March. The Craven Meeting at Newmarket was under way so, with even warmer weather, arriving to watch a National Hunt Flat race seemed out of synch. Still, it was unusual to be able to sit down and have a snack in Barry Cope's seafood bar – at the Festival this particular area looks as though a trawler has netted several hundred people and not released them. We were also able to gain access to the Lawn Bar for Owners and Trainers, and of course stood in the famous paddock when Doris paraded for her race. Unusually for a bumper, it was not the last race on the card, and even more unusually, it was televised by Channel 4.

There were sixteen runners in the field with the powerful yards of Nigel Twiston-Davies, David Nicholson, Mickey Hammond and Paul Webber being well represented. Doris was 20–1 in the betting and clearly would do well to get a place on form. With my dear wife in attendance, the opportunities for plundering the betting ring were limited anyway. Twenty pounds each-way on the Tote seemed the most reasonable investment, as Doris was trading at bigger odds in the pool betting.

Still, this wasn't really a day about winning money. It really did feel as though I'd taken the Olympic pledge about the 'taking part that's important'. I was in the most famous paddock in National Hunt racing. My horse looked fit and healthy – although she took fright when she saw the huge electronic 'scoreboard' that towers over one end of the parade ring. Nigel had booked a senior jockey for the occasion too, Brendan Powell, the very popular Irishman who could boast several significant wins in his career, including the Grand National on Rhyme 'n' Reason in 1988. He'd also won the most recent Festival bumper on 50–1 chance Monsignor, so hardly needed any advice from Nigel about how to ride this particular race. Something similar would do fine. Despite the relative modesty of this assignment Brendan seemed incredibly enthusiastic, and gave no hint that he might be 'slumming it' on our humble mare.

Even so, the race proved something of a disappointment. The ground was officially 'good' but was probably drier than that. Doris took up a decent position in mid-field, but when the pressure came on three furlongs out, she never looked like getting in contention. Watching her through the binoculars, it seemed to me that she didn't really handle either going or course, being unbalanced several times by the undulations that make Cheltenham such a test. Nevertheless she stayed on up the straight to finish ninth, so it wasn't a total disgrace.

Afterwards, Brendan gave us a very detailed and articulate

assessment of how she'd run – 'still a baby, definitely needs cut, probably a flatter track, two miles round here is like two-and-a-half anywhere else' – that suggested he had a great future as a television 'colour' commentator once he retired. Not that this was on his mind – two days after riding Doris, he won the Scottish Grand National on Young Kenny.

After absorbing Brendan's comments, we regrouped at the Lawn Bar. Nigel confessed to being a little disappointed with Doris's run. (I noted in the *Racing Post* the next day that somebody had had £420 on Doris at 25–1, so I hope it wasn't him.) But Nigel doesn't stay down for long, and had quickly turned Brendan's de-briefing into a statement of 'what we now knew' about Doris – slightly shorter trip, a less demanding track, going with the word 'soft' in it. It was also the end of her bumper experiences. She would school over hurdles now, and perhaps take in a race before the season was out, although softer ground looked unlikely now that spring was upon us. Of course it then pissed down on the drive back to Wiltshire.

Still, Wendy seemed to have enjoyed her day out at the races – seafood salad is her idea of bliss – but I would have to be wary of assuming that her support for the venture was unqualified. I don't think she will ever quite tune in to racing's wavelength, in the sense of being aware of its subtler pleasures as well as its obvious ones. But then she probably feels the same about me going around an art gallery with her, making comments about 'Does nice colours, doesn't he, that Matisse' or 'Do you think Picasso could have made that picture a bit bigger?'

I would like to report that Doris's subsequent career has been one of startling achievement. I would like to, but I can't. Her two races after Cheltenham were nothing brilliant. Nigel somehow thought it might be a good idea to take her to Cartmel in May for her hurdles debut. I have never been there, but from pictures I'd seen of the course, set against the backdrop of the Lake District, Cartmel is, as the BBC's *Holiday* presenter Craig Doyle would say, 'quite literally stunning'. There are only a handful of meetings there every year, but they tend to take place around Bank Holidays and attract crowds of over 10,000. Unfortunately the course is also a very tight oval, undulating all the way, with sharp bends and a long run-in. To my eyes, I couldn't conceive of a less suitable track on which to introduce Doris to hurdle racing.

In terms of my travelling there, I managed to plot a pro-gramme using Railtrack's Internet site that basically indicated a two-day round trip. So, for the first time in my brief owning career, I blanked a trip to see my horse run. I went to my local Backhouse betting shop instead and tried to affect cool indifference as the race unfolded on the SIS screen. Doris jumped neatly enough, but she was losing time and ground just regaining her balance after every flight, being almost constantly on the turn. The ground was also listed as good-to-firm. She stayed on well enough to finish fifth out of sixteen, but it appeared to me that she still wasn't able, or willing, to go through with her effort when it came to the business end of a race.

The same thought occurred when she raced at Hereford – yes, that Hereford – a short while later in early June, although there were mitigating circumstances. The ground, again, was firmer than she liked; she managed to get a cut on her leg in the race, not a serious one fortunately, but enough to hurt her. And Hereford's little rises and dips just seemed enough to unbalance her. After five races in ten months, a couple of virus infections and a few dodgy blood-counts, Doris had had enough for the time being.

'She's still learning and still growing,' Nigel pointed out to her glum-faced owners, who were both resolutely sober despite the odd drink. We gradually cheered up, as most owners must do, I suppose, taking crumbs of comfort and turning them into complete loaves again. Still, Doris had had a better time of it than Crowning Glory, who despite reports of good work on the gallops, was also hit by viruses throughout the season. She then spooked and fell off a horse-walker, putting paid to any late debut, so her season was entirely blank.

Despite the intentions to make a reasonably quick start with Doris in the autumn of 1999, she didn't actually get to the track until mid-November. Another virus and unseasonal firm ground were the usual impediments to a run. At least the five-month interlude had allowed some optimism to build up again. Doris looked much better and stronger too, bigger even than when I'd last seen her. Warwick had become one of my favourite courses too by now, having had a bizarre but enjoyable day out there back in February.

The intention to meet up with Jon Holmes and Simon Kelner that day had been achieved but not as we'd planned it. Instead of having lunch in the members' restaurant, we found ourselves invited up to the stewards' and officials' luncheon-room in the old stand. One of Jon's clients, the Channel 4 Racing presenter Brough Scott, had tipped off the Clerk of the Course that his agent, the Editor-in-Chief of the *Independent* and *Independent on Sunday*, and a hack writer were coming, so our party was elevated to what might be called 'Jockey Club Class'.

Despite the obvious cultural differences – Simon and I are state grammar school boys from urban Lancashire, and Jon, though an Old Oundleian (or whatever), still speaks with a gruff East Midlands accent – we were made very welcome and didn't quite feel like class warriors storming the castle at all. There was a bit of hunting chat around the table that we couldn't quite get on with, and a fair amount of over-emphatic greeting ritual along the lines of: 'How are you, Robert?'

'I'm *extremely* well, thank you! A good morning's hunting. How are you, Tristram?'

'I'm *extremely* well too!'

Returning to Warwick felt like the start of term, seeing Nigel, Liz, Steve and Doris again. Doris looked much more relaxed than she had been previously, standing quietly while being saddled and parading with confidence. This was reflected in her run – over 2 miles 4 furlongs now – in which she jumped well and stayed with the leaders until about two flights out. Within a few weeks, it became clear that the race, though dismissed in the *Racing Post* analysis as featuring 'the usual quota of no-hopers', had been quite a strong one. The winner, Hati Roy, the second Mini Moo Min, and the fourth horse Belle Derrière all won subsequently, with other finishers below Doris also being placed. Having completed three hurdle races, Doris would now be allocated an official handicap-mark, giving us a true measure of where she stood on the great ladder of racing achievement.

In the interim, Crowning Glory finally made it to the track, showing up quite well at Hereford before tiring, and then, with almost unbelievable bad luck, getting 'struck into' – kicked by another horse during the race – in her second outing at Ludlow. The cut just missed vital tendons, so it wasn't career-threatening in itself but Cliff reported it to be bad enough to keep her out for the rest of the 1999–2000 season. I didn't make it to either race, having being trapped in meetings and what is rightly known as 'development hell' on a drama project for BBC Wales. I did manage to catch sight of her on the bookies' TV screens, and she looks a real chasing type, strong-bodied and with a long pounding stride. Cliff said that she had a good temperament and stressed that this would be needed during the weeks of box-rest that would be required, the biggest danger to her recovery being the prospect of opening up the wound by sudden movements.

Doris missed several possible engagements in January 2000 due to the usual niggles and dubious blood-cell counts, but Nigel eventually nominated a Class F hurdle at Hereford for her next appearance. He knows how I feel about Hereford.

I'm better disposed to the place since my first visit, and can see that it is trying hard to improve facilities and that its meetings provide much-needed entertainment for race fans in Wales and the Borders. And though the garden shed and its turnstile are still there, there is at least a lap-top computer inside now to speed up the admission of owners with the use of a 'swipe' card. My reservations are not so much aesthetic now as practical. I just happen to think that horses like Doris don't act on the track. But with the entry made, it was basically a case of either having a moan at Nigel, or gritting one's teeth and accepting his decision. I chose the latter for now.

So the first Valentine's Day of the new millennium saw me taking the train up to Hereford, despite the fact that the train in question is not listed in the Wales & West Trains timetable – have they got a down on Hereford too? Doris's race, the first on the card, was entitled The Wedding Day at Hereford Novices' Handicap Hurdle, and the sports-writing fragment of my brain began to summon up phrases such as 'always the bridesmaid, never the bride'.

There were sixteen runners, three of them from the top-class yards of Venetia Williams, Henry Daly and Nigel Twiston-Davies. Doris had been allocated a handicap rating of 80, not exactly a great testament to her ability, but not downright insulting either. Mysteriously, the form preview in the *Independent* and in the Hereford race-card itself each mentioned the possibility that Doris could be the surprise horse in the race.

Emboldened by these hints, I decided to get my Tote Credit bets on early, although no early price was available on the race. So I had £20 each way at the starting-price and £10 each way on the Tote pool, and this without even having had a drink first. I began to convince myself that 'Today was The Day', a bleak Monday in February when my love for Doris would finally be requited. And then I found Nigel in the main bar/cafeteria, and his first words were 'don't expect too much today'. It transpired that the latest blood-test had revealed a not entirely healthy picture. It wasn't bad enough to stop her running, but it suggested that she might be about to go down with yet another bug.

Subdued, and sober, I watched Doris parade, standing alone with Nigel, Steve having made no-show. Ross was riding her again, claiming three pounds off her allocated weight of 10 stone 10 lbs. Nigel warned him not to be too hard on her if she tired suddenly, leaving Ross to judge as to how well or badly she was travelling in the race. Doris moved fairly easily down to the start, but it was one of those moments when you wished that horses could manage basic communications like 'I feel like shit' or 'Let me at 'em!'

I checked the betting in the ring. Doris was hovering between 16–1 and 12–1 on the bookies' boards, with the odd 14–1 also available. And then she started to shorten as some poor sods, who obviously couldn't know what we did, put their money on her. I had a superstitious tenner on at 16s and retreated to my chosen vantage-point. One other minor irritation of the Hereford track is that the far straight is such a distance away that you don't so much need binoculars as the Hubble telescope to see what's going on. But even with the naked eye, it was possible to see that Doris started to lose her place just past the half-way point. She hung on to the leading pack until the third-last flight, but then Ross conspicuously began to nurse her home, and she finished eighth. She'd jumped as neatly as ever but was plainly not one hundred per cent healthy, and blew for about fifteen minutes after the race. Nigel assessed that every five-minute period of breathless recovery was the equivalent of her being one training gallop short of full fitness. Well, he should know, I suppose.

Doris was washed down and rugged, and Liz walked her around until she had relaxed before placing her back in the racecourse stable. Happily, Doris's appetite for Polo mints hadn't been affected, and she demolished the packet that I'd brought along as a prize for her anticipated win. I would think it's almost impossible for an owner to have a down on his or her horse, especially when all the signs are that it's not quite right. There are some out-right head-cases and rogues who won't race or who will down tools as soon as possible, and I can imagine that having one of these would test the patience. But whatever shortcomings Doris may have, there's no doubt that she tries her best.

I know for certain that she'll never be a champion, although a lot of horses are late developers who need to go down in the ratings before they begin the climb back up. Given the right type of course, the minimum distance of two miles and a bit of cut in the ground, she'll win a race one day, and I'm sure that's not a delusion brought on by a few disappointments. On the way home on the train, I began to make a list of her finishing positions in her seven races and the number of horses she'd beaten. Only in two of her races had she finished more than half-way down the field and then only just – ninth out of sixteen at Cheltenham, fifth out of eight on her first run at Hereford. In the other five races she'd finished in the top half, and the total number of horses that she'd finished in front of in all her races was sixty-one.

Owning a racehorse, I now know, involves a constant process of rationalisation. It has to be this way, otherwise we'd all pack it in as soon as the disappointments start to kick in. I also now realise that though costs are important in the context of not throwing good money after bad, there does come a point when you stop keeping a literal count because it can't tell the whole truth. Owners develop an innate sense of the value they are getting from their involvement with horses, one that doesn't involve prize-money or winnings from bets. The value comes in all sorts of ways – the escape from drudgery or pressure; the good-humoured camaraderie of the racecourse; and the necessary triumph of optimism over cynicism. Try putting a price on these.

The Costs

The expenses listed below relate only to my two ventures into ownership and the races they involved. For the purpose of clarity, and of preserving my marriage, I have not detailed any expenses for other days of racing and betting that are referred to in the book.

Tally-Ho Partnership share	1,120.00
Warwick races (Rowley John)	229.50
Rebate on Tally-Ho share	(400.00)
Towcester races (Nova Scotia)	241.80
Hereford races (Nova Scotia)	101.90
Video of Di's Last	10.00
One quarter-share in Deadly Doris	5,000.00
Training Fees 1	130.00
Training Fees 2 (incl. colours)	213.68
Training Fees 3	135.87
Training Fees 4	148.37
Training Fees 5	148.37
Lunch with Nigel Smith	33.00
Membership of Racehorse Owners' Association	50.00
Worcester races (Deadly Doris)	97.79
TOTAL COSTS	**£7,260.28**

THE WRITING
OF ART

THE WRITING
OF ART

OLIVIER BERGGRUEN

PUSHKIN PRESS
LONDON

© Olivier Berggruen 2011

First published in 2011 by

Pushkin Press
12 Chester Terrace
London NW1 4ND

ISBN 978 1 906548 62 9

Reprinted 2012

Cover Illustration Cy Twombly Installation Shot
Bacchus exhibition
© Cy Twombly

Frontispiece *Olivier Berggruen*
Luchino Visconti di Modrone

Set in 11 on 14 Monotype Baskerville
by Tetragon
and printed in Great Britain
by CPI Antony Rowe, Chippenham, Wiltshire

www.pushkinpress.com

CONTENTS

For Ana and Tobias

THE WRITING
OF ART

INTRODUCTION

You might think that aesthetics is a science telling us what's beautiful—almost too ridiculous for words. I suppose it ought to include what sort of coffee tastes well. [1]

IN A SET OF LECTURES delivered during the summer of 1938 at Cambridge University, Wittgenstein cautioned his students against the delusion of treating aesthetics as if it were a prescriptive science—a set of rules that would ensure our emotional or critical satisfaction. Since aesthetic objects evoke emotions such as delight, rapture, joy, melancholy or sadness, we might be misled into thinking that they share a common essence. For each individual response, the actual experience is different and only the medium of language provides a common measure that unites these feelings.

My essays tend to take descriptions of aesthetic reactions to works of art as a starting point, weaving in other lines of argument thereafter. This involves finding a language that is sufficiently attuned to shifting sensations and a wide range of properties that works of art tend to have. The act of seeing things from an aesthetic point of view gives a range of structures a sense of worth—a chair, a funerary cloth, a tiara or falling snow. However, our attention is not focused on such objects merely because of their intrinsic properties. We cannot avoid looking at them from the perspective of a shared cultural environment. That is because aesthetic appreciation is linked to the cultural practices of a particular time and place.[2]

In other words, aesthetic contemplation is never pure, and it does not take place in a void; it is never quite innocent. (In the wake of Impressionism—the movement that proclaimed faithfulness to one's immediate impressions—Cézanne dreamt of a virginal eye, realising that his objective of faithfulness to one's sensations could not be attained.) Yet I believe it is still worth describing the realm of aesthetic experience in purely subjective terms, trying to provide a literary expression of one's sensations. Sustained vision, prolonged engagement with the work of art, being attuned to the shifting qualities of our sensations, description of various flashes of vision—these are revelatory of a truth that the surface of things does not entirely conceal. Works of art lie on the ashes of history, containing many accumulated layers hidden from our immediate grasp and the promise of further revelations. The act of looking is already an exercise in reclaiming deposits of the past, of salvaging fragments that may divulge a truth worth spelling out.

The first time I came to think of art in descriptive and literary terms was during the course of my studies at the Courtauld Institute. My tutor, Anita Brookner, encouraged me to read the Goncourt brothers. Although they were renowned for writing well-researched and realistic novels, the Goncourts were first and foremost historians and connoisseurs of Ancien Régime art.

They devoted their existence to artistic endeavours, as though fleeting glimpses of feverish aesthetic insights were enough to reveal a distant beauty far removed from nature and life. They kept declaring that all great writers were destined to sacrifice their lives to such an end. Thus it was not by chance that they subscribed to Charles Baudelaire's conception of art in opposition to life, in which the world of images offered compensation for the reality of modern life and the industrial age that filled them with such horror.

In the face of disenchantment and a debased century that was founded on mediocrity, the Goncourts drew from the realm of sensations the resources they needed for life and creation. Art had become a refuge for their bruised sensibilities. They wanted to escape the vulgar tendencies of modernity by seeking refuge in the rare feelings that inanimate artefacts could offer them. From this bloodless, exhausted world sprang subtle, fleeting, joyous sensations. Literature became the medium through which these euphoric moments of aesthetic contemplation could be translated.

What the Goncourts termed *l'écriture artiste* was their attempt to correct constantly changing, ephemeral sensations. The pen could no longer be content to act as a mere follower of the eye. Instead it became analogous to it, taking into account individual states of consciousness without even arranging them according to rational criteria. They accepted that writing could be discontinuous. Amidst this muddle, the eye sought to create links between objects, surfaces, materials, textures and colours. They strove to communicate the exact quality of their sensations, especially with regard to colours—even if that involved writing in a convoluted manner.

I would never compare myself to the Goncourts. Yet what I have derived from their writings is that the eye benefits from being trained to look carefully and slowly at a wide range of objects, and that ultimately looking and writing complement each other, often going hand in hand. This is because the act of recording our sensations forces us to dwell on such a process. Even if the Goncourts were pursuing an elusive dream, striving for an ideal perfection with descriptions that were refined and detailed to the point of becoming burdensome, their writing nonetheless heralded a charming way of writing about art. It was not unlike the English aesthetic tradition later embodied by John Ruskin, Walter Pater and Adrian Stokes—they all shared an ideal of describing visual sensations borne out of the immediacy of experience. Even if their writing reflected some awkwardness, staying within the realm of sensations became an intoxicating pursuit.

These essays are devoted to a small number of artists who belong to the canon of twentieth-century art. Yet my acquaintance with their work was not formed by art books and museum visits as much as by personal experience. I grew up in Paris's Latin quarter surrounded by the works of art that my father, Heinz Berggruen, had assembled over the years: a delicate watercolour still life with a fan by Cézanne, a rather mysterious-looking cubist Picasso (*Hommage à Cortot*), a *Contraste de formes* painting by Léger, two canvases by Bonnard, a collection of watercolours from the Twenties by Paul Klee, an Uli polychrome sculpture from New Ireland, amidst stiff-looking Louis XIII chairs and furniture designed by Diego Giacometti. It was this early education of the senses that influenced my later studies, and all the artists included in this collection of essays are connected in one way or another with the spirit of early modernism embodied by my father's art collection. I have such a deep admiration for their works that I felt compelled, for better or for worse, to write about them, and not always with the distant gaze that the history of art supposedly offers us.

The central figure in my father's aesthetic upbringing was the English art critic and collector Douglas Cooper (1911–84). At a young age Cooper had a sizeable inheritance, enough to start a collection of modern art, which he later displayed at the Château de Castille in the south of France. He shunned the established artists of the École de Paris (Bonnard, Vuillard, Rouault, Matisse from the Nice period) in favour of what he termed the "authentic" cubism of Braque and Picasso, Léger and Gris. He viewed cubism not so much as a style but as a form of artistic expression by a generation that was as brilliant as the one that had allowed the Italian Renaissance to flourish. Although it remained controversial, Cooper's vision shaped our understanding of modernism; it became common currency at New York's Museum of Modern Art under the aegis of its legendary director, Alfred Barr. My father, for one, was deeply influenced by Cooper's ideas, and eventually collaborated with him on exhibitions and catalogues; he also succeeded in acquiring some works of art from Cooper's famed collection.

Cubism has also played a central role in my aesthetic upbringing. In particular, the notion of assemblage derived from Picasso and Braque's *papiers collés* offered a radical questioning of traditional illusionistic painting. Reality was shown to be much more fluid as cubism found ways of transplanting things from their usual positions in space, thus creating new metaphorical associations. Thus, it should come as no surprise that this collection of essays starts with a text on Picasso; though not the Picasso of the "heroic" years of collaboration with Georges Braque, but of the so-called Classical period, often considered a time of regression from the avant-garde spirit of cubism. From 1917 until the mid-Twenties, Picasso worked mainly for Diaghilev's Ballets Russes, and although their first collaborative effort, *Parade*, is justly celebrated, it is the last of the ballets (interestingly enough commissioned not by Diaghilev, but by the arts patron and society figure Étienne de Beaumont) that is the subject of my essay. *Les Aventures de Mercure* (*The Adventures of Mercury*, 1924) came at a time when Picasso began to tire of the more conventional aspects of ballet, and Étienne de Beaumont's fairly liberal set of instructions provided him with the opportunity to deconstruct and reduce to its bare essentials an art form that was perhaps in danger of becoming formal, rigid and overly codified. In this venture, Erik Satie, who had composed the score for *Parade*, was the ideal partner, as the two of them engaged in an exercise of mockery—seen at the time as a vulgar masquerade of a noble art form—and parody of the conventional ballet.

Although *Mercure*'s sets and costumes were long ago destroyed, there is plenty of documentary evidence, largely thanks to photographs from the original production. The images reveal pared-down sets and decorations devoid of traditional stage props. The overall effect is reminiscent of Picasso's two-dimensional works from that time. For Picasso all pictorial situations were theatrical. If painting can be likened to a stage set, then the stage for *Mercure* looked very much like one of Picasso's late cubist constructions, conceived in the spirit of formal experimentation and assemblage of forms. The performers were not so much dancing as sketching lines that moved through space. Furthermore, in some of the scenes, Picasso devised some mechanical elements that were interacting with live dancers. That is not to say that the two were one and the same thing, but they certainly coexisted and merged to form an eccentric vision of ballet.

The essay on Paul Klee addresses aspects of language, particularly the way in which the artist pursued the Romantic ideal of pure, transparent expression; a renewed search for truth and innocence that sets Klee apart from his contemporaries, including his friends at the Bauhaus. If this ideal was somewhat elusive, it was nevertheless worth pursuing as a way of counterbalancing all learned

21

skills, those that were felt to be restricting the growth of one's imagination and freedom.

Yves Klein, the subject of the next essay, was at heart a Romantic too, even though his art was cloaked in futuristic appearance. The search for a holistic experience and his desire for a radical form of expression through the notion of the Void—emptiness as conceived in the Buddhist tradition—were not devoid of Romantic aspirations. Klein conceived of art as a ritual rooted in ancient sacrificial cults that had to be repeated daily in order to bring about a sense of peace. Such art had not only aesthetic but also therapeutic goals. By looking at his work, I chose to emphasise ritual—which Klein would have experienced in his judo practice before becoming an artist—as a point of entry into the Void. The scenarios he wrote for the publication *Dimanche* are expressions of specific rituals that one could imagine and perhaps act out, just as other forms of ritual-inspired gestures are allowed to coalesce into his trademark *Anthropométries*, *Feux* and *Cosmogonies*.

I was a teenager when I first saw Ed Ruscha's drawings. Their poetic quality appealed to me instantly. Much later, during an exhibition of works on paper I had curated for the Gallery at Windsor in Vero Beach,

I grew more interested in the conceptual aspects of art and language. It became clear to me that perhaps Ruscha's works were difficult to classify due to their multiple layers of meaning, somewhat reminiscent of the symbolist poetics conceived by Stéphane Mallarmé, albeit in late twentieth-century America. Ed Ruscha's famed gunpowder drawings from the Sixties offer stimulating visual paradoxes questioning the boundaries between art and language. In *Ribbon of Words*, it is the asymmetrical relationship between the two realms that forms the bulk of my investigation.

Two short essays are devoted to two very different artists—Jean-Michel Basquiat and Agnes Martin. The first was written as a summary of Basquiat's production as a printmaker. The silk-screens he produced around 1982 make striking use of a limited range of colour and surely deserve a wider recognition. In the second I reflect on the ethereal simplicity of Agnes Martin's art; her awareness of the spirit of modernism, yet removed from contemporary life.

The essay on Cy Twombly is perhaps more ambitious in scope. By examining his *Bacchus* paintings (2004), I emphasise the notion of movement, as fluid paint becomes a metaphor for the flux of existence. If

23

Twombly's multiple lines, with all their breaks and hesitations, manage to create fields of accumulated energy, once we remove ourselves from the image it becomes an object of meditation. Initially we perceive movement and then, perhaps, beyond the repetition of a continuous pattern, we see stillness.

But as visual objects, Twombly's paintings testify to something beyond the mere formal aspects to which I just alluded. For him, graphic marks are an expression of his emotional life, like a gathering of significant elements that permeate his consciousness, shards of extinct civilisations, Greek and Roman poetry, the landscape of his adopted Italy. In his early works, reality is abstracted and forms a matrix for increasingly free and instinctive markings. The picture's surface becomes a depository for multiple, accumulated fields of awareness, including trivial traces of writing taken from daily life and seemingly imperfect gestures. The obsessive scrawls of the *Bacchus* paintings reflect a desire to unearth the fragments of his own consciousness. In this sense his work is a kind of archaeology. As a form of excavation, it aims to reclaim and rewrite the deposits of this past, like salvaging fragments of writings from a vanished library.

If art, in a literal sense, can be written, as in Ruscha's word drawings and Twombly or Basquiat's graffiti-like scrawls, the history of art is constantly being rewritten. In the last few decades, a number of alternative narratives to those written by Douglas Cooper or Alfred Barr have emerged, derived from perspectives as varied as Marxism, psychoanalysis, anthropology or sociology. It is not my aim to challenge or even to rewrite such narratives, but simply to show that there is still room for educating the senses through the medium of writing and that a carefully considered probing of sensations could be conducive to reclaiming our understanding of twentieth-century art.

NOTES

1   Ludwig Wittgenstein *Lectures and Conversations on Aesthetics, Psychology and Religious Belief* ed Cyril Barrett. Oxford Blackwell 1966 p 11.

2   See for instance ibid pp 6–11.

PABLO PICASSO—*LES AVENTURES DE MERCURE*

La Nuit from *Mercure*

Danse de tendresse from *Mercure*

Signes du Zodiaque from *Mercure*

Mercure tue Apollon avant de ressusciter from *Mercure*

Danse des Grâces et Cerbère from *Mercure*

Le Bain des Grâces from *Mercure*

Fête de Bacchus from *Mercure*

Rapt de Proserpine from *Mercure*

PABLO PICASSO

LES AVENTURES DE MERCURE

A<small>FTER A SUCCESSION OF</small> ballets designed for
Serge de Diaghilev's Ballets Russes, Picasso embarked on yet another theatrical commission, this
time for Comte Étienne de Beaumont's "Soirées de
Paris"—a series of performances held in Paris in
1924. The premiere of *Les Aventures de Mercure* was
held at the Théâtre de la Cigale in Paris, a small
music-hall venue in Montmartre. It was also the occasion for Picasso to be reunited with Erik Satie and
Diaghilev's protégé Léonide Massine, his accomplices
from the ballet *Parade* (1917).[1] In the programme, the
storyline for *Mercure* was infamously described as a
series of *"Poses plastiques en trois tableaux"*, a new artistic form combining the human body's movement in
space with the body conceived as a pictorial surface.

37

THE WRITING OF ART

It presented Picasso with a perfect opportunity to permeate every aspect of the production with his post-cubist aesthetics.

With cubism, Picasso started dismantling the traditional separation between artistic modes of expression. *Papiers collés*, construction, sculpture, paintings and works on paper were manipulated in a variety of ways such that painting could become sculpture, as in the much later *tôles découpées* of the early Sixties. cubism allowed Picasso to experiment with techniques of assembling and rearranging all the elements within a painting or a drawing. At times, different artistic styles were made to coexist within the same work. This aesthetics of discontinuity was achieved through various techniques of assemblage, ways of transplanting things from their usual spaces to new, positions thereby creating incongruous relationships and offering metaphorical associations. Furthermore, assemblage allowed the artist to transform the meaning of objects by taking them out of context.[2] In creating cubism, Picasso gave himself the tools to develop novel ideas, including those for the stage.

In 1917, Jean Cocteau asked Picasso to work on *Parade* for Serge de Diaghilev's Ballets Russes. After listening to 'Trois Morceaux en forme de poire' ('Three Pieces in the Shape of a Pear') Cocteau also sought to enlist Erik Satie into the production. In the spirit of early modernism, Satie invented a sparse style of music called *musique d'ameublement*, a new genre with minimal structural change and clear sounds. Overall *Parade* and *Mercure* were conceived in the iconoclastic spirit of Satie's witty, ironic compositions.[3]

The idea of *poses plastiques* and *tableaux vivants* first appeared on the amateur and music-hall stage. This tradition involved static poses, stylised movement and a taste for the grotesque, all of which went on to inspire Picasso and Massine. *Mercure* was also devoid of any real narrative; instead, it was conceived as a slide show of scenes that were hardly connected, each one of them alluding to a different episode in the life of Mercure.[4]

In the early Twenties, Picasso and his wife Olga spent summers along the French Riviera. Among Picasso's most celebrated works from that period are his studies of bathers, goddesses, nymphs and other mythical Mediterranean beings. A certain formality characterises the figures lying or playing on the beach, so much so that they are made to look like actors in an antique play. In his drawings of bathers from that period the formal poses of the models seem to contradict the playfulness implied by the subject matter. Almost certainly inspired by antiquity, they anticipate the *poses plastiques* of *Mercure*.[5]

Picasso and Satie also derived inspiration for *Mercure* from the opulent balls staged by the aristocracy in Paris during the Twenties. In 1923, Étienne de Beaumont devised a ball under the title of "L'Antiquité sous Louis XIV", requesting that Massine choreograph a series of *tableaux vivants* in which guests were invited to take part. One of these scenes was 'La Statue retrouvée', the story of a statue coming back to life. Picasso designed the costumes while Satie provided the musical accompaniment. Strangely, there was practically no dancing involved. Instead, all of the action was focused on carefully choreographed entrées, often under the supervision of Cocteau or Christian Bérard.[6] These soirées culminated in Countess Pecci-Blunt's "Bal blanc" of 1930 with the guests imitating statues harking back to the Ancien Régime's taste for antiquity.[7]

Picasso's *Mercure* consisted of thirteen *tableaux vivants*, some lasting as little as thirty seconds.[8] Each tableau

40

Three Women by the Shore

Three Nudes Reclining by the Shore

evokes a different aspect of *Mercure* in Greek and Roman mythology. The first part starts with a night scene, in which the dancers actually moved around with placards marked "*étoile*" (star) instead of an actual rendering of the night, followed by a love scene between Apollo and Venus. Subsequently Mercure appears, killing and then reviving Apollo with his caduceus. The second part opens with the famous bathing scene in which the three Graces come out of a pool. Mercure is then seen stealing their pearls while being chased by the wild hound Cerberus. In the last part, Bacchus hosts a party in which Mercure, Pluto, Proserpina and Pulcinella feature, and where the guests even dance a nostalgia-tinged polka—perhaps a throwback to the pre-war era. With the help of Chaos, Pluto kidnaps Proserpina and leads her to Hades.

The premiere was held at the Théâtre de la Cigale on 15th June 1924. Henri-Pierre Roché, in his account, writes that shouts and clapping and a generally agitated, boisterous crowd drowned out Satie's music.[9] Apart from Beaumont's aristocratic friends and Picasso's followers there was an outspoken fringe of supporters of the surrealists who disapproved and subsequently tried to shout down the entire performance.

43

They were opposed to it because proceeds were going to benefit widows of soldiers killed during the Great War. It was generally perceived as right-wing propaganda. The police were called in to restore order. However, André Breton quickly apologised to Picasso whom he considered a most valuable friend.

In *Mercure*, Picasso radicalises some of the ideas that could already be found in *Parade*. Foremost among them, he treats the stage not as a three-dimensional construction, with the illusion of depth that the theatre stage usually affords, but as a flattened space, almost devoid of perspective, with a few layered elements and a linear theme and impulse derived from his balletic drawings of the time. Let us consider several ballets that preceded *Mercure*. Firstly, *L'Après-midi d'un faune*, which was evoked by flattening the stage and emphasising horizontal movement across it, and which was also set in antiquity. Secondly, Paul Claudel's *L'Homme et son désir*, which was produced by the Ballets Suédois around 1921 with music by Darius Milhaud. Yet again, one finds hieratic horizontal movement, a night scene and the body being treated as sculpture. Finally, there are Cocteau's "spectacles", *Le Boeuf sur le toit* and *Les Mariés de la tour Eiffel* (for the Ballets

Suédois). In these works parody, caricature and the adaptation of film techniques such as the freeze frame and slow motion are all evident. Together they emphasise mimetic gesture and narrative action, leaving little space for dance.

Gertrude Stein, in her famous book on Picasso, saw in his preliminary designs for *Mercure* a revival of calligraphy with straight lines, arcs of geometry, and fluid sweeping lines, as well as an astrological theme with asterisk-shaped stars.[10] Some of the scenes consisted largely of calligraphy superimposed upon cut-out images.

The spectacle unfolded as a series of mostly static scenes—thirteen altogether—not unlike turning the pages of a photo album. The whole thing was about eight minutes long. Just like a photographic image, the scenes could be seen as arrested developments that freeze the appearance of things; they also achieve a temporal density of sorts. It is ironic that all that remains of *Mercure* as a performance is a set of photographs, since the decors and costumes were destroyed. The subtitle *Poses plastiques* takes into account the fact that Massine broke up the choreography into a series of fixed images reminiscent of the masked balls as well as entertainment like the Moulin Rouge and the Folies Bergère. There seems to be little cohesion or logic linking the various scenes Picasso chose from Beaumont's script. We should bear in mind that each scene was like a complete work in itself. The stage curtain, which still survives, represents Pierrot and Harlequin, and has little to do with the storyline of *Mercure*.

The dancers entered the stage in an eloquent manner, just as Beaumont and his friends were used to doing in their *bals costumés*.[11] Rather playfully, Picasso replaced the dancers in some of the scenes with moving mechanical parts made out of wood or bent wire. Cerberus appears in the shape of a moving cut-out amidst live dancers. The rape of Proserpina by Pluto takes place amidst a party scene with real guests, like a parody of Beaumont's masked balls, with the two main characters represented by elements Picasso had crafted in the shape of arabesques mounted on wheels.

According to Douglas Cooper, the static poses of *Mercure* were inspired by antique bas-reliefs and Etruscan drawings. Picasso first saw those during a visit to Rome and Naples with Diaghilev in 1917.[12] Each scene of *Mercure* featured a more or less harmonious ensemble with the dancers appearing on stage in the manner of a sculpted or drawn group.[13] Alternating between the burlesque and the sculptural, the dancers of *Mercure* offered a witty parody of the ballet.

The stage was framed by architectural elements made out of canvas, painted pale grey and white. The curtain at the back of the stage was plain, either black or white, depending on the scene. The overall aesthetic was pared down to simple colour schemes and sparse scenic elements. For instance, in the zodiac signs, Picasso made grey and white costumes to match the set. The sets had moving elements, such as mechanical arms, that made them akin to live dancers, while the actual dancers moved in a hieratic way inspired by antique statues and Greek drama. At the centre of the Night scene, there was a wooden structure, which represented a woman reclining on a divan. It had some mechanical elements, such as the woman's limbs being manipulated by strings like those of a puppet.

In the feast of Bacchus, Picasso displayed a playful mixture of seemingly unconnected elements, with Venus being carried by Chaos and an animated horse made out of wire. Apollo and Venus were dressed in white, wearing pleated skirts and blue tights. Each of the men making up Chaos were covered, from head to toe, in a single stocking: pale rose; sky blue; mauve; yellow; green; with the costumes designed by Picasso himself.

In his *tableaux vivants*, Picasso played with contradictions—an exaggerated stiffness, as in the unwieldy cardboard transvestites with red breasts, while still lifes were infused with movement and suppleness. By animating elements ranging from still lifes to figures, which could be defined as theatrical, Picasso managed to create the dramatic action that he desired. In the still lifes that he painted for his dealer Paul Rosenberg in 1924, one could already see the seeds of the frozen scenes that make up the *tableaux vivants* of *Mercure*. All objects looked corrupt and slightly unnatural, as if engaged in a performance.[14]

All the elements of *Mercure* contributed to undermining conventions leading to dissonance, which was already a feature of *Parade*, its false gaiety and the deceptively simple, almost indigent, musical score by Satie. From the outset the spectator realised that *Mercure*'s creators were engaged in an exercise of demystifying conventions of live performance. Behind the mock-classical curtain (depicting two Harlequins tracing sweeping, undulating lines, where colour was nonetheless disconnected from the outlines), one discovered a set design consisting of movable elements such as panels, screens and the ubiquitous figures made out of wire and metal that could be manipulated and thus made to move from behind. These mesh-wire constructions were anticipated in a series of zodiac-like drawings with a similar graphic emphasis. Ultimately, classicism is impure, veering towards the baroque, at least in the Charleston dance that is reminiscent of Picasso's painting of 1921, *Three Musicians*. Hieratic, artificial, cloaked in exaggerated rigid gestures, rhetorical in their frozen expressions, as if to inflict permanent damage upon the neoclassical mode of which Picasso had clearly had enough, the actors of this drama laid bare the conventions of theatre, and furthermore those of reality as seen through its prism—since theatre made the reality of everyday situations explicit. It should be added that in many of Diaghilev's ballets of the Twenties one notes dissonance and also what Lynn Garafola has called "an intentional juxtaposition of the incongruous", a Charleston dance in *pointe* shoes, muses in flapper dresses, or a Parnassus crowned with putti.[15]

If the mocking spirit of *Mercure* is reminiscent of *Parade*, the convention of the illusionism of theatre, made to look like a world compressed and reduced to an all-encompassing totality, exposed what was a mere formal and arbitrary device. Later in life, Picasso declared—"For me, painting a picture is to get involved in a dramatic action during which reality gets torn to bits. This drama sweeps it along over all other considerations. The three-dimensional act is only secondary as far as I'm concerned. What matters is the drama of the act itself, the moment where the universe escapes only to encounter its own destruction."[16] It seems that this drama was attainable. Sometimes the scene was painted in the antique manner, the artist never failing to introduce a corrupting element—a slight disfigurement of the face, a sudden shift in perspective, the painting of exaggerated limbs in monumental paintings, such as in *Femmes à la fontaine*, lines running all in the same direction in some of the beach drawings. By introducing an element of discontinuity in a seemingly classical scene, reality is indeed torn apart (*"la réalité se trouve déchirée."*)

Furthermore, the cubist experiment, carried through in the groundbreaking work for the stage, allowed Picasso to assemble and dismantle all the elements of his craft until creation and destruction were revealed to be symptoms of the same basic impulse. If dance is synonymous with creation and regeneration, in the painting from 1925, *La Danse*, the convulsive, frenetic action of the left-hand figure can be seen as a metaphor for the creative impulse—one that contains the seeds of disintegration and rebirth. A few months later Picasso offered the beholder a presence that contained the promise of drama—a ritualised fragmentation of the body reduced to a scaffold of bones (as in his surrealist drawings from the Dinard sketchbook of 1927); the body transformed, mutilated, distorted and dismembered. Perhaps the first signs of this dismantling of the human body can be seen in *Mercure*: first in the curtain of Pierrot and Arlequin, in which the artist made a point of dissociating colour from contours around the figures; secondly in the wire and metal figures—ersatz bodies fragmented into numerous virtually independent elements, yet infused with a playfulness reminiscent of the astrological line drawings.

Reality needs to be torn apart—Picasso said that harmony was not necessarily interesting, rather what mattered was a convincing representation of reality (he appealed to the concept of *"écarts"*), one that could include distortions and emphasis on particular aspects of the visible. With *Mercure*, the reality that was being taken apart was that of neoclassicism and the tradition of ballet—by necessity neoclassical—but also the relationship between the theatre stage and painting. The stage poked fun at painting, its rhetoric as embodied by gestures of the late eighteenth century and early nineteenth century. Through the flattening of the sets and decor, the stage becomes an animated painting. We are given the signs of a minimal theatrical presence. Just as the score by Satie embraced simplicity, and Massine's entrées were reduced to a few steps, Picasso's sets strove to erase the boundaries between stage and painting.

I have tried to look at *Mercure* within the context of the historical links between theatre and painting, two different forms of art that shared a common rhetorical purpose. Picasso offered proof that one could aspire to the condition of the other. In his late period, he kept showing that his paintings were a form of theatre, as in *Guernica* and the numerous *tableaux vivants* in his later works. The ritual and symbolic significance of representing various elements in a theatrical way held its promise for the rest of Picasso's life.

Drop curtain for *Mercure*

NOTES

1   It was Jean Cocteau who urged Picasso to work on *Parade*. The theme of *Parade* is that of a circus performance, reminiscent of popular vaudeville theatre. Cocteau conceived the fairground setting with a succession of burlesque scenes. Picasso's sets reveal a kind of cubist shorthand that stood in contrast to the neoclassical style of the drop curtain. A multitude of painted dots stood for the windows of New York's skyscrapers. Although the characters were inspired by the traditional *commedia dell'arte*, Picasso added two modern "managers" as well as a horse to Cocteau's original script, all looking like cubist-futurist constructions.

2   During his adolescence and early twenties, Picasso was increasingly drawn to the ways in which the artificial nature of a situation was represented and exposed. What may have appealed to him was the symbolic significance of representing various elements in a dramatic fashion, borrowing from a shared repertory of images inherited from a long tradition, including the popular theatre of his early Parisian years. Picasso also realised that theatre, stage decoration in particular, provided him with a metaphor for assembling his paintings and other works, a method he first devised for his cubist constructions.

3   Apart from *Relâche* (1924), film music for René Clair, written for the interval between the two parts of a ballet with decor by Francis Picabia, *Mercure* was to be Satie's last endeavour before his death.

4　See Ornella Volta *Satie et la danse*. Paris Éditions Plume 1992 p 78.

5　See for example *Groupe de quatre baigneuses* 1921. Christian Zervos *Pablo Picasso*. Paris Éditions Cahiers d'Art 1949–86 vol IV no 287.

6　Étienne de Beaumont's taste for costumed extravaganzas was the inspiration for Raymond Radiguet's famous novel *Le Bal du comte d'Orgel*. 'La Statue retrouvée' gathered Olga Khokhlova and Daisy Fellowes in Picasso's costumes. Ever since the *comédies-ballets* at the court of Louis XIV in which the King himself appeared in various guises, the idea of putting oneself onstage had appealed to the aristocracy.

7　Although Paul Poiret was the first to hold elaborate balls in Paris just before the First World War, Étienne de Beaumont organised them at his Hôtel de Masseran. Often complicated themes were devised by the host, such as historical figures under the reign of Louis XIV, Perrault's fairy tales, playing cards, mythical heroes or creatures of the sea. Other hosts followed suit, often outdoing each other in invention and pomp: Mimi Pecci-Blunt's "Bal blanc" in June 1930, Marie-Laure de Noailles with the "Bal des matières", the Faucigny-Lucinge "Proust" ball or Luisa Casati's "famous couples" ball.

8　*Mercure* was part of a series advertised by Beaumont as the "Soirées de Paris", a title borrowed from a magazine founded by the poet Guillaume Apollinaire. Although he never took any credit, it was Étienne de Beaumont who conceived of the plot—three mythological episodes in the shape of *tab-leaux vivants*, the style of which was inspired by the costumed balls that he had hosted a few years earlier. The overall atmosphere was that of a *fête foraine*, also in the spirit of the Folies Bergère.

9   See Henri-Pierre Roché *Écrits sur l'art*. Paris André Diman-che 1998 pp 296–8. Here is what Lydia Lopokova, who was asked but declined to appear in *Mercure*, wrote to John Maynard Keynes the day after the premiere—"*Mercury* to me seems a decadence, Picasso perhaps wanted to pull the noses of the public, the colours are very good but the way they brought on, or executed, or what they represented is beyond my measure of comprehension. It is no ballet, no parody, but somehow a stupid fake." Polly Hill and Richard Keynes, eds, *Lydia and Maynard—Letters between Lydia Lopokova and John Maynard Keynes*. London André Deutsch 1989 p 221.

10   See Gertrude Stein *Picasso*. Paris Librairie Floury 1938 p 129. As Picasso embarked on a collaboration with Diaghilev's Ballets Russes, an increased fluidity of line permeated his drawings, including many depictions of his ballerina wife, Olga Khokhlova. The flowing lines convey a sense of movement that seems to reflect his observations of a dancer's trajectory into space. A similar sense of freedom seeped through Picasso's large paintings from the mid-Twenties when he was asked to design the costumes and stage sets for *Mercure*.

11   In the nineteenth century, actors often studied famous paint-ings and sculptures to perfect their poses, to the extent that

their poses on the stage became static (as in Sarah Bernhardt's portrayal of *Phèdre*).

12 See Douglas Cooper *Picasso Théâtre*. Paris Éditions Cercle d'Art 1967 p 66.

13 Hence the series of drawings of the three Graces Picasso made while in Cap d'Antibes in the summer of 1923 bore a direct resemblance to the scene of the same subject in *Mercure*. See for instance *Three Nudes* 1923 illustrated in Zervos op cit vol VI no 828.

14 See for example *Mandolin and Guitar* 1924. Oil with sand on canvas, 140.6 x 200.4 cm. Solomon R Guggenheim Museum New York. Reproduced in Zervos op cit vol V no 220. See also Christopher Green, *Life and Death in Picasso—Still Life/Figure c1907–1933*. New York Thames & Hudson, 2009 pp 129–30.

15 Lynn Garafola, private correspondence with the author, 2011. I am grateful to Professor Garafola for her comments.

16 Françoise Gilot and Carlton Lake, *Life with Picasso*. New York McGraw-Hill 1964 p 59. I am grateful to Anne Baldassari for drawing my attention to this quotation.

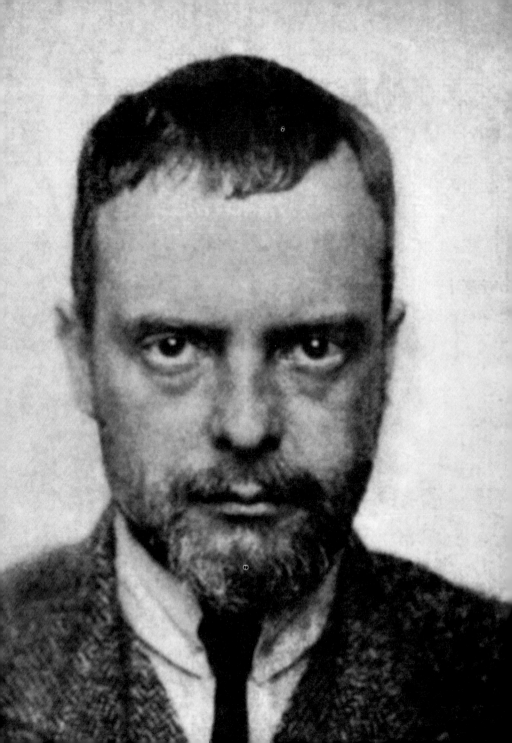

PAUL KLEE—IN SEARCH OF NATURAL SIGNS

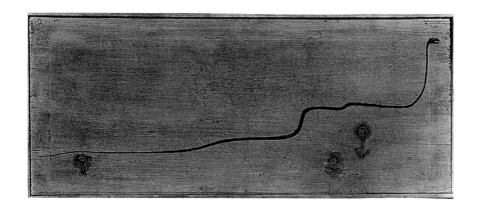

Die Schlange

PAUL KLEE—IN SEARCH
OF NATURAL SIGNS

T OWARDS THE END OF 1929, Paul Klee embarked on a two-week trip to Egypt. Travelling from Cairo to Luxor and Aswan, Klee was enraptured by the North African landscape. In the desert, the sun's intense rays seemed to envelop all living things, and at night, the movement of the stars felt even more palpable. In the architecture of the ancient funerary monuments Klee discovered a sense of proportion and measure in which human beings appeared to establish a convincing relationship with the immensity of the landscape; furthermore, he was drawn to the esoteric numerology that governed the way in which these monuments had been built.

Upon his return to Germany, Klee executed a series of paintings reminiscent of Egypt, including a little-known painting of a serpent deployed horizontally along the surface of a canvas (*Die Schlange, The Snake,*1929). The line it traces is fluid and slender, while its gaze is strangely self-absorbed, as if to suggest that it beholds magical powers. It inhabits regions close to the earth with nothing around it except for the burning sun high up in the sky. A handful of anaemic flowers are scattered along this barren ground; thirsty and impoverished, they seem to be longing for more auspicious forms of life.

During his time in Egypt, Klee became acquainted with ancient rites that conferred upon nature—plants, stones and living creatures—a magical and super-natural character. In ancient Egypt nature assumed a sacred character because it represented the eternal forces of the universe. The gods took the shape of sacred symbols with powers to dispel bad spirits, while animals were intermediaries between human beings and supernatural forces. Divine invocation was thought to be a way of influencing demigods. In the Book of the Dead, the serpent Apopis represents the forces of darkness and assumes a malevolent role by trying to prevent the sun's progress. Ancient Egyptians held the belief that a sense of order—the daily victory of the sun over darkness—could be maintained through rituals directed against Apopis; in funerary texts it is quite common to find depictions of Apopis being threatened by Re's warriors.

The artist's newfound simplicity of form, with its emphasis on graphic marks and fragments of a poetic shorthand, coincided with his attempt to do away with the complexity that had characterised his works from the Twenties. Once Klee had returned to the Bauhaus at Dessau from Egypt, he executed a series of watercolours in which horizontal stripes in different hues covered the entire surface of each sheet. Some of his other works also derived their inspiration from ancient Egyptian architecture and hieroglyphs.[1]

If ancient Egypt emphasised symbolic and mythical forms of thought, in the modern world such expressions of the magical link between human beings and the natural realm were no longer in fashion, having been replaced by scientific belief. Yet for centuries, various living creatures had been revered as quasi-divine symbols of nature. The serpent could be seen as the symbol of irrational forces. It is part of a more general process of the pagan worship of nature that is common to many ancestral belief systems.

Klee never ceased proclaiming his desire to be at one with nature. The trip to Egypt did much to reimmerse the Swiss painter in nature. To his students at the Bauhaus, he said—"The artist is a human being, himself nature and a part in the realm of nature". For Klee, the feeling of being at one with nature was born out of the "discovery of unsuspected relations from one element to another".[2] One may recall that he had assembled a collection of natural-history specimens—herbs, leaves, flowers, algae, moss, butterflies, stones and crystals—of which he studied the colour, shape and structure. He also dissected various plants or fruits in order to learn about their internal structure beyond exterior appearances. The vein of a leaf; the grooves of a tree's bark; a snail's shell—this vast dictionary of forms can be reproduced endlessly, providing a model of artistic creation to be manipulated through growth, repetition or extension.

Klee's desire to be in tune with the realm of nature coincided with his quest for greater innocence. Here he echoed the Romantics' preoccupation with trying to discover how painting could free itself of the weight of constricting traditions. By the end of the eighteenth century, Jacques-Louis David deplored the conventions of artistic education responsible, in his view, for the decline of the arts, while Joshua Reynolds proclaimed that it was necessary to relearn the craft of painting away from all stifling rules. For his part, Philipp-Otto Runge declared that in order to succeed, we had to become like children again. Could the artist reach a state of innocence and purity that would give an unmediated image of the world by turning his back on academic rules? Was language that was stripped of its arbitrary symbols not the most direct way of embracing the realm of nature?

During the course of the nineteenth century, it seemed as though the relation between man and nature had suffered a decisive blow. Nature was no longer felt to be innocent and it was uncertain whether it could be retrieved. This kind of disenchantment took many forms, not least the Baudelairean attitude according to which nature could no longer provide a refuge from the suffering of existence. Under the influence of Mallarmé's poetics, the following generation sought to redirect the experience of nature into an imaginary realm that was divorced from the immediate and present reality. Symbolism stressed feeling over intellect, suggestion over description. Above all, the work of art had to be evocative and emotionally resonant. According to this aesthetic stance, intuition was crucial to artistic practice, and one had to strive to communicate ideas and feeling derived from nature using the simplest of forms. When it came to depicting reality, the symbolists generally disdained anything too literal or too mimetic. Klee was deeply influenced by the belief that images did not simply depict something but were irremediably subjective and remained open-ended in their symbolism.

The discovery of the Rosetta Stone in 1799 had a profound impact on the first generation of Romantic artists. Runge saw living forms in the hieroglyphs, mysteriously conjuring up a vanished world that had not yet been deciphered. For the Romantics, hieroglyphs fulfilled their quest for a natural, spontaneous artistic language; one that turned away from the kind of history painting that had become so prevalent by the end of the eighteenth century. The appeal of hieroglyphs stemmed from the belief that these characters, which were transparent emblems of their own signification, revealed the last fragments of language in its natural state. (Novalis saw in hieroglyphs a sign of an intelligible unity between nature and God, word and image.)

The ways of articulating and signifying this form of writing were considered more immediate and accurate than any other representational system—form and symbol, signified and signifier were merged, as if the distinction between pure form and more or less conventional symbols had been erased. The sign was identical to what it referred to, and constituted its best formulation.

The dream of writing transparent signs, whereby even the untrained observer could grasp their meaning immediately, in which an icon in the shape of a snake stood for a snake, proved to be mere illusion. After all, hieroglyphs had to be deciphered, and only Champollion's discovery allowed this to become possible. The ancient Egyptian language was shown to be just as arbitrary as modern forms of language. If we accept that writing is altogether different from image-making, would it be possible for images to speak to us with the precision that characterises language? In other words, could images aspire to the condition of the written word? In 1915, Klee executed a drawing entitled *Dichter-Zeichner* (*Poet-Draughtsman*) in which the action of the draughtsman is likened to that of the creation of writing.[3] This drawing-poem is written on what appears to be a Chinese scroll. Here writing and drawing the likeness of an object are considered to be related activities. It is the act of writing that is important—the writing of symbols and signs that resemble objects. Taking this simile one step further, the *Schriftbilder* (*Word-Pictures*) from 1918 provide a visual expression to writing characters in order to merge form and content.

In the watercolour *Einst dem Grau der Nacht enttaucht* (*Once upon a Time in the Grey of Night*), each sign seems to waver between its mimetic function (as the letter of a readable text) and its expressive function (as an autonomous visual sign).[4] Here Klee acknowledges Braque and Picasso's cubism by turning away from imitation, thus proclaiming that painting and sculpture are forms of writing, symbolic modes of representation rather than distorted images of the exterior world. Klee realised that the Romantic project of a virgin, transparent writing could not be achieved; there were no transparent images of nature. (Novalis saw in the Egyptian script the sign of a unity between nature and God, word and image.) The materiality of the sign always interposed itself between the beholder and what he was looking at; the sign was condemned to retaining its autonomy within language. The relation between what the sign showed and what it meant was arbitrary; it was inscribed within a conventional semiological system.

So if the sign, given its simplest expression, such as a hieroglyph, was not as pure as the Romantics had hoped, could there not be another way of finding a novel language away from constricting traditions? Perhaps it is the flowing line—the arabesque—that provides a sense of that search for purity. For Klee, drawing in particular was like a seismograph that responded to his every inclination. The line functioned as a guide, in stark opposition to academic draughtsmanship. And perhaps the arabesque that the serpent of the 1929 painting described was a way of reaffirming the natural cohesion of things.

Such simplified means and compositions became a dominant feature in Klee's late oeuvre. *Blau-Vogel-Kürbis* (*Blue Bird-Pumpkin*) from 1939 is the deceptively simple depiction of a bird standing next to a pumpkin.[5] The image could well be seen as a cluster of signs, a graphic presence that verges on the abstract. The picture is an arrangement of hieroglyph-like symbols, rendered with thick black outline, reminiscent of the

THE WRITING OF ART

outline of archaic ancient Egyptian art. Forms such as birds and fruit are simplified abstractions reminiscent of ancient forms of notation. Although it would be difficult to deny that this process of abstraction is arbitrary, the mimetic element plays a role in constituting a sign. The image shifts between abstraction and representation. It is caught between two realms—as a symbol, but also as pure linear energy that finds its fulfilment in representation. If the motif is reduced to a mere sign, an element among others within the semiotic system, it gains added weight through the picture. Paradoxically, by adding a deep, radiant blue, the actual materiality of the picture is undermined, perhaps due to the artist disassociating contour (in black) from colour.

Although the image is framed conventionally, and presented in a formal manner, it is brought into the observer's field of vision with unusual, pervasive directness. It follows a standard organisation of the image-field as a rectangle. The thickness of the outline makes the bird look larger than it actually is. The pumpkin feels quite modest, yet the overall feeling is that the vibrating colours and black strokes are closer to us physically than in conventional easel paintings.

The distance between the observer and the painting narrows, gaining some form of immediacy—an unmediated quality of feeling for which the Romantics strove.

Klee's recurrent motifs—the arabesque, the hieroglyph—become ways of resurrecting the Romantic ideal of unity, connecting nature and man-made things. The natural world as it appears to our senses and the idealised vision of the artist are brought together. This art is intent on exploring the correspondence between the interior landscape of the soul and the desire to give a plausible image of nature. Klee offers us pictures of reality that probe deeper than the ordinary gaze. His paintings display signs that stand out among a multitude of other more mundane signs, which we experience on a daily basis; and their meaning is found somewhere between memories of things from the past and the writing that bears traces of them.

Blau-Vogel-Kürbis

NOTES

1   Several paintings by Klee can be traced back to hieroglyphic script, such as *Das Augenbeintier* (1922).

2   René Crevel, *Paul Klee*. Paris Gallimard, 1930, p 10.

3   *Dichter-Zeichner*, 1915. Pencil on paper, 24 x 15.4 cm. Paul Klee-Stiftung, Bern.

4   *Einst dem Grau der Nacht enttaucht*, 1918. Watercolour, pen and ink over pencil on paper, 22.6 x 15.8 cm. Paul Klee-Stiftung, Bern.

5   *Blau-Vogel-Kürbis*, 1939. Gouache on paper laid down on cardboard, 27.9 x 43.2 cm. The Metropolitan Museum of Art, The Berggruen Klee Collection, New York.

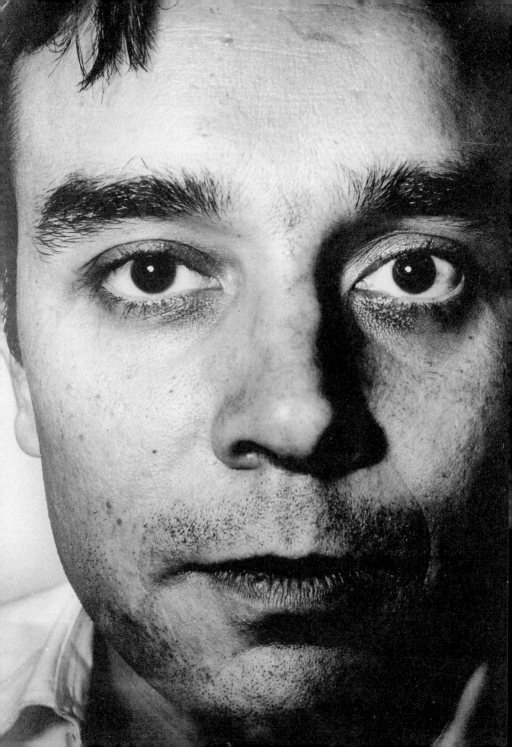

YVES KLEIN—THE VOID

Leap into the Void 5 rue Gentil-Bernard
Fontenay-aux-Roses October 1960.

YVES KLEIN—THE VOID

THIS ESSAY AIMS to explore a fundamental tension in Yves Klein's work, between the impulse to preserve ritual, linking the artist to a society where he fulfils a role that is not unlike that of a medium, and the dissolution of all worldly relations into the Void. We might ask whether, in terms of freedom (Louis Frédéric described his friend Klein as one who strove for total liberation), any kind of action—especially if it serves to maintain our sense of connection to the world—would not become irrelevant. How could we advocate this concept of the Void, whereby the artist sought emptiness—almost rendering all artistic rites that integrate mankind with society null and void—without provoking the end of art?

Yves Klein's conception of art was deeply tied to ritual but also offered a way of breaking from artistic

conventions. This emphasis on the profoundly subversive, transformational dimension of ritualistic activity would go on to permeate every aspect of his life
and creative output. In order to familiarise ourselves
with his work, we must interpret his view of art as
something that is never purely confined to the aesthetic realm, but also something that encompasses a
devotional—and spiritual—practice.

For Yves Klein, ritual activity was independent of
any particular religious belief system, although he
explored various spiritual disciplines including fringe
Catholic movements, judo and Eastern philosophy.
This came at a time when most artists had grown
weary of ritual with religious undertones. Nevertheless, the ways in which Klein enacted ritual affirmed
his spiritual and soteriological preoccupations. He
never slid into a detached, ironic attitude, but brought
instead an earnest and dedicated approach to his artistic praxis. Klein's interest in ritual took on a variety
of forms, though none was closer to his heart than
his commitment to judo.[1] Having spent nearly two
years in Japan studying judo from September 1952
to February 1954, he was aware of the philosophical
connection between martial arts and Zen Buddhism,

Anthropométrie

and the latter's search for emptiness may have played a key role in shaping his own interest in the notion of the Void.[2] Klein used martial arts to weave ritual into his artworks, which in turn allowed him to reassert his commitment to art through the repetition of codified actions. As we shall see, ritualised artistic activity gains significance by applying and codifying rules; it moves towards abstraction, not towards a specific set of beliefs.

Rather than focusing on a particular sign or an object, Yves Klein used pure colour as a starting point for his entire *oeuvre*. Colour functioned as a material and spiritual medium capable of inducing independent sensations and opening onto the boundlessness beyond the material surface of paintings. For Klein, blue became the symbol of the immaterial, the Void. It also helped him define his identity as an artist, so much so that he even tried to trademark it. To apply this deep ultramarine blue, Klein would employ a commercial roller used for house painting. Needless to say, such a gesture was not personal but mechanical and pure in that it carried no trace of any given identity. According to Emmanuelle Ollier, "Thus the act of painting requires a special ability to apply colour. To obtain areas of colour there has to be a certain mastery and manual control on the painter's part. This technique, which Klein developed, helped make the physical act of painting as detached as possible. The gesture had to be confident, rapid and spontaneous".[3] Years of practising judo had enabled Klein to use the human body—including his own—in a number of ways, so as to ensure that these works were executed with a great deal of precision. Judo also allowed him to objectify some essential aspects of artistic production.

In February 1960, Klein started using the human body as a living paintbrush, applying this monochrome blue onto nude participants whose smeared bodies would then be pressed against the surface of a white sheet of paper or a canvas. Klein called them the *Anthropométries*. Shortly after, in 1961, he created another series of works known as *Feux*, in which the act of burning a surface resulted in tarnished works of art.

In the *Anthropométries* Yves Klein devised a careful choreography of women leaving imprints of their bodies on the surface of the canvas. The precision of the artist's gesture was confounded by the uncontrollable mechanism of the model's body, which smeared the paint in ways Klein could not have foreseen. Not only was it a trace of that process, but it was also an action in time. In these works action does not refer to self-expression, which differentiates them from American action painting, but conforms instead to an existing practice; action is the result of codifying and applying rules defined by the artist.

The question of physical energy and movement, how such a transfer of energy could become the subject of a work of art, was particularly relevant to Klein's later *oeuvre*, including the *Anthropométries* and the *Feux*. As a highly codified ritual, this sense of movement could not have been conceived without an accompanying aesthetic dimension.

The slightly later *Cosmogonies* bear the hallmarks of natural events such as raindrops (a sheet of paper would be left outside overnight or affixed to the roof of his car while he drove in inclement weather). This was taken a step further with the *Feux*, in which the action of fire was cancelled or modified by that of water. The earliest ones, made in 1961, bore traces of soft-fire industrial burners. Later, Klein varied the effects by manipulating the intensity of the flame, playing with longer or shorter exposure times.[4] He also perfected a process in which the support (in the form of cardboard plaques) was primed with water and, in some instances, paint. Water was applied carefully during the combustion process, often with the help of a make-believe firefighter. In some of the *Feux* we can see the impact of water dripping down on the surface of the work before being consumed by the action of fire. In other works, Klein combined the *Anthropométries* with the *Feux* by asking his models— usually female—to leave wet traces of their bodies on the cardboard.

Yves Klein displayed a real talent for theatrics in his work. The execution of the *Anthropométries* was carefully staged and shown to the general public. In addition, he enjoyed devising original ideas such as the scripts making up his play of sorts known as *Théâtre du vide* (*Theatre of the Void*). It was to be staged on Sunday, 27th November 1960, and was advertised in the one and only issue of the mock newspaper *Dimanche* (an imitation of France's popular *Journal du Dimanche*).[5] Let us consider an example taken from one of the articles making up *Dimanche*, 'Projet pour un institut national théâtral' ('Project for a National Theatrical Institute'), which involved a group of spectators who "take an aptitude examination administered by a psychiatrist before being cleansed in a pool by young women."[6] They were to be taken to a sauna and then to an oxygen chamber where their sense of touch was to be stimulated by feeling the bodies of nude men and women through holes in the walls. Touching bodies through a hole in the wall was meant to reduce an actual visual registration of the body's boundaries and to draw instead on a sensation that brought to light an almost subconscious awareness of the sexual possibility of merging bodies. The ensuing period of artificial sleep relied on the unconscious aspect of the ego, as it appeared to go beyond the intellectual to the vital essence within. The participants were then to be thrown outside violently, showered and fully clothed. Their transformation echoes Klein's own sense of rebirth in another piece from *Dimanche*, 'Capture du vide' ('Capture of the Void'). That this process of psychological and physical purification assumed the guise of a ritual bathing offers further proof that the devotional aspect of Klein's work is not really tied to a particular religious doctrine.

In the *Anthropométries*, the art of Yves Klein is like the process of soaking something up utterly—both in the literal sense, as in sponges being soaked in blue pigment, and in the figurative sense. On the one hand, the body is a sponge, but when it does not soak up paint, it is also an impermeable surface. Everything in this work is striving towards a totality, which becomes ineluctable, and so everything is blue, or is thought to be blue. (In Buddhist Tantra, this technique is referred to as *laya yoga*. *Laya* can be translated as "absorption" and refers to increasingly refined states of matter that lead the practitioner towards absolute bliss.) The article from *Dimanche* entitled 'Capture du vide' highlights Klein's own missionary goals. In this text, he recounts a situation in which all the inhabitants of a city returned home and locked themselves in; outside, there was no one, until Yves Klein was thrown "into the Void" by his friends.[7] As someone who was enlightened and had created a void as the extension and greater part of himself, Yves Klein's disappearance into the Void presaged the goal of all those who followed him. It is important to see this story in terms of Klein's description of his monochromes, the *Anthropométries*, *Feux* and

87

even monopinks, each of which was made with the idea that they would eventually become his trademark blue—that they would all become monochrome in the end. In the same way, Klein used 'Capture du vide' to show that ultimately, one could capture the inhabitants of any city or country through the "void" of their own actions.

The dream of the Void is the dream of dying temporarily and leaving the everyday world and then being reborn as an entirely different being, one that represents freedom and release. Yet liberation, it seems, is rarely given to us once and for all; rather, it is a path towards release, which constitutes the state of release itself. The notion of absorption provides a metaphor for this gradual progression towards release and the steadying of the mind. As in the gradual soaking of all things into Klein's blue, our consciousness stops making distinctions and reaches a point where the colour blue sheds its materiality. Klein's ultimate goal was to create such saturation through colour. His blue certainly has a metaphorical character. It invites the world of everyday objects to recede from our consciousness by merging them into a seamless unity, a dream that the work of art is capable of enacting.[8]

In Yves Klein's discussion of levitation (such as in *Dimanche*), it seems the only obstacle standing in his way was his attachment to the earthly artistic ego that defined him. The struggle to let go of this ego preoccupied him until the end of his career, so much so that as he neared death he said he would only be making pneumatic sculptures. Once he shed his shell, he would exist only as the Void, which, as he saw it, was the non-existence of those of us he called "the living dead". His struggle to relinquish his artistic ego in order to achieve levitation—and ultimate oneness with the Void—took many forms, especially since he used rollers or living paintbrushes to distance himself from displaying any trace of a personal style. He was attempting to leave behind his exasperated ego. Once he had wholly embraced the Void, he could no longer exist as an artist, and since his art had merged with his life, he could not exist without it.

In another piece from *Dimanche*, entitled 'Du vertige au prestige' ('From Dizziness to Prestige'), Klein devised a performance in which he would free himself from the enslavement of gravity—represented in traditional sculpture by pedestals—by rising a few metres above the stage for a little under ten minutes.[9] This passage from *Dimanche* illustrates the important role levitation played in the thinking behind Klein's paintings, sculptures and performances. Levitation—the artist's flight towards weightlessness—is a metaphor for the artist releasing himself from the ego, and as his aerostatic sculptures demonstrated, Klein developed a literal space between the lived world of the contained ego and the utopia of the Void represented by the absence of ego. Through levitation, the artist hoped to straddle two poles of a contained and dissolved self corporeally, while setting an example for the viewer.

A well-known essay by Klein entitled 'Le Dépassement de la problématique de l'art' ('Overcoming the Problematics of Art') raises questions about how we are to go beyond the work of art itself.[10] The question is really one of boundaries. The ritual engagement with art offered the promise of freedom and release and thus the realisation of the Void. But once the Absolute was reached, art was no longer necessary, and would have to be discarded like the rest of human activities. Perhaps the Void's logical consequence was the end of art.

In other words, the work of art only fulfilled its mission to some extent. Yet what Klein truly wanted, as an artist, was to overstep the object as a physical trace of mental processes. It is remarkable that he

90

realised how that could have helped him re-enact a creative gesture in the first place. Yet the certainty or possibility of release came about only once the artist had realised that overstepping had been the result of a precarious equilibrium. To come to this conclusion, the artist had no other choice but to carry on with his artistic practice.

The Void implies some kind of renunciation that at first glance contradicts man's obligation to perform rituals. Indeed, inaction would seem to be the Void's logical conclusion. Yet we can see how the Void can enjoin the artist to continue his actions, to take responsibility for them, while distancing himself from them. He does so by seeing them for what they are, namely social duties. Yet Klein realised that if these activities were performed correctly, they could reinforce his belief that art was worth making. Therefore, with a requisite degree of detachment and selflessness, ritual could become an instrument of freedom.

Feu: FC 5

NOTES

1 Emmanuelle Ollier has patiently reconstructed the links
between judo and Yves Klein's work. Klein discovered the
martial art in his late teens and only gave up the rigorous
practice—and teaching—of it when towards the end of his
life his health began deteriorating. By the early Fifties, he
was already travelling to Japan and immersing himself in
the study of judo. Klein's devotion to judo culminated in the
publication of his book *Les Fondements du judo* in 1954, which
focuses on the katas of this martial art. "A kata is a form, a
mould," according to Ollier. "It designates a sequence of
technical moves that unfold according to a fighting plan
executed against one or several adversaries attacking from
different angles. It is usually performed with one partner and
comprises holds, throws and immobilisations". It is not surprising that, as gestures with a distinct aesthetic dimension,
Klein would emphasise the katas, which supply the essential
moves of judo. Not only did they give him a way to take
the body—his own body—as a starting point for his artistic
practice, but they also provided him with a sense of technical
virtuosity, an aesthetic sense of movement, and an economy
and efficacy of means. As Ollier observes, the kata succeeds
in "being the mould into which man begins to pour himself,
in apparent rigidity, the better to free himself of it and recre-
ate himself". An individual's practice grows by repeating
specific movements which offer him or her the opportunity
to become enlightened, bestowing upon such an individual

a structure that permeates the core of his or her being. See Emmanuelle Ollier, *Yves Klein—Artiste-peintre et judoka* (MA thesis). Grenoble 2002 pp 16 186.

2   For a discussion of Yves Klein, judo and Zen, see Sidra Stich, *Yves Klein* (exhibition catalogue). London Hayward Gallery 1995 pp 39–40.

3   Ollier op cit p 191.

4   All in all, he produced well over one hundred *Feux* between 1961 and his death the following year, not counting the *Feux-couleur* in which he combined painting and burning techniques.

5   *Dimanche—Le Journal d'un seul jour.* Paris, 27th November 1960.

6   Stich op cit p 212.

7   Ibid p 211.

8   "The picture is only the witness, the sensitive plate that has seen what happened. Colour in its chemical state as used by all painters is the medium most capable of being struck by the 'event'. Therefore I can say—my pictures represent poetic events or, rather, they are immobile, mute, static witnesses to the very essence of that movement and that free-running life that the poetic flame embodies during the pictorial moment." Yves Klein, 'L'aventure monochrome', in *Le Dépassement de la problématique de l'art et autres écrits*, ed Marie-Anne Sichère and Didier Semin. Paris École Nationale Supérieure des Beaux-arts 2003 p 230.

9   See Stich op cit p 212.

10   See Klein op cit pp 80–117.

ED RUSCHA—
RIBBON OF WORDS

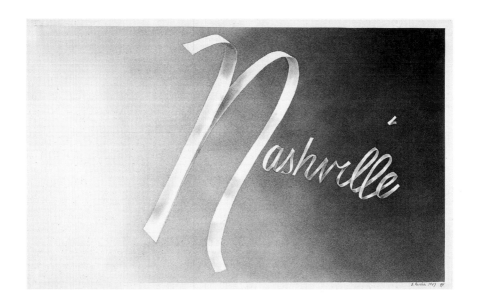

Nashville

ED RUSCHA—RIBBON OF WORDS

O VER THE PAST FOUR DECADES, Ed Ruscha has been painting and drawings words. At first sight, such a seemingly narrow focus on the relation between the pictorial and the literal may be puzzling. In Ruscha's own words, "it seems difficult to untangle the relationship between art and language".[1] How do we actually "read" or perceive the word-pictures, as language or as aesthetic objects? I will look at the play of these contradictory aspects—apparent visual paradoxes—that are embedded in Ruscha's work, only to argue that there remains a sense of continuity within our field of vision. But within the flashing forth of contradictory aspects—as words to be read or as aesthetic objects—there emerges a space for a new kind of object, one that cannot be characterised in terms of exclusive alternatives. Rather, the artist moves away from the traditional conception of the work of art as a purely aesthetic object. With Ruscha's word-pictures, poetic utterances shed their material body in order to inscribe themselves within the context of the modern world of media and advertising.

Ed Ruscha's early years are now the stuff of legend—born in Nebraska and raised in Oklahoma, he arrived in Los Angeles in the early Sixties and studied graphic design and painting at the Chouinard Art Institute. His first exhibition took place at the Ferus Gallery in 1963. He quickly made his mark by fusing seemingly unconnected sources such as Pop Art, commercial design, Marcel Duchamp's *objets trouvés* and surrealist paintings. Visual stimulus came from the urban landscape of Southern California. Its highways seemed to build a flat, repetitive scene littered with road signs and the occasional billboard. Automobiles, gasoline stations, street furniture, some scattered palm trees—the greater Los Angeles landscape displayed a steady and pervading uniformity, inescapable when seen from the road, all the more impressive as speed and movement amplified its monotony. Highways unfolding like ribbons, customised cars, cheap Hollywood dreams on candy-coloured billboards—a spirit of relentless image-making and recycling informed Ruscha's early paintings and drawings. There was no need for the artist to dig deep if he could make use of preconceived, seemingly weightless images, of everyday words that popped up along the road or re-emerged through memory. Words, often glimpsed through the ubiquitous car's windshield, asserted their presence as horizontal objects underscoring the repetitive flatness of the urban landscape.[2]

Words started appearing in Ruscha's paintings and drawings from the early Sixties onwards. They were often single words, like "Ruby" or "Trust" or "Promise", later followed by slogan-like expressions that seemed to float in an ethereal, atmospheric space, in a manner that was reminiscent of the studio penumbrae found in academic painting. Some images are suggestive of vast expanses of space, albeit hazy. Others, such as the "Liquid Words" series from 1967, sit on flat, ductile surfaces. Ruscha's various design schemes are suggestive of the techniques of graphic design, bearing witness to his fondness for illustration; technique is the foundation for what is only loosely representational. Or to put it differently: representation is given to the viewer through the prism of commercial

101

image-making devices, a kind of technical shorthand that produces highly artificial images. Ruscha was fond of experimenting with unusual media, such as black-berry juice and egg yolk, or gunpowder. In the mid-Seventies, Ruscha's drawings involved longer, more elaborate word sequences, often with a witty edge to them—*Chili Draft, Hollywood is a Verb*—done in the cool manner of sans-serif typography, thus giving the "printed" word the utmost impact. Here background suggests an empty space, and the black gunpowder is so rich as to confound the viewer's ability to imagine, let alone perceive space. Ruscha's works from the Sixties display a cinematic quality that runs like a thread through his career (he directed two films in the Seventies). A more recent series of drawings features the words "The End" apparently behind a foreground of calculated imperfections—a witty allusion to the scratches on celluloid. In Ruscha's recent paintings, words are superimposed over postcard-perfect views of snowy peaks (the Rockies or the Himalayas), the landscape conveying an idealised view of nature, bor-dering on kitsch. Such a background is just as manu-factured, illustrational, as in Ruscha's earlier works, acting like a stage set.

Words become objects—and as objects, they are lifted from an environment in which all words compete for maximum impact, like road signs along the highway seen by a driver. How much time are we prepared to give them? What is glimpsed through the windshield is quickly forgotten, only to reappear, perhaps in a predictable way, elsewhere. This indicates that Ruscha's works stem from an overwhelming and relentless parade of images and signs that make up the Southern California landscape. Visual data becomes omnipresent, each tiny element competing for our attention. There is a clear shift, whereby the notion of representation is secondary only to that of decontextualisation. Just like Duchamp invented the "readymade"—found objects that were given the status of artworks—Ruscha borrows "found" words that he rescues from the seemingly endless stream of information. That is not to say that words have lost their roots or the power of the very environment from which they were removed. In this sense, the analogy with Duchamp is ambiguous, as found words tend to behave differently from found objects.

It is now obvious that the words "depicted" by the artist behave in a variety of ways. Some, such as *Sea*

103

of Desire have slogan-like qualities that are suggestive of advertising, reminiscent of billboards; others, like "Punk", are American vernacular and live in a space that is cinematic (as is often the case with Ruscha); a work from 2009 proclaims "The greatest ride of my life was about to come up" (a quotation from Jack Kerouac's *On the Road*). It has an iconic quality, suggestive of the American counter-culture of the Sixties, conjuring up not so much the written page as perhaps a line from *Easy Rider*.

In Ruscha's pictures, words are clearly derived from everyday life; they are fragments encountered by chance, or at least, they do not intend to convey anything of a deeply personal nature. To a certain extent, as far as the individual is concerned, this rules out any notion of words as a means of self-expression; rather, what is at play here is writing that adapts and transforms language already used by others. In the case of Ruscha, the artist's activity is not to compose sequences of words but to reproduce and thereby transform them—just as graphic design replicates existing patterns. The "found words" are redirected by the artist towards a medium where they command a different kind of attention—that of the work of art.

THE GREATEST RIDE
IN MY LIFE
WAS ABOUT TO
COME UP

The Greatest Ride

Cut Lip

Now let us look specifically at some of the words
and expressions used by Ruscha. As a starting point,
we could say that in these pictures, words emanate
from an array of sources. Some are rather obscure
expressions—the word "Dude", for example, was
American vernacular slang when Ruscha used it in
the Sixties, and not common currency. Words such
as "Hollywood"—which is a synecdoche for an entire
culture—are imbued with iconic powers. Some words
or clusters have narrative meanings attached to them,
as in the use of quotations from Shakespeare or Jack
Kerouac. They have many ways of asserting their
presence, on the written page and on the picture
surface.

Apart from the obvious fact that words are made
into objects, as in the ribbon series of the mid-Sixties,
words in Ruscha's pictures are bent towards a variety
of meanings, not necessarily linguistic ones. Ruscha
offers a considerable variety of words, not just single
words (and not just nouns, but also prepositions,
such as "Of"), but slogans, catchphrases ("Let's be
realistic"), quotations ("Words without thoughts
never to heaven go"). Ruscha acknowledged the
irreducible variety of linguistic expressions, never

forcing his word-drawings to become paradigmatic, interchangeable expressions.

In Ruscha's works from the late Sixties, ribbons of words float ethereally in the picture space again and again. These ribbons are depicted as paper unfolding in the shape of words. To the artist, these ribbons offered the same sense of direction and movement as Los Angeles's maze of streets and highways. All words—such as *Self, Promise, Cut Lip* or *Cherry*—are thus transformed into ribbon-like structures that makes them into objects.

There is a fundamental ambiguity at the heart of these pictures—they involve perceptual issues, as the works function equally well as a visual thing (an "image" or an "icon"), but also as a verbal thing or a statement. The artist said—"I like the idea of a word becoming a picture, almost leaving its body, then coming back and becoming a word again".[3] These word-pictures are both words and pictures, without forcing the beholder to ask which side is winning the contest over the other. In some rather isolated cases one aspect dominates the other. For instance, in some ribbon-like drawings such as *Palm* (1970), the ribbon unfolds in such eccentric ways that it renders the word it forms almost illegible; before we can decipher the word, we are aware of the ribbon as an aesthetic object. We see a ribbon, and realise that it is a ribbon in the shape of letters. On the other hand *Scales of Justice* (1975) offers little of the presence of an object; rather, the stark black background accentuates the impact of words even further; past embellishments are banished. But these are perhaps extreme cases, as most works seem to occupy Ruscha's centre stage as words and images.

Of course these images can be read as one or the other, as in Wittgenstein's famous duck-rabbit paradox. Not only is Ruscha keenly aware of the multidimensional nature of the works, but he draws upon the asymmetrical relationship between words and visual symbols, as in the drawing entitled *Pool* (1968)—certainly a good example of an arbitrary sign, but then the artist blurs the line by introducing a naturalistic element, drawing the letters making up "Pool" in the shape of liquid puddles, thus alluding to the presence of water in both linguistic and visual realms. In general, Ruscha himself recognised that "there are no rules to observing the drawing".[4] Shifting perceptions come to the fore as soon as the beholder switches from reading the words to perceiving them as objects. A more global and continuous perception of the work as word and object emerges over time.

One could think of Ruscha's word-pictures in terms of resonance. This is true in a literal sense. Yve-Alain Bois, in his essay on Ruscha's *Liquid Paintings*, introduces the idea of the word paintings as inscriptions to be read aloud.[5] And on the subject of his works from the late Sixties, Siri Engberg wrote—"Like his drawings from the period, such as *Pool* (1968), Ruscha's first Tamarind prints used single words—'Rodeo', 'Anchovy', 'Mint', 'Carp'—chosen as much for their evocative power as for their phonetic quality".[6] The word projects its own vibration. The French symbolist poet Stéphane Mallarmé laid special emphasis on the suggested meaning of words, referring to the symbolist conception whereby the poet is capable of liberating words from their everyday usage.[7] The symbolists realised that artistic forms had meanings that were not directly connected to the things they depicted. Instead, meanings are dependent upon the functioning of the image as a whole. The artist insisted—"It is important to think that the drawing should not reflect the meaning of words."[8] It would be too facile to paint the word "Hot" in red, for example.

110

Pool

Hollywood

Like Mallarmé, Ruscha espoused notions of ano-
nymity; the emphasis on graphic design allows for
some traces of authorship to vanish. Mallarmé embraced the notion of literary products that were not
tied to a name and an author. (He even went as far
as to disapprove of bookshop windows displaying
the latest novels, likening them to a false glorification
of writers.) But perhaps even more significantly, the
French symbolist poet viewed the written page as a
multifunctional object—visual, commercial, literary,
social and material. His poems allowed for alternative
meanings, which were not evident. He produced a
series of short poems written on fans, which served as
poetry and aesthetic objects. With the flashing back
and forth between these two aspects, one could argue
that this movement is analogous to the actual oscillat-
ing movement of the fan. As we saw, Ruscha's works
are also at the crossroads between different realms of
experience. In this respect they are firmly inscribed
within contemporary society, not as static objects to be
contemplated, but as things that find their place within
other forms of life, that are part of a range of usages.

The word-pictures allow us to think of the work
as something beyond mere object. This is due to

language's fluidity; its capacity to be embedded in a variety of media, from the printed page of the book to TV screens, computers and billboards, as well as in artworks. As Ruscha developed a habit of collecting words while on the road or travelling, it is not surprising to see that some of the works have the allure of billboard signs. He displaced language by making pictures out of words—mental objects of sorts.

The poetic quality of Ruscha's pictures lies in their irreducible nature, their resistance to being categorised in any shape or form. We might offer a description of isolated aspects that come to the foreground—surfaces, words and objects. Such exercises can be rewarding. But once we are no longer tempted to see these images as one particular thing or another, and we let them sink into our consciousness, they will have fulfilled their promise. The work exists differently, not only in relation to other commodities, but also as language temporarily embedded in objects. As such it is open to new possibilities. It may succeed in displacing the object within discourse and within the sphere of societal activity. "Hollywood" is a place that becomes a sign that becomes an *objet trouvé* to which the artist comes back ever so often. Impurity and irony creep in. Words also become fiction. Ruscha emphasises their unique visual, graphic and phonetic characteristics; what we might call the existential experience of the word. Ultimately, Ruscha's works offer the conclusion that our cognitive understanding of the world is permeated by language.

NOTES

1   Ed Ruscha in conversation with the author Venice CA 2003.
2   While working on his early paintings and drawings—such as the series of Los Angeles apartments from 1965—Ruscha was also creating a series of beautifully manufactured books. Through these "travelogues", he gathered photographic data. *Every Building on the Sunset Strip* (1966) exemplifies this approach and shows the young artist's talent for transforming the most ordinary landscapes—a mile-long section of Sunset Boulevard—into an imaginary, almost cinematic space.
3   Ed Ruscha Lecture at the Getty Center Los Angeles 17th July 1998. Quoted in Siri Engberg, 'Out of Print', in Siri Engberg and Clive Phillpot eds *Edward Ruscha—Editions 1959–1999 Catalogue Raisonné* vol II New York 1999 p 14.
4   Ed Ruscha in conversation with the author.
5   Yve-Alain Bois, 'Thermometers Should Last Forever', in *Edward Ruscha. Romance with Liquids—Paintings 1966–1969* (exhibition catalogue). New York Gagosian Gallery 1993.
6   Taken from an interview with Howardena Pindell that appeared in *The Print Collector's Newsletter* (January–February 1973) quoted in Engberg op cit p 23.
7   The connection between Mallarmé and Ruscha was first established by Yve-Alain Bois. Bois stresses the recontextualisation of words through typography. See Bois op cit pp 15–20.
8   Ed Ruscha in conversation with the author.

SOME NOTES ON JEAN-MICHEL BASQUIAT'S SILK-SCREEN PRINTS

Untitled (from Leonardo) one of five

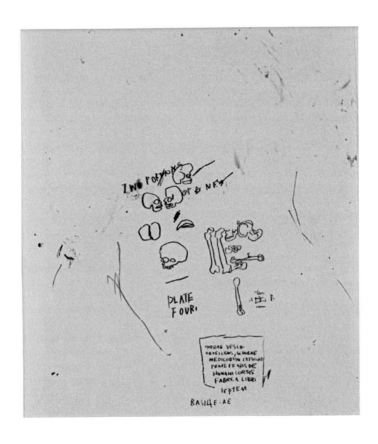

Untitled (from Leonardo) two of five

Untitled (from Leonardo) three of five

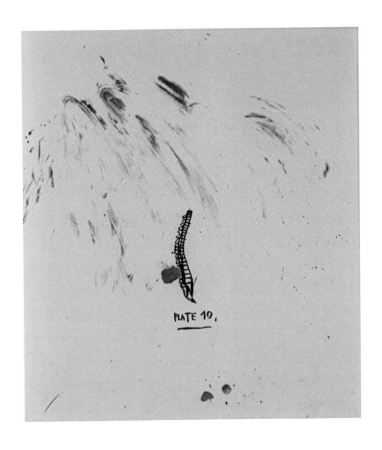

Untitled (from Leonardo) four of five

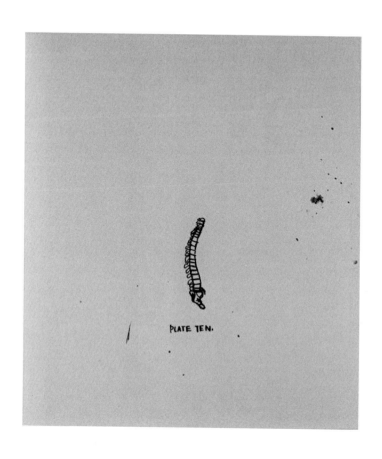

PLATE TEN.

Untitled (from Leonardo) five of five

SOME NOTES ON JEAN-MICHEL
BASQUIAT'S SILK-SCREEN PRINTS

F ROM THE LATE SEVENTIES up until his premature death in 1988, Jean-Michel Basquiat depicted subjects related to his experience of growing up in New York. These included images that harked back to his childhood, such as cars, planes, skyscrapers, policemen, black heroes, children's games, cartoons, comics, graffiti, pervasive symbols such as ©, or images common in storybooks such as the crown. This latter symbol asserted his authority, in a somewhat sarcastic manner, and his glorified status in the art world.

Basquiat was seven years old when he was run over by a car as he was playing in the streets of East Flatbush in Brooklyn. He suffered a broken arm and had his spleen removed. He was forced to remain at King's County Hospital for a month, where he studied

Gray's Anatomy—a book his mother had given him—in great detail. It made a lasting impression on him and went on to influence his later works. He also named his rock band Gray after it.

In 1982, Basquiat started to include body fragments in his paintings, as in *Portrait of the Artist as a Young Derelict*, which portrays, among other things, the artist's ankles.[1] It was during the same year that he unravelled the traumatising memories of his childhood through a series of drawings that were soon made into prints by his art dealer, Annina Nosei, in collaboration with the printmaker Jo Watanabe. Watanabe—who was renowned for his meticulous work with some of the best-known minimalist artists such as Robert Ryman and Sol LeWitt—transformed these drawings into crisp, animated prints through the process of photographic transfer. Each of the one-colour silk screens was the reversed image of the original black-crayon-on-white-paper drawings.

Anatomy, a portfolio of eighteen screen prints, was published in 1982. Each plate depicts what could be an anatomical fragment or dismembered limbs that have been drawn with some degree of artistic freedom, and is usually strewn with words, something of which

Basquiat was fond. One example is an illustration of a skull that is surrounded by a series of medical terms such as "great wing of sphenoid"; "nasal"; "notch"; "spine"; "styloid process"; and "zygome".

The silk-screen prints, which had now become white on black—and looked somewhat like chalk on a blackboard—also bring to mind X-ray images, as if the artist was willing to reveal the nakedness of his condition. The human body is dissected across a series of plates, like an anatomical study. This could be a parody of *Gray's Anatomy*. It also creates an aesthetic of the body as damaged, scarred, fragmented, incomplete or torn apart, once the organic whole has disappeared. Paradoxically, it is the very act of creating these representations that conjures a positive corporeal valence between the artist and his sense of self or identity. The creative act of representing a fragmented body probably helped Basquiat regain a temporary sense of fullness.

Apart from his obsession with the fragmented human body, working in multiples had also become customary for Basquiat. He would repeatedly glue parts of a colour Xerox drawing onto numerous canvases, in which painted elements, photocopies and the actual construction formed to create a unique work.

The rest of Basquiat's prints were produced between Thanksgiving 1982 and late spring 1983, when he was staying at Larry Gagosian's house in Venice, California. Starting with *Untitled* and *Tuxedo*, they were made in collaboration with Fred Hoffman, a young art historian who had just started his print-publishing business in Venice. *Untitled* is a beautiful mixed-media work consisting of twenty-eight sheets of paper covered with Basquiat's compulsive writing onto which he painted a face.[2] It was then made into a one-colour silk-screen before being printed on canvas. Soon after, Basquiat made *Tuxedo* from a set of sixteen drawings that were arranged vertically. Over that patchwork of words and symbols he painted the ubiquitous crown, giving them a royal seal of approval. (The original drawings are believed not to have survived.) The resulting one-colour silk screen is perhaps Basquiat's best-known printed work.

Basquiat went on to produce a five-part print known as *Untitled (from Leonardo)* and a further two prints entitled *Leg of a Dog* and *Academic Study of the Male Torso*. He created all of these works by drawing onto clear acetates that formed the basis of silk screens. In the "Leonardo" prints the image bears traces of unexpected shifts in lines and composition, in a manner that is reminiscent of Cy Twombly (whose influence Basquiat openly acknowledged). Some symbols appear regularly, such as the crown in *Tuxedo*; and fragments of writing have been crossed out. His very last print, *Back of the Neck*, was produced without aphotomechanical reproduction device. It was drawn directly onto the screen, and printed in various colours not unlike Andy Warhol's famous silk screens.

Fred Hoffman has generously provided additional information on the origins of these prints; in particular the set of five that were inspired by Leonardo da Vinci's study of the human body. One of Basquiat's paintings from 1982 is entitled Leonardo's Greatest Hits. Hoffman offered Basquiat his book of anatomical studies as a gift after he realised the artist's interest in Leonardo da Vinci. Basquiat produced some composite images of Leonardo's studies in which image and text were juxtaposed. One of them, *Leg of a Dog*, refers to a specific Leonardo sketch, which Basquiat drew directly onto acetates. The acetates, which consisted of a clear plastic film, were then projected—with the help of a lens—onto the actual silk screens and printed in two colours. Basquiat produced most of the prints in Hoffman's studio. He placed them on the floor and trod on them repeatedly to make them look old, as though they had been soiled by time. The traces of grime and soil that gathered on the surface of the acetates resemble accumulated energies of the past and the present. According to Hoffman, "These extra scumblings and marks gave the final prints a feeling of age and patina. Basquiat, the neophyte printmaker, was astute in understanding that his studio process could link his latest creations to manuscript pages created more than five hundred years earlier."[3]

Basquiat's childhood trauma after his accident and his study of *Gray's Anatomy* shaped his vision of a fractured human personality. The many fragments, such as carved-out, dismembered limbs in the form of Afro-Brazilian votive offerings to a saint, rid Basquiat's anatomical drawings and prints of conventional hierarchies. Dividing and reuniting, giving and taking away parts of a whole, can be seen as the principles governing this tearing apart of the human body. Humanity is reduced to a mere idea, a ghostly presence. Eerie zombie-like creatures that appear to be coming back from the dead, with remnants of fading and furiously scrawled writing, mark Basquiat's attempt to bridge the abyss between life's disappearance and its existence. The fragmentation and dislocation of the human body is performed symbolically, reminding us of ancient sacrificial rites in which such gestures were the cost of reclaiming a sense of wholeness.

His later works echo this vision. The large canvas *Riding with Death*, which he painted after his friend Andy Warhol died suddenly in 1987, is one such example.[4] In this representation of a skeleton riding a ghostly horse, the human body has lost its flesh; all that is left is the premonition of death. In an ultimate display of energetic gesture, the artist attempts to "repel ghosts", as he was used to saying. Basquiat died of a drug overdose on 12th August, 1988, aged 27.

NOTES

1   *Portrait of the Artist as a Young Derelict* 1982. Acrylic, oil and oil
    paintstick on wood 203.2 x 203.2 cm. Illustrated in Richard
    Marshall ed *Jean-Michel Basquiat* (exhibition catalogue).
    New York Whitney Museum of American Art 1992 p 124.
2   *Untitled* 1982–3. Graphite, crayon and gouache on paper
    mounted on canvas 248.8 x 320 cm. Collection of Fred
    Hoffman. Illustrated in *Jean-Michel Basquiat* op cit p 144.
3   Fred Hoffman in conversation with the author 2008.
4   *Riding with Death* 1987. Acrylic and oil paintstick on linen
    248.9 x 289.6 cm. Private Collection Switzerland. Illustrated
    in *Jean-Michel Basquiat* op cit p 231.

AGNES MARTIN—
THE LIGHTNESS OF ART

Flower in the Wind

Untitled 4

AGNES MARTIN—
THE LIGHTNESS OF ART

A PART FROM A DECADE spent in New York in the early Sixties, Agnes Martin lived away from the noise and trends of the art world. Discovering the desert of the American south-west was a crucial experience of her early years. She returned to the foot of the Sangre de Cristo mountains in New Mexico in the late Sixties, where she was able to work in desirable solitude. She was still aware of what was happening among abstract expressionists she had met in New York. Nevertheless, she always claimed the experience of the open landscape in the American west as decisive: silence, vastness, contemplation, an order of nature that absorbed her sense of selfhood.

Agnes Martin started devising geometric grids displaying horizontal and vertical lines over square canvases in the late Fifties, by which time she was exhibiting with Betty Parsons in New York. She used a limited range of colours, with black, white and browns giving way to some pastel colours in later years.

It has been said that among her contemporaries Agnes Martin had a somewhat unusual position, on the fringes of the mainstream but not detached from it. That is to say, despite her idiosyncrasies, she was neither irrelevant nor unaware of her stance within twentieth-century art. *Flower in the Wind* (1963) is close to the spirit of minimalism; within its over-all ordering there are elements of discontinuity, of chance perhaps, with overlapping vertical stripes drawn in pencil that are not entirely straight. The grid has had its mechanical character softened by the distinctly human touch of approximate pencil marks. A delicate blank border frames the painting with the central image appearing all the more iconic.

Some works, such as *Untitled 4* (1987), reaffirm conceptual and geometric characteristics, while others display a greater degree of freedom. In *Untitled 4* (2002), the soft edges of the contiguous vertical stripes are blurred, until the beholder's attention switches to the white dividing line in the middle of the field, creating a feeling of symmetry that grows as the eye distances itself from the picture surface. *Untitled 12* (2002) follows the painter's common scheme of vertical graphite lines that run over loose, grey horizontal stripes, forming bands of colour. At first glance this grid seems uniform. Gradually, it unravels discontinuous elements within the geometric concept governing its composition. The artist declared—"My formats are square, but the grids never are absolutely square, they are rectangles, a little bit of the square, making a sort of contradiction, a dissonance, though I didn't set out to do it that way. When I cover the square surface with rectangles, it lightens the weight of the square, destroys its power".[1]

The late works, such as *Gratitude* (2001), are more seductive, executed in delicate pastel colours such as celadon greens and pale blues. The eye of the beholder is allowed to wander between the floating bands of colour. The overall sensation is one of lightness although the works are sufficiently complex to create alternative movements within the viewer's mind.

These works seem to have been conceived as part of a series. Each one discloses something slightly different. We come to apprehend them as seismographs of the mind; the sparseness of these paintings shun all possible sources of inspiration other than intuitive ones while espousing certain ideals of order and geometry.

There is one aspect of these paintings that comes back, almost haunting us; one that perhaps points to the artist's originality. Surely, these pictures are conducive to contemplation. However, they lead the beholder to a place unlike the ones traced by any other painter: neither Cézanne, especially the Cézanne of the watercolours, who was wholly consumed by the realm of optical sensations; nor Rothko, who wanted to draw us into the picture to such a degree that we lost ourselves within its ridges, as a way of succumbing to the picture surface; nor Yves Klein, whose monochromatic surfaces came into being as a matter of principle, in an almost metaphysical way. What Agnes Martin's canvases succeed in doing is tied to a variety of sensations, all within the same range of colour, line and proportion. They achieve an immense lightness in which the viewer is left feeling elated and graceful treading the world ever so gently, somewhat like the Greek poet Pindar. Meanwhile, gravity is left lingering, like an afterthought.

NOTES

1   Agnes Martin *Writings—Schriften*. Winterthur Kunstmuseum
    Winterthur 1991 pp 36–37.

CY TWOMBLY—THE SUMMONS TO LIVING THINGS TO RETURN HOME

Untitled V

CY TWOMBLY—THE SUMMONS TO LIVING THINGS TO RETURN HOME

CY TWOMBLY'S EARLY PAINTINGS display a variety of seemingly random marks, creating a precarious balance between inscription and effacement, a seismic line that is occasionally suspended. Their surfaces are intensely lyrical, built up of signs that are suggestive of meanings that are not revealed to us entirely, thus reminding us of the famous dictum *"ut pictura poesis"* ("as is painting, so is poetry"), often interpreted as suggesting that painting should aspire to poetry. The canvas is like a silent elegy. Yet behind that seductive surface, the variety of inscriptions that punctuate the dense and hazy white expanse of canvas ever so lightly, something else is palpable. As Linda Norden has observed, "Twombly's beautiful effects undermine themselves".[1] How could we fail to see that the painter offers us not only poetic fragments of a drama, but tragedy itself? For Twombly, to paint is to acknowledge that beauty is inherently fragile, since violence and destruction are its unexpected accomplices. If, in the course of the last century, the condition of the artist has often been one of losing expressive powers, Twombly's series *Bacchus, Psilax, Mainomenos* (2005) speaks eloquently—painting appears as a field of generalised transformation, in which artistic creation contains the seeds of its own dissolution. The first signs of this underlying tension are visible in Twombly's Roman works, created in the Fifties. Smears and splashes of paint, sparse markings of lightly scribbled lines and scrolls are loosely applied to the canvas's virgin surface. In his essay on Twombly, Roland Barthes likens the line to an action made visible.[2] It constitutes a kind of writing, a gesture that mimics the impulse that lies behind language without quite reaching fully formed meaning. With these inscriptions the painter offers us glimpses of words or forms (Barthes likens them to the erotic), the promise of meanings never affirmed. Names of distant gods are evoked through seemingly random scribbles. Scrawled graffiti are the vestiges of Rome's defaced monuments. Every inscription holds the promise of its erasure, so that writing and its negation appear to be related to one another. Some paintings veer towards effacement and dissolution. They seem to testify to a lack of confidence in the ability of visual signs to convey meaning; yet they conserve the gesture of writing. Not all of Twombly's early paintings offer the muted sounds of seductive, scattered marks and impulsive lines that are devoid of resolution. Some of them are marked by convulsive turns, line breaks and occasional splatters of a vivid red, artless smudges that are the colours of life and death (as in *Leda and the Swan*, 1962).

In the mid-Sixties, the lyrical effects of the Roman paintings gave way to new works painted on a dark background the colour of slate, somewhat like a blackboard. Looped lines swirl across the surface of the canvas in a wavy manner. The handwritten scrawl is divided and ruled by horizontal lines like school exercises. Twombly still remained faithful to his graffiti aesthetic but the pictorial strategy was free of literary references or fragments of writing. The regularity of painted marks seems to adhere to a procedure. The sequential method he used appears to offer a response to the pervading spirit of the Sixties and the rise of minimalist and conceptual art. (Sequential repetition and logical progression are characteristic of minimalism.)

It is also a device for reducing the individual marks to a more logical programme. However, the cypher-like loops conserve the mark of a personal gesture, and their inflections are contrary to any notion of a mathematical model.

It would seem impossible to look at Twombly's Bacchus paintings without referring to the blackboard paintings from the Sixties. Thirty years later, the looped trajectory of the line has acquired an even more insistent edge, recalling the action of a lasso; it is the colour of blood. Not the pouring of blood or a slow impregnation; instead the dissemination of paint in a frenzied scroll-like movement. Here, the impulse behind the work—the repetition of a gesture—is released through skilful action: the circular motion leaves strong residual traces in the form of coagulated drips of paint running down the surface of the canvas. Some of the effects are the result of the circumstances in which the works were painted in the artist's studio in Gaeta—the canvas was folded over the floor, hence the accumulation of dripping paint along that crease. In these paintings art becomes quasi-liquid. The wave of blood is there to remind us that beauty is linked to violence; that convulsion cannot be absent from the work of an artist who is better known for the lyrical, poetic qualities of his paintings. This physical engagement with the materials of art is an affirmation of life, more eloquent than the scraps of life that adorned the surfaces of earlier works. Here the painter's gesture is at its most visceral; where the blackboard paintings articulate a naturally elegant, rhythmic outline, forty years later the movement of the brush is more forceful, at times messy. No longer a ghostly trace, the line is given much added weight with a thick paintbrush. An orgy of paint spreads across the vast expanse of the canvas, which is monumental in size even by abstract-expressionist standards.

The scale of each of the Bacchus paintings is unprecedented. Seen together, their effect is overwhelming. The sense of physical domination has its antecedent in Giulio Romano's extensive decorations for Federico Gonzaga, Duke of Mantua at the Palazzo del Te. The Sala dei Giganti illustrates the victory of Zeus over the rebellious Giants. It gave Giulio an excuse to indulge in a fantastic exercise of theatrical illusionism—by creating a continuous space in which all the architectural elements are integrated into the design, the visitor is drawn into this play of irrational forces. The sheer size of the Giants contributes to an overall sense of oppression. Some of them are seen crushed by falling stones, as their foolish attempt to overcome Zeus's temple fails, unleashing waves of destruction. In Twombly's work, the painter's gesture—his assault on the whiteness of the canvas—by taking control and losing control, is also a symptom of violence. It bears the mark of an action in which the contagious intoxication of painting degenerates into a raging battle.

Traditionally, serenity and detachment were ideals associated with ancient Greece. It was also assumed that these lost ideals lay at the heart of the Italian Renaissance. Today a different perspective has emerged, largely due to Aby Warburg's investigation of Florentine paintings, for he saw in them traces of ancient contradictions—ones that presuppose violence and irrationality instead of harmony and order. According to Warburg, in the Renaissance the old conflict between Apollo and Dionysus, between reason and passion, rationality and madness, is once again woven into the fabric of art. In Warburg's groundbreaking studies of quattrocento painting, the serene beauty of the gods is exposed as a myth. Botticelli's *Birth of Venus* is a farewell to classical solemnity—its deities wear floating dresses, their hair loose and their bodies contorted. Instead of a static display of hieratic gods, we behold the convulsive beauty of the dancing Maenads, Bacchus's female devotees. Botticelli's serpentine line serves as the concrete expression of vital energy.[3] Painting becomes the field in which various figures are prone to a trance-like agitation. The frenzy animating them is like "an immobilized sparkle, a petrified wave at the moment it comes ashore", to use the words of Goethe contemplating the ancient Greek marble sculpture known as *Laocoön and His Sons*. If in their orgiastic frenzy Twombly's recent paintings recall antique bacchanalia, it is perhaps because they embody an attitude in which Dionysian forces have reclaimed their preeminent position, conveying the violence of our impulses. The title of the series, *Bacchus, Psilax, Mainomenos*, alludes to the dual nature of Bacchus, caught between exhilarating feelings or worldly pleasure (*psilax*) and debauchery leading to annihilation (*mainomenos*).

The contradiction between Dionysus and Apollo, and pathos and ethos, resonates in Twombly's Bacchus paintings. Caught between continuity and disruption, a frenzied impulse sets the irregular line into motion. It is hardly surprising that one of the new works bears the title *Mainomenos*, which alludes to the raging debauchery of the Bacchic rites. Sudden, scattered breaks undermine the trajectory of single lines, their traces barely visible under new layers of paint. Those towards the edges are wiped off. In denser canvases, links between different parts of the picture are lost once the structural transparency of multiple layers is obscured. At times the painting is made up of layered outlines that produce tangled-up loops. Twombly's expressive marks refuse to settle down spatially. The Bacchus paintings can be read as compelling visual images of a wave-like movement that engulfs the surface of the canvas. At the same time they are free of mimetic constraints. Twombly's hand is guided by a fundamental gesture, a circular motion that is only partly aware of where it is going. This motion also resonates within us, as though we could perform it ourselves. The spiral movement is intoxicating; it spreads like a relentless wave that is not confined to individual canvases, but one that is reinforced through the mutual vibration of panels that are exhibited together. In their original gallery setting, the paintings' swirls of red paint permeated the whole room, and a reddish tinge seemed to hover in space.

In a collage from 1968 Twombly includes a reproduction of one of Leonardo da Vinci's Deluge drawings. Entitled *Deluge II—Proem*, it belongs to a series made towards the end of Leonardo's life. It appears to reveal something of the artist's fascination with motion and displaced energy. Leonardo's drawing offers the graphic expression of a fairly constant yet relentless ripple of energy that disturbs the water's surface. It depicts a town that has been ravaged by a storm, with constant looped waves unfolding and toppling buildings. The cataclysms (*diluvio*) they illustrate were also fashionable literary subjects. However it seems that Leonardo's Deluge series is not based solely on literary accounts, but on a careful observation of storms and floods in France and Italy. In his journals we find moving accounts of scenes of utter devastation caused by flooding. In these drawings, he records the movement of waves with swirling lines reaching a level of intoxicating profusion. Towards the top of the page Leonardo's distinctive mirror-script writing appears, a feature that must have appealed to Twombly.[4]

The significance of Leonardo's Deluge drawing is twofold. Firstly, as the image of a natural disaster, it serves as a metaphor for violence and destruction. The wave represents a moment when tragedy erupts and spills into our lives—it is the symbol of the continuum of life energy. Leonardo saw nature as a perpetual movement from creation to dissolution, and he viewed storms as "the raging of Nature against that which she has created", "the summons to living things to return home".[5] Destruction is part of nature's cycle, which contains the seeds of regeneration. Secondly, for Leonardo these studies derived from nature become cosmic images in which the movement of the seas is like an image of our souls. If "man is the model of the world", nature is just like ourselves on a different scale, and water is the blood of the earth. We cannot ascribe such metaphysical undertones to Twombly's paintings. Nor can we deny the association of the looped line with notions of flux and instability, violence and paroxysm. The wave has yet another dimension. It has become a metaphor for the creative act—a scrawl that leaves its inexorable trace. In its scroll-like effect the line resembles an oncoming wave, destined to repeat itself incessantly. It is not always fluid graphic energy; it bears traces of discontinuity, of losing control. It dies before regaining its powers. The lesson here seems clear—the work is entirely consumed by the gesture that produces it. Leonardo's metaphor suggests that artistic creation is subject to a cycle of violence and destruction. Although his attitude is less analytical than Leonardo's, some paintings by Twombly echo such conceptions. As the material of the work emerges throughout the painting process, the spectator is allowed to feel various forces at play. What his art seems to insinuate is that there is nothing more eloquent than this action, with the line serving as a tool of generalised transformation. For Twombly painting is a form of writing that lives impulsively, a gesture that eludes figuration and coalesces into signs that float in their own space, forming a new reality. As Roland Barthes wrote, "Twombly's art desires to take possession of nothing at all".[6] Leaving a mark, a trace, is more important than conveying meaning. This activity is defined by a fracture between the urge to find a voice and realising that language is futile. Yet, largely due to Twombly's meticulous approach, these paintings regain a voice that leaves an imprint, which is anything but disorderly. In the words of Leonardo, "there can be no voice where there is no motion or percussion of the air".[7] Leonardo's wave has been unleashed again, this time with joyous abandonment by a painter who was fully aware of his position amidst the contradictions of history.

NOTES

1 Linda Norden, 'What Painting Can Contain', in *A Gathering of Time—Cy Twombly—Six Paintings and a Sculpture* (exhibition catalogue). New York Gagosian Gallery, 2003.

2 Roland Barthes, 'Non Multa Sed Multum', in *Cy Twombly—Fifty Years of Works on Paper* (exhibition catalogue). New York Whitney Museum of American Art, 2004.

3 Aby M Warburg, *Sandro Botticellis 'Geburt der Venus' und 'Frühling'. Eine Untersuchung über die Vorstellungen von der Antike in der italienischen Frührenaissance*. Hamburg and Leipzig, 1893.

4 For a general discussion of the relation between Leonardo and Twombly, see Kirk Varnedoe, 'Inscriptions in Arcadia', in *Cy Twombly—A Retrospective* (exhibition catalogue). New York Museum of Modern Art, 1994, p 41.

5 Quoted in Ludwig Goldscheider, *Leonardo da Vinci—Landscapes and Plants*. London Phaidon Press, 1952, p 8.

6 Barthes, op cit, p 40.

7 Jean Paul Richter, *The Literary Works of Leonardo da Vinci*. London, New York and Toronto Oxford University Press, 1939, vol II, p 252.

Untitled VII

Pablo Picasso

La nuit, Danse de tendresse, Signes du Zodiaque, Mercure tue Apollon avant de ressusciter, Danse des Grâces et Cerbère, Le Bain des Grâces, Fête de Bacchus, Rapt de Proserpine. Photographs of scenes from *Mercure,* 1924, provided courtesy of the Archives de la Fondation Erik Satie.

Three Women by the Shore 1920
Pencil on paper 49.2 x 64.1 cm
The Metropolitan Museum of Art New York
Bequest of Scofield Thayer 1982

Three Nudes Reclining by the Shore
Pencil on paper 49.5 x 64.1 cm

The Metropolitan Museum of Art New York
Bequest of Scofield Thayer 1982

Drop Curtain for Mercure 1924
Distemper on canvas 392 x 501 cm
Centre Georges Pompidou Musée National d'Art Moderne / Centre de la Création Industrielle Paris

Paul Klee

Die Schlange 1929
Oil and pigment on panel 31.5 x 74.5 cm
Private Collection

Blau-Vogel-Kürbis, 1939
Gouache on board mounted on cardboard,
27.9 x 43.2 cm
The Metropolitan Museum of Art New York The
Berggruen Klee Collection

Yves Klein

Anthropométrie 1960 (ANT 130)
Dry pigment on paper laid down on canvas

194 x 127 cm
Museum Ludwig Cologne

Feu-couleur 1961 (FC 5)
Dry pigment on charred pasteboard on wood
116 x 89 cm
Private Collection

Ed Ruscha

Nashville 1967
Gunpowder on paper
33.6 x 55.7 cm
Private Collection

Greatest Ride 2009
Acrylic on board
71.4 x 75.9 cm
Private Collection

Cut Lip 1968
Pigment on paper
35.5 x 56 cm
Courtesy Gagosian Gallery Los Angeles

Pool 1968
Gunpowder on paper
58.4 x 73.7 cm
Private Collection

Hollywood 1970
Gunpowder and pastel on paper
56 x 76.2 cm
Private Collection San Francisco

Jean-Michel Basquiat

Untitled (From Leonardo) 1983
A five-part print
Each a two-colour screenprint
88.9 x 76.2 cm
Edition of 45

Agnes Martin

Flower in the Wind 1963
Acrylic and graphite on canvas
190.5 x 190.5 cm
Daros Collection Switzerland

Untitled #4 2002
Acrylic and graphite on canvas
152.4 x 152.4 cm
Private Collection courtesy PaceWildenstein New York

Cy Twombly

Untitled V 2005
Acrylic on canvas
325.1 x 494 cm
Private Collection courtesy Gagosian Gallery

Untitled VII 2005
Acrylic on canvas
317.5 x 467.4 cm
Private Collection, courtesy Gagosian Gallery

Cover Image
Bacchus Psilax Mainomenos Installation shot Gagosian
Gallery Madison Avenue New York 2005.
Photograph by Rob McKeever

Portraits

Picasso Courtesy of The Cecil Beaton Studio Archive at Sotheby's. Thanks to Natasha Mendelsohn for her help.

Paul Klee Photograph by Hugo Erfurth © ProLitteris Zürich / VG Bild-Kunst Bonn.

Yves Klein Courtesy of Roger-Viollet, Paris / The Bridgeman Art Library

Leap into the Void Work © Yves Klein, ADAGP, Paris Photograph Shunk-Kender © Roy Lichtenstein Foundation

Ed Ruscha *Large Trademark with Eight Spotlights* © Joe Goode Studio

Jean-Michel Basquiat © The Andy Warhol Foundation for the Visual Arts/Artists Rights Society (ARS) New York/DACS, London 2011
Image courtesy of the Galerie Bruno Bischofberger

Agnes Martin, 1979 Photograph by Dorothy Alexander
Courtesy of The Pace Gallery.

Cy Twombly, courtesy of The Gagosian Gallery ©
Bruce Weber

BIBLIOGRAPHY

Roland Barthes 'Non Multa Sed Multum' in *Cy Twombly—Fifty Years of Works on Paper* (exhibition catalogue). New York Whitney Museum of American Art 2004

Yve-Alain Bois 'Thermometers Should Last Forever' in *Edward Ruscha. Romance with Liquids—Paintings 1966–1969* (exhibition catalogue). New York Gagosian Gallery 1993

Douglas Cooper *Picasso Théâtre*. Paris Éditions Cercle d'Art 1967

René Crevel *Paul Klee*. Paris Gallimard 1930

Siri Engberg and Clive Phillpot *Edward Ruscha—Editions 1959–1999 Catalogue Raisonné*. Minneapolis Walker Art Center 1999

Lynn Garafola *Diaghilev's Ballets Russes*. New York Oxford University Press 1989

Françoise Gilot and Carlton Lake *Life with Picasso*. New York McGraw-Hill 1964

Ludwig Goldscheider *Leonardo da Vinci—Landscapes and Plants*. London Phaidon Press 1952

Christopher Green *Life and Death in Picasso—Still Life/Figure c1907–1933*. New York Thames & Hudson 2009

Polly Hill and Richard Keynes eds *Lydia and Maynard—Letters between Lydia Lopokova and John Maynard Keynes*. London André Deutsch 1989

Yves Klein *Le Dépassement de la problématique de l'art et autres écrits* ed Marie-Anne Sichère and Didier Semin. Paris École Nationale Supérieure des Beaux-arts 2003

Richard Marshall ed *Jean-Michel Basquiat* (exhibition catalogue). New York Whitney Museum of American Art 1992

Agnes Martin *Writings—Schriften*. Winterthur Kunstmuseum Winterthur 1991

Linda Norden 'What Painting Can Contain' in *A Gathering of Time Cy Twombly—Six Paintings and a Sculpture* (exhibition catalogue). New York Gagosian Gallery 2003

Jean Paul Richter *The Literary Works of Leonardo da Vinci*. London New York and Toronto Oxford University Press 1939

Henri-Pierre Roché *Écrits sur l'art*. Paris André Dimanche 1998

Gertrude Stein *Picasso*. Paris Librairie Floury 1938.

Sidra Stich *Yves Klein* (exhibition catalogue). London Hayward Gallery 1995

Kirk Varnedoe 'Inscriptions in Arcadia' in *Cy Twombly—A Retrospective* (exhibition catalogue). New York The Museum of Modern Art 1994

Ornella Volta *Satie et la danse*. Paris Éditions Plume 1992

Aby M Warburg *Sandro Botticellis 'Geburt der Venus' und 'Frühling'. Eine Untersuchung über die Vorstellungen von der Antike in der italienischen Frührenaissance*. Hamburg and Leipzig 1893

Ludwig Wittgenstein *Lectures and Conversations on Aesthetics, Psychology and Religious Belief* ed Cyril Barrett. Oxford Blackwell 1966.

Christian Zervos *Pablo Picasso*. Paris Éditions Cahiers d'Art 1949–86

ACKNOWLEDGEMENTS

F IRST AND FOREMOST I would like to thank those who were involved, in some shape or form, with the inception of these essays: Doris Ammann and Georg Frei, Paloma Botín, Larry Gagosian, Max Hollein, David Landau and Alannah Weston.

I owe an enormous debt of gratitude to the following who have been most helpful in a variety of ways: Anne Baldassari, Nuit Banai, Asya Chorley, Mary Dean, Stefan Frey, Lynn Garafola, Fred Hoffman, Venetia Kapernekas, Rémi Labrusse, Alison McDonald, Daniel Moquay and Rotraut Klein-Moquay, Emmanuelle Ollier, Sabine Rewald, Almine Rech, John Richardson, Nicole Root, Nicola Del Roscio, Ed Ruscha, Esther Schlicht, Philippe Siauve, Luchino Visconti di Modrone, Ornella Volta, Desiree Welsing and Diana Widmaier Picasso.

Finally, I would like to thank my editor, Mebrak Tareke, whose patience and guidance have proved invaluable.

The essay *Picasso—Les Aventures de Mercure* incorporates material previously published in 'The Theater as Metaphor' in Olivier Berggruen and Max Hollein eds *Picasso and the Theater* (exhibition catalogue). Ostfildern Hatje Cantz 2006.
The essay *Paul Klee—In Search of Natural Signs* appeared in an earlier version in *Paul Klee—The Berggruen Collection* (exhibition catalogue). Santander Fundación Marcelino Botín 2006.
The essay *Yves Klein—The Void* incorporates material previously published in Olivier Berggruen Max Hollein and Ingrid Pfeiffer eds *Yves Klein* (exhibition catalogue). Ostfildern Hatje Cantz 2005.
The essay on Agnes Martin is reprinted, with some minor changes, from *Agnes Martin* (exhibition catalogue). Zurich Thomas Ammann Fine Art 2008.
The essay *Some Notes on Jean-Michel Basquiat's Silk-Screen Prints* is reprinted, with some minor editing, from *Print Quarterly* vol XXVI (2009) no 1.

The essay *Ed Ruscha—Ribbon of Words* appeared in an earlier version in *Ed Ruscha—The Drawn Word* (exhibition catalogue). Vero Beach Florida Windsor Press 2003.

The essay on Twombly is reprinted, with some minor editing, from *Cy Twombly: Bacchus—Psilax—Mainomenos* (exhibition catalogue). New York Gagosian Gallery 2005.